THE TURNING POINT

After their first embrace, Christine realized how much she needed and wanted Jack. The warmth of his lips and the softness of his caresses were too much to resist. She was filled with passionate desire —a feeling she had almost forgotten.

She never knew lovemaking could be so beautiful, so fulfilling. And when Jack said, "I love you," she didn't know how to react. Thoughts of her husband and children flashed through her mind, but she couldn't ignore her pounding heart.

"I love you too, but I'm not sure what it means," Christine said. "And frankly, Jack, I'm afraid."

"Honey, don't be afraid—go with your feelings."

"But what about Carl and the kids? I can't abandon my family!" she cried.

"I can't believe how programmed you are: the lady of the house, the Mom, the fixer. Don't you think it's time you enjoyed yourself?"

"Don't say any more," she warned, feeling hurt by the truth. Her choices were clear: the security of married life or the excitement of a young lover . . .

BESTSELLERS FOR TODAY'S WOMAN

THE VOW (653, $2.50)
by Maria B. Fogelin
On the verge of marriage, a young woman is tragically blinded and mangled in a car accident. Struggling against tremendous odds to survive, she finds the courage to live, but will she ever find the courage to love?

FRIENDS (645, $2.25)
by Elieba Levine
Edith and Sarah had been friends for thirty years, sharing all their secrets and fantasies. No one ever thought that a bond as close as theirs could be broken . . . but now underneath the friendship and love is jealousy, anger, and hate.

CHARGE NURSE (663, $2.50)
by Patricia Rae
Kay Strom was Charge Nurse in the Intensive Care Unit and was trained to deal with the incredible pressures of life-and-death situations. But the one thing she couldn't handle was her passionate emotions . . . when she found herself falling in love with two different men!

RHINELANDER PAVILLION (572, $2.50)
by Barbara Harrison
Rhinelander Pavillion was a big city hospital pulsating with the constant struggles of life and death. Its dedicated staff of overworked professionals were caught up in the unsteady charts of their own passions and desires—yet they all needed medicine to survive.

Available wherever paperbacks are sold, or order direct from the Publisher. Send cover price plus 50¢ per copy for mailing and handling to Zebra Books, 21 East 40th Street, New York, N.Y. 10016. DO NOT SEND CASH!

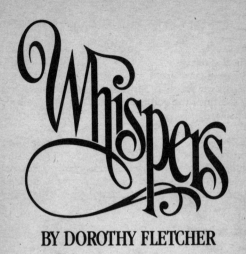

Whispers

BY DOROTHY FLETCHER

ZEBRA BOOKS

KENSINGTON PUBLISHING CORP.

ZEBRA BOOKS

are published by

KENSINGTON PUBLISHING CORP.
21 East 40th Street
New York, N.Y. 10016

Printed in the United States of America

1.

Christine Jennings sat, at ten in the morning, drinking her breakfast coffee. The *Times* lay on the floor at her feet, neatly folded and still unread. She would get around to it sooner or later, but she was a person who came together slowly in the mornings, not ready, at first blush, to slog through its pages. The dining room table, with the detritus of the others' morning meal, was sun-streaked in random patterns: four flowered table mats looked like individual small gardens blooming on the polished wood. The terrace, with its massed plants and bright blooms, seemed an extension of the room itself: beyond sliding glass doors the brilliant vista was rather like a fanciful *trompe l'oeil*, inordinately pleasing to the eye.

It was a big apartment, like a house, with a private feeling to it, spreading out expansively, rambling, almost. They had lived here for just under three years and Christine was still, at times, able to see it with a fresh and favorable eye. In the mornings like this, with the rest of them gone and the place her personal domain as she listened to the sounds from the street outside, all seemed well. She had left her bed from childhood with a sense of great expectations: something wonderful would happen today, because why not? She was an optimist, she supposed.

She buffed a fingernail thoughtfully. The trouble was that in these latter days she had been unable to put her finger on what wonderful thing would be likely to happen. Everything she had considered one's rightful due had come to pass. What was left to anticipate?

You tell me, she said to the newspaper, nudging it with a slippered foot. You know everything, you prepotent rag. Even if your typos rapidly become insupportable.

The coffee urn was empty. Well, that was that. She must get going, she told herself, but sat there twisting a strand of her hair. She must get going, granted, and since she knew exactly where she was going *today* there was no need for a decision about that. How about tomorrow, though, and all the other tomorrows: what was she going to do with the rest of her life now that the children were no longer children? Go out shopping every day? Play bridge? Join a health club?

She wasn't sure how many of the women friends she was lunching with today had reached this unpleasant crisis point, but she did know, having discussed it at length with her, that Ruth Alexander was in similar straits, which was one reason, Ruth confessed, that she could scarcely bear to remain indoors, as all she ever did was brood. Ruth said she had difficulty even reading a book, not being able to keep her mind on its contents for drifting into endless introspection and self-examination that led nowhere.

She said that sometimes these fruitless trains of thought—where was she going and why did a woman have to come to this stinking impasse—made her hyperventilate. "I press the panic button and it's anxiety time, then I start to gasp in this *awful* way, ending up with a migraine." This was something that happened to weak sisters and Edith Bunker types, Ruth had always thought, certainly not to intelligent persons, enlightened women, women with *minds*.

Christine didn't hyperventilate and she didn't have migraines. She was not as passionate about this textbook, case history, housewife blues syndrome as Ruth was. She was inclined to feel grumpy about it, or aggrieved, or even wryly amused. So it hits us all, she reflected. The kids grew up and Daddy was out in that big wide world and what did you have left? A house. It's happened to this woman and it's happened to that woman and now it's happening to me. And I always thought I was so special. But it didn't make her gasp in any "awful" way and most of the time it seemed to her that she was overstating the case, that most of it was a very natural fear of the future that anyone would have as the years wore on, that a lot of it was not wanting to grow old.

Nothing, of course, had changed for Carl. Her husband, working to the limit of his capacities, admired in his profession, gifted in it and dedicated to it. He had only, in some ways, just begun: he was growing all the time, learning all the time, new methods, new professional operandi, meeting people in many walks of life, an octopus with arms reaching out in all directions, a big man physically and a big man in his field. *He* certainly wasn't in danger of having an identity crisis, not Carl.

There was their son, Bruce. On the brink of manhood, in some ways a man already. Leaving for Yale in another year, ready for new worlds. There would be lovely young girls and eventually one special girl whom he would marry. And who would one day sit at a breakfast table wondering where all the glitter had gone. There would be, for Bruce, Med School and internship and ultimately a practice. *Tel pére, tel fils.* LIFE, in caps, held out a welcoming hand to him.

As it did Nancy. She was pretty now; she would be exquisite, a blend of a healthy father and a healthy mother. She would almost certainly have a

8

glittering future, as she was selfish enough to insure for herself what she wanted. When she was sure of what it was she would go ahead and get it. Nothing would stop her, certainly not pity. She had only contempt for what she called mawkish dogoodism.

And what about Mom? Not that they called her that, thank you very much. She had never allowed it. It was Mother, though she wouldn't have minded Mama, which sounded European and quite classy, but Mom, or Ma, had been verboten from the very beginning. What about Mother, the lady of the house? Now that the rest of them had been accounted for, with everything coming up roses, what about Christine?

She lit another cigarette. The truth was she was ambivalent about this apartment. It added to the general finality of things. They would not be moving on, not from here, this symbol of the American dream, the costly cooperative that would only increase in value over the years. This was it. Here she was and here she would stay, with the proverbial "jewel" of a woman to do the cleaning and only meals to think of for herself. She would wake for God knew how many mornings with her hearty dreams and her appetite for living and face it anew, this arrogantly esthetic cluster of rooms with their Ethan Allen and Henredon pieces and spool beds and butler's table and the Schumacher drapes. There it would be, complacent and orderly, everything in its place and staring at her smugly, the breakfront and the Georgian tea service and the Cuisinart and the microwave oven and the blender and the terrace that looked—or had been designed to look—like one of those charming overhanging balconies in Napoli. It had all cost thousands and thousands of dollars outside the purchase price and she sometimes hated it.

Or something very like that. It was a fake, it seemed to her, like a stage setting that looked authentic and homey to the audience but didn't house real people, only actors who were there every night to say their lines and give a performance. It was just a replica of a home, in some arcane way, and it had nothing at all to do with her, not her soul and not her psyche. She would have preferred . . . well, almost, something like the apartment in the Village that had been hers and Carl's first home. Bleecker Street, with most of the furnishings picked up at Good Will. That was real enough and it didn't have to insist on anything. It had housed a young man and a young girl who loved each other and who knew, really knew, their priorities.

She hadn't changed, not a bit. She was still Christine Elliott Jennings and she was a fun-loving broad with a passion for music and books and the graphic arts and she liked to wear her hair in different and various ways and keep her long legs smooth and shaved and entertain people with her mimicry and go out to dinner at lovely places and enjoy the eyes of men on her and wear sleek swimsuits and be admired and go to small Hungarian cafes where a zither tinkled out schmaltzy tunes and open her legs out of love for a man and lie on a hill of a summer's day with sheep-in-the-meadow clouds you wanted to reach up and touch with your fingertips. She was only forty years old and it was her turn now.

Why not? She had done her stint. Cooked and scrubbed and ironed shirts, catered to the Man, made him comfy and filled his belly, listened to his discourse, accommodated his sexual needs. Christine done good, like a good wife should. *And* mother. So now what?

Once more she thought of a job. It chilled her. Nine to five, and in all sorts of weather. She had loved working once, being part of a crew, coffee breaks, gossip in the ladies' room, friendship, common gripes, drinks after hours, the Barberry Room, Tony's Wife, Piazzetta. But that was rather a long time ago. It would be stepping down now, and she wouldn't fit into a *little* job, not her. A receptionist, something like that: that was what would be open to her at her age. A fancy, important post was out of the question. Young blood, that's what they wanted. Crass kids, arrogant little sluts with crazy hair and blusher smeared all over their faces. Like her own Nancy.

Oh, but she loved Nancy. It wasn't *that*. Just that there was, and had been for some years, a kind of war between them, but that was textbook too, and it didn't hurt too much. When the chips were down it was Christine Nancy turned to. Feminine gender concerns, even if your father was a doctor, called for confabs with a female parent. "Yes, Mother, if the time comes when I am simply dying of love, we'll talk it over and then decide." That was in reference to the Pill, or at least about preventive measures for a headstrong girl: you had to anticipate these things. Nancy had used that poetic phrase and Christine had thought of the

11

Song of Solomon. "Comfort me with apples, stay me with flagons, for I am sick of love . . ." And tried to imagine Nancy sick with love, her little girl.

She certainly did love Nancy, though it was not always easy. Bruce, who "took after her" and who didn't despise do-goodism and who, after all, was her firstborn . . . well, there was a fierce maternal feeling for Bruce. Her son had a gentleness, a softness that sometimes turned her heart over. Like the time they'd watched a rerun of *Frankenstein* on TV. He was about ten then. At the end, when the poor, bewildered creature had been trapped in the flames, Bruce had struggled with tears. He had plumbed the allegory, sensed the symbolism. There was no savage hate in his heart.

"Darling, it's only a movie."

"I know, It's just—"

"He's out of his misery. It's better so, isn't it dear?"

They were worthy kids. No longer belonging to her, as once they had, but to themselves, to what they would make of their lives. It was up to them now, her guardianship was just about over. Where were the infants she had carted around in buggies and taken to school on their first day? Why gone, gone forever, as was the little girl she herself once had been. You could never get those children back.

Well, time to rush now, she had dallied too long and would have to race the clock. Her lunch date was for twelve-thirty and it was a few minutes to eleven. She had to shower and do her hair and get dressed. But as she was meeting the girls at a restaurant not far away it was okay. Her spirits had risen. There would be Meryl and Clover and Ruth and Helene, and they had known each other for lots of years, were more au courant with each others' daily lives and ways of thinking than were their own siblings. They got together, in a group, roughly once a month, for a lunch at places like Mercurio's or La Grenouille or Le Bistro, and at La Scala, on the West Side. Sometimes they trekked down to Michael's Pub, for a little pizzazz. Someone's husband might be there, in which case there would be some table hopping, some kidding. "What's this, Ladies' Day?"

She got up and left everything just the way it was on the dining room table. Mrs. Chamberlain would clear it, wash the dishes, make some fresh coffee for herself and then get out the vacuum cleaner. In order to escape the housekeeper's chatter about the latest lies in the *Enquirer*, Christine closed the door that separated the sleeping quarters from the rest of the apartment, and began her preparations. She was humming now, once more tranquil as she was a naturally cheerful personality, able to slip from one mood to another with the same casual unconcern with which she closed a door between one part of the apartment and the other.

Out on the street, at twenty past twelve, she felt content and at ease, the knowledge that she was an attractive, desirable woman a quiet delight in her. She was pleased that Nancy had beauty too. It would simplify things for her, grease the ways. She walked down Lex toward the restaurant, which was on Park, but stayed with the busier thoroughfare because it was livelier.

This was her city, almost the heartbeat of her body. She felt secure and serene on its streets, with the rumble of the buses and the gleaming storefronts and the welter of people, the familiar, well-loved hodgepodge of types. She could understand shopping bag ladies, who, going down in the world, preferred the intimacy of the streets to sterile shelter in some eleemosynary refuge, fettered by stone walls and pious structures. A fierce independence to which they clung tenaciously.

For herself, Christine would have had to think twice if asked to make a choice between New York City and her family. It was her turf, it was herself really, and leaving it would be like a demand to relinquish her identity.

She breathed deeply and easily, her face bright and anticipative. It was only in the confines of her luxurious prison, her well-appointed home that she wavered. There, she was categorized, committed, immured in a domesticity that seemed to have lost its meaning. I love you, she was thinking, meaning the scene of which she was now a part, but she thought too that she might mean herself as well, just herself, a woman and a person, an entity apart from the others, and of some awesome importance, in the middle of her life, and certainly of some true and meaningful worth. She thought, I can be selfish too, and was buoyed by the resolve. After all, you only passed this way once.

The four women who sat at a corner table adjacent to a window in the sun-filled, ivory-walled Upper East Side restaurant might have been stamped from the same matrix, Christine reflected as she crossed the room. Groomed, easy, assured, they were examples of a certain time and culture, and of a place, which was Manhattan, U.S.A. They were at home here because they had been raised here, never having to learn the idiom, the topography or the mores. They had matriculated only in other ways and now, having reached a certain plateau in their lives, were at liberty to come and go as they pleased, as well as where they pleased, which today happened to be Le Perigord Park. What had once been hurried lunch hours when they worked in the same business office — and then continued their friendship as they moved on to other fields — had become more leisurely, as well as more expensive. That the latter was not of any grave concern to them was gratifying.

"Sorry I'm late," she apologized, easing into the leather banquette. "Aren't you nice, you ordered my drink. Well, cheers, ladies, how's everyone?"

Everyone was fine, how was she, and have some of these adorable miniature asparagus, so teeny-tiny, so crunchy. "Aren't they darling, I asked the waiter, he said they're Progresso."

"They're new to me. Yes, very good, I'll look for them at the market. I used to love those marinated mushrooms they gave you at Ca d'Oro with your drink. I feel so bad Ca d'Oro's gone."

"We had good times there."

"So many places have dropped out of sight. Don't tell me this isn't a Depression."

15

"It's because of night business, it's fallen off so. People are afraid to go out to dinner in the evening. How can you expect a decent restaurant to operate on lunches only?"

"It's so discouraging."

"The times they are achanging."

"You can say that again."

"The times they are—"

"Ah, shut up, Clover. How's the agency?"

"Same as ever, business as usual in spite of the shaky dollar."

"Speaking of restaurants going out of business, I was just remembering one Ralph and I were fond of," Meryl said. "At one time we went there almost every Friday evening. "Italian . . . would you believe I can't recall the name? Anyway, it was in Murray Hill, somewhere near Park . . . yes, between Madison and Park, and on one of the worst winter nights of the year, with a wind like a cyclone, absolutely dreadful. We had scheduled to meet some friends there, as a matter of fact a cousin of mine and her husband. Helen and Ted. We gave them directions, they were to go in and get a table if they were there first and vice versa. Well, they were there first, standing in the gale cowering, need I say that Marconi's was shut up tighter than a drum. Marconi's! Of course, Patsy Marconi! And it was so out of the way, near Altman's. You know how there's absolutely nothing going on in that part of town at night. Naturally, not a taxi in sight. But we did love that place, they had the most fantastic zabaglione."

"And now it's kaput, yes, it's a shame. I'm still

wild about them tearing down those two marvelous Italianate mansions across from the Metropolitan Museum."

"There won't be anything left soon."

"You get used to it after a while. You have to."

"No," Helene said. "I don't. I'm a mossback. I can't stand to see the devastation."

"You should live in the South Bronx."

"God, isn't that a crime?"

"Whither are we drifting?"

"What about Italy? The kidnappings . . ."

"What about everywhere. Oy, let's quit this gloom and doom. Chris, you know what I was thinking about the other day?"

"No, what?"

"The time you and Carl were pfft for a while. When he twisted your arm about getting married and you wanted to wait. Money and all that he was earning that teeny-weeny intern's pay and you told him it wasn't possible. You were like a zombie at the office, it was when we were still at Elliman's, you and Meryl and I. We dragged you off to lunch, and you—"

"And I cried the whole time. God, Helene. It was Reidy's. Yeah, sure, of course I remember that, all too well. My *crise de coeur*. That's that, Carl told me, when I said no, finding it impossible to think of setting up housekeeping just then, and I just couldn't believe he meant it, that he'd throw me to the wolves. Then I saw he did mean it, he didn't call me and he wouldn't answer *my* calls. Finished! No more busing down to the Village, the San Remo and Minetta's and that gloomy cavern-

17

ous coffee house on MacDougal. No more Waverly Inn, that garden with the big old trees, where a bird messed up my salad once, plopped his shit into it."

She laughed. "I started crying there in Reidy's and Meryl said, 'Gee,' and then I spilled my drink trying to get up and leave."

"We didn't go to Reidy's for a while after that."

"It was a disgrace."

"Well, you got back together again and you have two kids to show for it."

"We all took our lumps in one way or another."

"We had a lot of fun, though."

Yes, they did, Christine thought with a certain wistfulness. It was light years ago and yet it seemed, in some ways, more real than what had happened just yesterday. Now they were all married, except for Clover, who was a successful travel agent with a prestigious firm on Fifth Avenue, Rockefeller Center. Clover was the one who had eluded the tender trap, with a chic little apartment on East Eight-third Street.

She was extravagantly pretty, small, slight, honey-blonde, like a stylish waif, somehow. They used to call her "little Clover." They had all worried about her because she was not "taken care of," and no children to succor her in her old age, no grandchildren sitting on her knee. They didn't worry about her anymore, though, but had come to feel faint twinges of envy. Sure, the rest of them had achieved what was reputed to be *the* goal of woman even if she realized other goals: the rest of them had the chatelaine's keys firmly in their grasp.

But they were chained, shackled, when it came right down to it. In a rut and wondering what came next. Not Clover, though. She was free as a sandpiper, with travel perks that enabled her to fly off to Paris for a weekend, or go to Vienna at Christmastime. There were always men in her life, perhaps lovers, perhaps simply escorts, friends. Sometimes for a long period, just as often a passing fancy, here today and gone tomorrow.

Then, almost five years ago, she had mildly astonished them, with news of a liaison (her word) with a man much older than herself, and now she saw only this man. He was married, with a grown son himself married, and Viennese-born, a refugee of the Hitler era; he was a Jew. Clover said, "Some of his family went to the ovens, I don't know which ones, he doesn't enlarge on it. He's a brilliant man, much too good for me. He was of considerable importance as a journalist in Europe—London, Paris —also a short story writer, but in this country he's gotten short shrift in that regard, though he has a superlative P.R. job and has reconciled himself to being a writer *manqué.*"

By this time Clover spoke, *en passant*, about Anton (Anton Ehrenberg) just the way the others made mention of their own spouses, and by this time it was accepted by the rest of them that Anton was the man Clover had been waiting for. Or if not waiting, at least hoping for, one imagined. She appeared enormously content with her "situation:" Ruth said that Clover had the best of both worlds, and it did indeed seem that nothing was lacking.

Christine, over her second martini, studied her

friends. They were case histories too. Anyone their ages was bound to be. Pattern set, the die cast. They had reached the point of no return. Maybe Clover was the exception: her destiny seemed unfixed as yet. Aside from that, they were prototypes, alive and well and living in New York, and they would never, alas, have lengthy obituaries in the *Times.*

Ruth Alexander, like Christine, had had an uneventful passage from young womanhood to matron, the same "normal" progression from one stage to another. It was Ruth that Christine was closest to, not only because they were near neighbors but because their minds ran in similar directions. You didn't know who lived next door to you in the Manhattan of today, so it was a joy to run into Ruth on the street, striding along in her Ferragamo shoes, or to bump into her in one of the aisles at d'Agostino, coming toward you behind her overflowing shopping cart. There was a coffee shop on Madison where she and Ruth had many a sandwich together, and they often walked, meeting by chance, down to Washington Square, maybe not even talking very much, but just being together. Ruth was your typical Jewish princess, with a vivid little face like an Irish colleen. You would have sworn she came from County Cork.

Now Ruth was having migraines.

Meryl was tall and thin and broad-shouldered, big-boned and flat-chested. Regular features, an oval face and not pretty except when she smiled, then a kind of radiance came over her face. She was the one with really tough times behind her.

She had gone into computer programming, eased into a top-flight job at IBM and then, thrown over by a man she loved and had planned to marry, went into a tailspin. Funked out in slow, sinister stages: psychiatric sessions failed to ameliorate the situation and she landed in a psych ward. As a matter of fact, she insisted on being admitted . . . or else, she told her shrink, she'd overdose, it was up to him. His name was unpronounceable, with a lot of z's, so that you settled for calling him Dr. Cosy, or something near that. They had all talked to him at the hospital: he was grave and pontifical and he spoke in a kind of iambic pentameter, with an accent like Peter Lorre. "Full of himself," Ruth said, biting off her words. "She should have gone to a big fat jolly type who'd pinch her fanny. I hate these holier-than-thou shitheads, he really thinks he's Dr. Freud."

When she was released from the psych ward she had a mad, frenetic gaiety, telling them every detail of her experience, and almost at once began hunting down people she had met at the hospital, other patients, filling her apartment with them. You couldn't find a single line of communication with these crazies, young men with ponytails and beads and girls who drew their mouths with brown eyebrow pencil. Meryl lost her job and was in no condition to look for another and had to go on Welfare. Then she lost her apartment because of the crazies crashing there whenever they felt like it. She would have been put out on the street, except for her friends, who succeeded in getting her into a Y branch, where she had a horrid little room with creepy-crawlies. Bad days for Meryl, but she had pulled out of it. Even boyfriends lent a hand in a spirit of Christian decency, and after a while Meryl got a job at the East End Hotel for Women, renting rooms for them, and had a small but clean room as part of her salary. Also two meals a day, breakfast and dinner.

Then at a party at the East End Hotel she met a very fine young man who had something to do with television, and it went on from there. Now she was married to the television man and seemed no different from anyone else. You would never have guessed that she had had such horrendous zero hours. She had two children, twin girls, and after that underwent a tubal ligature. She said that with her history she really shouldn't have reproduced at all.

It was Helene who had really fooled them, though. Helene, whose father had died when she was only six years old. An only child, she had had a single-parent upbringing, as her mother never remarried. She put all her chips on her daughter, took really good care of her and worked hard to do it, and then later on became an albatross around Helene's neck. It was like having a cat: you couldn't do this and you couldn't do that because the pet had to be fed and watered and its litter box changed. Helene never went to the movies with them in the evening because she didn't want to leave her mother alone. There was a reversal of roles as Helene slowly became the mother and her mother became the child.

Helene was a big, robust, creamy-complexioned

girl whose splendid build and dimpled Nordic face easily attracted men, whom Helene invited home to dinner rather than date outside because she didn't want to leave her mother alone. Therefore, the gentlemen friends never lasted very long: they could easily see that anyone who wedded Helene would be wedding her mother as well.

Once Ruth, in her blunt way, had suggested to Mrs. Sonnenberg that she must be a little lonely. "You're so young to remain a widow," was her wily ploy. "It does seem such a waste, I feel."

"Lonely?" was the instant reply. "With Helene? Why, we have the happiest life! We're like sisters! Why should I be lonely?"

"What will happen to Helene when she dies?" became an almost tedious refrain. Then they decided darkly that she would outlive Helene. "She'll bury us all." She did die, though, at the age of forty-nine, and it just went to show that the things you didn't expect to happen sometimes did, while the things you did expect often never came to pass. It was a seven-months' illness, cancer of course, and it left Helene many, many pounds lighter and hollow in the face. Her friends outdid themselves in making things bearable for her, taking her to dinner at Longchamps and Gaetano's and Giovanni's and every place they could think of, places Helene had never been before.

Then after about three months Helene announced that she was going to Italy for a "breather." She said maybe a month or two, maybe longer, she'd see. Well, there must have been some money, insurance or whatever, but you would have thought it would be France, because Helene was a French major, using a lot of French phrases like *faute de mieux,* and so forth. But she said she had always wanted to go to Italy, and go she did. Not only that, but she stayed for almost a year, sending postcards of the Blue Grotto and Capri and Firenze and Verona and just about everywhere. She loved the hill towns, she wrote, and made X's to indicate her room at the hotels where she stayed. "This is my room, note the balcony. I sit there after a day's wandering, with a glass of Campari. Everything sublime, love Helene."

When she came back it was with a husband, a man she met in Anacapri and married in Rome. There were two daughters as well, Diane and Lucy. Their father, Harold, was a widower of four years and he simply adored Helene. He treated her as if she were made of Murano glass, of which he had shipped back a great quantity to the States. There was the usual uneasiness between stepmother and stepchildren, but time told the tale: Helene had catered to her mother for a good bit of her life, she was well equipped to take on the challenge of another woman's children. There was no question of any more additions, she told them. She had all she could handle, and Harold was in full agreement: he got himself vasectomized.

This was all, of course, yesterday's news by now, assimilated, digested and part of their history, running through Christine's mind because she was in an analytical frame of mind. What they had come from and what they had done. That was unchangeable. And now there they sat, five women of varying backgrounds but now with parallel outlooks, women who lived within a radius of a few miles, in the city they had been born and raised in, and who had "kept up." They saw each other at regular intervals, gathered together like the disciples, drank martinis and broke bread and were more real to Christine, more substantial and enduring than almost everything else. Their concerns would very likely be meshed until they died, one by one. She couldn't imagine life ending without their spirits wishing her Godspeed in her final journey and then remembering her, lifting a glass at some reunion far in the future, making a toast to the dear departed.

"Gee, it's weird not to have Chris here. Remember how she used to imitate Marlon Brando as the Godfather? Hell, she was so damned much fun . . ."

2

There were the usual protracted leavetakings outside the restaurant, though Clover, who had to get back to her office, dashed off with promises to keep in touch, sure, and see you next time, ladies. "I'm coming down fast," Ruth said. "How about a walk, anyone?"

"Let's go to Bloomie's," Helene suggested.

Meryl was game, but Ruth said no, it was too

nice a day to stay indoors, she wanted a brisk hike. "Christine?"

"You've got it. Alongside the park?"

"Be fine."

"Well, have a pleasant stroll, you two, and be well. See you eftsoons."

"Eftsoons? How Elizabethan can you get?"

"An acrostic word. Chic, ain't it?"

"If you say so," Ruth agreed, chuckling. "Okay, go shopping, spend the old man's money, serve him right. Bye bye."

Waves and smiles, and then Meryl and Helene headed over to Lex. "You don't mind if we stop in that outlet place of Carrano's first?" Meryl asked.

"What's that?"

"Carrano's, you don't know the store? They have stunning shoes, and they have this cut-rate store on Fifty-sixth. Okay?"

"Why not?"

Meryl didn't find anything, but Helene did, as a matter of fact two pairs. "Never been here before, thanks for telling me," she said when they left. "Terribly good stuff."

The light changed at Fifty-seventh Street and they crossed to the other side of the avenue. Lexington, at this point, was like a sewer, junky, odorous and a cacophany of hideous sounds, a spot where you had to keep a firm grasp on your pocketbook. Alexander's, the mecca of bargain hunters from points all over, was on one corner and a fast food place, from which hot and greasy smells emerged, on the other. There was a subway entrance that spewed forth hordes of milling bodies, much jostling and clamor, and street kids who looked as if they had never seen the inside of a school scrambled about chaotically, screaming and cackling with an ear-splitting intensity.

One of these kids, out of his mind with mischievous deviltry, ran to the curb, unzipped the fly of his ragged jeans, and peed in the gutter. He was about nine, rips in his dirty shirt, a little Hispanic kid with wild, handsome dark eyes that were snapping with delight at the way people darted away from his stream of urine. The other kids squawked with delirious laughter; he was a hero in their eyes.

"What chance does someone like that have?" Helene wondered "He'll O.D. before he's fourteen."

"Bet you a dollar he ends up on the City Council, maybe will be mayor some day."

"You may be right, he looked smart. He certainly has chutzpah."

A big, battered car, an old Chevy, was parked on the side next to the fast food place. The trunk was open, displaying great plastic-wrapped cuts of meat, bloody red slabs that were plainly steaks, nicely marbleized; you wouldn't mind having some of them in your freezer. That was, if you didn't quail at the thought of the probable consequences, salmonella or whatever. Maybe it was horse meat at that. We were almost a hundred percent sure it was hot, stolen, but there it was, massed in the car trunk in crimson heaps, peddled by two tough-looking men who looked as if they spent their spare time stuffing bodies under bridges, and they had every reason to be nonchalant about what they were doing without a license: there was never a patrolman in this vicinity.

Across the way, hunkered down and fiddling with some object on the sidewalk, a workman, or bum, squatted, a big, burly creature with an enormous behind. He looked prehistoric crouching there, clad on top with a skimpy sweatshirt that, positioned as he was, bared his massive back from midsection to buttocks as his pants strained down due to his crouch. You could practically see his sit-down, though thankfully not quite the whole of it, but the cleft between the two beefy haunches was almost fully exposed, and hairy as an ape.

He wasn't mooning, it wasn't exhibitionism. He was simply absorbed in something only he was cognizant of, and oblivious to anything else. It was *his* street, *his* city, *his* territory. He wasn't aware of the unlovely spectacle he presented, and wouldn't have cared if he had been.

Meryl said she had once seen a bag lady doing her business where the meat truck was today. She even had toilet paper, with which she wiped herself and then dropped alongside the pile she'd made. "It was so depressing, I couldn't think of anything else all day."

"And here I am with two new pairs of shoes."

"As if that would help, not buying shoes. I just always tell myself I'll avoid that side of the street down here, and then I always forget."

A block later the Boschian scene was left behind, and they slowed their steps. "You can't help appreciating this beautiful day," Helene murmured. "I think I'm getting spring fever."

"Yeah. There ought to be a hurdy-gurdy. Like when you were a kid, that tinkling music, it was like a siren song. And the monkey in his little suit. I'd love to see a hurdy-gurdy right now."

"I don't think they have them any more," Helene said, and they went into Bloomingdale's.

Clover, reaching Fifth, scratched the idea of taking a cab downtown. It would be no faster than walking, or not enough to make a difference; a few minutes more or less wouldn't mean anything. She had a lot of work to knock off this afternoon, though, so she walked rapidly, mentally deciding what to tackle first when she got back.

She didn't work late on the evenings she was going to be with Anton, and she was seeing him tonight, so she hoped there would be no hitches. Air fares were fluctuating so dizzyingly these days it was impossible to keep up with them. You quoted a price and the next day it went up, which was difficult for clients to understand. They thought you were gypping them. Some of them did, anyway, though in the main she had a comfy little nucleus of tried and true regulars who trusted her and she made it a point not to handle the "pushcart" trade, the people who were out to make deals.

She should be able to clean off her desk for the night at just before six and then hie herself up to Fifty-seventh Street to join Anton. He worked in the Genesco Bulding and they met outside it, whereupon they stolled up to her apartment on Eight-third, stopping off at a Gristede's for whatever food shopping might be necessary.

She and Anton were together three evenings a week. Monday, Wednesday and Friday, though Anton didn't stay overnight. He left at around eleven, unless they had guests, in which case it would be later. Clover always went downstairs with him to be sure he got a cab. Otherwise he might have decided to walk home. He had an arrogant disregard for even the simplest safety measures, no street smarts. She thought it was probably because he had lived through such grisly times in Europe, and everything else seemed picayune to him.

They were also together all day on Sunday. This was the way Anton apportioned his time between wife and lover. Clover had no idea how this arrangement sat with Mrs. Ehrenberg, but it suited her well enough. She was not one to cry over spilled milk, bang her head against a stone wall about things she had no power to change. She would have liked very much to be the sole possessor of this man she loved so much, but then it seem reasonable to assume that so, undoubtedly, would Mrs. Ehrenberg.

And my goodness, she was used to living alone after many a long year. Maybe it would be hard *not* to live alone for someone so accustomed to it. It wasn't that she had planned *not* to marry, but then she had never planned *to* marry, the way girls—even today—simply took it for granted that whatever course their lives took it would include the altar and the delivery room. She had always been comfortable with herself, not so much egocentric as simply at home with Clover Martinson, though she had often wished her sister April hadn't

31

married either, that the two of them had just gone on, in a companionable spinsterhood, with apartments close to each other's. April had married, though, and now lived in Connecticut, as did their mother, who had left New York when their father's firm relocated there. Now Daddy was dead, so it was nice that she had April within visiting distance.

She didn't miss April the way she used to, thankfully, since she had Anton now. It was just that her sister was almost like an alter ego, with the same ready spontaneity as herself and the same avid greediness for all the things there were to do and see and learn. They had always been best friends when they were growing up, doing rash things, absolutely in tune with each other, guessing what was in each other's mind and finishing each other's sentences as if they had a common brain pan. They had no formal religious beliefs, but she and April had always admired Jesus for his unstudied humility, his joyful poverty and his simple enjoyments, walking about in the fresh air and rapping with all sorts of people.

Before she met Anton she had plenty of fun and no lack of attention from guys. There was a period of a few years when her refrigerator was almost bare, just bread, milk, butter and so forth and in the pantry coffee and a few tins. Food was no problem because she was asked out to dinner just about every night in the week. Men wanted her, not only for her looks but for her easy, reckless abandon. She was never a great lay: her lust died quickly and maintaining a sexual relationship was difficult for her. She would rather go out to dinner, or a movie, or the opera, or take a walk. Ex-lovers found themselves gravitating back to her, for friendship and a good time. She was genuinely liked, which was primarily what she wanted.

That was over, there was Anton now, and she was just like any of the other of her married friends: she was happily hog-tied.

In her office at shortly after three, she pored over schedules, using the phone, writing out airline tickets. She had lengthy conferences with a client who had become a friend as well, and one with a male client, a lawyer who generally drove her up the wall but who today was a pussycat. All went smoothly and at five-fifty-five she paperweighted a few piles of material, locked her desk, and left.

She could see him standing there, as she neared the Genesco Building, a cigarette stuck between his lips, lean and handsome and looking expectant. She raised a hand, grinning, and he did the same. "Hi," she called, rushing up to him.

They kissed and then walked, hand in hand, uptown along Fifth. It was that lovely time of day with the sun at its strongest, like a fiery eye, so that a kind of golden sheen glazed streets and structures. "How was your day?" she asked him.

"Çi, ça. Yours?"

"I had lunch with the girls. Meryl, Helene, Ruth and Chris. I'm stuffed. Can we have a light dinner?"

"An omelet?"

"Yeah. With a green salad. Summer's nice, isn't it?"

"It's barely spring."

She was completely happy. She couldn't imagine any other life but this one with Anton. Everything had led up to this unalloyed contentment, and it was all she would ever want.

Ruth and Christine, after making their way over to Fifth, crossed to the park side and started downtown. "You didn't want to go shopping, did you?" Ruth asked.

"No, I wanted to take advantage of this heavenly day, stay out in the fresh air."

"It's probably anything but fresh, but pollution or no it feels like champagne."

It was indeed a rare day, a bonanza after the bum winter. Blue skies, like enamel. Cloisonné skies, speckled with delicate clouds that looked like pointillism. "How's this for an improvement in the weather?" Ruth demanded. "I guess we're set now, I doubt we'll revert to icy blasts."

"No, I don't think so. Just about time too. I'm so sick of wool scarves and lined gloves and bundling up like an Eskimo."

"It was a nice lunch."

"It was great. I missed Meryl the last time, when she was laid up with the flu."

"She looked fine today."

They walked down to Fifty-seventh Street, watched the Hare Krishna crew with their shaved pates and jingling bells. High-stepping it, cavorting and chanting. Ruth shrugged. "I suppose if they want to make jackasses out of themselves."

"Yes, well."

They retraced their steps, starting back. "Ever

worry your kids will go overboard for something like that?"

"Nancy's too ambitious and Bruce is too square. Like me."

"The trouble is you're not square."

"I wasn't once but I am now. Sad to say. I've become a bore."

"Okay, what shall we do, go back to school? Pick up where we left off?"

"I'd like to open a tiny shop somewhere. Over on Second, I guess. Gifts. Not run-of-the-mill garbage. Mad things, insane things nobody else has."

"Where would the capital come from?"

"I haven't thought that out yet." Christine laughed. "Just kidding, of course. I can dream, can't I? Let's go down and say hello to the seals."

They turned in at the entrance to the zoo area, down the steps and across the brick-tiled walkway that led to the central esplanade. On this sun-bleared day of early spring the crowds were out in full force, the vendors' stands enjoying a brisk business. "Well, all right," Ruth said, throwing her head back and breathing deeply. "This is more like it. I was here a week ago, I thought I'd be blown away. I can hack cold, but I detest and abominate wind."

The seals too seemed to vibrate to the change of seasons; they were as skittish as kittens, barking croupily and sliding off their rocks to splash in the sparkling pool. Screaming kids mimicked them, volleys of admonitions from harrassed parents rang out, babies bawled, English, Spanish merged to make a great clangor, noise pollution bombarded one's ears; it was a lovely bedlam. "You know," Ruth murmured, "it's little things like this that make you happy in the most idiotic way. Oh, I love New York."

"Even if it is dying."

"Bull. Well, maybe, who knows. So I'll die with it."

"You'll get no argument from me."

"Let's have a soft ice cream."

"After that lunch? Well, okay."

They lapped it while sitting on a bench. Chatting idly for a bit and then falling silent, sitting close to each other, companionable and glad to be together and just as pleased to sit quietly and watch the passing parade. "Duty calls," Christine said regretfully at shortly before five. "Let's catch the hour at the clock and then we'd better get on our sticks."

"Okay. I've so enjoyed today."

"Me too. Better hurry, it's a few minutes to."

They made it in time, and stood smiling as they joined the attentive throng in front of the Delacorte clock, where the beguiling bronze animals revolved slowly and with an endearing pomposity, beating their drums and wielding their batons. "Five o'clock and all's well," a smiling mother said to her toddler. "Wasn't that fun, Jeffrey?"

"Well, back to the salt mines," Ruth said briskly, and they left, arm in arm, and ambled back home. Ruth turned off at Sixty-sixth, her street. "Take it easy," she called.

"You too. We'll do something next week."

"I'll probably see you at the supermarket on Saturday."

Three blocks farther the complex that was Christine's own home grounds loomed, the Colonnade, so named because of some architectural features that were functional but gave the impression of decorative pillars if you stretched your imagination a bit.

It was an enclave, housing God knew how many souls within its confines, and a kind of superhuman effort must have been required to prevent the block-long, block-wide structure, in its elephantine proportions, from appearing to be either a hospital or a penal institution. Miraculously, whoever had mapped out this sprawling monstrosity had been in the main successful. There was much lush planting inside girdling stone walls that gave the clever impression of being built out of adobe brick, like that of an old Mission, and winding, woodsy little paths where you half expected to see an elf or two. There were imaginatively-shaped espaliered trees and dappled expanses of lawn dotted with lacy benches and chairs. It was rather like a Maxfield Parrish conception of paradise.

The Colonnade had been one of the first luxury houses to employ concierges. Just like in Paris, some residents commented with only marginal irony. Where you lived in this monolithic beehive determined which concierge was assigned to you and which elevator you used. Also which maintenance men got your money at Christmas. It was a fortress in the jungle of Manhattan: there were many such. It had gone co-op some years ago, though there were still, it was said, some nonsubsidized units. Famous people lived there and some infamous people. Money was the requisite, though controversial political figures and flamboyant film personalities had a tough time finding their way into the bastion. It was well patrolled and there had been relatively few burglaries and there was a marked absence of small children, though there were many pint-sized dogs with cranky barks who had been trained to wait until they were out on the sidewalk before emptying their bowels.

Carl Jennings had had the foresight to see the wave of the future, that cooperatives and condominiums would swallow the rental market, a shark wolfing down smaller fish. You didn't have a prayer these days unless you had lots of money in the bank. If you had it you thanked God for it and tried not to think of less fortunate people. For the eight-room apartment Carl had bought in 1977, he had paid the sum of $190,000 which, at the time, had seemed a princely sum but which inflation had beggared, so that by this time the asking price would be something like three times that amount, and he never tired of reminding Christine of that fact.

He arrived home while Christine was putting the artichokes in the steamer. "What's to eat, honey?" he asked her, accompanying the question with a pat on the rump.

"Linguine with clam sauce. Artichokes, and I made a flan for dessert."

"Sounds tasty." He kissed her. "How was your day?"

"I had lunch with the girls. You?"

"So so. Anything I can do?"

"No, sit down and read the paper or something. This will be ready in half an hour. Tell Nancy."

No one had to tell Bruce; he was setting the table. He was increasingly thoughtful, maybe a little apprehensive too, wistful, clinging even, for he would be going away to college next year, and anyway he had always been her shadow. Nancy was Daddy's girl, but Bruce and Christine had a dialogue that was very precious to her.

Next fall he would be vamos. Home for the holidays, but no longer under her aegis. His room would be empty.

God, I'll miss him, she thought.

It was a good dinner, she was a good cook. Many years had accomplished this, and these days it was her only duty around the house. It irked her that Nancy was picking at her food. "Aren't you hungry?" she asked her daughter.

"Not very."

"I can imagine why. You had junk food after school. Why do I bother to cook?"

"Why don't you hire a *chef de maison*, then you won't have to slave over a hot stove."

"There's little enough for me to do as it is. At least I can make a meal for my family. Damn it, Nancy, why do you do that?"

"Eat junk food? Live dangerously, I always say. You should be grateful I don't go in for angel dust."

"You go in for angel dust, you look for other accommodations," Christine said calmly.

"May I be excused?"

"No you may not. Sit there and move the food

around on your plate. What did you do with your hair?"

"Got tired of it and threw it in the trash can," Nancy answered sassily, and Carl laughed.

Christine smiled. "Look who's picking me up on semantics, of all people. However you fixed it, it looks nice. I used to part my hair in the middle."

"I remember that," Carl said. "You looked like a Renaissance Madonna."

"She's not a bad-looking chick," Bruce conceded. "Not that she'll ever be any competition for you, Mother. She'll go downhill fast, she'll be blowsy in her thirties."

Nancy threw a crouton at him. "What's for dessert?" she asked.

"I made a flan."

"Oh. So I'll hang around."

"I thought you would."

We're really a pretty nice bunch, Christine thought, sitting at her end of the table, the day dying, the prospect of a good documentary on television later on. Her daughter was blooming, getting to look more like Ali McGraw every day, and her son had those soft, velvety eyes. Facing her husband, she had to admit that he was a fine-looking man, though his hair was thinning at the back and it wouldn't hurt him to lose some weight around the middle. Still, and all things considered, they weren't such a bad lot.

The burst of sun that snaked in from the terrace cast a glow on the domestic scene. The classic American portrait, father, mother and offspring, along with a well-filled table. Like a Norman

Rockwell. Why then should she feel this malaise, this nagging discontent? There were no monetary worries, far from it. Carl's earnings as a doctor were gargantuan, neither of the kids was in reform school and it would soon be summer, when the living was easy.

She poured herself some more Beaujolais, forked up the last of her salad and molded her face into a smile. This was hers, this was what she had, it was all she would ever have and she wouldn't have it always. She sat there, with that fixed smile, which encompassed them all. Her family, two of whom she had brought forth from her own body.

And now it was time to get up and clear the table, bring in the dessert, the pot of coffee, fresh napkins. Bruce would help her, though Nancy would remain seated, keeping her father company, the two of them grinning at each other and he asking about her day at school. She would do one of her imitations, having inherited this dubious talent from her mother. Some instructor or other, mimic his speech or his stance or his pedantry. Carl would smile anticipatively. After a while, from the kitchen, she would hear his deep-bodied laugh, while she and Bruce exchanged amused glances. "There they go again," Bruce would say.

Immobility claimed Christine this evening, however, and the entr'acte between the meal and the dessert was unduly prolonged. She had eaten very little, after the hearty lunch earlier in the day, so it had been for her mostly the green salad. She was still dwelling on the lunch, and her friends, and thinking that the walk later on with Ruth had been sort of idyllic. Two old friends strolling the well-trodden paths of Central Park. The sky had been so blue, like the portals of heaven. How lovely, how lovely . . .

Her eyes were heavy—too many martinis. Three. Surely no more than that? She couldn't quite remember. But three at the most, she never went past three.

She heard the sigh escaping. It came from her. "Well," she said, to no one in particular. "Everyone finished?"

Everyone was, it seemed. But she didn't get up, just sat there. There were no remarks, no one made a crack at the unwonted delay, not even Nancy asked were they going to stay there all night or what. They just sat there waiting, sort of arrested in motion, almost unmoving, with the sun hitting Carl full in the face, so that he had his head slightly lowered, as if in prayer, and his eyes half closed. She thought of the ossified bodies in Pompeii, lying in their glass showcases on their backs, just the way they had fallen when the terrible blow struck, their voices stilled forever by the awesome force that ended the course of their lives in the midst of whatever they had been doing at the time. Maybe cooking, maybe tending a child, maybe getting ready for a party, maybe screwing, maybe waiting for their dessert to be served, who would ever know now?

But it wasn't that, after all, and it wasn't a Norman Rockwell drawing, all folksy and heartwarming. It was Duane Hanson, of course, of *course*. They were Duane Hanson figures, cast in plaster and then clad in store-bought clothing, large as life and real as life, artfully posed in the most natural postures imaginable, a striking facsimile of honest to God people. There they were, right in her own dining room, to add to the decor. Pretend companions, that's what they were. She was playing house and force-feeding them, the way she used to do with her dolls. *Eat that up, you bad girl* . . .

What did she know about them anyway, these days? Everything and nothing. What did they know about her? She was chief cook and bottle washer, the fixer. It was her fault, it must be her fault. She should have realized, years and years ago when there were two babies in the house and an attractive young man for a husband, that this present situation would arise, that she would be taking a back seat, that Carl would turn into a busy man in a busy world outside her own and that Bruce and Nancy would grow up, assume other identities, become *people*. She should have known better, should have farmed the kids out to a woman for daily care, found a top job somewhere, lived a separate life the way Carl did and the way the children were doing. She should have *been* somebody.

"I'll get the dessert," she said, pushing back her chair, and went into the kitchen, with her son, carrying plates, close on her heels.

3

It was always a delight to get one of those pale blue, tissue-thin airmail communications; you immediately placed yourself in the city it came from, in this case London. There it was, wedged in with the nuisance mail, the flyers and department store circulars and the utility bills. It was from Peggy Thornley, and it started the day off just right.

Peggy Thornley was a woman Christine and Carl

had met on one of their trips abroad; she was now a valued acquaintance. They saw each other infrequently, but had a sporadic correspondence and Peggy's letters were always a cut above those annual Christmas card things in which you scribbled some stale news and info about the weather in your parts. And this particular letter was pleasing because it offered some diversion for Christine.

It seemed that Peggy's son, the older one, would be wending his way to the U.S. for what Peggy termed "a year of American seasoning, Henry James in reverse." Ventures, and *ad*ventures, she asserted, were few and far between in these days of an empireless Britain. "For 'this scepter'd isle' substitute sequestered isle." England was dying, she added elegiacally, and no one felt it more keenly than the young.

Then she got down to business. "You remember Rodney," she penned, in her non-American handwriting, all round and firm and positive. "He had quite a crush on you when you visited us at our vacation place in Annecy. He's twenty-one now, very tall and thin as a walking stick. Quite the grown man, or so he thinks, but in reality a silly young ass. But he's quite well behaved, I've seen to that."

He would have to find a flat, Peggy explained, and went on to ask if it would be too much of an imposition for Christine to assist him in this undertaking. And could she possibly book him a room until he was settled?

It was like a present, like a gift. Christine was elated. Something to *do*. And of course he would stay with them until he found a place to live during his "year of American seasoning." She would unearth some cute little nest for Rodney, help him furnish it, make it a small showplace. She remembered the Thornley boys as charming, with beautiful manners. And yes, Rodney had had a bit of a crush on her. Carl had remarked on it. "That boy has eyes for you, Chris."

She and Carl had visited Peggy and Tony Thornley in Annecy, France, a lovely little canal city where for that particular summer the Thornleys had rented a villa. It was the first time they had encountered the Thornley children, Rodney and Douglas. They had been teenagers, but British teeners, with the polished manners of British children.

The younger boy, shy and—well, something like Bruce, soft and brown-eyed—had been very much in his brother's shadow, as Rodney—hazel of eye and sun-streaked of hair—was like a young prince, almost arrogant, and wonderful to look at. "A bit of a showoff," Carl had said. "But a fine kid all the same."

And Carl was right, Rodney hadn't been able to take his eyes off her, those large and brilliant gray eyes with secrets behind them, secrets of growing up, of being between boyhood and manhood, God knew what he was thinking when he looked at her like that.

She wondered what he was like now, at twenty-one. Worriedly, she realized it wouldn't be the easiest thing in the world to find a low-rent apartment in a safe neighborhood. She would have to

46

begin combing the real estate ads right away. But it was a delightful assignment, something to look forward to.

She dashed off an answering letter. She would meet Rodney's flight, of course, and they had a spare room for him for as long as he needed it. "It will be such a pleasure," she effused. "Such an unexpected pleasure and Carl, as you may imagine, will feel the same way, as will Bruce and Nancy."

She sealed the envelope and, dressing, went out and mailed it, then bused down to Bloomingdale's to see what goodies she could spot for the apartment-to-be of Peggy's son. Modern, certainly. In all the British films she saw there was a heavy emphasis on what was called industrial modern, with a lot of Beylerian imports and chrome-framed posters. Knock-down furniture—it came cheap and was suited to a short-term "adventure." Too bad Nancy was only fifteen, otherwise she'd have a hand-picked date. But at twenty-one, Rodney would probably consider her beneath his notice. It was she herself who, in the end, would benefit most from Rodney's sojourn in this country. It would be an adventure for her too, and the sofa in the study was a daybed, so that he would have all the comforts of home until she got him settled.

They met on the lower level at Kennedy, he with an enormous suitcase plus a rucksack across his back. She had recognized him from the gallery, after dismissing one or two other young men who somehow didn't look British, though she was a bit tentative in her greeting, not absolutely sure. "Rodney?" she hazarded, walking up to him.

"Mrs. Jennings?" Then he laughed. "I don't know why the question mark in my voice, because I knew you right away. Well, here's the nuisance arrived at your doorstep. I must say you put a good face on it, because that smile looks genuine."

"It is, it is! Hello, Rodney dear. It's *lovely* to see you . . ."

He sighed. "You *are* a brick." Then he put his arms around her and hugged her. "So," he said, when they let each other go. "How are you? I haven't even asked."

"I'm fine, Carl's fine, everyone's fine."

"Good. I'll be happy to see Mr. Jennings again too."

"Why don't you call us Carl and Christine? You're going to be part of the family for a while and there's no reason to be formal. You're a big boy now. Come, we'll find a porter and get your stuff in a cab. You must be tired after your trip. Was it a good flight?"

"Yes, splendid. It's really okay if I stay at your house until I'm shored up in a flat? My mother said I was not to be a bother."

"We wouldn't hear of anything else. We have a study that's scarcely ever used, with a very good sofa sleeper and you'll have your privacy. A bath to yourself, though for showers you'll have to share with Bruce. My son. Rodney, you've grown so tall!"

"Douglas is catching up to me."

"How is Douglas?"

"A pain in the you know what, younger brothers

always are. No, seriously, he's okay. A bit full of himself, quite the *grand seigneur.*"

Again the laugh, the hand reaching up to toss back the shock of fair hair, the display of excellent white teeth. Christine hid a smile of her own. Saying his brother was full of himself! But she loved his youthful assurance. Why shouldn't he be egotistic? Youth was the time for that.

"We're going to have a marvelous time," she assured him in the cab. "I've all sorts of things planned. Also I've started looking in the paper for apartments. So far nothing much, but we'll find something just right. You won't mind if I help you fix it up?"

"You'd do that?"

"You may regret it. Possibly I'll get in your hair, be bossy, and . . . Rodney?"

"Yes, Mrs. —" The smile flashed again. "I mean, yes, Christine?"

"Could you give me some idea of how much rent you had in mind?"

"No idea at all," he said cheerfully. "I expect it will take me some time to think in dollars rather than pounds."

"I see." That wasn't much help, she thought. It was true the Thornleys had all kinds of money, but still . . .

"So this is America," he remarked, looking out the window.

"This is America," she agreed. "I suppose you're starved. I've made a festive dinner for you. It's cooking away in the range right now, a standing roast. Will you like that?"

He put two of his fingers to his mouth and kissed them. "La la," he murmured, then put a hand over hers. Just for a second, but it felt so warming, it made her feel right at home. Though why she should think that when it was she who lived here she had no idea. She supposed it was because Rodney had been, in a way, an X quantity, and it had turned out that he was everything she had hoped for. Nice, friendly, companionable. Not at all ill at ease. He would fit in very well with the rest of them.

"It's a big place, this town," he said a little later.

"We're far from "this town," she told him, smiling. "This is no-man's land, just a lot of dumps and factories, but before long you'll catch a glimpse of this wicked city."

"It's wicked?"

"Just another metropolis with good and bad. Like London or Paris or Rome and so forth. Honey, you're to be cautious, though, you must learn the no-nos. For example, Central Park. Off limits after five at the latest. My kids will set you straight."

"How old are your kids, Mrs. Jennings?" He caught himself up, his smile mischievous. "What did you say your name was?"

It was like that all the way into town. Bandying back and forth; he was a bit of a tease, this Rodney. She felt as if she had known him all her life. How's that for triteness, she asked herself.

"Remember, in Annecy," he said at one point, "when you couldn't find a snapshot in a roll of film you'd just had developed? It was one of you, standing in front of the Casino. We were all passing the snaps around and then that one was missing. I filched it. You never could figure out where it disappeared to. I still have it."

"Rodney Thornley, you imp! I'm not sure I recall that—well, perhaps vaguely. Anyway, I'm flattered."

"I was a prurient little bastard, I expect. Well, then, I thought that would get a rise out of you, Christine."

"You sound like a native," she objected. "Get a rise out of me indeed. You're supposed to teach my kids the proper way to speak. I've sort of been depending on it."

"I shall try," he said solemnly. "Then you can tell my Mum what a lovely boy I am."

"You are a lovely boy," she said warmly. "Rodney, how is your mother?"

"Very well, thank you. Garden Club, lawn parties, lending a helping hand where a helping hand is needed. You know, small philanthropic enterprises." He slid down in his seat and chuckled. "Quite the English gentlewoman."

"While I vegetate and don't engage myself in a single worthy cause. No, don't shake your head, I mean it."

"A worthy cause is sitting beside you at this moment," he reminded her. "That is if you really mean it about giving me aid and assistance in my haphazard peregrinations."

"You seem so much older than American kids your age," she told him, wishing her own offspring had his verbal gifts. "Older and—well, different. A kind of different I very much like. And the way you take things in stride . . ."

"Yes, well," he said slowly, "we English are very good at maintaining a facade. The sky could fall and we'd still have tea at four of an afternoon. Don't—uh—let it fool you. At the moment—"

He cleared his throat. "I wonder if you'll believe this. I'm scared. It's true. I want new experiences, but when they come my way I go all bonkers. Right now I feel about twelve years old, and that's one reason I came, to get out of the bell jar. As you said, I'm a big boy now."

"Oh, Rodney," she said, concerned. "Don't be scared, don't go bonkers. Don't be homesick! I know, we're just people you met a long time ago. Not so long for us, but practically eons for you. Relax, darling. You're with friends. Take your time, take it slowly. Remember, you're with people who love you. I mean that, Rodney. Carl and I have never forgotten you, or those lovely few days we spent in the Haute Savoie with you boys and your parents. It's a precious memory."

"I never forgot you either," he said, and straightened up in his seat, his face composed again.

4.

Rodney, the charmer, made instant inroads with all and sundry. Naturally Nancy made Cleopatra eyes at him, and he told her she was Titania, should wear a jewelled diadem round her hair and that if all American girls were anything like her he would very much enjoy being in this part of the world.

"That's a bit thick," Nancy retorted, though

clearly satisfied with his assessment of her. "You must have met dozens and dozens of American girls. I thought only Italians laid on the baloney like that. I thought British men were too busy admiring themselves."

"You probably think we all wear bowlers and go to the city every day with furled umbrellas."

"Don't you?"

"Some. The rest of us idle our time away at pubs and clubs and sleep late of a morning."

"Then you should mend your ways."

With Bruce Rodney was very matey, treating him like someone his own age, very man to man. He asked Bruce question after question about his studies, career aspirations and when informed about the latter turned to Carl with a congratulatory expression.

"You must be frightfully proud," he said heartily. "Your son following in your footsteps. It's just what every father wants. Good for you, Bruce, I think that's splendid."

As for Christine, he kept glancing her way every now and then, with a kind of conspiratorial look, as if they were in this together, he and she, a sort of Hansel and Gretel pair, venturing into the company of others and on their best behavior. She was amused at his proprietary manner toward her: he entertained the others rather like a host putting guests at their ease, but with her there was an air of insouciant camaraderie. She wouldn't have been one bit surprised if, leaving the dining room after the meal for coffee and liqueurs in the living room, he had slapped her on the back with a pally hand

and called her "Ducks."

He seemed, in fact, to have adopted her, rather than the other way around.

They all stayed up rather late that night, discussing conditions abroad, the state of the dollar and fluctuations of all currency in these latter days, talking about employment and unemployment: all the polite things people talked about when they were still relatively strangers. Carl asked Rodney what his own career aspirations were and Rodney said, "Oh, I expect banking, or something beastly like that."

Then he slid down in his chair and shrugged. What he would really like to do was write. He thought he might have some aptitude for it. "Of course," he admitted, "in England it's not the same as here, an author sort of, you know, just barely gets by. In this country you have all kinds of juicy plums, large advances, big reprint sales, *enormous* advantages we don't have. Anyway, I expect it's something I'll get over."

"Hey, why?" Bruce demanded eagerly. He was a serious reader. "Something creative, that's the best."

"Time will tell," Rodney surmised, and covered up a burp behind a hand. "Sorry," he murmured, glancing at Christine. "I ate far too much, I fear, but it was such a splendid meal. We don't get haute cuisine at home, not like that. Mum's good at putting up jams and jellies and conserves, but as for anything else it's quite ordinary."

"You have a cook," Christine reminded him, smiling. "So don't try to fool me. Furthermore, this may be the only showy meal you'll have in this house. It's not one of my pet occupations, chopping and dicing and braising and all that. I'd rather read a book."

"Bully for you."

"Maybe I'll be reading one of yours some day."

"I shouldn't count on it."

The conversation was petering out. For the first time Rodney looked tired. Young and dewy and sleepy-eyed and, Christine thought probably dying to crawl into bed. It had been a long day for him. It was about five in the morning in the city he had just left, and Christine was abundantly familiar with jet lag.

She got up. "Come, I'll show you where things are in your room," she said, beckoning. He dragged himself up and followed. "Good night to you all," he called back. "Thanks for everything. Thanks so much, you're all so kind. Cheerio and God bless."

"God bless," Nancy replied, and the rest of them said simply "Good night, Rodney."

"You'll be comfortable?" Christine asked him, pulling out the sleeper. It was made up, she had done that earlier. "Plenty of extra towels in the bathroom closet. Oh, and the refrigerator is raidable in case you wake up dying for a snack."

"I shall be just fine," he assured her. "Everything, simply everything is super. I can't thank you enough. I feel so at home."

"That's the way you're supposed to feel. We love having you. I love having you."

"And now you'll tuck me in, surely?" He twirled

an imaginary mustache.

"It's not in the contract," she said, laughing. "Good night, my dear, and sleep well. Sleep as late as you want. The kids will be off to school, Carl will be at his office, and you won't have to hang a Do Not Disturb sign on your door. I'll see to it that the housekeeper knows this room is off limits."

"I shall be up at dawn's early light and ready to go," he stated. "I have a whole set of plans, places to see, places I've heard about all my life. I'm not even sure I'll be able to sleep for thinking about it."

"You'll sleep, you look half dead already. So good night, and pleasant dreams."

"Good night, love," he said, his eyes following her. "Good night, sweet princess."

She was snickering as she went to her room. Nancy was Titania, she was a princess, Peggy had certainly raised a courtly boy. Carl lay on his side, his eyes closed. She thought he was asleep, but just before she got into her bed he opened one eye. "Chris?"

"What are you doing still awake? Do you realize what time you have to get up?"

"Just wanted to say good night."

"Good night, dear."

She snapped off her night light and lay on her back, her arms under her head. It was pleasant having company. He was a dear boy. Tomorrow they'd go sightseeing. Herself and Rodney, of course, since the others would be in absentia until the weekend. She would see that he had a really good time, and in the process have a good time herself, have a little holiday.

Lord, he certainly had a huge appetite.

He had claimed to be shy, or at least a slow starter when embarking on new horizons, but so far as Christine could see, Rodney didn't have a timorous bone in his body. He crossed avenues against the light, learned the bus system almost at once, and had a natural sense of direction. It had been a Monday when Rodney's flight landed in New York. By the time the weekend arrived, with Bruce and Nancy free to do the honors, Christine and the boy had covered a large portion of Manhattan, had even gone to Brooklyn at Rodney's insistence: he wanted to see the Brooklyn Bridge.

With Rodney's itinerary of places to see and Christine's own preferences for him, they didn't miss much. South Street Seaport, the Village, Gramercy Square, Henderson Place, Times Square (of course), Broadway from Forty-second Street right up to the Nineties. There was a blister on Christine's heel, the right foot, which she covered with a Dr. Scholl's plaster, and she was finally reduced to the walking shoes she saved for trips to Europe. She felt like a first-timer herself, seeing it with a newcomer's eye, and to boot about fifteen years old. She was wiped out by the time Saturday came, but happily so.

However, she bowed out for the weekend. "You're not coming with us?" Rodney demanded, when Bruce and Nancy champed at the bit to get a good early start doing the town with their guest.

"Dear, it's their turn. After all, they have only

the two days. They don't want me barging in. They can do without the authoritative presence of Belinda the witch. Enjoy yourselves."

"It won't be the same," he mourned, looking dashed.

"You should be happy to be with your peer group. They're not that much younger, after all. Now go on, the three of you, and give it a whirl."

"He leans on you," Carl said when they left. "You don't think he's a fag, do you?"

"What in the world would make you think that?"

"They always form these attachments to older women. You know that, it's common knowledge."

"Thanks for referring to me as an older woman. That makes you an older man, you understand."

"I only meant—" he laughed, put his arms around her and told her of course he could see why that boy had a thing for her. "Anyone would, you're a sexy broad."

"At the moment I'm a bushed broad. Let's eat out tonight. They won't be home till late. I gave Bruce plenty of money for lunch and dinner."

"Okay with me. Let's decide where to go and I'll make a reservation."

"No, we'll go to some place we won't have to make a reservation. Just something quiet and relaxing, no fancy stuff. We don't have to decide until later on. I'll get these dishes done, you just take it easy."

It was a long, pleasant day. After trudging about all week she was glad to take it easy too, just laze around, listening to music on the stereo, Schubert, Liszt, Mozart, Saint-Saëns (that gorgeous organ symphony). Changing from grubbies into the street clothes later and walking over to Tre Amici for veal piccata. The wanderers got home at a little after ten. "You took a cab, I trust," Christine said quickly. "You weren't walking around at this hour?"

"We took a cab," Nancy said patiently. She looked quite set up, Rodney must have buttered her up plenty. They had a wonderful day, they enthused, gone to the Statue of Liberty and to Staten Island on the ferry. "I hope you ate well and sensibly?" Christine probed.

"Yeah, sure."

"Did you have enough money?"

"Of course."

The next day, Sunday, tended to drag, there was a kind of letdown. Empty rooms, a quiet house. "Mind if I put on some music?" Christine asked Carl in the early afternoon.

"Of course not, you don't have to ask permission, you know."

"We *could* take a walk."

"Yeah. Maybe before dinner. How about eating out again tonight?"

"No, not particularly on a Sunday. I have a capon in the fridge, I'll put it on around five. I have a feeling they'll be home early tonight, there's school tomorrow."

She chose some records at random, put them on the turntable. They sat there in the living room, she in a caftan Carl especially liked. Sections of the Sunday *Times* were here, there and everywhere. Carl was reading the business section. It was possible he'd get a call from the hospital. Or some patient. Someone in trouble. Maybe not, though, at this time of year. The cold months brought flu and pneumonia and then he was out of the house a lot. She was a doctor's wife, she expected that. But the phone was silent.

Once they had taken to bed when the children were out. That was long ago and far away, she thought, undismayed. There was love between them. Sex had a part in their lives, naturally, but it was not a compulsion. Carl wasn't a man to insist on his connubial rights, he had never asked for submission. But as a doctor he regarded sex as not only pleasurable but therapeutic as well, essential for one's well-being, the best exercise there was, and fine for the plumbing, not to mention its salutary effect on soma and psyche.

It was not passion, it was exercise. No matter. His body was dear to her, a familiar body that was always a comfort, that was there, together with hers and had been together in good times and bad. One of her aunts had said once, shortly after her husband died, "I loved going to bed with your uncle. I don't mean for sex. Chrissie. That is, not just sex and certainly not always sex. Just having him lie close to me. I don't know. I felt, somehow, like a pioneer wife. As if we had crossed the plains, under great duress and with terrible hardships, and had conquered the hardships. It seems so wrong that he should have been taken from me. I feel, you know, as if a terrible mistake had been made. As if it weren't supposed to be that way, that there was a grievous error of some kind, and now it can't be undone."

61

Of course her aunt and uncle, like her own mother and father, had slept in a double bed, whereas she and Carl had single beds. It must be so sad and wrenching to reach out to the other pillow and find it empty.

But then, she reflected, it must be just as hard to turn over and see that empty, single bed beside your own.

Why was she thinking about death?

Why not, it would happen some time.

Upset with her train of thought, she got up and went to the kitchen, made some coffee. She now wished that the others would come home, wished that laughing voices would conquer the quietness, vanquish the somnolence of the hours that were passing without event.

When she went inside again with the tray with coffee urn and mugs Carl was asleep, his head back against the chair and his mouth slightly open. Soon he would start to snore.

She wasn't annoyed. Why shouldn't he be fagged out? He worked his butt off and he merited a weekend's relaxation. She was, however, unwilling to drowse along with him, the two of them sitting there together, like Buddhas in their chairs, Darby and Joan. She felt like doing something and she did. She scanned the theater section, found an Italian flick playing at the Plaza. She left a note: she would be back at around five.

Then she left the house, flagged down a taxi on the street and got to the Plaza in plenty of time to catch the next showing. It was an engaging little film, with a charmingly aging Marcello Mastroianni. She enjoyed it very much and wished, when she left the theater, that she could go to some simple place for dinner and a drink, which she would very much like to do.

She thought of Clover, who could do things like that. No dependents. A man she loved but not someone she was conventionally yoked to. And no children for whom she was responsible. With a kind of startled astonishment, Christine Jennings thought — and truly for the very first time — I should never have married. I should never have had children. They ate you. Little bites over the years, like predators, or parasites, feeding on a host.

But when she let herself into the house she was heralded with welcoming cries. Carl had made a pitcher of drinks, Old Fashioneds. Nancy had prepared a tray of hors d'oeuvres. They sat her down and waited on her. Carl looked refreshed after his nap. Nancy and Bruce plopped down on the sofa beside her, Rodney sprawled on the floor at her feet. The sun, the late day sun, made a glory of the room. They asked about the film she had seen, and said they themselves had walked their feet off.

"We're going to the Copenhagen for dinner," Nancy said, glowing. "No cooking, no cleaning up. Isn't that nice?"

Okay, so they took something away from you, children always did, it was more or less nature's law. But would she really change places with husbandless, childless Clover? But there could be no ready answer to that. She couldn't imagine

Clover's life any more than Clover could imagine hers. Their lives were, quite simply, entirely different. At the moment, right here and now, she was supremely content.

Tomorrow she might feel differently.

And she probably would.

5.

When two weeks had passed, Rodney announced
that he really must get cracking and look for a flat.
"You don't know what you're in for," Christine
told him. She had been poring over the *Times* ads
even before he had arrived. It was as she thought:
it would be a hassle. Studio apartments were few
and far between, there was only a column and a
half of listings each day and the rents were

astronomical. True, there was a sprinkling of moderate-priced ones but you knew damned well they were—to say the least—dingy, if not downright rat traps. In the main, studios were renting for anywhere from $475 up, depending on location and desirability.

And of course *everything* was going co-op.

"It's because the whole world is gravitating to New York," she informed Rodney. "All the moneyed parasites, the kind of people I despise, they're coming here. Leaving Rome and Paris and Geneva and coming here, damn them. They're pissed off at taxes and insecurities and kidnappings and the threat of another Europe-based war. How dare they barge in with their Swiss bank accounts and their petro-dollars and take over this city? It's a rape, it's plunder, ordinary people can't afford to live here anymore."

"It's also inflation," he said, unruffled. He had his own copy of the *Times* now, so that they could compare notes. "How about this, Chris? Two and a half rooms, full kitchen, clean, $225."

"Where is it?"

"Amsterdam Avenue."

"Forget it," she said crisply. "I *was* wondering about this. Seventy-third Street, just off Second. $240, a studio. Oh, it can't be anything! Something over a greasy spoon."

"A what?"

"Some crummy eatery. Let it go. Or no, we won't let it go. There are few enough leads as it is, we'll have to investigate them all, anything that sounds in the least feasible."

She got up. "God, it's discouraging. Okay, let's get started. I've circled a few possibilities. I'm not very hopeful."

The first day was the worst because even though you knew it was going to be a rat race the full impact only hit you when you actually got out there and faced it. Rodney lost a bit of his composure when he walked into some of the "airy studio" and "sunny L-shaped room" offerings. He did a lot of throat-clearing and he didn't have very much appetite when they stopped off at The Brownstone for a three o'clock lunch. "Never mind," Christine said bracingly. "We didn't expect to find something first crack out of the bottle, did we?"

"I didn't realize they'd be so seedy," he admitted.

"We simply had phenomenally bad luck today. There *are* things around, I know that as well as I know my own name, even if it doesn't look that way. We must be patient, you see."

"Yes, of course, patient."

And after a few days he began to perk up, taking this hound and hare exploration as a kind of lark, so that before long his gusto returned, along with his appetite, and they set out each morning with Rodney in fine spirits. Now he took along his camera, as if they were once again sightseeing.

"We haven't time for that," she protested, when he kept asking her to pose over there beside that tree, or in front of some building he fancied would make a good background.

"It's only just for a moment. Smile, please."

She smiled and he snapped the shutter. "You're

very lovely," he said.

"I'm just a Mum."

It became almost a way of life after a while, getting up with the roosters each morning, weekends included and both of them very practiced now. "No, not there," Christine would say, in regard to a listing. "Don't you remember? We were on that block a day or so ago, the whole street is a decaying shambles."

A morning's fruitless search and the real estate page thrown in a litter basket, its usefulness over for that day. Lunch somewhere in the late afternoon and then back to the Colonnade. Carl stopped asking, "Any luck?" because she had snapped at him and said if they had any luck he would be the first to know about it. She sensed he was restless about the status quo. Men didn't care for disorder in their lives, he wanted everything as usual, for her to sit beside him and watch television of an evening. He'd had a busy, hectic day and now he wanted peace and quiet, not somebody else's kid yakking away in his British accent and interrupting an otherwise quiet evening.

She finally phoned Peg Thornley about what limit she would set on rent and Peg said, in her chipper Mayfair voice, "Oh, I should think about two-fifty, perhaps three hundred. That should do it, don't you agree?"

"No, Peg. Not in this city. Well, I'm sure it's the same in London. I'm afraid it will be far more than that, unless you want Rodney in some questionable neighborhood."

"Good heavens, certainly not! It's really of so

little importance, I shall leave it up to you."

"Could you set another limit, a more realistic one?"

"It's only for a year or so, you must use your own judgment. You're being so frightfully kind, love, it's a great deal I'm asking of you."

"Not at all, Peg. We'll find something perfectly splendid."

"I say. What about a hotel?"

"Same as in London," Christine said dryly. "A hotel would break the bank, my dear."

The conversation at the dinner table was invariably centered on the treasure hunt. "Find anything perfectly splendid today?" Nancy had been privy to Christine's London call.

"No splendid, much sick-making." Rodney, rueful, admitted that the quest was a tour through the lower depths. "One flat really gave me a pause. I simply can't tell you. As soon as we left Christine told me that on pain of death I must not put my hands to my face until I'd washed them. She made me go into a department store and find the loo, told me to use a great quantity of soap."

"Well, he *touched* things. We should really have worn masks."

"That bad?"

"I can't tell you. Grease on every surface, and some beastly animals."

"Animals?"

"Mr. Feelers," Christine explained.

"Yuck."

When at last they did stumble onto the Sixty-first Street place it was without confidence, because why should this day be different from all other days? It was the first ad they answered, with a phone number to call: the location was "low Sixties," which could mean anything at all. It was only $365, which by now seemed a widow's mite. Of course, Christine said gloomily, it was probably over a store.

"A greasy spoon."

"Uh huh. Some smelly souvlaki place. A one-bedroom for $365? I must be crazy even to give it a second thought."

"It says "small" bedroom."

"That's why I'm willing to consider it, it's probably a walk-in closet or a plyboarded L. All right, I'll phone."

It was Sixty-first between Third and Second, she announced hanging up. "All ready to go, Rodney?"

They cabbed down to Sixty-first, where Christine suddenly recalled a few visits to a podiatrist on this very street: his office was just off Second. This was a street of brownstones, or limestone row houses, tree-lined, not a highrise in sight. The cabbie pulled up in front of one of the five-story row houses and she said, "This can't be it, what's the number?"

"The one you gave me." He turned in his seat. "See? There it is, right over the door."

"Why shouldn't it be here?" Rodney wanted to know.

"Does this look like the kind of shit we've been seeing? Excuse me, Rodney, don't tell your mother I use bad language." She consulted the slip of paper on which she copied the address the man had given her over the phone. "Well, okay, let's get out."

She paid and stood looking up at the building. It was the number she had written down, all right. "There must be some mistake," she insisted flatly.

"I hope not. It seems so dignified, don'tcha know. Rather like London."

"It seems divine, but far too good to be true."

Some of the houses had stone steps leading up to the first floor level, some had been stripped of these attractive, old-fashioned appurtenances: this one had the steps. At the top was the "stoop" and then a heavy, carved door through which you entered on a small vestibule where there was a bank of brass mailboxes, one of which bore the name E. Manson, the man spoken to on the phone. "Here we go," she said, and put her finger on the bell.

The inner door, of heavy glass behind iron grillwork, was opened by a woman who had a worn but pleasant face. "It's about the apartment," Christine said. "I spoke to a Mr. Manson."

"That's my husband. He's there now, it's the third floor."

"Thank you. Coming, Rodney?"

They climbed. Three flights up, but who cared, Christine thought, still darkly suspecting some error in the listing, because the entrance hall was clean and vacuumed, with no musty food smells and the stairs were carpeted in a soft taupe, would you believe it. Beautiful old banisters, a fine, dark wood and niches in the bend of the stairway with old-fashioned busts, one of Shakespeare. "I say,

71

this is more like it," Rodney said enthusiastically. "I shall certainly take it, Christine."

On the third floor a door stood ajar, the one leading to the front-view flat. It was apparent that there were two apartments on each floor, which meant about ten units altogether. "I'd like to live here myself," Christine said pensively. "I wonder if this is a dream or something."

"Or maybe Mr. Feelers is in residence," he murmured.

They pushed open the door and went in. She knew at once that this was it. They were in a large, high-ceilinged room, rectangular in shape, with a fireplace that was sealed off but which nevertheless lent grace and elegance, its moldings adorned with carved caryatids. Oyster-white walls and parquet floor with the patina of age, and the ceiling was festooned with plaster moldings, in the center a great sunburst design. The sun, strong and effulgent, blazed in through almost floor-to-ceiling windows.

"Oh, Rodney . . ."

"Oh, *Chris* . . ."

"You're sure you have your checkbook now."

"Yes, of course." He patted a pocket.

"It will be a month's security, maybe two. And the first month's rent."

"Right."

Voices, coming from another room, grew louder, and a couple of men appeared in the doorway that led beyond the living room. Or drawing room, Christine thought, it was a gracious, oldtime drawing room. A middle-aged man and a younger one.

"Mr. Manson?" Christine said to the older one.

"Yes, Ma'am."

"I'm Mrs. Jennings, I phoned a short while ago. This is Mr. Thornley, who's interested in the apartment. May we go through and see the rest of it, please?"

There was an exchange of glances between the two men. Uh oh, Christine thought. The young man was also looking for a place to live. "My friend isn't just interested," she said quickly. "He wants it. Just let us know what the deposit will be and he'll write out a check for that and the first month's rent."

"I'm sorry," the young man said, "but you're just a little too late. You see I've already written out my check."

"But we came right away!" she cried. "I mean, when I phoned it was still vacant! If there was any question you should have said so, Mr. Manson. Well, really! Couldn't you at least have waited for us to see it before deciding?"

"It's a hard, cruel world," the younger man remarked. "First come, first served. I'm truly sorry."

"My God."

She felt like weeping. Beside her, Rodney stood glum. She felt his disappointment, his letdown. Shock, too. Hell, she herself wanted to hit somebody.

"You know, this is really too much," she said furiously. "It isn't fair, *I* don't think it's fair. You have to be given *some* chance. We've been looking for days and days. We've turned this town upside down. We've—"

"I know," the young man said. "Take my word for it, I know. People look for years. Just the same, though, I have an idea. If you can stick around for a few minutes I may be able to help."

"How?" she asked scornfully.

"I'm serious."

"I fail to see how we can stick around. Stick around and lose out on other listings? You're *sure* you want this place?"

"Very sure."

"I see. Well, it's all very depressing. Finding just what Rodney wanted . . . he can't afford to pay very much."

"I can't afford to pay very much either. I was reckless enough to ditch my job, which if I still had it would enable me to move aside and let you have this place with my compliments." He smiled. "It's not easy to turn a deaf ear to the entreaties of a lovely lady."

"Compliments won't get us an apartment," she retorted, but found herself, with great reluctance, answering his smile. He was a prepossessing sort, interesting-looking and very dark in his coloring, dark eyes and dark crispy, curly hair, quite a lot of it and rather undisciplined, though not long and shaggy. He was a little too thin for his considerable height and he had a strong face you couldn't help noticing, strong and thin. Artistic? Maybe a painter, except that a painter would want north light. He would have been attractive to her under any other circumstances.

"Did you want something more, then?" the super asked, the check for the rented apartment in his hand.

"No, I think we've settled everything, Mr. Manson. I have the keys, it seems to be all for now. I'll let you know my moving date, of course. And many thanks."

"Well then, good day and I hope you'll be happy here." He nodded to the other two. "Good day to you too."

Christine, sulkily resigned, was curious. "Why is the rent so low?" she asked when the super had gone out. "The dives we've seen for higher. Why *is* the rent so low?"

"One of those lucky strikes you never expect to come your way. The last tenant was here for a hundred years, so the rent was low for a hundred years, no turnover. Now they can only take the standard hike."

He shook his head. "Who would have thought it would happen to me."

"If you hadn't beat us by a scant few minutes it would have happened to us."

"Oh. Look, I said I had an idea, and I think I can save the day, fix you up. By the way, I'm John Allerton."

"Christine Jennings. This is Rodney Thornley, he's the one who needs a home. What is this save-the-day idea of yours, Mr. Allerton?"

"I have an apartment for you."

"What do you mean you have an apartment for us?"

"I put down a deposit on another one this morning. First ad I answered, but I also wanted to see this, so I hopped over here and knew right away I'd found pay dirt. Would you be interested in the other one? It's on Eighty-first between Lex and Third."

Hope soared. "It's not as nice as this one, I take it?"

"This one's brighter, more sun, which I wanted if I could get it. The other one's great, though, or else I wouldn't have plunked down the money for it. It has a bay, like this one, I'm pretty sure you'll cotton to it. Rent's $315."

"Rodney?"

"Yes, of course. What was wrong with it?"

"Nothing. Except no bedroom, which I certainly didn't expect to find anyway, but mainly it's just enough below ground level that there isn't all this strong light. Otherwise—"

"You mean a *basement* flat?"

"No, nothing like that. You don't think I'd consider anything like that? Do you want to see it? I'll be glad to go on over with you. If you decide on it you can return my deposit to me. That is if you're so inclined. I know I have no right to ask for it."

"Of course we'd return it."

"Then let's get a move on, before something goes wrong on that end."

"I appreciate it, Mr. Allerton."

"Not a bit. If you're satisfied with it I won't be the villain in the piece. I'm not partial to being a heavy. I'll just lock up here and we'll be there in a jiffy."

They flagged down a cab on Third, rode up to Eighty-first, where Allerton told the driver they'd get off. "It's just up the block," he told the others. "Here, let me get that."

"You're not paying for our cab," she said, surveying the environs, which of course were familiar to an old New Yorker. "I know this street, it's a good one. Trees, Rodney. I suppose it's that rickety building with the peeling stucco? Still, it doesn't look too run down."

"No, it's the one with the diamond-paned window, the one with the bay."

"Oh, I've passed it before, any number of times. I always thought it was very sweet, sort of quaint. Rodney, it looks nice, doesn't it?"

"Very nice indeed," he said judiciously. "Rather like a small cottage. Mullioned windows. I shall feel I'm in the country."

"It's small inside, but very well laid out, very compact and serviceable. As I said, I was all ready to settle in there myself."

Rodney had gone to look in the bay window, leaning forward to peer inside. Of course there were drawbacks immediately apparent, Christine was thinking. Where would he put an air conditioner? Naturally the thought wouldn't have entered his head. You couldn't put one in the bay unless you wanted to spoil its appearance, and they were the only front windows, so where would he put a unit? And there would certainly be easy access for a burglar. A ground-floor dwelling, it would be a piece of cake for someone to jimmy open a window and go right in.

Which was, when it came right down to it, something a burglar wouldn't bother attempting, in plain sight. A burglar would jimmy open the door to the apartment rather than risk being spotted outside.

Well. Lots of people lived with fire escapes, what easier entry was there than a fire escape?

It did seem a creditable building, on a pleasant street, and if the plumbing left something to be desired, *tant pis*. Rodney would just have to learn to live with it. It would be a blessing if this were the last one. She was suddenly very, very weary of looking at apartments. "Could you see anything inside?" she asked Rodney when he came back.

"It looks good," he said, sweeping back his hair. "There appears to be some built-in shelving. It doesn't seem dark, either."

A few minutes later they were inside the building, after being let in by a Mr. Scanlan, who unlocked the apartment door for them and who complained that he was being kept busy by people responding to the ad. "I can't hold it any longer," he said severely. "Deposit or no deposit."

"I can understand that," Allerton agreed. "Just give us a few minutes. You'll have your answer right away. Okay?"

"Okay," he said, and pushed open the door so they could go inside. Ten minutes later Rodney was writing out his check, and they had the key. Mr. Scanlan, relieved of his responsibilities, went his own way and they surveyed the rooms again. Rodney was overwhelmed by his find. He kept returning to the bay, where there was a window seat, presently covered in a faded chintz, but even though it would need recovering the overall effect was very pretty. It would provide extra seating, he informed them unnecessarily, and you could sit there reading a book.

And the light. Such a soft light, quite mellow and soft, like amber. Plus the built-in shelving, one hadn't expected that. "Thank you, Mr. Allerton, I say, thanks a million. Oh, I must write *you* a check now. Three fifteen, right?"

"Unanticipated but welcome," Allerton said, pocketing the check. "I think I'm as glad to get you people settled and off the hook as I am to see the money again. As I said, I know what it means. We're a frantic fraternity, we apartment hunters. I've seen the same people frequently."

"It's terribly wearying," Christine agreed. "But thanks to you we're taken care of, no more trudging all over creation. I feel like buying you flowers, Mr. Allerton. You saved the day after all."

"All's well that ends well."

"As for you, Rodney, congratulations. You're a homeowner! You must call your mother tonight and let her know."

"I shall. And now let's celebrate, a smashing lunch, with champagne."

"Lunchtime's about two hours away, it's only ten."

"Oh. So it is."

"And Mr. Allerton, now you have to get yourself back to your own apartment, don't you? Please, I insist on paying for your cab back there."

"Now listen," he said. "I know I protested I couldn't afford to pay much for my digs, but I'm not on Welfare. But I'd like to take you both to lunch, that is if you can manage to do without the champagne, which I confess might strain my resources a bit too far."

"Well, wonderful! Instead of buying you flowers I'll buy you lunch. Oh, please. If it weren't for you—"

"Not at all," Rodney said expansively. "I'm in a celebratory mood, this will be my treat. And not another word said. Well, though, as it's only tennish, what shall we do until then?"

"Maybe you wouldn't mind coming back with me to admire my own acquisition? I wasn't there very long so I didn't have much of a chance to gloat."

"Fine. Let's go back to your own acquisition and help you gloat. We'll start our rounds of furniture stores tomorrow, Rodney. Today we gloat. Lock the door. Got it? It's a good Medico, but do you think he should have the bolt changed, Mr. Allerton?"

"I don't think it's called for, no. I'm not going to replace mine. By the way, please call me Jack."

"Okay, call me Christine."

"Would you like to walk down? It's a nice day."

"I'd love to walk down."

"And now I really feel I belong here," Rodney said, pocketing his key. "Now I'm really a resident."

If she was a trifle uneasy about Rodney's reaction to Jack Allerton's much larger place she needn't have worried, Christine was glad to see, as they went through his newly-acquired apartment. There was abundant praise but no envious glances, Rodney was clearly preoccupied with his own plans. He had a kind of vacant look, as if he were present only in the flesh. He had found what he had set out to find, and nothing could distract him from his complacency.

Christine herself enjoyed wandering along with Jack through this empty, high-ceilinged apartment, their footfalls echoing, voices as well. The bedroom was not a plyboarded L, but a real room, even if small and with a not very roomy clothes closet. "It will do," Jack said. "I'll have to make it do. There's a better one in the hall between the rooms, and there's a broom closet. I'll manage."

He opened a door. "Do you think this bathroom's tacky? I was stunned when I looked at it. All these multicolored tiles. Like a circus. I wonder what smartass dreamed this up?"

"I don't know, I feel it's rather jolly. It's certainly cheerful. And it looks clean as a whistle."

"I suppose I'll get used to it."

"You're being overcritical. I like it. I think it's fun."

He shrugged. "Anyway, it's a minor point. Beggars can't be choosers."

They went back to the living room. "This," he said, and swept his arm in an arc. "This is what you hope to find and rarely do. These ceilings, the room proportions, the fireplace. Be nice if I could use it, but just having it for appearance' sake is terrific, that formal mantel, the carving. The hell with everything else, this room's what sold me."

"It's beautiful," Christine agreed. She could imagine what the room looked like when it was in prime condition, years ago when this house was in its heyday, a mansion—modest in its way but nevertheless a dignified town house some prosperous merchant owned at the turn of the century—and this one of its front parlors, a sitting or morning room, with heavy brocaded drapes at the handsome windows and a magnificent crystal chandelier where the sunburst radiated in the middle of the lofty ceiling.

There were louvres at the windows, built-in shutters that pulled out of the side wall, a feature you found in some of these old houses, closing off the room at night or parted, according to your wish, to subdue the glare of the sun when it became too dazzling. "Thank God I won't have to have Venetian blinds," Jack said. "They always look so tenementy to me."

"I don't like them either and they're so hard to keep clean. You don't have shutters in the bedroom, do you?"

"No, that's not a wide-silled window. Of course, as you noted, it looks out on nothing, just a few yards of space between this house and the adjoining one, but it provides light and air, and you can't have everything."

"At least it's not an airshaft. We saw plenty of places facing on airshafts. Just put some cheerful curtains up, or a slatted bamboo blind, something in a warm cedar or so."

"And I'll have to buy an air conditioner for the bedroom. Just a small unit, install it myself. The one I have is a very good unit, 9200 B.T.U.s, I'll get that installed right away, even before I move in." He pointed. "In that window, not the one near where my desk will be. It won't look too bad, it has an ivory-toned front panel, unobtrusive."

"I say, must I have an air conditioner?" Rodney demanded, a little disconcerted. "But where?"

"I'm afraid it will have to be in the bay," Christine explained. "I know it seems a shame, but—"

"In the *bay?*" He bristled. "But that will spoil it! How can I do *that?*"

"There isn't any other place, my darling. Don't worry, it will be scarcely noticeable. Besides, the planting outside will help a bit. Rodney, dear, you must have an air conditioner. You haven't experienced one of our New York summers yet."

"Well, I must say this is a bitter blow. One of those horrid things sticking out of my casement window?"

"Why don't you rent one?" Jack suggested. "Then you can have it taken out for the colder weather. Unless, of course, rental prices are exorbitant, I really can't say about that. I can ask when I have mine moved and installed here. Shall I do that?"

"Oh yes, would you then? I'd very much appreciate it." He shook his head, crestfallen. "I'm afraid I didn't give it a thought, rather stupid of me."

"Not at all, you're probably not used to such details. I'm glad I have mine and don't have to buy one. The bedroom unit won't amount to much expense."

"So you see, Rodney, your problems will be ironed out in no time. And if you rent a unit for, say four months or so, it might be the best all-round idea. Well, Jack, congratulations to you and I'd like to apologize for throwing a tantrum earlier this morning when I found someone had beaten us to the draw. I'm sorry, really sorry. You've been marvelous, I'll never forget it."

"I'm glad I could assist. So did you, don't forget. I might have had to forfeit my deposit otherwise. At the very least, I would have had a lengthy argument about it." He looked at his wristwatch. "I'm afraid I've bored you to a fare-thee-well. I didn't realize we'd been here all this time. And nothing to sit down on. It's one-thirty, where'd the time go to? God, I'm sorry to keep you hanging around here all this time. You must both be starved. As a matter of fact so am I. Now. Where would you like to have lunch?"

"Rodney? If it's your treat you should decide."

"No, no, just wherever you'd like."

"I guess it's up to you, Jack."

"There's a place quite near here I go to a lot. Sure you have nothing special in mind? Well then, I'll just lock up and we'll get going."

Christine noted his smile of satisfaction as he gave a last look at the rooms that were now his. Turning, his eyes met hers. He laughed sheepishly. "Yeah, the cat that swallowed the canary," he said as they went down the stairs. "If you could see the place I'm leaving you'd know why. A building that used to be good, but now they're milking it, doing nothing, just letting everything fall apart, practically brick by brick. A recurring leak in my bathroom ceiling, the plaster hanging down like someone's skin peeling. Insufficient heat in the winter and as often as not none at all. I had to go to the Hyde Park Hotel two nights this past February, otherwise I probably would have frozen to death. Never reimbursed for it, of course. Twenty-one degrees and cold radiators. When Gristede's, which was on the corner, closed its branch there, all the Gristede roaches scrambled to find other quarters, which needless to say were the nearest houses, including mine. It was a day by day skirmish between me and the roaches, the survival of the fittest."

"Jack, how gruesome. Rent controlled?"

"No. Low, admittedly. I know it's next to impossible to maintain a building for rents that haven't kept pace with the economy, but they could have some kind of landlord-tenant discussions. I for one would have been glad to pay an increase, and I think most of the others would have. You know what's happening these days. These old brownstones aren't bringing in any profit, so they hang on to them until such time as some developer buys up a whole block of them, tears them down and puts up a highrise. What are you gonna do?"

Out on the street, he directed them toward Third. "Then we'll head for Lex," he said. "We're going to Anthony's. It's quiet, leisurely and they have good drinks."

It was in the Fifties and it looked like a saloon from the outside, but then so did Clarke's, and when they went in Christine felt comfortable right away. It was cool and dim and hospitable, with a big, weathered, dark oak bar and comfy chairs around fair-sized tables. A few booths. They sat in one of the booths, Rodney sliding in beside Christine and Jack opposite. It was a man's place, you knew that immediately, but it was not raffish in any way, and there were two young women at one of the tables. They looked like office girls on their lunch hour. "I'd like a martini," she said, when a waiter came over.

"One martini for the lady. Olive, twist, onion?"

"Olive, thanks."

He greeted Jack by name. "Hi, Jack, Canadian Club for you?"

"As always. Rodney?"

"I'd like a gin and tonic, please."

"This is nice," Christine said when they had their drinks. "I must have passed it a lot of times and never noticed it."

"It's a respectable watering hole and the food's really very high quality. Well, shall we heft a glass to our respective good fortune?"

"Here we go. To you both, gentlemen, and all the best. Jack, an additional toast to you, and heartfelt thanks."

"I second the motion," Rodney said, grinning. "You're the undisputed hero of the day."

"Okay, enough already, you'd think I saved you from drowning. You're British, Rodney, what brings you to these parts?"

"Just thought I'd pop over and see how the Colonies were doing." He shook his head. "No need to worry about them, they're in great shape. Actually, I'm here on a visit, a bit of a holiday, that's all. What do you do, Jack? You said you ditched your job, I believe."

"Yes, a few months ago."

"You're looking for another one then?"

"As a matter of fact, no. I'm working on a book, I decided to take the long chance."

"A book? You're a writer?"

"More or less. That is, it's been less to date, just a few pieces published, which netted me an agent, and four or five short novels, strictly hack stuff. Now I'm involved in something more—" He made a solemn face. "More substantial. Ta da da."

"I'm most impressed."

"Rodney would like to write," Christine said. "So you're an author, Jack. That's great. I guess you're the first one I've met. My husband's a doctor, so I meet a fair amount of doctors. They're not very interesting. As a matter of fact they're—well, at least in my opinion, dull as ditchwater, and monstrously pompous."

She laughed. "I'm not referring to my husband, he's a very nice guy."

"So is his wife."

"Christine?" Rodney put in. "She's more than nice, she's Aphrodite with a soul."

"You sound like a groupie," Jack remarked. "I can't say I blame you."

"And her name, Christine, it sounds like shimmering glass. Christine, that was the name in O'Neill's *Mourning Becomes Electra*."

"Oh, she was a bad lady," Christine objected. "You're not going to compare me with her? She did away with her husband. I have no plans to murder mine."

"Neither did she, but he showed up at an inopportune time," Jack observed.

"She must have known he'd make an appearance sooner or later."

"She probably thought he'd be killed in the war. And she didn't reckon with that daughter of hers. Vengeful bitch."

"Whose side are you on anyway, Jack?"

"I guess I always felt sorry for Christine/Clytemnestra. Love is a many-splendored thing. I'm on the side of love."

"No matter who gets hurt?"

"Someone always gets hurt. So you'd like to scribble too, Rodney."

"I always have wanted to, you know. But it's only a remote possibility."

"Writing for a living is chancy at best. As I'm sure I'll discover when I've been at it long enough. It's so damned reassuring to have that job, a structured life, you can't flake off in a job."

"Why did you leave it? Couldn't you do both?"

"I decided you couldn't. Or I couldn't. Well, there were other flies in the ointment. I was in publishing, moved around a good bit, got shafted one too many times. So I thought I'd be an independent guy and let them publish *me*. It would be easier that way." He smiled. "Famous last words."

"Are you having trouble with what you're working on?"

"I'm having trouble sitting still. No, the work's going along creditably, it's just a long, long process. I have to find the pace for it."

He picked up his drink. "You aren't interested in all this."

"But we are, very much so."

"I've done nothing but talk about myself, a lot of crap. No more about me. So, how do you like my apartment?"

Laughter all around: he was fun, Christine thought, very attractive, very entertaining, someone she would like to know better. She tried to guess his age. It was hard to tell. He could be twenty-eight, he could be thirty-two. He lived alone, it seemed: he could be single or he could be divorced or in the process of separation. She didn't see any reason why she shouldn't ask him.

She didn't have to. Rodney asked him. "Are you—ah, married or something, Jack?"

"More like something. I'm divorced."

"Oh, I *am* sorry."

A quick laugh. "Don't be, Rodney." Another quick laugh. "Just one of those things. Ever notice when things go wrong between people the reason is always that it's just one of those things? How about you, Rodney, found any delectable girls to take out since you've been here? And how long have you been here?"

"A month now. Girls? I daresay they're about."

"They are indeed. I'm surprised they haven't started ringing your doorbell."

"It's still early times."

"Were there any children, Jack?" Christine wanted to know. "I don't mean to pry."

"No children. Thank God for small favors. Children always make it hairier."

"Yes, of course. Could we order, Jack? I'm beginning to get light in the head; we haven't been eating much in the way of breakfast lately. Too eager to get out and answer ads."

"Sure." He caught the waiter's eye, menus were brought over. "What's good here?" she asked.

"You can safely take your pick, but the eggplant parmigiana's tops."

"Fine, I'll have that. Rodney?"

"Yes, the same for me, please."

"Okay, Mario, we're all agreed. Three eggplant."

"Coffee with?"

"Later for me. Rodney likes his later too."

"Can we have the garlic bread right away, though, Mario?"

"Garlic bread coming up. You want some Chianti?"

"How about it?"

"Not for me, and I think not for Rodney either. These are lusty drinks."

"We'll skip the wine, Mario."

He was back with two baskets of the bread in a second or two, the smell of the garlic preceding him. "Guaranteed to put hair on your chest," he said with a wink, and went away again. "Wow," Christine said, putting a piece in her mouth. "This is garlic bread to end all garlic bread. Lord, it's fantastic."

"It's great butter too. Sweet as field flowers."

"Isn't this marvelous. I suppose I shouldn't have scotched the Chianti. It's just that the two of us are pooped after killing ourselves for two weeks looking for a place for Rodney. I don't particularly care to fall flat on my face. In Florence we drank Lacrima

Cristi. Teardrop of Christ. I loved the name."

"A great many of our friends live in Florence," Rodney said.

"That's not surprising. There are more English in Florence than there are native Florentines."

Jack said he had spent a month in Florence. "Loved it, absolutely unforgettable. Crossing the river at nightfall, after spending the day on the Oltrarno, with the sun flaming and then dying down, everything purpling, the bridges like misty webs. It stays like a dream landscape in your mind. Italy's so preposterously beautiful. Lacrima Cristi —yes, I drank it too."

"Italy's God's country. I suppose you've been there often, Rodney, not having to cross an ocean to get there."

"Twice, to be exact. I'm fonder of France, though."

"Nothing wrong with France."

"Aha! Here comes lunch."

"Hot plate," Mario said. "Okay, folks, *buon appetito*."

"*Grazie*."

"It looks super," Rodney said, digging in. "Whoops—careful, it's hot."

"I'll have some more bread." Christine wiggled her fingers. "Please? I don't know how you managed it, Rodney, but both baskets are on your side of the table."

"Oh. Sorry. Here you go."

"Jack, you were right. The eggplant's sublime. Say, how'd you find this place?"

"Ah, it's very well known among us cognoscenti.

Stick with me, kid, old Jack knows where it's at."

"I bet you do," she replied, laughing. He was really charming. "You come here a lot," she said. "Now I know why."

"Yeah, it's a haunt of mine."

"Do you cook for yourself?"

"Maybe a chop once in a while. Mostly it's TV dinners."

"They're supposed to be nourishing enough."

"They'll do. With a green salad. No work entailed, why not?"

"I'm sure it's what I'd do if I lived alone."

"Rodney, now that you're setting up housekeeping, what's your plan of action?"

"Why, I suppose about like yours, Jack. Something prepared, just shove it in the oven. Or else dine out."

"If you really mean 'dine,' you won't have any trouble finding restaurants," Jack told him. "If you mean just fill your stomach and refuel, there are a few places around. I mean that won't cost an arm and a leg."

"And of course you'll be at our house for dinner a lot," Christine reminded him. "No invitation necessary, I'm sure you understand you're always more than welcome, Rodney. And yes, we must not forget to call your mother tonight. Be sure to outline some kind of budget, so you won't run low on cash. She has to have some way of knowing what your essentials will be."

"Christine, I'm perfectly capable of managing things," he objected, flushing. "I'm not, after all, a teener."

He put down his fork. "Sorry, love, I didn't mean to be shirty."*

"You're right, though," she said good naturedly. "You must be left to live your own life, and I *am* a smothering sort."

"You're an angel. I adore you."

"That's nice. Jack, I'm a horrible pig, but do you think he'd let us have some more garlic bread? It's all gone, alas."

"No sooner said than done. Mario?"

With coffee, Jack suggested brandy. "They're not much on desserts," he admitted, "so how about a brandy instead? The drinks have worn off by now."

"All right, fine."

"Rodney?"

"Yes, please."

They sat sipping, talking idly, smiling at each other. "I hope you've enjoyed this as much as I have," Jack said.

"I've had a lovely time."

"Can we do it again?" Rodney asked eagerly. "It would be super to meet again like this."

"Nothing I'd like better."

"Yes, by all means," Christine agreed. "I'd like to know how you're getting on, Jack. When you're moved and settled, why not give me a ring? Rodney, would you write down our phone number, please?"

He pulled out a pen. "When we get home I shall have to call the telephone company about a phone

*Shirty — An Anglicism meaning "huffy."

for myself. There, Jack, the Jennings' number."

"Many thanks. I'll write it in my directory right away."

Rodney, with a certain panache, paid the check. "It was my idea," he insisted. Jack said no, it had been his idea, but Christine murmured to him to let it go. "Of course he owes you, certainly Rodney will take care of this. It's little enough. Jack, you've truly been a godsend. I can't thank you enough."

"I'll look forward to seeing you again."

"And I to seeing you. You have my number. Good luck with the moving; that's not very much fun."

They parted outside the restaurant, with nods and smiles, and then she and Rodney walked home. "Nice chap," Rodney said. "Well, I must say this turned out to be a banner day."

"It certainly did. And now we must furnish your apartment. We'll go first thing in the morning with a yardstick, make our notes and then start in picking and choosing. I have a few ideas."

"Good. I shall have to depend on your expertise, Christine."

"You did point out that you were capable of managing things yourself," she observed.

"For which I could cut off my tongue. With all you've done . . . I just had a moment of rebellion, sometimes one feels so bloody juvenile."

She said be glad to be young, it didn't last forever.

6.

The house seemed quiet without Rodney's robust cheer, though Christine, who was up to her ears in making a "showplace" of his new flat, was far from regretful. She was glad to return home each evening, slip off her shoes and relax over a glass of Chablis. He had moved, suitcase and rucksack, into his snuggery, as he called it, just as soon as he had a bed, chest of drawers and two chairs. He was thereupon keen on filling up all the spaces pronto, ready to settle for anything that took his fancy. If she left it up to him, Christine told him, he'd be living in some kind of old curiosity shop. "No," she kept saying patiently. "No, Rodney, it's nice, but it's way out of proportion for your place, you must see that."

"But it's a smashing étagère! Chris, we seem to be getting nowhere."

"Rome wasn't built in a day."

Of course he had no way of knowing that she had earmarked pieces as they went along, for future reference, that she had a master plan which was slowly taking shape, and so his astonishment was profound when she informed him that now they had everything they needed for his place. All they had to do was return to the stores that had them and buy them up.

"Don't worry, Rodney, everything I chose was something you approved of, so I'm sure you'll be satisfied."

"But I don't understand."

"You'll see."

By the end of the month Rodney's flat was fully equipped. It looked, if she did say so herself, as elegant as something a decorator whipped up, and without the grotesqueries they always stuck in. It looked great, and Rodney was almost sickeningly self-congratulatory, though open-handed in his appreciation of all the "help" she had given him, as if the whole splendid orchestration had been conceived and executed by himself, with her as apprentice. She was vastly amused by his lapse of

96

memory as he completely forgot that almost everything he had wanted to snap up would have been totally out of scale and, to boot, without any overall scheme or harmony.

But let him preen, the darling: he was so twenty-one-year oldishly cute, like an urban squire, fiddling possessively with his bay window draperies on their traverse rods, plumping cushions and rushing out to the kitchen to empty ashtrays as soon as someone put out a cigarette. It wouldn't last long, she surmised; his householder's pride, his Craig's wife fussiness would give way to other serendipities. She just hoped he wouldn't end up leaving clothes all over the place, it was too small for that.

"And now," he said, "I can start to *do* things."

"You haven't been doing things up to now?"

"I mean New York things. Let's go to a film tomorrow. I have a whole list of ones I want to see. How about *La Cage Aux Folles*? I'll pick you up, we can go to the two o'clock showing."

"Tomorrow I rest."

"Oh please, Christine."

"Learn to go alone, Rodney. It's what I do. I often go to an art film by myself. I enjoy it and so will you."

"I'd enjoy it more with you."

"You'd enjoy it more with someone your own age. Find a perfectly adorable girl, which should be the easiest thing in the world. I can tell you that if I were some nubile maiden I'd give a lot to meet a dashing young blade like yourself."

"Gels my age are such wogs," he said jadedly. "I can't take them seriously. It's a woman I ap-

97

preciate, and for that matter almost any chap would say the same. There's a—well, a smoldering quality about a woman, a real woman."

"Smoldering?" she echoed, and giggled. "Do I, for example, smolder? If so I had no idea."

"Perhaps an ill-chosen word," he said off-handedly. "But you know what I mean."

"No, I don't," she said, and tweaked his nose. "Most of us women are not of the sultry variety. You've read too much Colette. I'm not Léa."

"Are you sure? I confess readily, you know, that there's a lot of Chéri in me. And it does seem rather a waste."

"I think I'll phone your mother and tell her you propositioned me."

"Oh, do. She'll laugh her head off. She thinks I'm about ten. About the film tomorrow. You'll go, won't you?"

"Some other time, thanks."

"Bother," he said crossly, but let her off the hook, though he kept trying for a while, trying to cajole her in subsequent days, obviously eager for company in his perambulations. He had them all over for Sunday afternoon cocktails a week later, preparing a very nice little spread, though it was mostly to show off his snuggery and be praised for its comfort and elegance.

There were frequent telephone calls from him, reports on his multifold adventures. He certainly did get around, discovering restaurants like Il Vagabondo, which was so "in" that most people had never even heard of it, and out of the way places like Sniffen Court and Amster Yard. He was seeing all the Fassbinder, Herzog, Buñuel and Bertolucci films he could cram in. He came to dinner once or twice, didn't stop talking for a minute, and ate like a horse.

Christine liked having him in the vicinity, Peg's boy, and felt that he had adjusted very well. She wrote the Thornleys and told them that their son Rodney had completely taken over the city and she expected to hear any day that he was running for public office.

Jack Allerton had phoned in early May, to say hello. She was astonishingly glad to hear his voice. He had moved, he said, was slowly getting things to rights, and would very much like to knock off some day this week and take her to lunch.

She was in the midst of project number two, she told him, furnishing Rodney's flat and the sooner she got that over the better. Could they table it until, say, the first part of next month, and by that time both he and Rodney would be in better shape.

"Me too," she added wryly. "What I really need is a rest cure. Jack, why don't I call you when this razzmatazz is over? I want your phone number anyway."

She didn't tell Rodney about the call, because he would only have wanted to slow up the proceedings and waste away an afternoon, and besides she wasn't sure Jack had meant both of them, Rodney as well as herself. She had the vague impression he had meant it only for her.

School was out at the end of the month and Nancy hied herself off to Massachusetts, where she was to spend June and July with her friend Amy Longworth, whose family had a country cottage in Hadley. Bruce had signed up for a summer job at the concession in Central Park, where he would waiter at the outdoor terrace. Carl thought it was unconscionable, taking bread out of the mouths of less privileged kids, but most of the kids came from just such homes as Bruce, so it didn't seem an inequity to Christine, and she liked his enterprise: she had certainly never suggested it.

At any rate, now she was more or less on her own again, just as she was when the children were at school. There was no reason not to call Jack Allerton, see how he was faring.

"Well, hello," he said. "Does this mean you're at leisure once more?"

"I have done my job well and truly. Results are fine, Rodney's like a clucking hen, you're afraid to disturb the position of a single·item, and he keeps jumping up to straighten lampshades. He's very happy. And how are you coming along, Jack?"

"Not bad, and I want you both over, but that will have to wait until it looks like something other than a junk shop. I have quantities of reference material, an overflow of books, and my working equipment. I'm trying to calculate just what I can buy in the way of cabinets that will accommodate things I don't know what the hell to do with. I'm not the most organized person in the world."

"I see. If I can help, let me know."

"You can help a great deal. You can help, for instance, by having lunch with me and *talking* to me. I've been talking to myself so much lately I'm afraid they'll figure me for a nut around here, that someone passing my door will call Bellevue. I've been cursing a lot, mostly at the top of my lungs. I move a pile of stuff, look for a better place to put it, but there isn't a place to put it so I set it down again. And then curse some more. I junked some file cabinets, in a reckless moment, because I didn't want to clutter up this stately room with file cabinets, than which there is nothing less stately, and now I have to find replacements. You know, good fruitwood pieces, preferably one good fruitwood piece with compartments. Roomy and serviceable and at the same time furniture, not officey stuff."

"That shouldn't be too difficult, Jack. You should easily come across something like that."

"Yes, but I want it day before yesterday. Now about lunch. When? Today?"

"Yes, if you like."

"You bet I like. Where do you want to go, Christine?"

"I'd just as soon the same place. Where we were before. Anthony's. There's no bustle there, it's very relaxing."

"You're sure?"

"Um hum. About one?"

"Great, I'll be waiting."

"See you, Jack."

He was at the bar when she walked in, talking to Mario, who greeted her with a smile and a hello. "Nice to see you again," he said. "Martini with olive, right?"

"You have a good memory. Yes, thanks. Hi, Jack."

"Hi, Christine. Come on, let's find a booth."

"Were you waiting long?"

"No, just got here a few minutes ago. You're right on time."

"One of my few virtues, punctuality."

It was earlier than the last time they had been here, and the place was very well occupied today, with two waiters serving and Mario behind the bar. It was cheerful and pleasantly lively, with men in business suits and a few young girls dressed rather well. This modest-looking midtown cafe-restaurant apparently attracted a respectable clientele.

They slid into one of the booths and then a waiter came over with the drinks. "This is something I didn't anticipate when I got up this morning," Jack said, and picked up his glass. "Here's to you, Christine, long time no see."

"To you," she said, lifting her own glass. "Long time no do anything except solve the many problems of Rodney Thornley, Esq., that's about it."

"And now they're all solved?"

"More or less one hundred percent. He doesn't know anyone his own age, but I can't figure out what to do about that."

"Isn't it up to him?"

"Except that he's a stranger in a strange city, which can throw anyone off."

"Otherwise how are you, Christine?"

"Why, tip-top. Cardiogram's good, blood pressure normal and nothing wrong with my appetite. How's your bill of health, Jack?"

His laugh rang out. "Is that the way it sounded? I guess it was for instead of the weather. Isn't it a nice day. Wonderful temperatures, not too chilly, not too warm. Dandy not to have to wear a topcoat. A lead-in. We're strangers, when it comes right down to it, no longer any housing perplexities to gas about, and my fervent wish is to sit here unhurried for as long as I can hold your interest."

"Aren't you funny, did you think I wanted you to perform? I'm very pleased to see you, Jack. Well, I called you, didn't I? Tell me about your apartment, why don't you, I've been wondering if it's come up to expectations."

"It has. Very much so. It's diverting to be in a new place. You wake up and wonder for a minute where you are, and then you realize, oh yeah, I'm in this new place. Nothing is where it was before. You reach for a light switch and now it's not there anymore, it's somewhere else. You have a feeling you've gone to another city, not just another neighborhood. Good for the soul, moving. Everyone should pull up stakes once every five years or so, it shakes you up."

"Maybe. Out of the old groove. I enjoy being in a foreign city. Opening your eyes to entirely different sights. And sounds. And smells. Other cities—that is, cities in other countries always smell so different. Don't you think?"

"Oh, sure. Paris smells like Paris. Paris has the most pungent smell of any city I can think of. Rome smells like newsprint, I've always thought, maybe it's just because they have so many newspapers there. Any city in Spain you're in, you know it's Spain, all right, it couldn't be anywhere else."

"Spain always smells like hot brick."

"That's because Spain is, let's face it, hot brick. Baked daily by the sun."

"Seville. I couldn't get dry after my bath. I sat on the edge of the tub and cried."

"In a *hotel*?"

"It was so ridiculous, we chose this hotel because it was a beautiful old monastery, one of those restored places, with a garden like Eden. It was late September, we were sure it would be cooling off by then. This beautiful old picturesque monastery hotel was not air conditioned. We knew we were taking a chance, but mostly it was naiveté."

"You picked the wrong city for a hotel with no air conditioning. Seville's more humid. Did you really cry?"

"Oh yes, I'm not kidding. I got sick too. Lived on tea and toast for two days. Maybe three. You seem to have traveled a lot."

"Yeah, bumming it. I think every young person should do that."

"So do I, if possible."

"It used to be possible, I guess it's getting tougher. The way the economy is these days."

"Everything's going out of reach. Rents are the worst, of course. My first apartment, I paid $160."

"Those were the days, my friend."

"I suppose people will be saying that until the end of time."

"No doubt. You've traveled a lot too, it seems."

"Quite a bit. Just Europe, not the East or Africa or places like that. I'm for where history was made.

I mean, the history I'm interested in. Kings and queens and dynasties, music and art and . . . you know."

"Yeah. You're a romantic. Me too."

"Glad to hear it. We're a dying breed."

"I don't think we are, no. I really don't."

"Is your building quiet, Jack? Any distracting TV sets blaring away at late hours? That kind of thing?"

"Thankfully, no. In the main tranquil and typically shabby genteel. Very comforting. There's someone in the apartment adjoining mine who wakes me up every morning at precisely seven o'clock. No sooner, no later. Seven on the dot. He sneezes. Just once, but it does the trick, snaps my eyes open as if he pulled a string. This loud, resounding sneeze that may eventually put a crack in my bedroom wall. I don't need an alarm clock."

She tittered. "Is that a plus or a minus for the apartment?"

"I would say a plus. There's a touch of intimacy about it, a kind of long-distance greeting. Friendly, in a way. Neighborly. I've never seen him."

"How do you know it's a him."

"My dear girl, no female could possibly unleash such a thunderclap."

"I don't know. I imagine Gertrude Stein, for instance, sneezed like a donkey."

"Possibly. But she wasn't really a gender, was she?"

"Apparently not. Did you find a shade for your bedroom window? I can't imagine you with cretonne curtains."

"I can't imagine me with cretonne curtains either. Yeah, I did what you told me to, bought a cedar-toned bamboo blind. It looks nice."

"What do you mean, I told you to? I suggested it, that was all."

"I knew you'd be right, so I did it."

She laughed. "Do I seem infallible to you?"

He studied her. "In a way, yes. I think I'd take your advice about almost anything."

"I'll have to be careful what I say, then."

"Oh, please don't. Anyway, yes, that matter's taken care of, and some progress in other directions, though storage space is high on the list of necessaries. I'll have to take some action soon. I have a tendency to think too much and do too little."

"Doesn't everyone?"

"I doubt Rodney puts off what he wants done. He seems a determined sort."

"The English are like that, I find. No flies on them, they forge ahead regardless. Has he tried to get in touch with you?"

"As yet, no. Will he?"

"Yes, I imagine. Right now he's too taken with his new toy to need bulwarks. He's happy as a clam. But I suppose he'll get your number from new listings and hit you with an invitation to survey his castle. He keeps saying, if it weren't for Jack . . ."

"Nice to be someone's savior. How do you happen to know him, Christine?"

"His parents are friends. I've known them quite a few years, met them on one of my trips abroad.

He's here only for a year or thereabouts. I've enjoyed having him on the scene. It's given me kind of a boost."

"Did you need a boost?"

"Yes, I guess I did."

"Why?"

"The usual. Everything sameish. This must be Sunday because there's no mail. That kind of thing, that's about all."

"I know what you mean. Particularly since I'm not dashing out to an office in the morning. The days don't have a specific meaning. It looks as if you're ready for another drink, so am I."

"Yes, I guess I am. I wonder if we could have some of that garlic bread with it?"

"Absolutely." He half rose from his seat, drew the attention of their waiter. "Two of the same, please, and may we have some garlic bread too?"

Their seconds arrived shortly, along with a napkin-covered basket of bread, its redolence steaming the air. A crock of sweet butter. "That's a-nice," Christine said contentedly.

"Yes, that is a-nice," Jack agreed. "A lot of garlic bread simply pretends, but Mario doesn't stint on the garlic, as you've noticed. I sometimes come here and order a big bowl of minestrone and this bread. It's one of the best lunches in town."

"I could go for that today."

"So could I, except that they have Calamari fritti on Thursdays, and today's Thursday. Or don't you dig it?"

"I'd kill for it. Not very many places have it on the menu. Man, oh man. The minestrone will have to wait for another day."

He got up. "Be right back."

When he returned he looked satisfied. "It occurred to me that the well might run dry," he told her. "I was afraid the Calamari'd be gone when we got around to ordering. Mario just laughed. He said, hell, Jack, you know I wouldn't let you down, especially with such a lovely lady, you think I'd cut your throat?"

"So we're safe."

"We're safe. Lord, this is great. Talking to a real live human being. Not going to an office means you can't unload a lot of stuff. You don't yammer with this person and that person, and after a while your voice gets rusty. Or it feels like that, as if it's drying up inside you. What you really want to do is cover up that threatening typewriter and go out for a whole day's walk, like maybe over to Brooklyn or somewhere. Or take in half a dozen movies. Escape. You try not to give into it, though, so you sit there with that blank sheet of paper in the machine. There's that dumb sheet of paper, blank as a wall, and you're not a Sunday writer anymore, but a working one, a seven-day-a-week one, and you type a few lines and it laughs back at you. I remember a *New Yorker* cartoon picturing just such a situation. This harried-looking author sitting at a portable. There's a piece of paper in the typewriter with one line, his beginning line."

He lit a cigarette. She waited. He was smiling faintly. "What was it?" she asked expectantly.

" 'Call me Ishmael . . .' "

"Oh, marvelous! I guess every author in the city

thumbtacked it on his wall. How about you, Jack? Ever find yourself starting with something like, 'Buck Mulligan came from the stairhead, bearing a bowl of lather . . . '?"

"Not yet," he admitted. "But it would be a damned, natural thing to do. Melville or Joyce or any of them. Their opening sentences are graven on your mind, so much so that you have to be always pushing them out of the way to find your own."

He regarded her. "As a matter of fact," he said, "the Joyce sentence isn't, to be perfectly truthful, graven on my mind with the same exactitude it appears to be on yours. I'm a little abashed. Now I'm trying to remember the rest of it. '. . . bearing a bowl of lather . . .' "

" '. . . on which a mirror and a razor lay crossed.' "

"Yes, of course." He leaned back. "You're full of surprises, Christine."

"Is that good or bad?"

"What do you think?"

"We were looking for your opinion, Jack. Now. About the last sentence. Do I remember that with such exactitude. As I recall it, it's forty-odd pages long."

"It's the last few words everyone knows."

"Of course. Your turn now, Jack. I started the book, you finish it."

" '. . . and yes I said yes I will Yes.' Some words for a guy to say, Molly Bloom's thoughts in the darkness."

"It must be fantastic to write something deathless."

"Even *Ulysses* will probably wither in the dust of time. Sad to say." He smiled. "Yours truly isn't aspiring to immortality, I'm quick to add. Just a little honesty and originality."

He had a voice that fitted him, Christine reflected. A deep-based voice that seemed to have a long way to travel, like the rumble of a train in the far distance, a dark voice, smooth and dark and subterranean in a way. It made her think of a handed-down record of her mother's, Chaliapin singing "The Volga Boatman." I like his voice, she thought, I like to listen to him talk.

"Do you ever have any doubts about having left your job?" she asked him. "Becoming self-employed."

"No," he said positively. "There was ample aforethought, it was no hasty decision. I wanted to write this book. It won't be an easy one to turn out, I may be overextending myself. I told you I'd done some yeoman work, half a dozen suspense novels which, very gratifyingly, and much to my surprise, netted more than the advance, which was modest in the extreme, admittedly. Foreign sales, two of them reprinted, unexpected money in the till. I'm not a raw novice, like these cab drivers who tell you they have a story, boy have they got a story, it's all there in their head, all they have to do is get it on paper."

"Do they do that? Cab drivers always discuss politics with me. They have very strong opinions, mostly fascistic."

"I like cab drivers, though."

"So do I. It's bus drivers I'm not fond of. Of

110

course they have a hard row to hoe, but they're so often mean to old people. Did your publishing house try to persuade you to stay when you said you were quitting?"

"Let's say they didn't twist my arm. It was a quid pro quo thing, one of those uncomfortable circumstances where the options had to be up to me. I was covering for a lush of a senior editor, a real baddie who was dumping the work load on me, I saved his hide a hundred thousand times. I never ratted on him, but everyone knew the state of affairs anyway, including management, who assured me on the Q.T., that the situation would be rectified, that this guy would be eased out and I'd get his title. *And* that corner office. It was an open and shut case, I was given to understand. Yeah, man. Okay, they dumped him, sure, and I waited. I wasn't about to dance a tarantella on the body of a dead man, rush in and say when, guys, when? So I went on with my double work load, meanwhile mentally moving into the corner office, I'd get a corn plant and at last have some decent working space and good, bright light. Okay?"

He crushed out his cigarette. "Do I need to go on with the saga?"

"You mean they replaced him with someone else?"

"Damn right they did. Jack, you can be a star, they'd been telling me, tacitly, but it seemed explicit enough. Many thanks, Jack, we want you to know how much we appreciate . . . a real crock. Yeah, someone else moved into that corner office, a guy from S and S, with a longer track record

111

than mine, and there I stayed in my cubbyhole, smilin' through my tears."

He shrugged. "Maybe I sound like an injustice collector. If I were hearing this it's what I'd think, this guy's a sorehead. It ain't so, and I'm not rationalizing. Taking some things lying down's bad for the old ego, but it can be just as bad for the old rep. If you don't hype yourself nobody's going to do it for you. I didn't truckle in the trade. You'd be surprised, word gets around that you're no schlemiel, it's a kind of advertisement in your favor. Of course I'll be in the business again. Some day. When I knock off this little masterpiece, start my *oeuvre*, I'll go back. If the book's any kind of success, that will sew it up."

He put an elbow on the table, leaned his head on his hand. "Christ. Why do I always dither about myself and my times when I'm with you?"

"It's only the second time we've been together, Jack."

"That's right. It seems like more than that."

"I think I'll take that as a compliment."

"You can. You most assuredly can. You must be starved. And bored. With my self-centered mewling."

"I'm far from bored. I'm having a lovely time. I like the place and the company. If we come here again it's my treat next. All right, let's do our ordering. I want some Calamari and I want it fast. I'm famished just thinking about it."

"They generally serve sautéed escarole with it, great stuff. Grated parmesan. Hello, there—ah, he sees me. This lady's famished," he told the waiter.

"Calamari for us both. And I know we're disgusting, but may we have some more of the garlic bread."

"Coming up right away," the man said, and was back in no time at all with their meal, a fresh basket of bread, and a brisk "*Buon appetito.*"

It was almost four when they left Anthony's. Mario had sent over a liqueur, Strega in tall, slender-slim goblets. "That was nice of him," Christine said, pleased.

"He's a nice guy. What are you going to do when we leave here?"

"Walk home. Do some food shopping on the way, rather a lot, the larder's dangerously low."

"I'd ask you up to my place, as a matter of fact I'd very much like to. I'm afraid, though, there's no place to sit down. I know it sounds wacko, but the thing is my sofa's out for reupholstering and hasn't come back yet, though it was promised for early this week."

"You don't have any chairs?"

"Junked the two I had. You can see I was very cavalier with my few possessions, but the truth is they were crummy specimens, I couldn't see hanging on to them."

"Where are you sitting in your spare time, on the toilet seat?"

"Not quite reduced to that, babe." He snickered. "No, I have my desk chair. I cart it around. Down to the bare essentials, that's me, no excess baggage. The simple life, of course primitive's more the word."

113

"Better call your place that's doing over your sofa and light a fire under them."

"I've been calling every day. To no avail, alack."

"At least you've got a roof over your head."

"And one that doesn't leak, praise the Lord." He rapped the table top. "Knock wood on that one."

On the way out she thanked Mario for the Strega. "And the squid was delicious, I never had better."

"Come again, please."

On the street Jack said, "Why don't I walk you home?"

"Why don't you go back and work? Don't you think you've wasted enough time today?"

"Wasted? Are you kidding?"

"Furthermore, I don't want you to see where I live. I'm ashamed of it."

"What does that mean?"

"It's a dumb place, a bourgeois bummer, it wasn't my choice."

"Now you have me all curious. The Excelsior? The Sovereign?"

"No, the Colonnade, you probably know it and laugh up your sleeve at it."

"Oh, that one, I don't think it's too outré, not like Le Galleria, which I'm sure has a golden calf in its lobby."

"Come on, I'll leave you at your street and then you get going starting on your *oeuvre*."

"A heart like a stone."

"Not at all. I don't intend to be a bad influence."

She held out a hand when they came to Sixty-first Street. "So long, Jack, and thanks very much for the lunch."

"Thank *you*, Christine. All right if I call you when that elusive sofa arrives, lay an invite on you for a modest housewarming? You and Rodney."

"Sounds great."

"Well, then. Take care."

"You too."

It was Rodney, she thought, continuing on up along Lex. Rodney's coming here had somehow picked things up for her. Nothing had changed, yet in a way everything had changed, for one thing her attitude. She felt light as a feather, buoyant, with her lips turned up in a faint smile. New people, that was what you needed, and Jack Allerton was a most attractive and interesting guy. She couldn't remember when she had liked someone so much, and she hoped the "elusive sofa" would make its appearance before too long.

In fact it was the following Monday when Rodney phoned to inform her that the chap who'd put him on to his flat had rung him up. "Jack Allerton, I was so pleased to hear from him. I had thought of asking info for his number, as I owe him a great deal, but I had some reservations due to his writing style of life, I presume he may not want to be disturbed in his battles with the Muse. But we had a very agreeable chat."

"Good."

"And he wants us over this week. He said he tried to get in touch with you this afternoon."

"I see, well yes, I've been out."

"He suggested Thursday. Is Thursday all right with you?"

115

"Yup. Thursday will be fine."

"He said if it isn't it can be another day."

"No, Thursday's okay."

"Anyway, he's to ring you up this evening. It's evening now, and he may be trying to get you, so I shall buzz off. Call me when you have it settled, will you? I'll pick you up."

She was in the midst of dinner preparations when the phone rang again. "Is this a bad time to call?" Jack asked. She said no, it was a good time to get her and if she sounded tearful not to wonder about it. "I've been peeling onions. Rodney said you tried to get me earlier. I've only been home a short while."

"As for the onions," he advised, "munch on a piece of bread. It does the trick, at least for me. I won't keep you long, I just wanted to know if you and Rodney could come over for afternoon drinks on Thursday. If not, what day would be better for you?"

"I can make it and so can Rodney. He said you had a nice talk over the phone."

There was a slight hesitation. "I—uh, didn't say we'd met the other day. Possibly I thought his nose might be out of joint. For some reason I—"

"It's all right, I didn't say anything either. It's of no importance at all. What time would you like us on Thursday?"

"About two or so?"

"Very good. I take it your sofa's back home?"

"And looking very posh, I don't even recognize it."

"So they did a good job."

"Fantastic. It exceeds my wildest expectations."

"And we won't have to sit on the floor."

"Or the toilet seat."

"I would call that a giant step."

"So would I. Now I can offer you a place to sit down, ain't that ritzy?"

"Seriously, I'm so eager to see the apartment again. I felt like moving in myself when I was there. It's just the kind of place I adore. Okay, Jack, around two on Thursday, and I'll be looking forward to it."

She went back to the onions. He said to munch on a piece of bread, she remembered, and broke off part of a slice from the loaf. It didn't do much, but then of course the damage had already been done. Thursday, two o'clock—she would take something, of course. Maybe a plant. Plants would do well in that big sunny room. Perhaps a little orange tree, it would be a cut above your philodendron or baby's tears.

"Keep the aspidistra flying," was one of Rodney's British phrases. She had no idea what an aspidistra looked like. Out of curiosity she might ask the florist, but it wouldn't be an aspidistra anyway, it would be an orange tree. He seemed like the sort of guy who'd enjoy eyeing those brilliant little fruitlings. Thursday, two o'clock, she scribbled on the counter-top calendar. Allerton.

She couldn't remember the address number, but it didn't matter, she knew the house. The house had reminded her of her first apartment building, after leaving home, on Ninety-second Street. She wouldn't live that far up now, in these changing

117

times, but in those days it had been a safe area. She had loved that apartment, and still thought of it with pensive fondness. The first home of her own. She never went that far uptown now, ending her walks in that direction at Eighty-sixth Street, which was only wise. But it was also because she didn't want to see the building that had housed her young self. Better to remember it with a sentimental affection. It would be like confronting a ghost to come across it again, in some careless moment. It would be like resurrecting the dead.

7.

"Oh, you brought a present too," Rodney said when Christine opened the door for him.

"Just an obligatory one, I couldn't really pick out anything else without knowing his tastes. This is just a plant, an orange tree. What have you got there, Rodney?"

"An ashtray for him. He smokes, and probably a lot when he's writing, so I got a big one."

"That's thoughtful. If you'll carry this I'll carry your package."

He hefted the foil-wrapped plant, which was of considerable size and weight. "It's heavy," she said. "We'll get a cab."

"No, let's walk."

"You don't want to tote that all the way over to Sixty-first."

"I don't mind at all."

"It's up to you."

"You said an orange tree? I'd like an orange tree."

"You can't have one in your place. You have a good, soft, gentle light, but you need strong, direct sun for a fruit tree. You don't think a plant's too chintzy for a gentleman, then?"

"Certainly not. I mean to buy some, I just don't know what kind. The ashtray I bought is ceramic, interesting design. I went to Royal Copenhagen, as I intended to present him with something magnificent, but everything in the size I wanted cost about a hundred and fifty dollars. So I found this elsewhere. I didn't want it to look ostentatious."

"How are you doing moneywise?"

"Managing."

"Talked to your mother lately?"

"You mean has she threatened to cut off my allowance due to wild extravagance?"

"No, I just meant how is she. Are you being wildly extravagant?"

"Not at tall. I'm really awfully tight. Stingy, you know. That's why the girl I met suits me very well."

"You met a girl? At last? Where?"

"Jack put me on to her. When he called on Monday. She lives in his old building, where he was before he moved to where he is now. She's a Gaslight Girl."

"A what?"

"She works at a place called the Gaslight Club. At night. It sounds seedy, but it's not really."

"You've been there?"

He was elaborately offhand. "I took her over there, so I could see what it was like. It's rather amusing, quite harmless, no leather jackets."

"Jack told you about her on Monday. You didn't waste any time, I see."

"I was naturally curious."

"Naturally. Well, she must be a decent girl if Jack suggested your getting in touch with her."

"As a matter of fact, very proper. I couldn't get in her knickers even if I cared to try."

She said it was nice to know that some girls were protective of themselves, but why *didn't* he care to try? "Isn't she comely?"

"Pretty as a pixie," he assured her cheerfully.

"Well?"

"Too many other things to do," he replied blithely. "Plus I don't get worked up over a girl who doesn't send out feelers."

"Just like a man, you all want to be cozened with Delilah ways and suggestive perfumes. If she works at night how can you take her out?"

"During the day, I expect. She had me to lunch yesterday. Not a bad little cook. She's a good stick."

She glanced at him. Rodney certainly seemed

unpreoccupied with sexual matters. Was he a fag, after all? But she thought not. He was very egoistic, even egotistic, absorbed with himself most of all. Also, he was lazy.

"She promised to make me a soufflé," he announced. "I told her I was keen on them."

"I see," she said dryly. "Is she going to darn your socks as well?"

He grinned. "Haven't got round to asking her yet."

"As a rule what do you do about meals? I mean at night, dinner?"

"Take-out," he enlightened her. "You can get a nice little roast chicken at a Safeway on Third, it does you for two meals. There's a good deli on Eighty-sixth Street. Madison Avenue. All sorts of juicy meats, roast beef, and things like smoked salmon. Sturgeon too. Potato salad and all that. It's not at all difficult."

He grinned again. "And once in a while a friend of mine invites me to dinner, Christine Jennings. I believe you have a nodding acquaintance with her."

"I'd ask you more often, but you have your own life to live, Rodney. I don't want to be a mother hen."

"I never think of you *that* way," he said rakishly, shifting the plant from one arm to the other.

"We should have taken a cab, you'll be muscle-bound."

"It's a bit awkward, that's all. Anyway, we're not far now."

A few blocks farther he indicated a corner spot

on the street. "A film crew was shooting a scene there the other day. Most interesting, you know. I'm told they make a lot of pictures in this city now."

"I guess they do."

"Two people running out of that house across the street, one in full chase of the other. I didn't recognize the players. They did it over and over, about a hundred times. I was exhausted just watching them. I couldn't see any difference in the way it was done, it all looked exactly the same. Much gesticulating and arm waving. It must be smashing to make movies, I know I'd certainly like to take a shot at it."

They turned at Jack's street, walking to Third, then down a little more than halfway to his building, Christine consulting her watch. It was two-ten. Just about right, give him a few last minutes' grace. These stone steps must be hazardous in winter, she thought. She pressed Jack's bell on the brass plate. The answering buzz sounded almost instantly.

Her original impression remained: this was a well maintained building, one of the better ones. It seemed there were still decent rentals at relatively reasonable cost left in this fast-changing city, . though scarce as hen's teeth.

Jack stood looking down at them as they hiked up. "I knew you were coming so I baked a cake," he said. "I'm kidding. Hello, Christine, good to see you again. Rodney . . ."

"I suppose I should have baked a cake," she said. "I brought this along instead."

"Ah, Christine . . ."

She watched him peeling off the protective foil. His hands were deft and quick. They were good hands, shaped well, long-fingered and with the nails clipped short and clean. He was such a dark-skinned man, with crisp dark hair extending from the rolled-up sleeves of his blue and white striped shirt to the wrist, where it came to a stop. He was probably six feet in height, but he gave the impression of being taller. It was because he was thin, markedly thin, and his bones were large enough to accommodate more weight.

He looked strong and capable, a sinewy type. He had a face that was grave in repose, sometimes even somber, but when he smiled it became open and boyish. He was smiling now, holding the plant in both hands, and he really looked delighted. "It's a beauty," he said. "Oranges, Christine, thanks. Thanks a hell of a lot. But you—"

"It's just a thought, nothing at all. And this is from Rodney. Here, you give it to him, Rodney."

"My God, I feel like crawling in a hole. I didn't think of you *bringing* anything, for God's sake. I hate to mess up this nifty paper, it seems a shame. But an ashtray—one that won't spill over, how great, how great. Rodney, it's beautiful, the colors I like, it's much too nice for a slob like me. Christ, you should both be spanked. I'm horribly embarrassed, I never thought you'd arrive bearing gifts."

"Mine isn't a gift, it's just a token. Ah, this *is* a lovely room, Jack. Simply luminous with light."

"I'm afraid it's really precipitate, my asking you here so early in the game," he apologized. "There's no way I can get all that crap off the floor until I find something to put it in. I hope you can close your eyes to it. And I want to scrap that godawful coffee table and get a better one, and I need chairs, a lounge chair and two straight-backed ones. What do you think of the sofa? It's a rather light color, the new stuff, but it's stain resistant, so—"

"It's perfect. It's not near the windows, so it won't get sooty. It's a beautiful fabric, sturdy too, it will wear well, Jack."

"I'm kind of proud of it. It looked pretty sick before I had the reupholstering done, as a matter of fact decidedly tatty, but it has good lines and I couldn't see investing in a new one. Listen to me, I sound like an old biddy."

"You don't look like an old biddy. You look very masculine and handsome and pleased with yourself."

"Oh, I am, very pleased with myself. I keep opening and closing the shutters at the windows, like a witless fool, I'm nuts about them. I stretch out on the sofa and smirk at the ceiling, all that fantastic rococo, like a ballroom. Ain't that something? Now if I can only fill in with the right items, get that shit off the floor and some seating other than the sofa I'll be able to marshal my thoughts at the typewriter."

He stood there, pounding one fist against the palm of the other hand, all energy and enthusiasm, so lean and tall and rangy, so dark-browed and lanky. She must have been out of her mind to let him get away, Christine thought, and wondered what bones of contention, mutual or unilateral, had led to that divorce. "About the stuff on the floor," she said. "Rodney and I saw something that would be fine for this room, would you be interested? An armoire. Not for hanging clothes, you understand, but the kind of storage piece you want. Compartmented, large, with two big, deep drawers. I'm sure you could shovel all those things in with room to spare for more."

She pointed. "Against that far wall. With a chair on either side of it. Very decorative, Jack. Grand Rapids, admittedly, but really very tasteful, with carved doors and brass handles with a dull finish."

"And not pricey," Rodney said. "I wanted it, but Chris said it was too big for my place."

"Sounds fantastic. Sounds like just what the doctor ordered. How much, do you remember?"

"I do," Rodney said. "Five hundred eighty-nine. I still wish I could have had it."

"We saw it at Sloane's. Well, their outlet store. You can get very good buys there, and no wait for delivery because they're not floor samples. I don't know whether you want to pay that much."

"No no, it fits into my budget okay. Will it still be there?"

"If it isn't we can find something else."

He threw her a glance. "You said 'we'?"

She laughed. "I didn't mean to take over. Well, yes, I guess I was thinking along those lines. You'd better tell me to mind my own business, I'm a bossy type."

"I'd give my eyeteeth to have you take over. Think twice before you go any further. You don't know what you might be letting yourself in for. Okay, you've thought twice? Thanks very much, I accept your offer of help, Christine."

They were all laughing now, Rodney saying that she should go in the business of furnishing flats for helpless bachelors, get a fee for her services. "Seriously," Jack protested, "I really can't ask you to go through all that again, Christine."

"I enjoyed helping Rodney, I'd enjoy helping you, Jack. It's just that I'm an old hand at this kind of thing, I have a good feel for where to pick up hard-to-find odds and ends. I know you're keen to be of serene mind."

"It would certainly be a Godsend," he admitted. "I have no imagination at all and I'm always intimidated by salesclerks, I feel rotten when they spend their time with me and I don't buy."

"A writer with no imagination? Impossible."

"That's as far as it goes, plots and all that. All right, sit yourselves down and I'll get our drinks."

"First, may I see the rest of your place?"

"Sure, come on. Rodney?"

"Yes—well, do you mind if I look at your books in the shelves, Jack? You have a smashing library."

"Not too bad. Go ahead. I don't lend, I'm a crank about that, but I just might make an exception in your case, Rodney."

"Oh, I wouldn't borrow. I'd just like to browse through them, if I may."

In the hall between the rooms Jack said he was going to put up a few prints. "Take the curse off its being so narrow. This is okay though, just the way it is," he said of the kitchen. "Maybe an iron rack for pots and pans, but that's about it. As I said, I don't make a production over meals."

The yellow wallpaper brightened the windowless room: it was cheery and cozy, with a white ice cream table against the wall. "You could have a couple of chairs for the table," Christine suggested.

"Why a couple?" he countered. "There's only one of me."

"Just for the sake of symmetry."

"For breakfast, you mean. I stand up at the counter."

"I used to do that too, when I lived alone."

He put his hands in his pockets, considering. "Maybe chairs, yeah. What kind should I get?"

"Ladder backs, rush seats. Simple and countryish. They cost very little."

"You know where to find them, I gather."

"I grew up in this city. I know where to find anything, everything."

"Are you really going to take time out of your life to give me aid and succor?"

"I have a lot of time."

"I would like to see that storage piece you spoke of. Where did you say it was?"

"Eighty-fifth between Second and Third."

"The chairs, the ladder backs. I could latch onto those at the same time, maybe?"

"Could be. Would you like to take a run over tomorrow?"

"I'd like very much to take a run over tomorrow."

"Then how about meeting me there at around ten-thirty?"

"It's a date."

"I hope it will fill the bill for you. I think it's lovely. I like your centerpiece on the table, Jack."

It was a glass liter filled with dried flowers. "It'll do," he said. "Understated. And with the rack for pots and pans—I thought I'd get some with copper bottoms. Mostly just for show. As I said, I don't bother much. I can make a pretty good pot roast, though."

"With a bay leaf?"

"Of course with a bay leaf. Eye of round, I don't dig brisket."

"Neither do I. This is fun. I like being here. May I see the bedroom?"

"Rather forward of you, but always glad to oblige."

"Oh, stuff it," she said, smiling, and followed him. "Voilà," he said at the door. "I don't plan to fuss this up, what's here is all that's going to be here. It's too minuscule to do much with."

"It's cute. A narrower bed would give you more walking space, though."

"I bought this from a friend, sight unseen. I was a little teed off, but it wasn't his fault. I just took it for granted that it would be a studio-sized job."

He shrugged. "You don't turn down a bargain, though, and it's nice to stretch out, though I'm practically touching the walls when I do. It's not much of a room, but it *is* a bedroom and you can close it off if it looks too messy."

"I doubt you're a particularly messy guy."

"If I'm in a hurry I can be slipshod about things. The closet is crammed, but anyway it has shelf

129

space." He showed her. "See? Not all that bad."

He shut the door and faced her. "Christ, I'm a drag. You must think I'm a jerk. Giving you the grand tour like it was Schonbrünn."

"I asked for the grand tour."

"There will be a small fee for the guide."

"Pay you later, my handbag's inside."

"Listen, I made Planter's Punch, I hope you have nothing against rum?"

"Planter's Punch? How festive. You went to some trouble, Jack."

"Are you kidding? This is big doings for me, it means a little something. Jack Allerton is giving a party. Some party. Christine, I'm not much of a socializer, at least these days. Lots of reasons for that. I need friends, I'm on my own and no responsibilities. For some reason I was lucky enough to meet you. Obviously you have another kind of life."

"Not all that much."

"When you're lonely yourself you're prone to think you spot it in others. No no, delete that, for God's sake. What a half-assed thing to say."

She gave him a cordial smile. "Not so half-assed. Who isn't lonely sometimes? Come on, let's get out that Planter's Punch. Rodney will think we've fallen out a window. I'll see the bathroom later, before I leave. I love this apartment, Jack. I hope I'll be asked here again. This whole place reminds me so much of Ninety-second Street, an apartment I had there. Gee, I was happy fixing it up. I must tell you about it sometime. Remind me."

"I will."

In the kitchen he opened the refrigerator door. "There's a tray on the floor, Christine. Yeah, behind the table. You want to put it down on the table and I'll set the pitcher on it."

Then he began pulling things out of the icebox. "*Caviar*," Christine murmured. "Aha."

"Poor man's caviar. Lumpfish, Romanoff's best. Are you insulted?"

"I didn't expect Beluga, my dear. What do you think I serve? What can I do to help?"

"You could open the crackers." He handed her the box. "You'll find a plate for them in the overhead cabinet, the one on the left."

She circled the crackers on the plate, reached for the cream cheese he had taken from the fridge. "All right if I put this in the center of the plate?"

"Great. Silver in the drawer under the counter, ditto napkins."

"Serving plates?"

"Ah, yes. Also in the overhead cabinet. This seems to be it."

"I'll take this in, you can bring in the drink tray."

"What did I ever do without you?"

They carried things inside. Rodney lay, hands folded under his head, on the sofa. He looked very much at home. "Get up," Christine ordered. "Three of us have to sit here."

"I'll bring over the desk chair."

"No, this is cozier. Sit down, Jack, there's loads of room. Just shove over a bit, Rodney."

"What is this we're to drink?" he asked interestedly. "It looks smashing."

131

"It's a punch, called Planter's," Jack explained. "Lime juice, Angostura bitters, sugar and a good, heavy-bodied rum. Like it?"

"Super. Super indeed, Jack."

"Anyone want more sugar? I generally err on the tart side."

Nobody wanted more sugar. Rodney commented on the crackers. "I see these are English biscuits."

"Carr's—they're popular here."

"And caviar—I say, I shouldn't have had lunch."

"You'll manage to eat your share," Christine said. "No, that wasn't a crack, Rodney. You're a growing boy, you're expected to eat up. Jack, the punch really is superb. I have a feeling you do Tom and Jerrys in the cold weather. Or Irish coffee."

"Sometimes. I go for cold weather drinks, though, you're right about that. Toddys and hot punches. Mead, negus, things like that."

"I gave a wassail party one Christmastime. It was a great success."

"I wish this was a working fireplace. We'd have a ball, drink our oldtime quaffs in front of a roaring fire. Applewood. Maybe I'd send to Santa Fe for piñon. Ever smell piñon burning?"

"I don't think so."

"There's no other aroma like it. You feel like eating its smell, I find it almost hallucinogenic."

"You've been to Santa Fe?"

"Yes, it's another world. Getting too arty, of course, but still a kind of fantasia, with the luminarios during the year-end holidays, it's be-witching."

"I used to read Sigrid Undset. *Kristin Lavransdatter*. I was fascinated with the food and drink passages. There was plenty of it too. They were eating so much all the time. Boars' heads and great haunches of meat, birds hot off the spit, and flagons of wine."

"I love visiting the chateaux in the Loire Valley," Rodney said. "You want so much to have been part of it. Rowdy communal meals at tables set for a hundred, you can imagine the din. Dogs snatching at table scraps and tossed bones. Serving wenches hurrying to and fro, bottoms being pinched. So bloody colorful."

"And no bathtubs."

"Oh, yes, those funny little measly tin things, of course very fancy for the gentry. I can imagine the plight of the lower echelons. Bloody lot of privation, frightfully sad. Still, no dreary telly."

"Don't knock television," Jack protested. "I don't know what I'd do without it. After sweating it all day at my Olympia electric I'm glad to sit in a bleary-eyed stupor in front of the tube."

"Some things are worth watching, you have to admit. Your Masterpiece Theatre, for one thing, Rodney."

"Polished soap opera. Still, yes, it's awfully good."

"It certainly makes Sundays special," Jack agreed. "I think it's one of the big things in my life. I'm not kidding. I doubt I could be fond of anyone who wasn't as hooked as I am. I don't know about you, but I find myself going off into Cockney at the drop of a hat. My frozen entrees call for a preheat of 400°, or the bulk of them do. I light the match, turn on the oven and mutter, 'Four 'undred.' Even as Hudson. Or Rose."

"Louisa's my girl," Rodney said dreamily. "Louisa Trotter, Duchess of Duke Street. I'd give a lot for a go with Louisa."

"I guess lots of men had a go with Louisa in her time. That series got me to reading Evelyn Waugh again. She was Lottie Crump in *Decline and Fall*. And *Vile Bodies*."

"I was a big Waugh reader," Jack said. "It was the early books, though, then he got religion and began to get solemn-serious. That's my opinion, anyway."

"Graham Greene got religion and he didn't get solemn-serious."

"My favorite Waugh is *A Handful of Dust*," Rodney said enthusiastically. "That's a book."

"No arguments about that, Rodney. But can we stop talking about writers? It makes me squirm, out of—well, fear. I try to stack myself up with popular writers, people whose work doesn't throw me for a loop. If I start thinking of all the good ones, I'm inclined to feel like going to stand in a corner. One reason I don't read the book sections when I'm working on something. I just get sick. Dazzling encomiums, and here you are just trying to do a workmanlike job."

"Which means that you care very much about excellence and are probably a born and scrupulous craftsman."

"Excellence and craftsmanship don't always bring in the checks."

"But since we know it *can*—"

"It would be nice to toss off a flashy bestseller and then get down to brass tacks."

"I guess lots of people had that idea, only it didn't pan out that way. I haven't met him, but my friend Clover is on *intime* terms with a writer. Or a former writer. I guess he doesn't do much of it these days. He was a journalist in Europe, where he was born, but apparently hasn't had much success at authoring here. An old story, he was a Jew in Nazi Austria, the usual horrors. Clover never married, but then she met Anton, and it's just as if she *were* married to him. She can't be, because he's already married and it seems there's been no talk of divorce. It's interesting, though. More than once she's referred to him as her husband, and I could tell she didn't even realize what she'd said."

"Is she happy?"

"She certainly seems lighthearted. I don't know about happy. Somehow the word doesn't trip lightly off the tongue. I don't mean just for Clover, I mean for anyone."

"Obviously that's because we overwork it so heartlessly. The English language isn't too rich in nuances. But I think it's because we're leery about overreaching. Or oversimplifying. The trouble is, we're inclined to equate it with happy forever, like the fairy tales. And they lived happily ever after. Well, you know damned well they didn't live in a state of uninterrupted bliss for every day of their lives. You know damned well they piled up a list of grievances against each other, thought of breaking each other's necks at odd and sundry times."

He broke off, grinned. "Sorry, I didn't mean to pontificate. I could have said right off, yes, happy's a word I'll stand by, I think it's what gets us out of bed in the morning, looking for it. Christine, you were telling us about your friend when I pre-empted the floor."

"No, just that her man is, or was, a writer. And yes, I think she's happy, there, I've said it. Certainly Anton must be an interesting companion, with his European ways, and his anecdotes and stories that give her a new look at like. Like the Schnorrer business."

"The what?" Rodney demanded.

"Schnorrer, that's a man who cadges, a down and outer, failed in his profession or else a victim of bad luck for some reason. A Schnorrer isn't able to earn a living, so he exists through the bounty of relatives and friends, managing to keep afloat on their largesse. It's not like a Bowery bum, we're talking about a man with creases in his trousers and a homburg on his head, maybe. A faded gentleman. Anyway, Clover tells us about these things and we're all fascinated. Sometimes I'm almost envious of her, of this thing she has. That she's part of another world, that she has this glimpse into another culture, and that she's *assuaging* this Third Reich survivor, Anton, giving him her strength and her love and her young prettiness when I'm sure he thought there would be nothing forevermore but bleakness. And now Clover, just one day running into someone like her, and he not young anymore."

She gestured. "The rest of us are living static

lives, stuck in a time warp, American provincials, supermarket types, but Clover knows about something else, sees it at first hand. In that way yes, I do envy her. And yes, I will have some more punch, apparently I've decided to stop counting glasses. More caviar too, Rodney, that is if you can spare some."

"Oh, was I pigging it? Frightfully sorry."

"Nobody minds, so don't look so dashed."

"By the way," Jack said, "I'm no stranger to the term Schnorrer. My mother's Czech, or at least by ancestry. It was called Bohemia in her grandmother's time, and it was all part of the Austro-Hungarian monarchy, as I'm sure you're very much aware. I've heard my own stories. As a matter of fact I was raised on just such fancifications— *Wind in the Willows*—just like any other child but also Schnorrer stories, and yarns about Baron Munchausen."

"It sounds like an interesting childhood, Jack. Imagine you knowing about Schnorrers!"

"Imagine you knowing about them."

"It's only because of Clover Martinson. Do you have a liking for lieder? And the Viennese schmaltz? Kalman and Lehar and Stolz—of course Strauss too?"

"Unabashedly. You?"

"Sure do."

"As for Strauss, *both* Strausses. Johann and Richard. Ah, yes. I think I could even do without books if it came down to a choice. I know I couldn't live without music."

"You don't have a stereo, though."

"I don't need a stereo. It's a lot of fuss and bother. I get all the music I could ask for, music is part of all my waking hours, except when I plant myself at night in front of the TV set. QXR, it's an old friend. That's an old Zenith radio near my desk, but it has an exceptionally good tone, it's my old familiar. I'm always afraid it will conk out, I think I'd consider tearing all my hair out."

"So you have music on while you're working."

"Certainly. Oh, I know some people demand utter quiet when they're concentrating, but not me. God, not me. There's that to keep me company, and the window view, seeing people moving around on the street; it's like having friends around. I couldn't work in a place where I wasn't able to see other people."

"Yes, it must be horrid not to have a window in your office."

"I worked in an office without a window once," Jack said. "Two of us, this young kid and I. He was a character, I liked him very much. He came from a very moneyed family and he had the job through connections, right after he graduated from college, it was noblesse oblige. He was incensed at being closed off that way, so he hunted through magazines and came up with a full page color photo of the New York skyline seen through a window frame. I came in one morning and there he was, sitting at his desk looking pleased as punch, with the photo tacked up on the wall next to him."

He chuckled. "Funny thing was, it was very effective. It made you feel there really was a window, quite remarkable. His name was Richard, I've never forgotten him. Rodney, I meant to ask you, how do you British feel about your new Prime Minister?"

"Thatcher? Mixed feelings, but on the whole no riots in the streets. She's very pretty."

"Yes, she is," Christine agreed. "She certainly dresses better than the Royal Family. I never saw such frumps."

"They seem to consider it de rigeur to look dowdy. Is there a reason for that, Rodney?"

"English women are tweedy types, that's all. Stumping along in layers of clothing, it's a cold country, you know."

"That's no excuse for those awful hats. Your mother doesn't stump along in layers of clothing. Peggy has incredible style. You'd think people in public life would want to— They all look like dressmaker's dummies. But oh, I do love England, with its misty moors and lovely leas and its thatched roofs in the provinces. Creamed teas and pubs and all that clipped speech."

"And its stiff-necked pride."

"You Americans make a mystique about it," Rodney said cheerfully. "You've all read too much Shakespeare."

Jack chuckled. "We've all seen too much Masterpiece Theatre."

"Maybe too much Maugham."

"I hate it that there's no Empire anymore, where the sun never set, and all that pomp. Okay, that's reactionary, but I can't help it."

"It's not what it was," Rodney admitted. "Still, nattering won't help."

Jack said he was a confirmed Anglophile too. "I felt so in place when I was there, as if after a long journey, I'd come home. Whitehall and Trafalgar Square and the Inns of Court, all those bewigged barristers. I put up in a hotel in Kensington, the door porter was costumed like someone out of Dickens. I couldn't believe it in this day and age. Kippers for breakfast. Marylebone and Christopher Wren and St. Mary's in the Fields. Nice."

"We went to a Lyons, for the fun of it," Christine remembered. "Not the Corner House, the one near Marble Arch. We just wanted tea and crumpets, but it's all divided into separate rooms, one for fish, one for meat, and so forth. Nothing that said tea. Except that I spotted a sign reading 'Restful Tray,' which proved to be where you got tea. It was so prototypically *British*."

"They have their ways."

"Listen, Jack, about an easy chair, which you said you want. Did they give you any extra material? They usually do. Not that we'd be able to match the fabric on this sofa, but at least it would give us the color tones. Don't you think?"

"Yes, as a matter of fact, there was a plastic envelope with some material. I'll get it now, before I forget. Be right back."

"And bring it along with you tomorrow."

"What's this about tomorrow?" Rodney wanted to know.

"We're going to look at that armoire. Maybe we can find some other things for this place at the same time."

"Good, I'll come along."

"Darling, no. *If* you please. You'll only get tired straight off, and want an early lunch. This is no laughing matter. Naturally Jack wants to get everything he possibly can off his mind, so just let the two of us polish off the necessary, it will be so much quicker."

"Well, if I'm not wanted."

"You know better than that. I helped you, it's Jack's turn now."

He returned with the material. Christine shook the fabric out of the envelope. "Oh, these are the arm pieces. See? Look, this is what you do with them, Jack."

She got up, fitted the shaped pieces properly, stood back. "For what, though?" Jack asked. "It's just another layer of material."

"People run their hands down the arms of a sofa, or a chair, for that matter. They get soiled quicker than the rest. So you have these for protection, you have them cleaned whenever necessary."

"I don't think I like them, Christine."

"Neither do I," she admitted. "I never make use of them. To me, they're simply antimacassars. Just keep them for match-up purposes."

"So you're going furniture hunting," Rodney said. "I offered to go with you, do my bit, but Christine said nothing doing. I'd be in the way seemed to be the burden of her refrain."

"I'm sure you want Jack to have a free mind too."

"I still think it's asking a hell of a lot. There are quite a few things I have in mind to look for. I'm afraid you'll start looking askance. Why the hell am I wasting so much time on this dithering dolt?"

"I have more time than I know what to do with."

"Somehow I can't believe that."

"It's true."

"Why, Christine?"

"I suppose it's because I'm in the middle, like maybe when you're writing a book, for example. There's generally a beginning, a middle and an end. Or a play, perhaps. The first act is over, the last act is still to come and the second act is in progress. And this second act is not particularly action-filled. If I were in the audience I don't think I'd bother to stay for the last act."

"I'd suggest some revisions," he said.

"So would I, but my mind's a blank. Maybe it's just a case of miscasting; the wrong person in the role. Maybe I wasn't cut out for keeping home and hearth together."

She was instantly aghast at what she had said. To a stranger. And with Rodney listening. A betrayal of sorts. Would he now report to his mother, via a transatlantic phone call, that her friend Christine Jennings seemed to be in some sort of snit?

"I didn't mean a single word of that," she cried, reaching for a cigarette. "Talking just to hear myself talk, that's about it. What nonsense! I think I'm just showing off, trying to impress you, Jack, with flashy metaphors. By the way, those books you had published. You belittled them, rather, but could I read them? Or anyway, one or two of them? I meant to ask you before. May I?"

He hesitated. "I wouldn't refuse, of course, and

I'm far from ashamed of them, it isn't that. I'd rather not, since they were outright potboilers, to make a quick buck, but I will because it would seem churlish and self-conscious to refuse when someone shows interest. The thing is I have no idea, until I can properly arrange my books, where my few little published gems are. As you can see—or maybe it isn't immediately apparent—I just shoved them in the shelves helter-skelter, no organization at all. So—"

"Another time?" he asked tentatively.

"Whenever, Jack." She understood, or thought she did. He probably would feel exposed: she could sympathize with that. A writer must cringe at possible criticism. Maybe he was fearful his work would meet with lukewarm praise, dutiful encomiums. She thought that if she wrote a book and had it published she would probably hand it out to strangers on the bus, but then that situation wasn't likely to arise.

"But thanks for asking, for being interested, Christine."

"Needless to say, I'm interested too," Rodney assured him. "As a matter of fact, it's one of the reasons I scanned your books, I was hoping to come across something of yours."

"Well, you're not missing much for now, the big project is just getting under way. That will keep me busy for a while." He looked uncomfortable. "I guess I am a little self-conscious about my output," he admitted. "Defensive. Oh, well, shut up, Jack, come on, you two, drink up, we have to finish this brew. Rodney, let me fill your glass."

"Thanks, Jack."

"Christine?"

"Okay, seeing as how there's just about enough for the three of us. I may be sorry later on, but right now it doesn't seem to matter. And then, in a very short while, we must go. I must, at any rate."

"I had hoped today would never end."

"What a superlative host. Not one of those who already have their minds focused on cleaning up the dishes in the sink. Oh, must you go, here's your hat."

"I told you she was endless fun," Rodney said, chortling.

"Have you two been talking about me?" Christine demanded. "When could that have been, may I ask?"

"On the phone. Monday, when Jack called. I told you we had a good chat."

"And yes, we did talk about you," Jack agreed, laughter behind his eyes. He did that sometimes. No overt smile, but in the depths of those deepset dark eyes a quiet amusement. He filled her glass, Rodney's and then his own. The caviar, thanks to Rodney, was down to nothing but a scrape.

And the shadows were lengthening. She realized, with a kind of mild astonishment, that she would stay on for the evening, if Jack should suggest it. She would simply make a phone call home and tell them to manage dinner without her.

"Well," she said briskly, finishing her drink and putting the glass back on the table. "May I use your john, and then, Rodney, we must go. Much as I regret putting an end to this utterly delightful afternoon."

"You know where it is," Jack said, rising. "Guest towels and all that."

The bathroom now boasted a shower curtain. It must have been hard going, with all those rainbow-hued tiles. He had been canny, however. The shower curtain was in a pale yellow, with a design that was at first just a shadowy pattern of lines and curlicues but which, on closer inspection, proved to be a subtle mosaic of mouths, women's mouths. At first almost indecipherable, their curved lips and dimpled chins popped out at you when you finally made out what they were. Smiling, soft, full-lipped mouths, delicate, gentle, and yet sensual and inviting.

Very amusing, she reflected. A little challenging too. He said he had no imagination beyond his authorship, but he had found this, and it was a first for her. It was—well, sexy, really. Of course maybe he had only wanted an almost plain shower curtain, with no discernible pattern, and so had chosen this without much thought or plan. Yet . . .

Very amusing, she thought again, and sat down on the seat, glancing round. There was a rack against the farthest wall which held two very large, very masculine terry towels in a mustard color, and a matching washcloth draped over the side of the tub. It was still damp.

There was also, next to the basin, a neat little row of fingertip towels, three of them, obviously the guest towels Jack had mentioned. One was yellow, one was violet and one Nile green. All of them were fringed and, when she looked, the label read 'Cannon.'

It was somehow so touching. This man living alone, a man who had once been married, perhaps even very recently. He had asked people to come and visit him and then one of the things he had done in preparation, besides making his Planter's Punch and buying the staples, was to lay out three pristine little towels in his bathroom. The amenities.

She washed her hands and picked up one of the towels, the one nearest the basin. It was the yellow one. She dried her hands and then, not folding the towel, replaced it on the rack. That way he would be sure it had been used, congratulate himself for his thoughtful provisions and know he had done the right thing.

Then she switched out the light and went inside again.

Their voices came to her on the way. Rodney's voice at the moment, that correct, perfectly modulated British voice that had a touch of the arrogant in it. She thought of Queen Elizabeth, those high-pitched, high-born accents, that mellifluous, monotonous drone. She couldn't picture that woman engaged in fellatio, but one supposed she must do it all the same. Did a queen cry out when taken?

"Like *The Magic Mountain*," Rodney was saying, very serious and pontifical, like some Oxford don. "Settembrini, you know, was to me simply such a tiresome *bore*. Of course I shouldn't have read that book when I did, I understood practically none of it."

Rodney swept back that abundant fair hair that

146

sometimes Christine felt like anchoring with a bobby pin. He gestured, very studied and theatrical. "I think," he said, "that certain books should be forbidden people until they reach the age of reason. Don't you agree, Jack?"

"No," Jack replied, shaking his head. "My feeling is that anyone of any age should have free access to all the libraries within walking distance. What makes no sense at one age will later on meet with comprehension. Ready or not doesn't matter. It's like coming across an old friend you might not have hit it off with years ago, but now you're on the same wave length. That's the way I feel about it, Rodney. Oh, hi, Christine, I have some ginger brandy around, we could get a little drunker on that. Someone gave it to me. I thought it looked like shit and was rather offended, but I find I like it very much. How about it?"

"Another time, Jack. It's been a perfect afternoon, I've enjoyed every minute of it. Coming along with me, Rodney?"

"Righto."

"So tomorrow morning, Jack? Ten-thirty at Sloane's."

"Eighty-fifth between Second and Third. See you there. I'm very grateful."

He stood there on the landing as they walked down the carpeted stairs. He was still standing there when they let themselves out. She knew that because she glanced back up, just before closing the outside door. He was there looking down at them, leaning over the railing, an arm, in its striped shirt with the rolled-up sleeves, visible as well.

She was very glad she had used the guest towel. It was such a silly thing to think of, but she did think of it, and she almost mentioned the towels to Rodney, but thought better of it. He wouldn't understand, why should he? Rodney was like a camel, and almost never had to go, which worried her sometimes: did he hold it in out of impatience with this tiresome function that would take him away from more interesting things, or was there something wrong with his kidneys? It seemed to her, if the former, quite unreasonable, seeing that men had so much an easier time of it. Zip in and out, back in and rezip. But then men were endlessly long-suffering about shaving, as if it were such a big deal, while women had to go through all sorts of rituals in order to achieve the desired effect.

She kept thinking, though, by now he knows I used one of the towels. It would please him, she was sure. The woman had dried her hands on his yellow towel. A very nice man, with his dark thick hair all curly and not very obedient, as a matter of fact quite wayward, as if it had a mind of its own. And the slow smile spreading across his face like the sun emerging from a cloud. Rodney, at the entrance to her building, kissed her on the cheek and asked her if she thought Jack had liked his ashtray.

"Of course he did, it was exactly the right thing, Rodney."

"Your orange tree looked super on the windowsill next to his desk, too."

She watched him walk off, jaunty as always, and then went inside, past the concierge's desk and into the elevator that Rodney called the lift. Riding up to her floor, she mentally began dinner preparations. What a nice day. She changed into jeans and a light shirt and then went into the kitchen, consulted the menu for the evening. Roast chicken, yams, petit pois and a tossed salad. She yanked the chicken out of the fridge, dank and submissive, poor thing.

When it was stuffed and trussed she popped it into the roasting pan. It would take an hour and a quarter, about. When Bruce came home she would send him down to Baskin-Robbins for an ice cream cake.

She sat in the kitchen, doing a *Times* crossword. The late sun of preevening shone in through the window, her pencil filled in blank squares. It was good to be alive. She wasn't always sure, but today she was. She had her own world, outside of the others, just as they had theirs. She kept forgetting that, but it was true. If disaster struck, say tomorrow, and she was separated from those near and dear to her, there would still be herself. It was the only thing anyone could ever really count on. They could all die in an accident. Carl, Bruce, Nancy. Who would be of support then, who would supply comfort and care? She would have to go on. It was true of everyone.

When the phone rang she answered it with the pencil still in her hand. "Yes?"

"Hi, this is Jack. Is this a bad time to call?"

"Hello, Jack. No, I'm just doing a crossword puzzle while waiting for my chicken to need basting. Did I leave something there?"

"No no. I just wanted to say thanks for being my first guest."

She laughed softly. "Jack, the pleasure was mine, I assure you. This afternoon—well, it put me in such a good mood. Don't thank *me*, please."

"My orange tree seems happy here, I thought you might like to know." A slight clearing of the throat and then, "Well, bye for now, Chris, see you in the morning. Have a good evening."

"You too, Jack. Thanks for calling."

She went back to the crossword, smiling. Carl came home an hour or so later. She heard his key in the lock and then his footsteps through the outer room. "How was your day?" he asked, brushing his lips against the back of her neck. "Something smells good. Capon?"

"Just your ordinary roast chicken. About an hour or so, or thereabouts. Bruce hasn't come in yet."

He filled a glass with water. "How was your day?" she asked him.

"A really rotten one. Thank God they're not all like today."

"Lie down for a while."

"I'd have a drink if I weren't determined to shed some of this flab."

"Carl, it's not flab, don't abuse yourself."

"Feels like flab to me. Okay, yes, I will stretch out on the sofa in the study."

He works hard, Christine thought. While I fritter away my time. Still, if he really wanted to know, she had had a good and satisfying day. She had probably talked too much, but nobody seemed to mind, neither Rodney nor Jack.

He seemed to like that orange tree, too.

8.

She ran into Ruth Alexander on the way to the
Villa d'Este, where group lunch was scheduled for
today. They must have taken roughly the same
route. Ruth was wearing a stunning pants suit,
Ultrasuede, she looked marvelous, but when
Christine caught up to her her friend looked glum.
Ruth, turning, had a kind of silent expression on
her face, as if what she had been thinking about

wasn't particularly pleasant.

"Fancy seeing you here, Chris. No, I mean hello. I tried to get you yesterday but no answer."

"What time?"

"About two. I'm not sure."

"I was out. Anything wrong?"

"What should be wrong?" Ruth asked rhetorically, because she followed that right up with, "Chris, Michael's come down with mono."

"Oh, no."

"Oh, yes. That means the whole bit. God knows how long it will linger. Isn't it loathsome?"

"God, I'm sorry, Ruth."

"I don't believe it, you know. That this had to happen. I simply don't believe it."

"Darling, fortunately it's summer vacation. It should be licked by the time school starts again. Don't you think?"

"Chris, you know as well as I do that it can mean months! We've paid his tuition for next quarter. It's just so damned discouraging."

She sagged. "Of course he's fallen completely to pieces. He's just a discouraged, wretched lump. He's reverted to about seven years old, all whining and hiding himself under the bedclothes. I feel so *sorry* for him, but who bears the brunt? Yours truly, as you can well imagine. What the hell's to be done? I got the news yesterday and after tucking him into bed went out and bought this thing I have on, which to tell you the truth I can't afford, but I've lost my looks and I've lost my spirits and I had to, simply *had* to spend some money on myself. Hag that I am."

"Ruth, you're a handsome, young, bright and delightful woman," Christine assured her. "You're lovely! And you know it, you dope. Don't let this get you down. Please. *Please.*"

"It's got me down," Ruth said grimly. "I ain't kidding, it's got me down to gutter level." Her lips tightened. "What I really want to do is stand on this street corner and swear, say all the most profane things I can think of and laugh in people's faces when they stand stock still and stare at me, the madwoman."

She put an arm through Christine's. "But I won't," she promised, one of her impish smiles suddenly appearing. "Hey, what would you do without your friends to spill your beefs to?"

"I say that almost every day of my life."

"Yeah. Oh, what the hell. Do you like this suit?"

"I saw the suit first, before I realized it was you," Christine said truthfully. "It's a knockout I was telling myself, all envy and greed. Where'd you get it?"

"Bolton's. At that, it set me back two hundred. Anne Klein, I was assured, sotto voce, and I believe it. It has good lines, and it hides my middle-aged spread."

"You're as thin as a stick."

"Not around the middle, dearie. It takes money spent to fool people into not noticing. But I *have* lost three pounds drinking not much but beef bouillon for several days, and to celebrate I'll have a whopping lunch. I deserve it."

"Give Michael my love, will you? And I hope this will be of very short duration. Sometimes it is, you know that."

"And sometimes it isn't, but I won't dwell on it. We're here for merrymaking, I won't cast a pall over the proceedings."

The others were already there, in a cloud of cigarette smoke and perfume. "Don't say anything about Michael," Ruth muttered in Christine's ear. "Let it go, just let it go, okay?"

Room was made for them on the banquette. "Greetings, you two." The waiter came over, an old friend over the years. "Don't tell me, I can guess," he said. "Martinis with an olive, be right back."

"I love your pants suit," someone said to Ruth.

"I love yours," she replied.

"I'm wearing a dress."

"So you are. Yes. Oh, I—one of those sedative hangovers. I'm seeing out of one eye."

"Valium?"

"I don't know, triple bromides, I can't remember."

"Which eye are you seeing through?"

"I'm not sure. The right one, I guess. I remember when I lost a contact in the elevator, starting out on a date. As a matter of fact, my first date with Lloyd. It fell out and I was in a panic, but I was so vain. I didn't even look for it. My contact lens! We went to the movies. I sat the whole time holding a hand in front of my eye. He thought I had a headache. It was ghastly, and I did have a headache after a while. I would have died rather than tell him I was nearsighted, and it was much, much later that I learned Lloyd had had a nose job, which he was too vain to tell me; his sister did."

"Oh, *poor* Ruthie."

Some confidences of Clover's. About Anton. "He's so darling," she said. "I love his phone calls, they're always interrupted with hellos. I don't know whether it's European or not. Maybe it's just Anton. He'll be talking away and suddenly he says, 'Hello?' As if he thought I'd gone, hung up. 'Hello,' I say back. A little later it's the same thing. 'Hello?' It's a little bit like Victor Borge doing a sketch."

"Does he have much of an accent, Clover?"

"Oh, very Paul Henreid. Charming, it is to melt. No, not one of those barking Kommandant accents, God forbid."

"Me?" Christine said, when asked what she had been up to. "Busy as ever. Now that Rodney's place is finished I have another assignment. How about that?"

"How about that?" Helene echoed. "Who is it this time?"

"A friend of Rodney's. No, not British, I've had enough Rule Brittania. We met him when we were looking for an apartment for Rodney. It won't be much of a challenge, he only needs a few additionals to add to what he has. Anyway, it's something to keep me occupied. He's a writer, I'll have you know."

"Who?"

"You mean a recognizable name? No. Anyone with a recognizable name would be better fixed financially. I guess. Just a guy."

"Why are *you* involved in all this?"

"A woman's sure touch. Or something like that.

He's a dear creature, a friendly soul and rather at sea. Divorce, or whatever."

"Or whatever? That's like saying someone's slightly pregnant. Is he or isn't he?"

"He did mention divorce."

"Is he nice?"

Christine laughed. "By that you mean is he toothsome?"

"Is he?"

"I hadn't thought about it. He's a younger man."

"Younger than what?"

"Than me. I like him. That's about it. Not very interesting."

"It sounds interesting to me."

"To me too. Chris, if you're tired of helping out bachelors and divorcés I'd be glad to take over."

"Thanks, but it's all rather fun. Tomorrow I'm going to wear him out again shopping for necessities and pretty trimmings. He's as helpless as a baby."

"Doesn't he work?"

"I don't think he'd thank you for the slur. He's self-employed, a free-lancer. According to him, it's no snap."

"What does Carl think of this new—" Meryl giggled. "Assignment, I think you called it?"

"Carl?" She thought it over. "Actually I haven't said anything."

There was a chorus of cries. "Why, it sounds positively *illicit*," Meryl said, leaning forward. "Secret trysts!" She turned to the others. "Do you realize none of us has ever mentioned our own secret trysts?"

"You must be kidding," Ruth said jadedly. "I've never had one of those. No one ever asked me."

"As for secret trysts," Christine assured them, "this is *work,* I'd like to point out. You knock yourself out finding little treasures for their pads and you go home feeling like a wrung-out mop. It's merely a favor asked and a favor done. Everyone ready for another drink?"

"I know I am," Meryl said. "I have to go to Campbell's tonight. A friend's father has died. I'm not looking forward to it."

"I'm sorry," Clover murmured. "Someone you know well?"

"Well enough. His daughter's someone I'm very fond of. Her kids are in the same class as the twins. Laura's an Electra personality, and I know this will be a great sorrow."

" 'I weep for Adonais, he is dead'," Clover said, sighing. "Okay, another drink. Art is long and life is fleeting, but a good martini goes a long way to vanquishing that old devil Weltschmerz. All in favor say aye. And after that I'll have to order, because I have an arduous afternoon, so time is of the essence. I guess I'll have to skip dessert and coffee today."

"I thought travel was dropping off," Helene commented. "You always seem to be the busy bee, though. How do you manage that?"

"I haven't lost any regulars. They keep on wending their ways hither and yon. It's not easy to get new people, though. There is, naturally, a lot of resistance. God, European prices are soaring, far worse than ours. I wouldn't want to go into the

157

business right now, start from square one, I can tell you that. But I'm doing all right, though I should throw salt over my shoulder or something for tempting fate."

"You're not the superstitious type."

"I'm a closet worrier, but on the other hand I'm stubborn, I refuse to let circumstances get the best of me. You have to believe you're lucky if you want to be lucky. Like that James-Lang theory I always felt applied to me. You're happy because you laugh, sad because you cry. Rather than the other way around."

"Which is just another way of saying keep a stiff upper lip."

"No, there's a big difference. All the difference in the world. Maybe it isn't your cup of tea, kiddo, but it has a very special meaning for me, and I've fallen back on it for years."

Meryl said it might be a good idea to try a little psychology on herself. "I have this sick feeling in the pit of my stomach just thinking about tonight. It's terribly infantile, but I can't help wanting to back away from death, and I think the whole schmear is barbaric, the body offered up like a trophy or something, and everyone praising it, admiring the mortician's handiwork. *How well he looks, how natural,* as if it was a copy of the real thing."

"Never mind psychology," Helene said. "Drink up, Meryl, gin's better than psychology any day in the week."

She didn't feel at all like going out tonight. She

generally didn't go anywhere on the evenings following one of the ladies' lunches, usually checked to be sure there was nothing on the agenda for later on. This was duty, though, and nothing that could have been foreseen. There was a condolence call to pay. You couldn't write down on a calendar or in your day book that you were going to visit someone in order to console them about a bereavement, since you didn't know in advance, did you, that someone was going to die.

A condolence call—she had heard someone or other refer to it in this manner. Probably Amy Vanderbilt had it listed in her *Book of Etiquette*. How to behave at a wake. But of course Amy Vanderbilt wouldn't say "wake." Nor would I, Meryl thought, so why did I use that word?

Anyway, she had to go. Ralph was off the hook. Her husband played chess on Thursday evenings with a neighbor down the hall. He had offered, half-heartedly, to scratch tonight's game, but Laura Morrison was really Meryl's friend, not Ralph's. Ralph and Hank, Laura's husband, had never hit it off, so the four of them didn't socialize. It was the women who were amicable, and quite fond of each other. Now Laura's father had died, was lying "in rest" at Campbell's, and although Meryl was not going to the funeral it was certainly incumbent on her to show up at the funeral parlor with Laura's other friends and relatives.

She cleared up the dinner dishes, rinsed them and then put them in the machine, turned it to ON. She went to the liquor cabinet, poured out a small measure of scotch, drank it straight, then lit a cigarette, which she puffed at quickly until it was half smoked, after which she crushed it out in an ashtray. Now she must hurry and get dressed.

Laura had said about eight, so there wasn't much time. Not enough time, really. She might not be able to get a cab, and at this time of the evening buses would be few and far between. Maybe she'd have to walk, but she hoped not. The days were long in this season of the year, but just the same most of the avenues were inclined to be deserted after seven o'clock.

She hoped the "piece" would be all right. She loved buying cut flowers as a general rule. Anemones, mimosa, African daisies. But funeral flowers were something else. "A basket, I think," she'd told the florist. "Something graceful and unostentatious. But of course fine blooms. Just not—oh, *solemn*. Or tortured. Simple and lovely. Quietly distinguished."

The end of a life and people went into florist's shops and bought posies to put around the bier, so it all came down to that. Duty and etiquette. The machine didn't work anymore, the machine had stopped running, a loose sparkplug somewhere, and what was left was thereupon exhibited and paid tribute to. An inoperative model, but it had worked fine in its day and the least you could do was give it a respectful send-off to wherever broken machines went to.

It was a topic of discussion, though, threshed out even at cocktail parties, where you ran into people who had made living wills. Wills that forbade un-natural means of prolonging life when there was no

160

further hope, wills interdicting against embalming and "laying out" for viewing. Instant cremation and instant privacy. She and Ralph were in agreement with this sensible kind of arrangement, but they hadn't got around to doing anything about it yet. After all, they were only in their early forties. Some day, though. She'd bring it up with Ralph again soon. She didn't want anyone paying condolence calls for her, or buying baskets and flowered wreaths. And yet . . .

Some of the most memorable occasions Meryl remembered had been just such gatherings. When someone died, and people who hadn't seen each other maybe for years met once again and talked their heads off. A funeral was often a reunion. Friends and relatives from far-flung places managing to get together to pay obeisance to someone they loved—or once had loved—and now had lost. There was a peculiar kind of festivity about it even, as if they were all celebrating the fact of their own aliveness and that of the others, a kind of tribute to life as well as death. A bonding together in the presence of death, like survivors of an earthquake or a plane accident. A kind of club, a fraternity to which they belonged, the living. It was a time for reminiscences, recalling events half buried in their minds, most of which included, gratuitously and out of consideration, the occupant of the coffin. Soft laughter and hands grasped in freshets of sentiment. *Remember the time when . . .*

Food passed and a drink in your hand and a little linen napkin on your lap. Cigarette smoke circling the room, the sun making a haze of it. The john, when you had to go and where you sat alone on a spotless toilet seat seen to by a helpful neighbor or friend who had later brought the potato salad and cold meats. You lingered in the bathroom looking in the mirror, glad as anything that the familiar face still stared back at you and was not lying on a satin pillow in an oak casket. You put your quiet and reflective expression back on and went outside again.

Maybe it made sense, Meryl thought. Maybe it wasn't so barbaric after all. She just didn't like to think of herself lying there dead while the others had fun. Which was terribly selfish. And thoughtless, of course. The close of kin weren't having fun. The close of kin, perhaps, were momentarily comforted by the support of friends and family. A temporary reprieve. Tomorrow they would weep.

She pulled on her dress, picked up her handbag and gloves, left her bedroom, snapping out the light. She wished, rather a lot, that Ralph was coming with her. It would be late when she left Campbell's. Someone would probably drive her home, though, or share a taxi. Whatever, but she had to leave now, right now.

The twins, Susan and Amanda, were watching TV. "You know your bedtime," she said to them. "Be tucked up before Daddy gets home. Understand?"

"Yes, Mom."

"What are you watching? Nothing violent? You know the rules about that."

"It's the end of a Disney," Susan said, offended.

"Next is that circus program we've waited all week to see."

"Oh, yes, that will be fun. And then bed."

"Um hum. Have a nice time."

"I'm going to a funeral parlor."

"Oh."

Out on the street, as if by magic, she got a taxi. The driver had his radio going. It was Mozart, the concerto 21 in C. Or as some people had come to refer to it, the Elvira Madigan concerto. "Sounds nice," Meryl said, settling back in the seat.

He regarded her in his rearview mirror. "You like music."

"Sure. Very much."

"Rock?"

"You can have it."

"I'll pass too," he said. "How do you feel about Mehta as a conductor?"

"I think he's excellent."

"I drove him one afternoon. Did you like Boulez?"

"Not enough dash, I'm a little old-fashioned. I'm happy about Mehta."

He had seen them come and go, he told her. Bruno Walter. Mitropoulos. Koussevitzky, Barbirolli. "You name it," he said. "I've been a long time around. I should be retired, but who can retire these days? I'll hack till I drop."

When the cab pulled up in front of the funeral parlor she had a good look at him. Yes, he must be going on seventy. He *would* probably hack until he dropped, she thought, in his cab with the radio turned on to his favorite music station. He was a nice guy, and it seemed meet and right that this cheerful personality should end his days at the wheel, his ears filled with immortal music.

"Nice to talk to you," she said as she paid him.

"You too, lady. See you around."

She was ushered into Campbell's by an attendant at the door. Inside another attendant, correct and formal, indicated the room she was to go to. His smile was pleasant and concerned at the same time. A professional smile, he probably practiced it in front of a looking glass.

She stopped at the doorway of the room assigned to her friend's family. It was only just past eight, but a very large number of people sat on folding chairs, with some grouped at the place where the casket stood on its catafalque, surrounded by flowers. The scent was almost overpowering. It was the goddamn flowers that were so macabre. Flowers belonged in fields and gardens, why flowers for someone who could no longer smell them? But of course it was for the family of the person who could no longer smell them. The final acknowledgment. Afterwards everyone said how many lovely flowers there had been. "Masses of them, absolute masses."

She sighted Laura, who was standing at the coffin, gesturing toward it as if she were displaying some rare work of art. Laura looked pale and tired. She looked as if she had been jogging around the reservoir at Central Park for about a hundred hours. There were lines in her face Meryl had never seen before. There was a kind of frantic determination on her drawn face: after all, she had to see this thing through to the bitter end, and then maybe she could let her defenses down, go to bed and fall to pieces.

"Darling," Meryl said when she gained her side. "Hello, dear."

"Oh, you came, Meryl."

"Of course I came. Did you think I could stay away?"

"I am so glad to see you. It's been such a strain."

"Of course it has. Laura, have you eaten? Have you had something to eat?"

"Eat—well. Oh yes, at four this afternoon Marcia Lewis—she's a neighbor—yes. She made a lovely little snack for me."

She smiled. A smile as professional as the man at the door. "I'm fine," she said. "Just fine." She tapped her handbag. "I have a little flask in here. Gin. It leaves you breathless. It *has* helped, Meryl. Oh, I *am* so glad to see you."

"This hits me," Meryl said simply. "I haven't lost anyone yet. I'd like to do something, is there anything I can do? I mean anything at all."

"After a while, yes, maybe. When the letdown comes along. Oh, Meryl, your flowers are beautiful. Let me show you. Where's Ralph?"

"He had a meeting," Meryl lied smoothly. "He was so sorry. He said to tell you he—"

"No matter. It's you I wanted. Come, you must see the flowers you sent." She chatted animatedly while guiding Meryl to the spot where they were. "I know people go and order flowers and then they never know what they're going to be like. I'm always fretful myself. You pay some ungodly amount, absolutely blind, and you have no assurance . . ."

She put an arm through Meryl's. "It's an awful expense," she said worriedly. "I think it's horrible. I never want to smell another flower in my life. I should have told people to contribute, instead, to a cancer fund, or muscular dystrophy or something like that. But my mother—"

"Of course, I understand."

"She did want flowers. Well, here they are. So lovely, Meryl. You must have spent a fortune."

Tears spurted to Meryl's eyes. "Christ, Laura, do you think I care about the money?"

"Still," Laura murmured, "It is a waste, you have to admit that. Anyway, thank you. I thank you, my husband thanks you, my mother thanks you. Oh come on over and talk to my mother. She's being incredibly brave. Thank God she'll be taken care of financially. It would be damned difficult for us to fit her into our lives. I mean moneywise. We just don't have it. And I'd hate to see her give up her home. That would be the last, the unkindest cut."

"I'm glad she won't have to."

"Listen, can we get together for lunch sometime soon? Not next week, too much to do. But, say, two or three weeks from now? I'd really like that, Meryl."

"I'm at your service any time you say. I love you, dear."

"I love you too. What would we women do without each other?"

It was a little before ten when Meryl took her leave. No one had offered her a ride home. Well, when it came right down to it, how many people owned a car in Manhattan? It was, for almost everyone, buses or subways. If money was no object, a rented limousine. Anyway, it was such a short distance home. You could walk if it weren't for not being able to after dark these days. So stupid not to be able to get yourself home on foot. A crisp, coolish early June evening like this. But of course no one did and, Meryl thought, she wouldn't be the exception. She stood outside of Campbell's, searching the far distance, in both directions, for the lights of a taxi. Those cheerful lights. Isn't that exasperating, she said to herself. All the taxis in this city and not one in sight.

The alternative was to walk over to Lexington, for a downtown bus. She remembered when Madison was a two-way avenue. A bus uptown and a bus downtown. That was long gone by the board. She didn't like the idea of trekking over, along lonesome streets, from Mad to Park and then from Park to Lex. Shit. She looked back toward the entrance of the funeral parlor. As she did, four people exited. She heard one of them say, "The car's just around the corner. Let's go, it's getting late."

How about me, she thought of saying. There she was, standing alone on the corner. They might have given some thought to her. Anyway, she didn't say anything, simply watched them round the corner. Then, stiffening her spine, decided to leg it over to Lexington.

With a last, longing look and still no cabs in

sight, she crossed the avenue. She felt queasy, very uneasy, and in her mind recalled the Manhattan of the sixties, when you could still go out at night and have a good time. Or anyway, the early sixties. Sic transit and all like that. She walked briskly along the crosstown street cheerily lit by those pretty, rosy bulbs that had replaced the dim and ugly green ones of yore. She used to hate that dismal green lighting. At Park she hadn't encountered a soul, but from Park down to Lexington sighted—with a feeling of ineffable happiness and relief—a man walking an enormous dog which, when she hurried to catch up to them, sniffed at her ankles.

His master said, "Hi," to her, and she returned the greeting, then passed him. She had a feeling that he had paused on the street, to watch her progress down to Lex. Sure enough, he was standing still, in the spot where she had come face to face with him. He raised a hand and waved. She waved back. And people said New Yorkers were unfriendly! It made her feel very good. She would have liked to thank him, but it was the better part of valor to get herself to the bus stop.

Which she did, and craned her neck for the lights of an oncoming downtown bus. In vain, alas. She saw nothing, not a sign of a bus. The avenue was barren of people. Daytimes it would be crowded, jammed with passersby and hurrying shoppers. Daytimes it was cheerful, neighborly. What was she doing here all alone at this time of night, she asked herself, feeling the first tremors of panic. She shivered, quick, convulsive. Where was the bus? She was afraid, she was suddenly terribly afraid.

What could she do? She wanted to climb up to the sky, or scale the wall of a building, beyond the reach of predators. Suppose there was someone lurking nearby? Watching her . . .

She hugged her handbag to her side, but she wasn't fearful for her handbag. She was fearful for her life. Why had she done this? Anger, powerful and overwhelming, seized her. Ralph should be here! She shouldn't be alone here. How fatuous men were, how self-serving, how rotten when it came right down to it. Here she stood, alone and defenseless, at this time of night in this dangerous city.

I hate him, Meryl thought savagely. I hate him. Even when I love him I hate him, have hated him for years, for taking everything and giving little. They earned the daily bread and never gave a thought to the women who kept their homes going. They all thought their wives were so protected and lucky. Staying home and taking it easy. Damn it, she thought, grinding her teeth. How dare they treat us this way?

A beam of light, from as far up as Eighty-sixth Street, caught her eye. A bus? It was! It was a bus, making its lumbering way toward her. Oh, thank God! Thank God! Two blocks away it made its last stop before coming her way. She had never in her life been so glad to see a city bus. She climbed in, put her change in the slot and sat down. It's the last time, she promised herself. You couldn't venture forth in this city at night without prearranged transportation. But she was breathing easily now, and when she debarked from the bus and made her way toward her home her thoughts were on her friend, on Laura, whose father lay in that casket at Campbell's, his face a marble mask. She would phone Laura in a day or two and whenever Laura was ready to face the outside world would take her to some lovely place for lunch. They would talk, and Laura would get a few things off her chest. It was fortunate that Laura's mother could provide for herself and not have to be a burden. I'd hate to be a burden, Meryl was thinking. Anyone would, that's one of the things that haunts us, one of the worries. What will happen when I'm old?

The world blew up in a violent explosion when she was just a short way from her building. The blast rocked through Meryl, bursting her lungs like a punctured bellows, tearing the heart out of her body, shattering her bones. The mighty hand of holocaust slammed down on her mouth, the hot breath of doom scorched her face.

The illusion was short-lived. It was natural enough, given the suddenness of the attack. She had heard nothing, sensed nothing, not a sound, not a whisper. Comprehension returned and with it the realization that she had been seized from behind in a silent, swift tackle, that the mighty hand was a human hand and that she was in danger of suffocating with her head wrested back so brutally that the slightest move on her part would surely cut off whatever breath she had left.

Her heart, far from leaving her body, was circuiting round inside it in dizzying revolutions, sending up jets of saliva to her mouth. There was all this distant awareness of what was happening, but no real response, certainly no protest. She stood still as a stone in the iron embrace, crushed against the mass of some powerful body into which she seemed to merge, as if she were united with it, as if she were now part of its contours. She was without will or wonder: her mind had ground to an abrupt halt. Something cold and hard was against her throat. There was no curiosity about what it was, her brain was functioning only minimally.

"Scream and I cut you to pieces," a voice muttered.

The hand on her mouth tightened. Her lips were twisted behind it, bruised and savaged. She didn't feel the pain, she felt nothing.

"You hear me?" the voice insisted. "You hear me lady? You want to be sliced up?"

The hand eased away from her mouth. She tasted blood, her mouth was wet. From her lips filtered an answer.

"Okay." It was a whisper. A knife, she knew. He was holding a knife against her throat. Her breath was dribbling from her in sick gasps. She said again, "Okay."

She was released, slowly, cautiously, begrudgingly. She saw the gleam of the weapon. Paralyzed, facing the dark shadow of the man as he got down to business, she nearly fell. Bile came into her mouth. She wasn't thinking anything. Except for the knife. As if she were in a trance, she proffered her handbag. It left her hands without power of determination on her part, it was purely automatic. She didn't do it, someone else did. It was what he wanted, here it was. She wasn't think-

171

ing of rape because she wasn't thinking. It was all mechanical, almost a natural gesture. She thrust it at him quickly and efficiently, as if they were transacting some prearranged business. There was a grunt as if from some desperate animal that had been offered, starving, food for its stomach. Then he stripped off her rings, her engagement ring and the wedding band. After that he took her wristwatch.

The lights from her apartment house were only yards away. She wanted, more than anything in the world, to reach those lights. If he killed her when she reached them at least she would be home. Dead or not she would still be home. Thoughts were beginning to coalesce in her mind now, sluggish but trickling painfully through her returning consciousness, and with them a horror and revulsion that brought the vomit into her mouth and the vomit gushed out and the man, surprised and taken unawares, muttered and then cursed as it spurted over him. He let out a stream of obscenities and his hands, flashing toward her wrists, almost stopped her forward plunge.

But she was strong now, she had regained her humanity. She streaked, silent and the breath wheezing out of her, the short distance to the entrance. She didn't scream until she was inside with Harry the doorman standing looking at her, his mouth agape. He wavered in her vision indistinct and blurry, standing stock-still as if he had seen a specter. Then she screamed. She heard the sound tearing through the lobby, quailed at it, at its echoes. She was still screaming when others came to her side. A tenant, roused from television by those frightful sounds. Harry, sitting her down on the velvet bench near the wall. More people and then, not much later, Ralph. "What?" he kept screeching in her ear. "What? *What?*"

She was in her bed after a while. A little later the doctor came, Dr. Corelli, quiet and considering. He gave her a shot. "This will calm you, just lie still, dear." "He has my handbag," she said just before she slid under. "My credit cards, everything. I must call. My check book. My keys. He'll kill us all in our beds. My rings. My watch . . ."

"Sleep now," the doctor said. "Ralph will see to everything in the morning. He won't kill you in your beds. He just wanted the price of a fix."

"Goddamn it," she cried, tears sliding from under her closing lids. "Where can you go to be safe?"

"Darling," Ralph kept saying. "It's all right. You could have been raped. Christ, you could have been raped."

"Then why didn't you come with me?" she shouted at him. "You and your fucking chess game! He has my keys and my credit cards and everything! All you're glad about is I wasn't raped. You'd have to live with my violated body. Wouldn't that just kill you, you male animal?"

Soon everything fell away. Peace stole over her. It was very wonderful. Part of her knew she'd have to face this horror in the morning, but another part of her rejoiced in being able to close her eyes and her mind to it. Thank God for opiates, Meryl thought. Thank god for man-made sopor, for the joys of forgetfulness. I'm alone, was her last conscious thought. Everyone was alone. You just kidded yourself that you weren't. That your husband and children were there, in your life and part of it. When it came down to the nitty gritty you were all by yourself, in a hostile world, and one day you'd end up in an oak casket, like Laura's father, with flowers surrounding you, mean tokens of the fact of your life, duty tokens that cost a lot of money and meant, in the scheme of things, nothing, nothing at all.

9.

Helene got the call in the morning. It was an eerie voice that came to her, eerie and whispery. She frowned, held the receiver closer to her ear. "Hello," she said sharply. "Who is this?"

"Me," the voice said, and became clearer. "Meryl."

"Meryl? What's wrong? You sound so—"

"I was raped."

"You were—"

It was as if clouds of smoke or perhaps some more noxious vapor swirled around Helene's head.

I was raped. The clouds whirled and were dizzying and then Helene found her voice again. "What did you say?"

"I wasn't raped. He said I could have been. That's all he was thinking."

"Meryl. *Meryl?*"

"Oh, I'm all right." A wild little laugh. "He doesn't have to face that shameful knowledge. No man forced his way into my body. Maybe he would have divorced me if it had been so, Helene? What would *your* husband do if you were raped?"

"Meryl, what's happened. Tell me. Tell me! Tell me right now, this instant. Where *are* you?"

"In the insane asylum. Where else?"

Before she could gather her wits about her, Meryl's voice came over the wires again, suddenly strong and clear. "I'm sorry, Helene. Forgive me. What are you doing right now?"

"I was having breakfast," Helene said, her lips pressed against the mouthpiece. "Meryl, tell me, please tell me. What happened?"

"Something rather nasty. Helene—any chance of you coming over here and having breakfast with me instead of alone?"

"But what happened?"

"I was held up at knifepoint last night. Practically right in front of our building. Naturally I'm upset. I'd love to have you with me."

"I'll be right over. Less than half an hour. I just have to put on some clothes. Meryl, are you all right?"

"Yes, but spooked. I'd love to have you here."

"Twenty, twenty-five minutes. Okay? Hang on,

my love, I'll be there almost right away."

"That's nice."

"Just hang on, hear me? Be there in no time all all. I'll bring some fresh cranberry bread I made."

"Just don't bring flowers."

"Don't —"

"No flowers," Meryl repeated and hung up.

God, Helene thought as she dressed. She was trembling, her fingers thick and disobedient. Held up at knifepoint . . . Meryl. Last night. Practically right in front of her apartment house. My God. Maybe she really had been raped. Maybe Ralph told her not to let anyone know. It would be just like what a man would think prudent conduct. The shame. All they thought of was the shame. Helene's throat was dry. A knife. It was as if a knife were cutting her throat on the inside. What would Harold do if *she* were raped? His fierce possessiveness . . .

She said she wasn't raped, she reminded herself. Why did she say it at all, though? It was almost the first thing she'd said. I've been raped. Fear numbed Helene. The girls. Perky Lucy and dreamy Diane. Growing up, a ready prey for some swift and vicious assailant. It could happen to them. It was always there, in the back of her mind, fear for her children. She had long since stopped thinking of them as Harold's children. No matter how careful you were the danger was always there. It could happen in a minute, without warning. Television show after show was about rape. You saw them listed in the guide and you maneuvered wilily to arrange that the girls were busy doing something else when that show was aired. It was bad enough to know it existed without watching it, being reminded of it.

Damn this city. This horrible, deceitful city that shimmered with beauty during the day and became a mugger's paradise at night. It was like two different cities. Daytime New York and nighttime New York. Everything was scheduled for daytime New York. The only restaurants that did any real evening business were hotel adjuncts or those in the theater district. The rest were strictly lunchtime places. You didn't go out to dinner at *night* anymore. Christ, most of your social life used to be at night. Now it was simply one lunch after the other. You went to the movies in the daytime too. As soon as dusk fell you scurried inside and locked doors.

Damn this damn city.

It didn't help to tell herself that it wasn't just this city, that it happened everywhere, anywhere, there was nothing new about cruelty and violence, there was just more of it because there were more people. Reason didn't help, or logic. It had happened close to home, for the first time, and now it was real, not just a nebulous distant menace. Whatever it was, rape or a mugging.

When she got to Meryl's her friend was in a lovely, floaty peignoir Helene had never seen before. She looked pale but not drawn. In fact Meryl looked very, very young, sweet and vulnerable and young. "Come in," she said, and shut the door, locking it quickly.

"I'm sorry," she said next. "My God, I'm sorry, Helene. I had some nerve imposing on you like this. The way I must have sounded! I'm sorry."

"What for? Are you all right? You look all right."

"I look gorgeous," Meryl said with a smile. "Tell me I look gorgeous. This is a very special housecoaty thing I save for special occasions. What I wanted was not to look awful. It seemed the thing to do. Therapy, you understand. Look, did I say something about rape? Ah, I did, I can see by your face. Lord no. Not that. You see, Helene, the doctor came and gave me some knockout stuff, it wafted me off to the clouds. I slept like an infant. When I woke up it was Ralph bending over me, looking like Christ on the Cross. He couldn't say enough about how sorry he was he hadn't come with me to Campbell's. He cried, too. Of course I was so groggy I just wanted him to beat it so I could go back to dreamland. I guess when I called you I was half out of it. I shouldn't have upset you that way. I didn't know what I was saying at all."

"But you weren't —"

"No, stop saying that! I wasn't raped. I'm intact, my pudenda uninvaded. It's okay. I was mugged, yes. Well, hardly even that. I mean he hurt my mouth when he clamped his hand over it. It's sore as hell and swollen, well you can see that. A nasty cut. But he didn't beat me up. Or cut me up. I guess I told you there was a knife. It kept me quiet, I assure you. What really kept me quiet was I blanked out, I was a zombie. I'll admit it won't be soon that I'll forget that little episode, but all he wanted was my money. My handbag. My jewelry. See? Gone with the wind, my engagement ring and my wedding ring. *And* my watch. I handed it all over and he didn't hurt me."

"Was he black?"

"I don't know what he was. A man. What does it matter if he was black or white or striped? He was a prowling animal and he got me. He was waiting for someone and he got me. Or rather, my possessions. I have to start calling department stores and Visa and Master Card and what all. Doug said he'd do it but I don't trust him. At the moment he's so stunned he doesn't know his ass from his elbow. I want to do it myself. I'd better start right away."

She laughed suddenly, her eyes wide and excited and her lips drawn back in an ugly way, and she breathed quickly, wildly. "I forgot to tell you," she cried, lacing her fingers together, uptight, uptight, it was easy to see the hysteria under the studied calm and the swishing peignoir. "I didn't tell you! I up-chucked all over him! I threw up my dinner right in his face, isn't it magnificent? Maybe he *would* have hurt me, maybe cut my throat from ear to ear, or —"

Chilling laughter bubbled from her. "Only I took him by surprise, ain't that a gasser? He didn't expect my puke, what do you think of that, Helene, it was better than Mace."

"Why don't you cry," Helene said, aching. "Darling, wouldn't it be better to cry? Much better than —"

"Oh, no." Meryl's voice was hard. "Not on your life. It's the anger I want to keep alive. You bet. It's what's holding me together. And now I'll start wading into those damn phone calls."

"Meryl, where are the twins?"

"With a neighbor. She owes me one. I wanted them to be in a less tense atmosphere for the day. They're staying overnight. Tomorrow the ambiance, shall we say, will be more tranquil, today's the worst."

"Can't I make the calls for you?"

"You could make some coffee while I get a start on them. That would be dandy, Helene."

"You haven't had breakfast at all?"

"I doubt I can eat anything. I'd love some coffee, though."

"I'm going to make bacon and eggs. Toast. I want you to get some food in your stomach."

"You're such a doll."

"A big, Brunnhilde blonde who probably will never be attacked on the street because of my in-timidating heft. I'd like to get my hands on that

180

bastard. I'm no doll, but I am a friend, sweetie, and I'm sorry as hell about your rotten experience."

"Thanks. Yeah, me too."

"What was that about the flowers?"

"The flowers?"

"You said don't bring flowers."

"I *did*?" Meryl laughed. A good laugh, a natural laugh. Her color was coming back too. "I don't know what I said, and I apologize all over the place for making a stupid fuss. I'll tell you about the flowers after I get these phone calls done. Then we'll sit down and have some coffee and I'll explain. You know my kitchen, I'm sure you can find whatever you need."

She went to the telephone, picked up the small address book that lay on the table beside it. She started leafing through the pages and then looked up.

"You know," she said, "when you really don't want to feel alone, or lost, or anything like that, what you want is a woman in your house. Women are wonderful. I think they're stupendous. I've had my sex and I've had my children and I've had the trappings of marriage. But I sure couldn't do without women. Men let you down, without wanting to or meaning to, but no woman has ever let me down. Thanks for coming over, Helene. Thanks for being here. Bacon and eggs would be nice, yes. As soon as I get this over with we'll have a nice long talk, just the two of us. I'm beginning to feel myself again now you're here. As I said, it takes a woman to bring you to your senses. What the hell would you do without your friends?"

10

"We'll have to finish up today," Christine informed Jack when they met on Friday. "So you'll be home for deliveries when they start arriving next week. Don't be too downcast if they don't all arrive when promised, though. You know how it was with your sofa."

"True, but that was different, that was labor. You really think there'll be unconscionable delays, Christine?"

She had to laugh. "It's possible," she replied, glancing at him. "Furniture—well yes, anything like that is somewhat unforeseeable."

"Sorry to hear that, damn it to hell. Well, I guess I can hack it. If it happens. There's still tomorrow, though, before next week comes along."

"Except that Saturday's a hectic shopping day."

"There's only the coffee table and the lamp left on the agenda."

"We should be able to find both today, Jack."

"The lamp has eluded us thus far."

"That's because you have a preconceived idea."

"You had a preconceived idea about *all* the chairs and we found them right off the bat."

"Because I'd seen them. How can I explain? I know what I like, so I know where to get it."

"What made you so sure I'd like what you like. May I ask?"

They were on their way to First Avenue, where there was a very large and very crammed lamp store Christine thought might yield what Jack was looking for, or at least tempt him with a suitable alternative. He had dismissed, up to now, every lamp in the city, it seemed to her.

His query, so like Jack, dry and understated, charmed her. He wasn't being accusative, just genuinely curious. He had trotted along at her side for three days, Monday, Tuesday and now today, obedient and submissive, taking her every suggestion as ex cathedra, and she *knew* he approved wholeheartedly of her choices. Just the same she had taken over, as she had a way of doing, almost forgetting she wasn't buying for herself but for someone else.

He laughed with her, taking her arm companionably. She said, "Jack, I hope I haven't steamrolled you in any way. Have I? I mean, have I picked out things for you that—well, would you have preferred a quite different look for your apartment? I don't know why I let my enthusiasm get the best of me. God, you've spent quite a bit of money, I'll have a fit if you're unhappy about the result."

"Hey, hey! Can't you see I'm tickled to death? Jaysus, I'm happy as a bedbug. And you're probably right about the chrome and glass coffee table. As you say, it emphasizes that *light* look. It doesn't loom large, or make a big massive block in the room. I think we'll settle for that table, Christine."

"The big brass tray on the tripod legs was striking too, Jack. You liked that, said it made you think of Morocco."

"It wouldn't hold much, though, I realized that later. No, it's true, I'm in full agreement with the cool and stark look you recommended. It's effective. And as you pointed out, as dust-free as you can get." He smiled down at her. "Obviously I do like what you like. It wasn't a loaded question, Chris, but how *did* you know it?"

"I'm afraid it was mostly because I'm a human bulldozer," she said, sighing. "Early on, when I went into a job, I was a real Uriah Heep, stuttery and ingratiating and people felt sorry for this shy mouse so they helped me, and I learned very quickly, got the hang of the work and once I did I went through this perfectly outrageous metamorphosis and started running the whole shebang. The funny thing is, I was popular. This Janus creature never seemed to alienate the rest of the staff. Of course I wasn't conscious of my behavior, not at the time anyway."

"Obviously an annointed leader."

"Ha ha. I'm a supermarket type, I told you that."

"You brought up a family, didn't you? You didn't do that buying groceries."

"They're not *quite* grown up yet."

"How old are they?"

"Fifteen and sixteen."

"They came close together."

"Yes, an assembly line."

"Fifteen and sixteen. I'd call that grown."

"So would they. Anyway, you said a leader. You don't lead kids, not if they can help it. You wangle them."

"Which is exactly what leaders do. They wangle." He tossed his finished cigarette in the gutter. "They call it diplomacy."

A little farther on he said, "It's hard for me to picture you as part of a nuclear family. The key pin. I can't seem to see you looking for lost collar buttons and worrying about sore throats and getting the right vitamins into the family diet. I don't know why, but I can't."

"Then don't." She added, "Women aren't just *kinder, kuche, kirche* any longer, Jack."

He was looking down at her intently. Waiting, he seemed to be waiting. She shrugged and felt foolish. She sounded like one of your militant

185

feminists. She was annoyed that he had brought other people into their casual friendship, a friendship that had come to mean something to her.

"Anything else you want to know?" she asked lightly.

"Not for the moment. The light's changed, let's cross."

They came to Fifty-seventh Street and Christine said the store she had told him about was very near here, maybe two or three blocks. It was three blocks, and they went in. "Never saw so many lighting fixtures in my life," Jack said, looking a bit befuddled. "What do you think, about a thousand? Or more like two?"

"Well, it's all they carry, just lamps. If you don't find it here you won't find it anywhere, not in the near future, anyway."

There were so many lamps, rows and rows of them, you couldn't remember what aisle you were in or what aisle you had just traveled. "A labyrinth of lamps," Jack murmured. "I think I'll be dreaming about this tonight, it's Hitchcockian."

"If I knew what it was you wanted I could start at one end and you at the other."

"I'll know it when I see it."

"You're sure *that* wasn't in a dream?" she asked. "I mean, the lamp you have in mind."

"Nope. No dream, I saw it. This may take a year or so, do you mind?"

He finally spotted it, way ahead of Christine by that time, as she had slowed up to admire one or two she especially liked, even coveted, though God knew she wasn't in the market for a lamp. In all the maze suddenly Jack's voice: a cry of triumph, like the roar of primeval man, sounded suddenly.

"Over here. Chris. Here, Chris?"

She had to admire his taste as well as his tenacity. It was a lovely thing, a monumentally large milkpail base in a luminous silvery metal that had a nacreous shimmer. It looked as if it had been cast up from the sea, a treasure washed ashore. "God, it's gorgeous," she said reverentially. "Where did you see the other one that sent you scurrying for its double?"

"I think in Sturbridge Village," he said, stroking the lamp. "I can't be sure, but maybe there. Anyway, I never forgot it. My Lord, here it is, I just can't believe it."

She flicked the price tag. "It's more than the coffee table," she said, scandalized.

"I don't care, it's mine." He eyed the tag, which read $295. "Wow. Well, what did I expect? I'll take it," he told the man who, sensing a sale, had come toward them.

"Do you deliver?" Christine asked.

"Oh, yes. Any Manhattan address, that is."

"If we took it with us would there be any concession on the price?"

"Oh, I'm very sorry, but—"

"Gasoline saved should be a consideration, I can't help thinking," she pressed. "Time, too. The city tax would amount to almost twenty-five dollars. I hate to be a bore, but do you think you could let us have it for—well, say, $275?"

"You must realize our profit margin isn't the highest," he said, but hesitated.

187

"Yes, I know," She turned to Jack. "The coffee table's only $265," she reminded him. "And this is, after all, simply a lamp."

"We *are* having a sale next month," the salesman said quickly. "I suppose I could stretch a point." He lifted his shoulders. "Very well, $275 if you take it out of the shop now."

"Okay, Jack?"

"Yes, please," he said, and behind the man's back made a face at her. "Never mind," she whispered to him as they went to the service desk. "We saved the tax, which is nothing to sneeze at."

They rode back to Jack's place in a cab, with the lamp between them on the back seat. He carried it up the stairs like a baby, set it down on a new end table, got out a three-way bulb. Then he plugged in the lamp, turned it on and he had that strong, white light he had set his sights on. "How's that?" he asked her.

"Lovely, wonderful. I'm so glad you found it."

"And now let's go to Bloomingdale's and get the coffee table," he said purposefully. "I've made up my mind it's the one I want. One thing more, but no rush about it, I'll go looking on my own some. I'll find it somewhere. A big fruit basket, hand-woven, to fill with dried flowers, those little pale sprays. You know what I mean."

"Baby's breath?"

"I guess that's it. I saw a lot of it in Provence."

He said, very seriously, "I put aside cash for all this, Chris. Allerton's still solvent, in case you're interested." He switched off the lamp. "Okay, the table and then that's that, and we'll get serious about lunch, how's that sound?"

Two hours later they were in a booth at Anthony's. They didn't even discuss it, just walked over as if it was what they were programmed to do, and went in. Christine had her martini, Jack his Canadian Club. He said, "And it came to pass, on the third day, that John, the son of John, had gathered together all the worldly goods needful for his dwelling and was therefore grateful unto the Lord."

A grin. "Not that the Lord enters into it. John the son of John owes present company a debt of gratitude. The Chinese are reputed to say that a person who saves another's life has the rescuee in his keeping forever. So you see, my life belongs to you, Christine."

"Far too much responsibility, I give it back to you, Jack. What did I do except bully a few salespeople? Big deal."

"Now that the shopping hassle is over, can't we think of something else to take my mind off my work?"

"All play and no work makes Jack a dull boy."

"That's your story. It's funny, but now that I have my lamp what I want most is the kitchen chairs. I can't even tell you why. I guess the kitchen looks unfinished without the chairs. And I didn't even plan to get any."

"A table needs chairs. Now you won't have to stand up to eat your Cheerios. Also if you have an overnight guest you'll have accommodations."

"Are you trying to sell me on a live-in relationship with some lady friend?"

"Like the girl you introduced to Rodney?"

His laugh erupted. "I hope you don't think I make a habit of passing on discarded loveresses like so many hand-me-down clothes. La Ronde—Jeannie Merrill, God. She's about nineteen. By the way, how are they hitting it off?"

"The last I heard it seemed to be fine and dandy. She's a good stick, he said. I imagine that's fairly laudatory, you never know with Rodney. It was nice of you, Jack."

"I thought it was time he had a whirl with a girl. Jeannie can hold her own, she's no pushover."

"I don't think she needs to worry about Rodney. He said she lived in the building you were in before Sixty-first Street. Where was it, Jack?"

"After things broke up I moved to Eighty-fourth, just off York. Not a bad building, in fact it was decent enough when I settled in there. Then it—well, I told you about that. Neglect and greed, it's the name of the game."

"You said the other day that you—well, something about needing friends. I wondered why."

"I gave custody of our friends to Phyllis," he said. "It was the least I could do, I thought."

"Oh."

He didn't say where he had lived when he was married. She didn't know for how long he was married, either. She didn't want to know anyway. She knew Jack Allerton as he was now, nothing else interested her. He had come into her life randomly. Rodney had come into her life in the same way, as had the women she knew. In a big city that was the way it happened.

"It's different in the suburbs, I suppose," she said.

"What's different?"

"I was thinking about how you meet people. In a metropolis like this. Of course when I was growing up—well, you knew your neighbors and all that. I don't know my neighbors now. The whole fabric of life has changed. In the cities, I mean. If you live in a suburban area I suppose it goes on the way it always has. Men coming home on the same commuter train, women having coffee at each other's houses."

"I wouldn't live in the suburbs if you gave me a house rent-free."

"I wouldn't either."

"I can see myself mowing lawns." He shrugged. "Nope. You can have the suburbs, they're the real pits."

"If I were alone, nobody else to think of, I'd like to live in Paris. Say for a year or two, the way Rodney's doing here. I'd like that. Paris is the most like New York, I think. I'm good enough at the language to get by. You pick it up so quickly anyway. Yes, Paris would suit me very well."

"I guess it would be Paris for me too. It's easy to get around in, it's a very manageable city."

"Do you ever think of shifting bases?"

"Not really, no. There's no reason for it. Oh, if you had a fellowship or something like that."

"I'm trying to decide whether to have the eggplant or the minestrone."

"Hunger pains got you down? Shall we order?"

"Let's have another drink first."

"I'd like to take you out to dinner sometime," he said. "Is there any chance of that?"

She considered. "Maybe sometime, Jack."

"All I've been able to offer you is drinks, lunch, no fancy-schmantzies."

"Why should you offer me anything more than that? Because I gave you a little help with your apartment? You don't owe me anything, Jack."

"That isn't the reason, but let it go."

He flicked his lighter for her cigarette, got the waiter's attention, ordered their refills. A basket of the bread was brought over with them, the smell of the garlic spicing the air. This was such a pleasant place, Christine thought. She was so *used* to it. Jack was right. The shopping expeditions were over, there was no reason for them to come here anymore. She hadn't thought of it before, but she was thinking of it now. It gave her an empty feeling.

"You certainly opened your checkbook quite a few times in these last few days," she said. "You spent a lot of money, are you worried?"

"As I told you, I was prepared to. Remember, I was in a low-rent apartment, able to save. I don't have child support. Anyway, I'm not really one of life's unfortunates, in fact rather the opposite. Nothing magnificent, you understand, but I do have a trust fund that was bequeathed to me by a dear old uncle who favored me and that's what keeps me going, that quarterly check. I would have been bananas to try earning a living solely by my writing efforts and as a matter of fact may have been bananas to chuck the job anyway. I should be holding down a post, it's important to be in the marketplace. I know that very well. For a spell, though, it's good to live without someone breathing down your neck. Time will tell."

He smiled at her. "It's nice of you to give it a thought, Chris. Not to worry, however, I'll get by. What drives me up the wall is that clock racing by, time and tide coursing ahead, and what have I done for immortality. That's what wakes me up in a cold sweat in the long and lonely nights. Nobody knows my name."

"Give yourself a break, why don't you. You do tend to flog yourself, Jack."

"Just a masochist at heart."

"Sometimes yes, I think you are."

"Not really. Impatient? Yes. I have my serene moments, though. Too bad it's not yesterday. Yesterday was Thursday, they were serving the Calamari."

"Alas. I've decided on the minestrone, though. Yesterday I had lunch with my friends. Five of us, we've known each other forever. It's about the only social life I have."

"It's a lot more than I have."

"Well, you've got your work."

"Yes," he conceded. "Anyway, I'm not one of those people who need people characters. That is, yeah, I need people in my view, the way I said I liked to face the street when I work, see the passing crowd, know they're there. But I'm not a glad-hander, I couldn't care less. I don't think you are either."

"No." She eyed him. "You said you miss going to

an office, though."

"Oh, that. Sure—well, it's actually Calvinistic. You know, you *should* go to an office. The work ethic. A good day's work for a good day's pay. You can work your ass off on your own but somehow it's not the same thing. You still feel you're playing hookey. That's more or less it except, yes, you do get that forlorn feeling sometimes, things are passing you by, the action's elsewhere. It's a penalty you have to pay."

"As long as it's worth it."

"It will have to be worth it. It's up to me, that's the first thing I tell myself when I wake up in the morning."

"Is the sneezer still doing his wake-up job?"

"Hasn't fallen down on it once."

"Haven't you seen him yet?"

"Nope. Still a mystery man. I've grown very fond of him." He gestured. "By the way, I meant to tell you. The orange tree's doing marvelously, did you notice?"

"No, I guess I didn't. So it's healthy and such?"

"It's fantastic. I talked to a florist, he told me how much water to give it. It seems to like me, it's behaving very well indeed."

"Glad to hear it. Well, I guess I'm ready for that soup, Jack, how about you? It's a long time since breakfast."

Later, he said he would call her the minute the kitchen chairs arrived, give her breakfast. "Not Cheerios, the works. A big country spread, the way mother used to make. Bring your appetite."

"I like my bacon crisp, please."

"Eggs how?"

"Once over lightly."

"I'll make a note of it."

They left Anthony's laughing, went out into the bright sunlight and the clamor on the street, stood smiling at each other. "It was nice," Christine said. "It's always nice, Jack. You know, you haven't let me pay for a single lunch."

"You should pay for lunch? After walking your dogs off getting my household problems solved? What kind of a heel do you think I am?"

"Just the same."

"What are you going to do now, Christine?"

"I have to go to Saks. They're having a lingerie sale; I want to see what I can find. Very boring stuff, you wouldn't be interested. Go home and have a love affair with your new lamp."

"You like it, don't you?"

"I think it's one of the most gorgeous things I've ever seen."

"Yeah, me too. Well, then—"

He reached for her hand. "I'll call you."

"Do that."

"When would be a bad time to call?"

"Is it your intention to call me at a bad time?"

"Why—ah, shut up," he said, and they grinned at each other.

"Call me in the early evening, why don't you," she suggested. "Around five, five-thirty, okay?"

"Right. Thanks a lot, Christine."

"Thank you. Bye now."

She walked off in one direction, he in another. She resisted the temptation to look back, though she wanted to. Now he would go home and sit at the typewriter. Maybe he'd work well today, maybe he wouldn't. She hoped he would.

It was almost five when she left Saks, with a shopping bag of goodies and a smaller balance in her checkbook. Five o'clock, rush hour, the bus jammed and about 110 degrees Fahrenheit inside. It crawled along. She couldn't remember what she had scheduled for dinner. The menu, so painstakingly orchestrated for the week, eluded her. They had had beef bourguignon last night, sole the night before. Why couldn't she recall what she had written down for today? There might be something she should buy on the way home.

She found herself coolly disinterested. After all, there was food in the house, none of them would starve. If something was needed someone could go out and get it. They were a community of souls, each of which was capable of fending for himself, they didn't need her to shovel food in their mouths. This should be a happy time of life for her, a time when she could stop thinking of herself as chief cook and bottlewasher.

Phyllis. His former wife's name was Phyllis. A winsome name, with echoes of Gilbert and Sullivan, *Iolanthe*. And now Jack was in his high-ceilinged room, at the desk in the right-hand corner, pounding away at, she hoped, a great rate. Later he would put one of his TV dinners in the oven.

She didn't feel sorry for Jack Allerton. It seemed like a very piquant life to Christine. He had his work, an apartment he obviously cherished and he had his freedom. She was inclined to view it as a little bit Puccini, la vie de Bohème. And now here she herself was, after a pleasantly tiring day, going home during rush hour. Sardine time. It made her think, in a nostalgic way, of when she herself had worked in an office and gone home with others of such ilk. The marketplace, as Jack had said, was good for the soul and the psyche. You were part of the forward thrust of things, in it and of it. It was a good life, a worthy life. You called it the salt mines and you griped about the regimentation and you always thought you were underpaid. But you were out there, in the madding throng, one of the movers and the shakers even if it was only in a modest way. She missed it still, even after these long years.

Shopping for a gift for Jack, because of course the plant wasn't really a gift, just—well, in place of a bottle of booze when she and Rodney had been invited. She would like to find him a fruit basket, since he had mentioned that, but she was pretty sure he had his own ideas about what he wanted, the way he'd had about the lamp. Something "different" was always hard to track down: you only saw something different when you weren't looking for it. What she meant, of course, was something imaginative, distinctive.

She didn't come across it on Saturday, but on Monday, passing a music store, quickly retraced her steps and stood in front of its window again. There it was, just what she had in mind, it couldn't be more *right*. It was a print of a sheet of music, a big blowup, the first few bars of Richard Strauss's *Death and Transfiguration*. It took her a second, because naturally the title was in German, *Tod und Verklärung*. It had been reproduced in all its yellowed and weathered state, and it was enormously impressive.

She realized that it was part of the window dressing, but she meant to have it, even if it meant waiting until the display was changed. "I have an odd request," she said to one of the men behind the counter when she went in.

"If it's possible we'll do it," he said. "If it's impossible we'll do it anyway."

"It's the poster in the window, the Strauss page. On the far wall to the right. I'd like to buy it."

"Poster?" He looked surprised.

"I guess it's part of the display."

He went with her to the window. "That? Oh, it's just a promotion item. I'll speak to someone in the back. There might be a few more lying around someplace. Wait here, I won't be long."

When he came back it was with something that looked like a parchment scroll which, when unfurled, proved to be the Strauss poster. "So you did have others," she said, delighted. "I can have this?"

"It's yours."

"I'm awfully grateful! How much will it be?"

"No charge. As I said, it's a promotion ad for Wallace."

"It's marvelous, just what I wanted."

"You're going to frame it? Good idea, it will look nice."

"Yes, I think it will. Thanks again, thanks very much."

She took it right around to a good frame shop in Lexington, not far from her own building. They showed her what would be suitable for posters and modern art. "Like so, how's that?"

"Yes, it's about what I had in mind. But no matting showing, just the page itself. That's important."

"I understand. For a musician, right?"

"A music lover. When do you think you'll have it ready? I'd like it to be this week, he'll be sticking close to home waiting for other deliveries."

"I'll do my best."

"You can't really promise?"

"Not a hundred percent, but we'll do our best."

"I'd appreciate it. How much do I owe you?"

He scribbled on a piece of paper. "Fifty-five. Plus tax. Fifty-nine forty."

"You're sure it will come out all right? No matting showing."

"Not to worry, it will be very stylish."

She hoped that when she next went to Jack's place the poster would be hung. Something of her own there, she'd like that. He had said he'd call her when the kitchen chairs arrived, but she knew he wouldn't; he'd wait until every last thing was in place before inviting her again. She was pretty sure of that.

When he called, it was on Friday. "Where did you find it?" he demanded, the rumble of his voice shooting up a bit. "And how? And what do you mean spending all that money? I think I'll kill you."

"Would you by any chance be talking about the

picture?" she asked.

"What else? Christine, you—my God, it's the most superlative—"

"When did it get there, Jack?"

"Just now! I almost refused to take it. I didn't order this, I was expostulating. What is it, I kept demanding. It was all wrapped up tighter than a drum in stout brown paper. The boy said take it, mister, isn't that your name, J. Allerton? I took it inside and unwrapped it and nearly fell over. How did you—"

"How did you?" she asked. "Know it was from me?"

"Who else? There isn't anyone else."

"Is it all right, do you like it?"

"Like it," he said simply. "Like it. Jesus, I think I worship it. Christine Jennings—"

"It was a very chancy thing to do," she said doubtfully. "Please, Jack, you must tell me if it jars with your own ideas. Afterwards I thought, well how nervy of me to stick you with something that—"

"Try and get it back," he said vehemently. "Just try and get it back. I'm insane about it. Listen, but you—"

"I just hope you'll be sure," she insisted.

"You must be crazy not to know I'd go for it. Wow, I can't wait to hang it."

"What else came, Jack? The armoire?"

"That, yes. I'm not shoving things in hit or miss, though. I want some organization, do it right, so I can find things properly. It's a temptation to sweep up everything off the floor and get it quickly out of

200

the way, but I'm resisting it. I'm glad it's here, though, and the table came. It marches, as the French say. Look, Christine, how's next week shaping up for you? I want you to see how the poster looks, I'm going to get it up tomorrow."

"Why don't we wait until the rest of the stuff gets there?"

"I don't think I can wait."

"I've had some terrible news. One of my friends. She was mugged. Needless to say it's been preying on my mind."

"Hell, I'm sorry to hear that," he said, making a sound between his teeth. "Is she—is she all right?"

"She was robbed, nothing worse. Except that once it happens, it—"

"Christ."

"But it would be nice to see you next week, Jack. Would you give me a call. By that time you should have all your new things."

"I'll do that. And—well, I can't thank you enough, Chris. There's no way."

"Just if you like it, that's what I hoped for. Talk to you next week, Jack."

She hung up smiling. What a nice guy he was. What an unusually nice guy . . .

11.

She was pulling on pantyhose when the phone rang. Why now, she thought crossly, can't you see I'm trying to hurry? "Yes," she said into the receiver.

"Christine?"

"Oh, Jack. Hello, hi. *Come va?*"

"*Bene*. Guess what?"

"I'll bite."

"The kitchen chairs are here. Finally. The last to arrive."

"Aha. How do they look?"

"Empty. Any chance of you coming over for breakfast?"

"I've had it. I'm rushing a bit because I have a dentist's appointment. Eleven o'clock."

"I'll make you lunch, then. When you've finished with the dentist."

"After a cleaning? I don't think I'll want to chew."

"All the more reason for some tender loving care."

"When do you do any work, may I ask?"

"In between times."

"Between what times?"

"The pleasurable ones. I'll give you pap then, soup and toast. And a stiff drink to raise your spirits after the dread ordeal."

"Oh, Jack—well, okay, how about—I suppose I could be there at around one or so."

Rodney phoned shortly after that. "I've been trying to get you for the last hour," he complained.

"I've been right here."

"The line was busy."

"I was on the line for about three minutes! Honey, I have to run, I have an appointment."

"Bother. I was hoping we could—"

"Darling, I really have to dash. Look, dear, come to dinner this week. Any night, just let me know beforehand. I love you madly, be a good boy."

The dentist was in his usual jovial mood. Before

she found Dick Altman, going to the dentist was indeed the dread ordeal Jack had called it. She was convinced he was the best man in the city, if not the whole world, and he had been talking lately about retirement, which depressed her. Not only was he a superlative craftsman but he inevitably left her laughing: there was always something amusing he had to tell her, an anecdote or story that sent her into gales of mirth just when she decided she couldn't sit, a victim, in that damned chair one minute longer. He referred to himself as the good gray doctor.

There was always music, from a stereo, as an accompaniment to the drill or his own steady stream of conversation. He was partial to 17th- and 18th-century Italian; Pergolese, Corelli, Boccherini. Today it was Vivaldi.

"Okay, you can rinse now," he said at last. "You've got good gums, Christine, you're a sure bet to die with all your teeth in your head. If everyone had equipment like that I'd go out of business."

"You're always so reassuring. Thank you, Dick."

"Mrs. Malaprop was in yesterday," he told her, washing his hands. "She came up with a string of howlers. I had the best time, even if I did nearly bust trying not to laugh."

"What did she say this time?"

"Let's see—oh yes, she was up in the arms about someone's behavior. Apparently this person did her dirt, and she was up in the arms about it. She claimed to be in a real 'dungeon' about it. You know anyone who says *dudgeon*, Christine, in this the twentieth century?"

"She must be deep into Thackeray or something. I love up in the arms! Sounds like a bad tailoring job."

"Here's the killer though, are you ready for this? She was very, very sore at this person, I could tell that because she's not a tough-talking gal. Her idea of profanity is 'Oh, sugar.' She wouldn't say the other thing if her mouth was full of it."

He dried his hands and beamed at her. "Imagine my astonishment, then, when she came up with this little gem. 'What she is,' she told me through clenched teeth, 'is she's an ass-polisher, a lousy ass-polisher.' After getting that off her chest she seemed to feel better."

When she could stop laughing, Christine went to the washroom, put on fresh lip color, blotted it and went out again. Another patient sat in the chair, being bibbed by the dental assistant. Dick came out and gave her a hug. "Love you," he said.

"Love you too. See you in six months."

It was just noon. Well, she would walk up to Madison and window shop; she had an hour before she was due at Jack's. Her mouth was sore, naturally, but as always after a session with Dr. Altman she felt, as she had told him, reassured. And what a day, 76 degrees, not humid and the sun blazing away. How splendid she felt these days! In every way, as if nothing could faze her, that she was in total control, pulling the strings like some master puppeteer, with quintessential ease: it was as if the whole world were dancing to her tune. She seemed unable to give the proper consideration to Ruth's plight, with one of her sons down with mononucleosis and his education in jeopardy. It was *awful* for Ruth, it was a disaster and, as for Meryl's ghastly attack on the street, how *was* Meryl going to weather it? Especially with her earlier shaky psychological history? What had happened to Meryl would ordinarily have given her sleepless nights and endless panic about her own family's safety.

Instead she was mindlessly absorbed in her*self*: she felt so gloriously alive, splendidly euphoric. But then she always did love summer and one supposed it was, in the main, just that. But now it was twelve forty-five and she had trotted all the way down to Central Park South, she would have to get on her stick in order to be at Jack Allerton's at somewhere around one o'clock. She'd be very firm with him today, tell him that he had been spending enough time away from the typewriter, praise his new acquisitions, that she was delighted to see what God hath wrought and now that all was accomplished he must get back to work full time. That was the most important thing, that he establish himself as an upcoming author.

Up the stone steps and into the lobby, a little breathless: she had walked rapidly all the way there. The bell on the brass plate pressed and then the answering buzz. She ran lightly up the carpeted stairs, smiling; he was in the open doorway, smiling too.

"For some reason I convinced myself you wouldn't show up," he said.

"Why?"

He shrugged. "I don't know. And then when you were late—"

"It's only fifteen after. If I say I'm going to show up, I show up. Hello, Jack."

Inside she gave a quick look round. "You found the basket!"

"What do you think?"

"It's very handsome. There isn't another man alive, or at least one I know, who'd go bonkers over a fruit basket."

"Bonkers. Rodney's influence again."

"Yes, I'm still doing it. Impressionable's what I am, a tabula rasa, write me off as a witless broad."

"I think not," he said, and watched her as she moved about the room.

"The armoire's gorgeous." She felt complacent about it. "I love it, I just love it."

"Do you like where I've hung the music page?"

"I saw it as soon as I came in. It looks nice."

"You know damned well it looks stupendous. It's the focal point of the whole room."

"It isn't supposed to stick out like a sore thumb."

"It doesn't do that! Come on, stop being so self-conscious, Chris, if I'd bought it myself you'd be falling all over yourself with admiration."

"All right, it's lovely. I'm happy you like it."

"Doesn't it amuse you about the German being a shorter word than the English? That doesn't happen very often, those long-winded Krauts with their Geldangelagenheits and their Gesetzessammlungs, tongue-twisters all."

She walked over to his desk, where a growing pile of typed sheets was accumulating. "You seem to be making progress, Jack."

"Not as fast as I'd like to. More or less at a snail's

pace. Note how well I turn a phrase."

"Jack, really, this whole place is terrific. Everything fits in so beautifully. I have a very *special* feeling for this apartment. I helped you find some things for it, and I have a feeling you're still not sure about that coffee table, but you know you can change it, just don't wait too long."

"No, I'm not in doubt about it, forget that. I was at first, I admit. I thought it might be too high-keyed, too modern. Now I agree with you that stuff with clean, sharp lines takes the curse off an old place like this. I sure wouldn't want a Victorian look."

"Nothing is jazzy, I wouldn't go for that either. Well, Jack, I had more fun fooling around with this place than I did with Rodney's. Don't ever tell him that."

"I haven't heard from him since he was here. My guess is he's moved on to greener fields."

"He told me he didn't want to interrupt you in your battles with the Muse."

"Did he? Actually it's just as well."

"Anyway I meant what I said. I feel part of this setup and besides money's no object to Rodney. I know I told you he couldn't pay too much for an apartment, but it was only because I was trying to do the best for him. His family is very well off, he can buy whatever takes his fancy. You can't afford to do that, so—"

She turned quickly. "Oh. You don't mind my saying that."

"No. Not at all. Or rather I do mind, but not in that way. What I mind is being such a slow starter, that the fucking returns are so piddling, that I can't turn out a big package deal. Reprint in six figures, movie interest, my name writ large. What I mind is not being Mario Puzo."

"I had the impression you were thinking more along the lines of Updike."

"Okay, later. After I hit the headlines with a Puzo type opus."

She sat down. "Mario Puzo was your age once. I guess he minded too. Anyway he was never as pretty as you are."

He sat down too. "I know what you're trying to say. That it takes time. I don't question that, but I don't like it either. I don't feel any more that I have that time."

"Jack, you're only—what, 28, something like that?"

"Ain't you the tactful one. I'll be thirty-one in November. And then that slow decline."

"Oh, excuse me. I keep forgetting I'm in a slow decline."

He laughed. "Not *you*. You don't have to make it, you've made it. You're there."

"May I ask in what way?" she queried, smiling faintly. "*I'm* forty, I'm an almost empty nester, I can't remember when I last had an orgasm and I never did a ground-breaking thing in my whole life."

"That's bull," he said flatly. "You know it too. You're on top of the world and here I am trying to drag you down."

"Drag me down?" she echoed wonderingly. "What do you mean by that?"

209

He looked at her for a long time. So long that she became uneasy. Then he rose. "Some host I am," he said, shoving his hands in his pockets. "Let's get you fed. By the way, how's your mouth, tender and such?"

"Not bad at all."

"Anyway, I have nothing jaw-breaking, I kept it in mind. No, sit still, you can see the chairs later. The kitchen's slightly in disorder at the moment."

"I thought we were going to eat in there, that's why you asked me."

"I changed my mind. We're having Chablis, I marinated some strawberries in brandy for it."

"Sounds ambrosian, Jack."

"Make yourself comfortable. I won't be long."

"Can't I help?"

"Uh uh. Want to go to the john or anything?"

"Not that I know of. Maybe later. Did you put out those nice little towels just in case?"

"Certainly. Excuse me, Chris, be back shortly."

She could hear him moving around in the kitchen. She smiled contentedly. It was nice to be waited on. It was nice to be here. She got up and ambled about, stroking the shutters at the window. In New England they were called Deerfield blinds. How she loved these old brownstones and town houses, and how melancholy it was that they were disappearing so rapidly. They were the old New York, which was quickly becoming a city of highrises, characterless and impersonal.

She sat down and lit a cigarette and just after she crushed it out Jack returned carrying an enormous tray. A plate of sandwiches, elegant little triangles, with the crusts cut off. He had spent a lot of time cutting those crusts off the soft fresh bread. There wasn't even a trace of what had once been crust. They were artfully pyramided on the platter and they reminded her of when Schrafft's, which was now almost a thing of the past, had served tea sandwiches at three in the afternoon.

A little bowl with green olives, another with Greek olives. A small feast. The glasses were iced. Beautiful crimson strawberries floated on the surface of the crystal-clear Chablis. Cocktail napkins with strawberries in the design. She said, "Why, Jack, how festive, but why? This was supposed to be soup and toast and on the run, you shouldn't have done all this! Good God, it looks like a wedding reception or something."

"Ah shut up and start eating. And drinking. How's the Chablis?"

She sipped. "Like nectar, it's like drinking May wine." She clinked glasses with him. "To you, Jack, and lots, lots of luck."

"Here's to you. Here's to us. To Rodney, when it comes right down to it. Thank God for Rodney. That's lox. There's chicken liver and there's smoked turkey. Oh, and Boursin."

"I can't believe this magnificence. It's like a cocktail party for the Windsors."

"Strawberries okay? Marinated in brandy. A good brandy too."

"You bet they're okay. Jack, all this because I went to some stores and browbeat a few salespeople?"

She smiled reminiscently. "I liked shopping with

you. It was like old times. When I furnished my own place."

"Where you live now?"

"Now? Oh no, that was just adding here and there, that wasn't really anything. I mean the place on Ninety-second Street, when I left my family's home and got one of my own. I quit college after two years, it didn't seem to be my thing, and I lucked into a pretty good job. Then I found this apartment, a big, airy room, square or almost, twenty by twenty-one, on the top floor of a brownstone. Or limestone, I guess, like your building. I bought two studio beds because I got a good buy on the pair, slept in one and the other was a sofa. A good buy—you must think of me as some kind of Arab trader or something. To this day I think in terms of a dollar saved is a dollar earned."

"It's one of the things I like about you."

"Well, anyway I bought the beds and then at one of those unpainted furniture stores I latched on to two chests of drawers, some stools, a room divider and little by little it all came together. I had the best time I've ever had. I was so proud of that place. When I was doing the dishes, there was this whistling tea kettle I had, and I kept that polished and shining, and I could see the other room from the shine in the kettle; I used to enjoy doing that. The room, the studio room looked like a fascinating picture, like the way you would see it in a bull's-eye mirror, all spherical and mysterious and lovely. My room, my home."

She bit into a sandwich. She could see that gleaming vision now, the big room with its pieces that had been accumulated, painstakingly and lovingly, bit by bit by bit. There had been times when, after paying rent and utilities and food and the pharmacy for cosmetics and such, she had had little more than bus fare in her pocketbook. She had never minded. Even going without had been fun then.

"Well," she said briskly, coming back to the present. "That was a long time ago. You can see I'm a sentimental sort."

"Nothing wrong with that. You mentioned that apartment before, Christine. The house on Ninety-second Street. It was a film, wartime, espionage."

"Only that house was on Ninety-third Street. I guess they changed it in the title for legal reasons, something like that."

"It's torn down now."

"Yes, I know."

"I saw the film for the nth time on TV the other night. It holds up pretty well."

"What made you think of making sandwiches like this, Jack? I must tell you they're the ultimate luxury as far as I'm concerned. When I was a kid I used to tear the crust off my bread and hide it on my lap. I hated the crust."

"When I was a kid I used to circle it around underneath my plate."

"I hated milk."

"That wasn't one of my hangups. I drank quantities of it. Once I ate practically a whole box of soda crackers and about six glasses of milk. I blew up like a balloon. God, it was gruesome."

"Oh, poor boy. Listen, can I take a doggy bag,

Jack? You made a lot of sandwiches."

"Getting sated?"

"Rather. I did manage to pig it, as Rodney would say. Of course I don't mean it about a doggy bag, you'll have leftovers for lunch tomorrow. I don't know when I've enjoyed anything like this. It was a splurge, did you get your quarterly check today?"

"No, that will be in August. I did get a check, yes, for a foreign sale. Italian, a Milan publisher."

"Well, great. Congratulations, Jack."

"I like to make Italian sales. I'm a pushover for Italy, it's a kick to think of some Roman or Milano or Florentino reading one of my things on the bus. Maybe in an outside cafe over a cup of espresso."

"You should have put your check toward a little trip to Italia. Instead of blowing it on me."

"It wouldn't have taken me very far. It was a very modest check, I hasten to assure you. What is this fuss about sandwiches and wine? It's true I did a little thinking about making some kind of a splash, yeah. The reason being that—"

He eyed her. "Well, you," he said slowly. "I keep worrying you'll say one of these days, no, I can't come over anymore, I have better things to do."

"Why would you think that?"

"For a very good reason. One of these days you won't come anymore."

It threw her a little. Well, his face, the way his face looked. She spoke quickly. She felt she had to say something quickly. She said, "There's a poem by Edna St. Vincent Millay. Well now, I realize she's a little out of fashion, so please don't look

214

pained. Anyway this poem—apparently it's about her husband or her lover or whomever—when he died. In the poem she says, 'He went down the hill this morning. He didn't come up the hill again.' I always found it incredibly moving. He went down, as usual, but he never came back up."

He didn't help her out at all. She needed some help, suddenly she realized it. He should take her cue, and ease over this peculiar, silent moment. His face was still and expressionless, and she felt odd. Lost, really. She remembered films—well, period films, where a woman enters a man's apartments and stands in front of a mirror and takes off her hat. She pulls out the hatpins and is framed in the glass and then the man comes up behind her and puts his hands on her breasts and then everything becomes hazy and the camera cuts.

"I always found that so—so moving," she said again, and put down her glass with the strawberries floating around in it. His face swam in front of her and then he leaned back against the sofa. And he still hadn't said anything.

Her ears sang and she was conscious of the faint whistle-hum of the refrigerator. Rodney's did that too. He said it sounded like a peanut vendor. She said with an effort, "You washed your hair this morning, didn't you?"

He regarded her. Then he replied, unsmiling, "Fussy, ain't it?"

"What do you use, Head and Shoulders?" she asked inanely, and knew at once where all this had been leading, where it had been leading from the very first, when Rodney had lost out on this apartment and he had told them about the other and she heard, as if from a far and ghostly distance their footsteps echoing in the empty flat, herself, Rodney and Jack. It had led straight to this quiet, heart-stopping moment, and she must have known it almost from the beginning.

"No," she said, when his head bent to her. It was girlish and ridiculous and stupid, and they both knew she didn't mean it. Anyone with half a mind could see that he had been sitting there quietly, waiting for the thing to jell. It was time, today was the time, and she sat tensely as he put his hands on her shoulders, the warmth of them a quick and surging pleasure that shuddered through her and for which, she now realized, she had long awaited, patient and impatient, expectant and unsure, all the while duping herself with pious little deceptions, guileful pretensions.

His mouth. At last, and the feel of him, his big bones strong and hurting, his body making its claim on hers. So long since this had happened, this unbearable and delirious time fragment, when you knew where it would end, lusted for it with your brain and your flesh and were still powerless to start the machinery going because you were in a kind of helpless inertia, not wanting to pull apart for even a single second. Lips and tongues and wildness, this animal and that animal, the straining.

He released her finally, pulled her up. They parted in an almost formal kind of way, but staggering, unsteady, silent. Silent and intent. Then they were in the bedroom, she was undressing, she could hear him doing the same. Something was knocked off a surface, a soft thud on the floor, but she didn't turn, she had to hurry. How did I hide this from myself, she wondered, trembling. That she wanted it so much. Not it, not just it, but from him. Jack. Even his name excited her, God knew why. John Allerton. Jack.

"Wait," he said hoarsely, and pulled the coverlet off the bed, then sank down with her onto the sheets, pushing her head to the pillow and covering her body with his own. Covering her like a blanket: she lay sheathed and swathed in him, his arms cradled round her head. He breathed deeply, as if they had come to rest to die together, he shielding her as if from some sudden, irrevocable disaster.

Not for long, their demands were too imperative. They must now know each other, what lay beyond the conversation and the laughter, the affection and the companionship, the public faces and the arrayed figures. There was another kind of knowledge, when you were all sensation, skin, flesh, feeling and heat, an assemblage of separate parts clamoring for appeasement. Avaricious and insatiable and questing. Every man smelled different, his own distinctive emanations: she reeled with this man's skin scent, inhaled it, memorized it, his body too, lean and triangled from chest to navel with a crisp mat of that dark, dark hair. Hair and bone and sinew. Jack . . .

Then his massive groan as he pulled away, towered over her again, rapid and rough, hands parting her thighs, fingers digging deep into the soft flesh, painful, elating, tears in her eyes from the hard pressure, exquisite hurt. Gasping, shuddering, he drove into her, his entry forcing a cry from her lips.

Even as her own frenzy peaked, even as she writhed and thrashed with him, a thread of tenderness, like a glimmer of light in a primeval darkness, inserted itself in her consciousness. Hair all awry, like some Paleolithic cave dweller, his eyes bloodshot, sweet, sensitive face now a tortured mask, sweat running in little rivulets. Laughter somewhere inside her, untimely and grotesque, but which she recognized as human and loving, and then she was all concupiscence again, blind and avid and climbing with him, both striving, straining, eyes wide and wild, the cries and the puffings, the heat haze.

Sliding down now, with the mind coming back and the beginnings of gentleness and the acknowledgment that they had taken this rough and ancient road together, together all the way. Spent and sweating and exhausted, tired and sated and together. Hands roving, slow and grateful and stroking, with a faint wonder, the body in the shared bed that had so recently given such incandescent delight. Quick, shamed apologies. "Your mouth. After the dentist! Did I hurt you?"

"It's all right. I'm fine. Hold me."

He held her. The sun, behind the drawn cedar blind, made golden stripes. "I'm terribly in love with you," Jack said. "You must have known that."

"Jack. I didn't realize I felt this way. If I did, I didn't think about it. Or I didn't want to think about it."

He held her, but he was a hungry man. Well, she was hungry, too. There were no cigarettes, no interludes with quiet whisperings. It wasn't long before she felt him hardening again. He said, forgive him for what had been, unintentionally, a quickie. He said he'd just plain lost control, he had been thinking about it too much, day and night as a matter of fact and he couldn't hold himself back. He would do better this time. "I want to make love to you in every way known to man," he told her. "Christine—"

"What?"

"Nothing. Just—oh, Chris, Christine."

He was tireless, Jack was. He had waited a long time, it seemed. She recognized need when she ran into it. Jack, for whatever reason, had been starving for love. Love or sex or just someone to lie with him, alone from the rest of the world. It didn't matter for what reason. He had his reasons, she had hers.

No afternoon lasted forever, though, and when the sun had lost its potency and fire and the last gold gleams from the window were gone you knew it was time to get back to your senses. "Jack, it's getting late, we must stop."

"Why?"

"Because it's getting late."

"Don't go."

"But it's getting late."

"Don't leave me."

His hair was so soft. He had washed it that morning. "Ain't it fussy?" She'd remember that too. And that first moment, when she realized what was going to happen. She'd like to have that first moment all over again. That first, dazzling moment, which would never come again.

She lay there, picturing herself going home, walking up to Lex and passing all the familiar shops on the way to the apartment. Checking her clothes to see they were all in place. Smoothing her hair. Legs unsteady and the indelible imprint of this afternoon fixed, unerasable. She'd go in the door and say hello to the concierge and then the elevator man. "Hi, Jimmy." Not the same woman she had been when she left this morning. A different woman, a woman who had made love to this man beside her.

"Darling, I have to go."

After a while he eased himself up on an elbow. "Is this going to change things? I mean, now you'll have second thoughts?"

She was honest. "I don't know."

"I'm in love with you. No, I don't mean that. I love you. I love you so much I can't stand it. I feel you're mine. I just feel you're mine, that's all."

"I love you too, that should be plain. But I'm not sure what it means. That is, in the general scheme of things."

"If this is the end, it's the end of everything for me. I don't have anything else. I don't want anything else. I don't want anything without you, anyway."

"You have a whole life ahead of you, Jack."

"That's what you probably say to Rodney. And then go home."

She was astonished. "Rodney? There's nothing

between me and Rodney! Why, he's just a child!"

"He's in love with you."

She slid out from under him. "That's silly," she said, unnerved. "Everyone's in love with me all of a sudden? Jack, what are you talking about?"

"Lots of men are probably in love with you. Why shouldn't they be? You're a beautiful woman, certainly the most beautiful woman I ever saw."

"Is that it?" she demanded, upset. "I'm a dish? Men want to lay me because I have good legs and—is that what it is, tits and ass?"

"Damn you," he said quietly. "I don't mean a face and a body and that's the end of the story. You know I didn't, and don't. So don't make like I'm a male chauvinist pig. You're someone a man doesn't meet, only I did, after being convinced I never would, it wasn't in the cards for me, and if you have any idea I'll let you walk out of here—so long, it was fun for an afternoon, thank you very much—forget it. I don't care what you say, you knew all along I was making love to you every time we were together. I was courting you, like some village Romeo, and you wouldn't have gone along with it if I hadn't meant something to you. What kills me is how *programmed* you are, wired for the role you're cast in, the lady of the house, the Mom, the fixer. That really makes me want to puke. I bet your husband complains he can't find his socks and there's static cling in his underwear. Honey, there's static cling in my jocks and a ring around my collar. How come, Mommy? All you have to do is keep this house in order, don't I—"

"Don't say any more," she warned, stung. Stung,

astonished and shaking. "I don't know why you're taking this tack, but let me tell you you can put your guest towels away unused, because I'm not even going to use the bathroom. I'll take a tub at home, a long, hot tub and soak in it—what's the *matter* with you?"

She was scrambling into her clothes. He looked at her and then turned away. In her undies, she stared at his back. "Jack, Jack!"

"I don't want you to go, and I'm saying a lot of half-assed things," he said over his shoulder. "Put it down to my being a total shit."

"Jack, please, I don't want to leave this way."

He turned again and walked up to her. His eyes filled with tears suddenly. Oh, she thought. Oh, Jack. Her own eyes misted. She looked beyond him at the bed. I left myself there, Christine thought. There's something of myself in that mussed bed. She glanced around the room. Never to come here again?

"Look," she said. "Maybe I understand. You must understand too. This kind of thing isn't what I do. What I ordinarily do. I mean, I never set myself up this way. Looking back, I realize it was in my mind, I was attracted to you, I just didn't admit how much. But in a way it was excusable, because other than physical attraction I simply liked you so enormously, I just loved being with you. Attraction—hell, I see a man on the street, or in a bus, or . . . and that man excites me. You know, Jack, that kind of thing happens all the time."

"Maybe."

"It does, and you know it! Yes, and I like it, it means you're alive, you're a woman, but I don't go to bed with—"

"Neither do I."

"But you can. You're not married, you have no responsibility to anyone."

She swallowed. "I'm married, and this is the first time, in seventeen years, that I've done anything like this. I don't want to think on its bearing on anyone else, I don't want to think about my husband, I don't want anyone else to think about him, have I asked you about Phyllis? Whether you're still missing her, wanting her? How many times you took her to bed? One thing I've respected and admired about you is you've never spilled your guts about her, never beefed or said it was her fault that you split. Or it was your fault. You never cried in your beer about any of it, you kept it your concern. We didn't bring other people into our friendship, that meant a lot to me."

"There's no way I can adequately tell you how much it means to me. But I can't go back to just being friends. Not now. I was off base, yes, what I said, that's because I can't get it out of my craw that you belong to someone else."

"I *belong* to *myself*. I do have duties and obligations to a few other people, and well I know it, but must you remind me of it? Right after we—"

Her eyes went to the bed again. "I never felt like that before," she said tremulously. "Not like *that*. Not even half like that. Even if we never saw each other again I'd remember it, cling to it. Jack, I have to get dressed."

"I know. Sit down for only a minute, let me try to make amends, there has to be some kind of —"

He sat down beside her, smoothed her hair back, smiled. "Promises," he said. "From me to you. Not ever any impertinences, no more querulous accusations, the mind is master to the tongue. I would go to my room without supper, except that I am in my room and you're still here with me. Will you be here with me, Christine? Other days? Will you be my Valentine? Just you and me, no intruders."

He threaded his fingers through hers. She was silent. His fingers tightened. After a while he said, his voice flat, "Have I blown the whole thing to hell, then?"

No, she thought. Nothing's changed. Not even their making love together had altered anything. She simply adored this man, she was not going to give up being with him as often as she could manage it. "Put your arms around me just for a second," she said. "Just so I can remember how they feel. Yes, like that, soft and —"

Then she disengaged herself. "Don't abuse yourself," she said. "You didn't say anything all that infamous, just something I didn't want to hear. Shall we try to do something on Thursday, that is if you want to and can."

His heartened smile. "Yes, Christine. I want to. And I can."

"Maybe we could meet at the Met. There's that new exhibit, the Vienna art showing. Clover told me about it, her man's Austrian, you know."

"What time, Christine?"

"How about noon? I'll meet you just inside the

224

entrance. All right?"

"Yes. Fine."

She headed for the bathroom. "Be right back."

When she returned he was in a bathrobe. She hadn't used a guest towel, she had dried her hands with a tissue. That way he wouldn't have to wash the towel. He stood there, his hands in the pockets of his robe, watching while she brushed her hair and slipped into her blouse and skirt. When she went he would be left here, in his bathrobe, with the soggy remains of the crustless sandwiches and the tepid Chablis with strawberries swimming in it. He would have to get dinner later on. One of his frozen meals. She should have used one of the towels, but he had to take care of his own *laundry*, for God's sake.

He was a lonely man, and he so much wanted to be Mario Puzo. Maybe one day he would, or the equivalent. Or maybe he would be an Updike, a Cheever, but that day was doubtless a long way off. He looked solitary, he looked abandoned, even though she was still there.

At the door she held up her face for a kiss. "I wish I could stay longer."

"Likewise. See you Thursday."

She walked home, thinking of his face. The way it had lightened when he sensed everything was going to be okay. And earlier, his tears. Very serious this was; she had never imagined finding herself in any real involvement; then she had met Jack Allerton.

So, she thought, walking into the lobby of the Colonnade. So. The world had changed, or at least her world. What did it matter, whom would it hurt? Lots of women had lovers. Why not Christine Jennings? The day after tomorrow would come, sure as God made little green apples. He was wrong, though. It wasn't his tears that had convinced her. It was that she wanted it, wanted it very much, and she would have it. No matter where it led, and that was the story, pure and simple.

12.

There he was, taking the steps in a kind of dog trot, his progress unimpeded: this was a weekday, the clutter of students and Sunday culture vultures who on a weekend sprawled uninhibitedly on the stone flight outside the Metropolitan Museum of Art on Fifth Avenue were otherwise occupied at school or office. Even the special exhibit wouldn't be too jammed on a Thursday. It was always a delight to have the Met almost to yourself.

There he was, not seeing her yet where she was standing just inside the doorway. She couldn't read the expression on his face, not yet. Jack Allerton, my love, look at you in your nice twill pants, your striped shirt open at the neck and a light tweed jacket slung over your shoulder. How beautiful you are, with your dark skin and all that wonderful, luxuriant hair and your rumble of a voice.

"Here," she called as he neared the top. "Hi."

He walked up to her, and his aura enveloped her. Her breath caught in her throat. "Hi," she said again. "Hello, Jack."

"Hello, Christine."

"Nice day, huh?"

"Terrific. Hey, how long have you been waiting?"

"You're exactly on time, don't be silly."

"I didn't mean to keep you waiting, though. Actually I thought I was early, I mean ahead of time."

"I just got here before I planned to, that's all. How are you, Jack?"

"Fine. You?" He put both hands on her arms, patted them, then righted the shoulder bag that had slipped down to her wrist. His smile was a trifle forced. Well, he was obviously nervous too. As for herself, she hoped he couldn't sense the turmoil inside her. Hi, she had called to him, cool as a cucumber, which she felt anything but. Worrying, brooding, ever since she had left him on Tuesday. Would she have second thoughts? he had asked her. It applied to him as well. Would *he*? Men could have second thoughts too.

"Say, this is a great idea," he said. "I guess I haven't been inside this place since the King Tut exhibit."

"I come here sometimes. When I'm taking a walk, maybe. I stop in and browse, generally in the Impressionist section. Wouldn't you just know it would be the Impressionist section?"

"I can't fault you for that."

"Sometimes, occasionally with a friend, we stop in and have a drink in the Fountain Room."

"Oh, yes. Well, say, why don't we do that now? Before we see the exhibit? We don't have to stay long. Want to do that?"

"Sure, that would be nice."

The Fountain Room seemed to be doing a brisk enough business, lots of people sitting at the marble tables beside the pool, lunching or simply lingering over drinks. Food smells and chatter that echoed in the white-columned chamber. Probably mostly out-of-town visitors who would later take a horse and buggy ride through Central Park. Jack didn't bother with a waiter, he went to the bar and came back with a martini for Chris and a Canadian Club for himself.

"It's nice," he said. "This is nice. I haven't been in here for a long time either."

"It's restful. I like to be where there's water. I'm told that's Freudian, which cuts no ice with me because I'm not one of his slavish followers. I like the Sculpture Garden at the Museum of Modern Art a lot more than this."

"Me too. I used to go there a lot."

"So did I. I had a Museum membership, mostly for the movies. I've seen some great ones there, *Birth of a Nation*, things like that."

"I love the piano player."

"Isn't he darling? He does a fantastic job. Bill Perry, or something like that."

"Yeah, something like that."

"All the film classics, that's where I've seen them. *Carnival in Flanders. Les Enfants du Paradis, Poil de Carotte.*"

"The Thalia, too. They bring back the old gems."

"Sometimes the Regency. And the New Yorker. Rodney's a film buff too. He tries to get me to go with him, but somehow I have a feeling he'd talk during the performance. Make judicious comments. I don't like to talk during a film. Do you?"

"No, I sit there and lose myself. No yakking. No popcorn either."

"Oh, I hate that! You don't find it in the art theaters. Anyway not in the daytime, and that's when I go."

"Have you seen Rodney?"

"Yes, he comes to dinner every so often. He's fine, same old appetite and always in fine fettle."

"Have you been to the Sculpture Garden lately?"

"No, not since they've been doing that work on the new addition, so I haven't seen what's happening."

"I hope they don't make a mess of it."

"Whatever they do it will never be the same."

"I wish they could leave things alone. What really kills me is having that damned Olympic

Towers right next to St. Pat's Cathedral. That's the real desecration. The way it dwarfs the cathedral, overshadows it. Jesus, it's the most blatant violation of all, it's a slap in the face to the whole city."

"Just the kind of casual cruelty that's going on all over. We'd better get used to it. As Rodney says, nattering won't help."

"It's a crime, though."

Two days ago we were in bed together, Christine thought. Now we're talking about city planning. The room was cool, even faintly chill because of its size and the marble ambiance, but she felt sticky and uncomfortable, the back of her neck slightly damp. The drink wasn't helping one bit, it wasn't taking the edge off her unease at all. This was all her fault, her greeting to Jack had been all *wrong*, cool and calm and impersonal. She hadn't meant it to be, she was simply inept today for some reason. If she could only start *over* again. A big smile, and her arms around him.

"Oh, I didn't give you your button," she said. "Here, Jack. I got them when I came in."

"Hey, you didn't need to do that, Christine. I would have taken care of it."

"Good heavens, the least I can do is hand over a couple of dollars for our buttons, Jack."

"Well, thanks."

He stuck it on the collar of his shirt, she folded hers over the string belt of her dress. "Now we're legit," he said, and flicked his lighter for her cigarette.

Then he lit one for himself. "I never asked you if you wanted something to eat," he said quickly. "I didn't think of it. Would you?"

"Oh no, not now."

"They used to have good roast beef. Prime ribs. I suppose they still do."

"I think it's one of their main attractions."

"You haven't seen this exhibit yet, have you?" he asked. "The one we're going to today?"

"No, but I understand it's excellent. A long time in the drafting stage, it should be stunning."

"I'm glad you thought of it, Christine. I have a tendency to pass up a lot of things. They're there, and you can go to them, and then somehow you don't."

"My friend Clover said not to miss it. I wouldn't have wanted to anyway."

"We're spoiled. There's so much offered in this city, we don't take enough advantage of it."

"It's the visitors that do. Like Rodney. He's certainly no slouch, he gets in on everything. But then I suppose when we go abroad we do things the natives don't bother to. That's generally the rule of thumb."

"Hell, I imagine half the people in New York have never been to the Statue of Liberty."

She laughed. "Rodney has. By the way, have you?"

"You bet your life." He laughed too. "Not since I was a kid, though."

"Me too, but then I went three times."

"I think it was twice for me."

"I doubt there's anything much in New York City I haven't seen. My record for the rest of the country could stand some improving, however.

New England. The South—there was one summer when I went with my family, I was only about twelve. Otherwise, *nada*. I'm your typical Europhile, the grass is always greener, et cetera."

"Never been to California?"

"Uh uh. I'm serious, this country's an X quantity for me, what do you think of that? I'm not even sure which state is next to what other state."

"I've been here and there," he said. "It's a country, it has its history. Hell, as you know I'm a Europhile too."

"After all, you do have some roots there, Jack. Your mother's family—"

"We all have roots there when it comes right down to it. I guess that's what does it, why it draws us."

"It's the *old* that draws us, past centuries. *Long* past centuries. Churches dating back to 1100. Castles. Rites and rituals that have been going on for hundreds of years. They know something about preservation, they don't scrap buildings, they honor them."

"I guess one thing is they've depended on the tourist business for a long time. But you're right. The key word here is progress."

"I'm against progress."

"I guess we're both against all the indifference and profiteering that goes on."

"It's more than indifference and profiteering. It's the whole society, plastic and neon."

"Let's write our Congressman," he gestured. "You know, London's doing a pretty good job of messing things up. In Cheapside, for example.

They've succeeded in hemming in St. Paul's with new and modern, undistinguished office buildings, it looks rotten. Of course it was practically all bombed out during the Second World War, but they could have done better than that."

"Yes, I've seen it. They've taken a lot of the grandeur away from the Embankment too. No, I won't have another drink, thanks. You go ahead if you want one."

"No, one's plenty. Okay, shall we go then?"

They made their way out. Again the central area, after that up the flight of marble steps. Jack's hand on her arm as they climbed. At the top a sign indicating their exhibit, embellished with Art Nouveau squiggles and swirls. Also now, quite a few people heading that way, and when they reached the gallery rooms a sizeable crowd. Jack bought a glossy brochure from someone sitting behind a rococo table, handed it to her.

"Well, then I'll buy one for you," she said.

"No no, this will be fine for us."

I should have said I'd meet him at his apartment, Christine thought. He's uneasy, I'm uneasy, I was only trying to be civilized suggesting we meet here instead of my going to his place, and now he's going to defer to me. What the hell were they *doing* here? They were behaving like two adolescents miserably unsure of the rules of the game.

She should have kissed him right away, then he'd know. Simply, naturally, just let him know where he stood.

All very well, but she was beginning to be somewhat uncertain of *where* she stood. This man

234

had had a disastrous marriage: it was highly possible that he wasn't keen on adding a second mistake to a first. Thinking it over, he might very well have decided that an involvement with a married woman would only add to his woes.

She should have kissed him right off anyway.

They wandered through the exhibit rooms, sometimes together and then, separated by groups of people who disunited them, on their own. She was glad for it, it relieved some of the tension. And it was admittedly a dazzling display, so that after a while Christine was able to shake off some of her queasies and appreciate it.

She hoped Jack was enjoying it. After all, he had that middle-European background, it should mean something important to him. The way it had for Clover's Anton. As for Vienna, Christine had been there for a week and a half: it had charmed her and chilled her all at once, that city with the split personality, Strauss waltzes and anti-Semitism, whipped cream and class consciousness, grace and sadism. Carl, she remembered, had not vibrated to Vienna. He said it was drearily provincial and all the gilt was turning brown.

But then Carl wasn't a romantic. The City of Dreams, in its twilight now, was for a romantic a kind of cosmos encapsulated, its dwindled glory reflected in thousands of ways, little showers of stars dying slowly but still shedding their light however feebly, the proud and arrogant old men in their berets sitting in coffee houses still reading their newspapers, the *Schlagobers* in pewter bowls, the insistent traditions and the chandeliers and the memories, beauty and barbarism.

And these artists, spawned in an epochal Vienna that was going to hell in a breadbasket depicted, with wild and almost cheerful abandon, the death throes of a crumbling order, Brechtian, a *Totentanz*. Even the most glittering Klimt fantasies, brilliant, shimmering and iridescent as they were, had their macabre comments: "Sleep" looked like death, an eyeless skull hovered over a young pregnant girl in a painting called *Hope*. Schiele and Kokoschka, with their splashes of vermilion gore and the ashy white of their dehumanized, gaunt bodies, made an appalling statement: a flayed mass of flesh was flaunted like a banner. Oppenheimer's *Bleeding Man* was a silent scream.

There was no hint of whipped cream or waltzes in this gallery, no celebration of a Belle Epoque. It was more like an abbatoir.

Jack finally sought her out. "Well?" he asked. "Had enough?"

"Just about, yes. It sure leaves you exhausted, doesn't it?"

They went downstairs again. "It's haunting, all right. You can't write it off as avant garde, the artistic mind thumbing its nose at the *Arbeiter* mentality, *épater le bourgeois*. It's horror with a grin." He glanced at his watch. "It's one-thirty. Let's have a drink at the Stanhope. We can't get lunch on the terrace, but we can go inside for that."

"Do you really feel like eating after that Kokoschka poster, *Pietà*?"

"That was grim, wasn't it?"

"Let's have a drink on the terrace and then walk

236

downtown. We can have a hot dog on the way."

"Just a hot dog?"

"Maybe two hot dogs."

"That's a funny lunch."

"All right, a hot dog and a Good Humor."

You couldn't get a table at the Stanhope outdoor cafe on a weekend, but you had no trouble getting one on a workday. You not only got a table, you got some decent service as well, when waiters were not too busy to be polite. They sat there, over their drinks, shaded from the midday sun by the red, white and blue canopy, eyeing occasional passersby and benchsitters on the opposite side of the avenue, talking about the Vienna exhibit and not much else because both were thinking—and were aware of it—the same thing. Where would they walk downtown *to*? A hot dog and then what?

There were lots of things going on downtown, movie theaters, other museums, hotels to have another drink in, the park itself, with its winding paths. "Downtown" extended to Wall Street and the Battery, if you wanted to be technical: downtown could mean anywhere. It could more than conceivably mean Jack's apartment, which was downtown, and it was the precise location Christine, when saying it, had in mind. She was sure Jack knew that, but on the other hand the cue would have to come from him. If for some reason he *had* had second thoughts, was going to bow out of this budding romance, he would certainly not tell her on the street while they were eating a frankfurter.

Or would he?

It had been many years since she was uncertain of her footing, and it was a distinctly unpleasant development. She realized now that you could be forty years old—or fifty, or any age at all: if you were a victim of Cupid's barbed dart age was no defensibility. She was as vulnerable as a twenty-year-old, as unshielded. Besides, Jack was no Chéri. He was a very positive personality, no preppie type, no vacillating youth. He might be a lot younger than she was, but he was formidably adult.

Her composure seemed admirably unruffled as she sipped her drink and played idly with the gold chain round her neck, but she was not. If they got as far as Jack's street, and he didn't pause, didn't say anything, but simply walked on. . .

Well, she would walk on too, and that would be that.

"How about another drink?" he asked, when her glass was empty.

"No, Jack. Thanks, one will do it."

"For me too, I guess," he said, and signaled the waiter.

Out on the street again he didn't say, "Let's cross over to the park side," and this seemed to augur that their minds were bent on the same destination, since *not* crossing over kept them on the side of the street that would more readily lead down to the farther avenues and the direction of Jack's house. There was the little matter of hot dogs, however, and at Seventy-second Street, with the entrance to the park ringed with stands offering franks and soft drinks, he took her arm and walked

238

her over. The last thing she wanted, at this particular moment, was the frank she had earlier suggested, but she was hoist on her own petard, after all the idea had come from her.

They had a hot dog each, sitting on a bench to eat it and then wiping mustardy hands with the postage-sized napkin provided. She started to rise, but Jack said, "No, sit. You'll want another one, won't you?"

"No, Jack, I couldn't possibly."

"Okay, then, I'll get us some Good Humors. What flavor for you?"

"My eyes were bigger than my stomach. No, really."

He sat down again, leaned against the bench. She gave him a quick look. He was grave and quiet, drumming his fingers in a rat tat tat on the bench. She looked away and opened her handbag for a cigarette. She couldn't find her lighter. He put a hand on her arm. She thought he meant to offer his own lighter for her, but instead he took the cigarette out of her fingers.

"Christine?"

"Yes?".

"Can't we go home now? That is, would you want to?"

She said, "Home?"

"To my place, Christine."

This was what was meant when people said their bones turned to water. She felt like that, as if she were a sack of water, just all fluid, every bit of her. He was waiting for her to answer, though any fool could see it in her face. She was so overcome with gratitude and relief she could scarcely speak. She nodded, and her voice came back to her. "Yes, let's go home," she said almost in a whisper, but he got the message. A quick, sharp intake of his breath, and then he pulled her up. Swaying slightly, she regained balance and locomotion when he thrust an arm through hers, steered her across the avenue, and then they continued their walk downtown, to Jack's place. Nothing to discuss now, nothing to speculate about. The test was over, there would be no more uncertainties, no further unspoken questions. This was home, he had said so, and so she felt; it was like finding something she had lost, or mislaid, a long time ago, and then given up, with sad reconcilement, for good.

As before, he was quickly propelled to climax and, as before, rueful about it. "It's the same damned old thing, I just have this on my mind so much, with you, thinking of being with you, and then when I am I go all ape."

"Can't you see I was in a hurry too? Eating that damned hot dog. I thought I'd choke. All I wanted was to get my hands on you. I love your body."

"As for yours, well you can see what it does to me. Listen to me still panting away, I sound like some animal in rut. It gives me a visceral, ass-aching pleasure to have you talk about my body. You never think of your own body, it's just something you tote about everywhere, feed it and empty it, but when someone you're insane about says, 'Your body,' you feel you have something there. Give me enough time, you telling me you like it,

I'll start flashing on the street."

"Oh, *don't* be a flasher, Jack. You'll end up in a police station and I'll have to come and bail you out. So shaming for me. Look at that nice lady, would you ever think she'd take up with an exhibitionist? Tsk tsk."

"Agreed, then, I won't flash. I'll phone you instead, breathe heavy into the phone, drive you nuts. 'Now I'm pulling it out,' I'll say. 'Now I'm erecting.' How about that? Yeah, maybe I'll dial your number and you'll be doing a crossword while waiting for the roast to cook. There you are, all calm and cozy and then this voice says—"

"How would I know it was you?"

"I'll say something. Some password. Something a random caller wouldn't know about. 'You've got a little beauty spot on your *toches*.' Incidentally, I've been dreaming about it."

"It doesn't take much to please some people."

"Everything about you does. Drives me crazy. It's sick, I suppose. Thinking about you, and you're not here, and I walk the floor, not seeing anything and bumping into furniture. You have no idea. The first time I saw you. With that boy. I didn't know who he was, what he meant to you, and then we went out to lunch. Don't close your legs. I don't remember what we talked about because I was beginning to lose my mind about you. Right away, right away fast. *Don't close your legs.*"

"I don't really like that," she protested faintly.

His voice, muffled. His dark head between her thighs. She stirred, tried to move. His hands forced her thighs farther apart. Why did she say she

241

didn't like his mouth there, she asked herself. Why was she still self-conscious? Let go, she instructed herself. Let go, give yourself up.

Then her body took over again, the way it had the other day, two days ago. All you had to do was forget time and everything else and let yourself go: There was no one else, there was nothing else, just this—the pain-pleasure, like a powerful stimulant zooming into her, drove thought away, she was body now, strong and passionate and driven, her legs had their own life, her arms theirs, her mouth, his mouth, they were inside each other's skins, sweat and hair and orifices. The room whirling, now the ceiling, now the pillow, her face buried in it, rolling, tossing, then the unbearable, the colossal, agonizing, mind-blowing sequence of orgasmic contractions, never like this. Oh no, never like this . . .

No more talking after that. No jokes, no funnies. Do it again. Rest for a while and then do it again. You had to feel like that once more before you looked at a watch or a clock and thought about leaving. You had to have it in your mind to remember. Walk around the house and remember, eyes filmed, abstracted, it was one of the things you had between you, no one else knew about it, what you could do together. It didn't happen all that often, it wasn't an idle pastime, it was a necromancy, this particular man and this particular woman. "God," Jack said, in a kind of stricken voice. "God."

They lay quietly, spent. The only thing Christine was thinking now was that she would very much like to stay right through, make dinner for him, with candles on the table, and in the morning find him beside her, that dark head on the other pillow. Anything else seemed almost obscene. It wasn't what she had intended at all, feeling that way. But then she supposed it wasn't what he had intended either.

She stirred after a while, sighed. "Yeah, I know," he said. "It's getting late, you have to go."

"I'm afraid so." She tensed, remembering the other day. Oh, please don't let him be resentful again.

But he only stroked her hair, smiled down at her. "If you have to go you have to go. Chris, when?"

She knew he meant when would they see each other again. "I promised myself I wasn't going to keep you from your work," she said hesitantly. "Jack, what do you think? It will be hard to stay away from you. Just the same, we both have to be reasonable. I just don't know what to say."

"I do. You may not realize it, but you can only turn out good work when you're living. Shutting yourself up all alone in a room is death. An empty mind, you can't work that way. Since I met you I'm turning out great stuff, I'm at the top of my form, I mean that."

He ran a finger down her nose, then traced the outline of her lips, chuckled. "Hell, I don't mean I'm writing about us," he assured her. "Just in case it's crossed your mind. No, I just mean I'm alive, my work is alive, it flows."

He raised himself on an elbow. "I want to be

243

with you as much as possible, as much as you can manage. You're here now, even when you're not here in the flesh, I see you everywhere, I even talk to you. I was thinking—"

He bent and kissed her, a long kiss. He felt her quick protest. "Don't worry, I'm not going to arouse the sleeping lion again. Uh, I was thinking —well, could we say hello to each other in the mornings? On the phone. I call you or you call me, just hello, how are you, I love you. Like that. Then—"

Thoughtfully: "Maybe we could be together at least two times a week? Not one of those Monday and Wednesday kind of things, but—"

His eyes questioned her. "I know nothing about your life, I only know about mine. It doesn't always have to be in bed, either. Maybe a couple of hours in the middle of the day—take a walk, have lunch somewhere. Be together."

He slid down again. "I guess I'll have to leave a lot of it up to you. I don't even know if this means as much to you as it does to me."

"It does," she said resignedly. "It does indeed. Well, Jack, yes, we'll do that, talk to each other in the morning, say hello and then work it out. Don't call me when your neighbor sneezes, that's too early, promise?"

"Good thing you told me, that's exactly when I had in mind."

"Revise your thinking, then." She threaded her fingers through his hair. "Who does your coiffures, honey? Kenneth? Cinandre?"

"No. A perfect little gem of a guy nobody's

discovered yet. My deep, dark secret, I decline to give out his name. Unisex, males and gays. I was wondering when you'd ask."

"It has that untamed look, I think I'll snip off a lock of it."

"Good idea, I'll give you a gold locket to put it in."

"I love your hair."

"Don't give me that shit, it was a crack."

"No crack. It's sexy, it feels pubic."

"Jesus Christ."

"Your hair was one of the first things to attract me. I kept thinking about it."

"Odd you should say that. It was your hair too. I couldn't pin down the color. Buckwheat honey, but that was a cheap, easy word, a magazine story word. Besides, it's tawnier, but that's all used up, it is to shudder. I can't find anything right."

"I can. Dishwater blonde."

"Say that again and you get a crack on the mouth."

"Okay, dun-colored." She sighed again, sat up regretfully. "What are you having for dinner tonight?"

"I don't know. Chicken divan, maybe. That's not Swanson's, it's Stouffer's. Pretty good. I might succumb to Mrs. Paul's fried clams. I have a big special for when I'm down in the mouth. Short ribs, it costs almost five dollars, I feel like Diamond Jim Brady."

"I'd love to make you dinner. I can't stay to do it, but I'd love to."

He laughed, watching her slide off the bed. "I

245

knew someone once," he said, "who corrected me whenever I used that phrase, make dinner. A Jewish lady who told me you 'prepared' dinner, you didn't make it. She said you make a cake, yeah, or you make a bed, and when kids had to do number two they said they had to 'make'. Did you ever hear a kid say that?"

"I think Jewish kids do, Jack. My friend Ruth's children did. You don't seem to have been around very much."

"Aha. I'm insular."

"Our first fight, how lovely."

He laughed softly. "You nut . . ."

"Now where did I put my bra?"

"I hid it. Now you can't leave."

"It's all right, here it is. This room's a mess, our clothes are strewn all over. Please get dressed, I can't bear to leave you wearing your bathrobe, it tears my heart out."

"It does? Makes you sorry for the poor guy? Okay, I'll put it on."

But he obeyed her, got into his regular things and came to her while she was giving a brush to her hair, put his arms around her. "What's really the right time to call in the morning, Chris?"

"Nine, nine-thirty. Okay, you call *me* tomorrow."

At the door he took her in his arms. "I'm loath to let you go. But then I always will be."

"Maybe on Monday we can take a walk somewhere. Or lunch at Anthony's." She pulled away from him. "It's only you I'm worried about, Jack. Your work."

"Don't worry about me. Chris—"

"What?"

"You make me incredibly happy."

She walked home at a leisurely pace. Her mind wasn't on this evening's menu at all, her mind was elsewhere. She would see him, probably, next Monday. Meanwhile, she smelled him, tasted him, heard his voice, that low rumble. She permitted herself all this delightful bemusement until she walked into the lobby of the Colonnade, then she shifted gears, became that other person.

"Hi, Jimmy."

"Beautiful day today, Mrs. Jennings."

"Perfectly lovely."

"Spring has sprung."

"Actually it's summer."

"You're right."

"About time, wouldn't you say?" Which was dumb, it had been excellent weather all along. It was the kind of thing everyone always said, that was all, like telling someone to have a good day. Carl was home almost on the heels of her own arrival, looking grim: he was greatly disturbed about the death of a thirty-nine-year-old patient who threw an embolism. "I'm so sorry," she said. "Is there anything I can do?"

"Short of raising her from the dead, I can't think of a thing," he said, unaccustomedly curt with her.

"I meant make you a drink, perhaps?"

"Chris, I can make my own drink." The fact was that a predinner drink was not his usual style, but he did splash some bourbon into a glass and then tossed it off straight.

"Are you all right, Carl?"

"What else can I be? These things happen, there was nothing I could do to foresee it. It's shit, but there you are, it comes with the territory. You just feel like a fucking jerk when you see someone seemingly in perfect health go down like that, you wonder what you're in business for."

He went through the swinging doors, was back almost immediately. "I didn't mean to be cross with you," he said.

"It's okay, I can imagine how you must feel. Read the paper, take a nap, dinner won't be ready for another hour. I love you, dear."

I couldn't be a doctor, she thought, looking out the kitchen window. I couldn't go through that kind of thing. He would pull himself together at the dinner table, though, for the sake of the rest of them. He was a very nice man, a good man. She didn't want to hurt him, and she wouldn't. There were things he would never know about her, she would see to that, and what you didn't know couldn't hurt you.

13

There were penalties to pay when you gave yourself up to duplicity, unexpected forfeitures, like hidden expenses in an investment: you hadn't counted on them, really, you dimly sensed that there might be some additional costs, though too titillated by the wonderful thing you had bought on a shoestring to think deeply on supplementary amercements. You had your treasure and the joy in it, so you waived fugitive doubts, relaxed and enjoyed it and told yourself you would deal with the devil when he decided to show up for further and final payment.

But you couldn't wholly put the old Adversary out of your mind, and besides he was clever, wily, exacting recompense even before it was due, relying on conscience to do some of his dirty work for him. He gave you the golden rose (take it, it's yours, kiddo) and then laughed up his sleeve when you pricked yourself on the thorns that lay so innocently concealed. But you didn't give back the rose, you might bleed a little, but you held on to it, gloating. Mine, mine . . .

Or so you would imagine, thought Christine, trying to sell herself a bill of goods on the guilt and worry she should be feeling. She didn't believe for a minute that an extramarital affair meant you were of low moral fiber: that was cant. Monogamy happened to be the law of the land and a fairly reasonable way of safeguarding the institution of marriage. Even if it was asking a hell of a lot. She didn't raise her eyebrows about it, but when it came down to brass tacks if you had an itch you scratched it and, all things considered, copulation with an outside party wasn't the whole point anyway. In fact was not really—because you were dealing with human vulnerabilities—the point at all, but was more or less beside it.

It was *awful*, for example, that she gave scarcely a thought to the man she was blithely betraying, i.e. Carl, who hadn't a notion in the world that another man was in the picture—in fact, was in

250

the forefront of the picture. She used to wonder if Carl, who must run into lovely and desirable women patients, strayed occasionally: she had heard a few bitter truths from the mouths of other doctors' wives. It had always seemed unlikely, since his habits were so regular and ordered, home for dinner when he should be, draped about the house on weekends. Possibly on some trip to another city, a Medical Congress—perhaps then he met some female on the loose, who knew? It had never troubled her. She had to confess to herself that it was of no large import. Was that indifference, lovelessness on her part?

No, it was not, she decided quickly. Her husband was part of her, part of the progress of her life, a good man if not an imaginative one, a little bit like a father, though he was only two years older, but he was steady and down to earth and somehow like a person of another generation: he even used some of the stock phrases her own father did.

If there was a faint, fugitive reservation, it was about the kids. No way in the world they could ever unearth this new facet of her life and yet —well, she was weirdly shy about Bruce and Nancy's regarding her as other than a parent. There must be something Victorian about her, but it made her squirm to think of their sensing in her a questing sexuality, that Mother had a lover, which meant stolen moments, a dark and dirty wallowing and then coming home to them brazening it out, the Mother-whore. That was the way they would view it!

And it wasn't like that at all. If it were, it would be far less disloyal to Carl.

But it wasn't like that.

In fact it was a gorgeous gift, a rebirth, a lustrous wonder, the knowledge of it bursting into her consciousness when morning came and sending her off to sleep at night with a thankful smile. In fact it was something to guard and cherish and protect, like some exquisite, orchidaceous bloom coarse hands could soil and sully, needing painstaking care and love. In fact Jack was not her lover, but her love, his apartment not a way station but a place she felt was home.

Even the mechanics of the situation dismayed her not at all, the careful arrangements, the delicate maneuverings, the dual roles she assumed seemed not so much double-dealing as a necessary evil she cheerfully took on. It was her tribute to Jack, a way to show her wholehearted devotion. She wasn't only cosseting him, he must be made to see, she was cosseting herself, which anyway was the plain and honest truth, and in a way a terrible truth. If there were to be a phone call, some unfamiliar voice saying there had been a bad accident, she must be brave, it would be Jack who instantly sprang into her mind: Jack had been killed in an accident, Jack was dead. He was dead, she would never see him again, never have his arms around her, never stroll the Manhattan streets with him, never . . .

This ultimate disloyalty, this calm betrayal of everything she had previously held dear, was so shattering that it made her tremble. At the same time there was a kind of piercing exultation: if there were penalties for this wondrous enchantment she would gladly pay them.

Their hours together were quietly domestic: she often thought of Clover Martinson, with her consort, maybe you could call it, her Anton Ehrenberg. Not living together either, but very much like a husband and a wife, certainly not like a bitch in heat with a sniffing hound circling: you could tell, talking to Clover, that it was quite different, an "arrangement," a loving and comfortable one. There were so many ways to live, weren't there, and now she herself was part of a new experience: God, she was happy, she could taste it, she was flooded with it, it ran through her veins, colored her speech and her laugh, glistened in her eyes, moistened her mouth.

"Gee, you look great," one of her friends said at lunch on a group day together. "Are you having facials or something?"

"Good heavens, you know how I hate beauty salons. Of course not. Why do you ask, was my skin showing signs of wear or something?"

"Silly. Nothing wrong with your skin at any time. No, it's not that. Just something or other, I can't pin it down."

"It's the summer, I'm a summer gal."

"Me, fall's my time. The air like wine, things starting up again after the summer doldrums."

"What do you mean, summer doldrums? I adore summer, how can anyone *not*?"

"New York summers? They're the pits."

"Not to me."

"Well, damn you, it's a little sickening the way you look so feisty and all. What's your secret, huh?"

"Nothing, I just feel good."

"How do you manage that?"

"Clean living and plenty of exercise, Meryl."

"I live clean but there's little to show for it. I'm beginning to hang back from the mirror in the mornings, naked fear. Or worse than that, afraid to go to sleep at night, not knowing what I'll find on arising. Oh, goodie, a brand new wrinkle."

"Listen to her, a face like a baby's bottom."

"You must be nearsighted, kiddo."

"Nope. Twenty-twenty, that's me."

"Gee, I used to be so vain about my chest and shoulders," Ruth said tragically. "But now—"

"Your *chest*?"

"I don't mean my boobs, darling. No complaints about them yet, but lately I see fine lines running down from my clavicles. I suppose I should train myself to sleep on my back. I find them very disturbing. Portents of the increasing years. I feel like screaming, I don't want to get old. Goddamn it, why do you have to get old?"

"Old is sixty. Seventy."

"Old is when men don't look at you anymore."

"Old is when you don't look at them anymore."

"This is a horrible conversation. For God's sake, we're in the prime of life, what do you *want*?"

"Remember that picture, *All About Eve?* When Bette Davis hits forty, and she says to someone, with that wild look of hers, those hyperthyroid eyes bulging, 'I'm forty! 4-0!' Well, friends, so are we.

Does it hurt all that much?"

"I'm not forty yet," Clover said mildly.

"Screw you."

"*And* the prime of life is for men. What isn't for men? They have the world by the tail, screw them. Look at Cary Grant, he's older than God and he could have any nymphet he had a mind to reach for."

"Yes, damn it, it's true, and true and true. A man can be any old age, four double chins and a revolting paunch. Even when they can't get it up anymore, they can still call the shots."

"Comes the revolution—"

"Dummy. Nothing will ever change it."

"God, I love Bette Davis."

"I wish I knew her, I'd hug her to death."

"You, Christine. You used to do that imitation of her in *The Moon and Sixpence.*"

"No no. *Of Human Bondage.* Yes, sure, I used to do that one a lot. 'And every time you kissed me, I wiped my mouth . . . wiped my mouth . . . you're a cripple, a cripple . . .'"

She laughed. "I don't think I'd do it for Rodney, he'd probably carp at my Cockney."

"Oh, it's great, it's great."

"Do Ann Landers."

"You want us thrown out of this restaurant?"

"What were we talking about before? Oh yes, male superiority."

There was a chorus of protests. "Well," Helene said, grinning, "anyway, about male supremacy, that's what I meant to say." She leaned forward. "You know, you do look sort of Renoir-ripe," she told Christine. "As if you just came out of a scented bath. You're not pregnant, are you?"

"Dear God in heaven," Christine cried. "What a hideous thought! Why are you all picking on me?"

"*I'm* not picking, I'm annoyed," Ruth said. "But then you always were queen of us all."

"I beg your *pardon?*"

"It's true. You don't have a bad angle. And your daughter's the same, they'll fall like flies for Nancy. I used to think your legs were too skinny, that the calves could be rounder. I was wrong."

"Tell me more," Christine said, dimpling.

"Uh uh. Fuck off, you don't need any admiration societies, you must know you've got it, so I've said enough." She smiled. "If I didn't love you I'd hate you. Me with my crow's feet."

"Look, let's not be idiotic, I just feel great, that's all. You feel good, you look good. Like Clover with her James-Lang theory."

"Why *do* you feel so good, then? Is Carl going to win the Nobel Prize for medicine?"

"Not that I know of, and I fear not that he knows of either." She hesitated, toying with her cigarette lighter. "It isn't anything like that. It isn't—"

They were waiting. She saw their faces looking at her. They were all looking at her and waiting for what she had to say. Ruth, and Helene, Meryl and Clover. Bright, expectant faces, the faces of her friends, curious, half smiling. She felt reckless. She wanted to say, "Why do I feel so good? It's very simple—you see, I'm in love. I'm very much in love."

It was an almost uncontrollable compulsion. Like when you're sitting in the balcony of some theater, with a bag of peanuts in your hand, and you think what if I dropped one of these peanuts down, it would land on someone's head — what if I did it? And you want, like anything, to do just that, so much so that you get scared and frightened that some devil in you will take over and your hand will reach in the bag and throw the peanut.

You see, ladies, I'm in love.

You didn't drop the peanut and you didn't say what you wanted to say, that you were on cloud nine because you had fallen in love and everything had changed and you would almost kill to keep what you had.

She laughed and reached for a cigarette. "Sue me," she said. "I feel good, period. I feel great and don't ask me why. I just plain feel the best I ever have."

They looked disappointed. Inquisitive too. It was accepted, however. How would they ever guess the truth? She had always been Caesar's wife, and she had no reason to suppose that the others weren't the same. They talked about men a lot, but if any of them had her own secret it was well concealed. They had certainly never discussed the marriage bed (my husband does it this way, how does yours?): they were not women who operated that way in their friendship. The compulsion to spill her guts was gone, she was relieved that discretion had come to the fore. What she wanted, she knew, was to shout it out to the world at large, her immense happiness, her stupendous well-being. It was, after all, only natural.

"Oh, I'm sorry," she said after lunch, when Ruth, as they all drifted out to the street afterwards asked if she couldn't · go for a walk somewhere. "Maybe even dinner, Chris? We could call home, I thought we might go down to the Village or something, browse around and then hack it back to Marchi's, make it a whole day."

"It's just that I promised to take a run over to Rodney's," she apologized. "He's having a few people in, I said I'd be there to help a bit."

"He's still intruding on your time?"

"Not really, he's doing very well on his own, I don't see him all that much nowadays. I did promise to be there today, though."

"Oh, hell. Anyway he lives uptown, let's amble on up together."

"I thought I'd go to Bloomies and pick up a few goodies for him. Some paté, a jar of those oversized olives."

"I'll go with you."

"It wouldn't be much fun. Ruth, I'll just pop in there only for a minute and then cab up to Rodney's."

"Well, okay. Listen, maybe we can go someplace next week? There's a dandy new exhibit at the Wildenstein. I understand some magnificent Seurats. Okay?"

"Absolutely. I'll call you."

"Fine. Well, dear, keep the kindergarten in good order, don't let them fingerpaint themselves to death. Yes, I know, his mother's a good friend of yours, greater love hath no man. Well, then, I'll hie myself over to Madison, for endives, I'm fresh

258

out. Have fun."

"You too."

She watched Ruth walk off, in her designer dress, all crisp, clean lines, and the Mark Cross handbag clasped in Ruth's summer-tanned hands. Friends. Friends had dwindled in importance, you lied to them easily and expertly, the way you lied about everything these days, it didn't even prick your conscience. All you wanted was to get off the hook as gracefully as possible, with a cordial smile.

She turned the corner and walked over to Park, waited for the light to change and then, crossing, walked the block farther down to Lex, staying with it until Jack's street, where she continued on down to Third. Now she quickened her steps. She had said it would be—oh, say, around three-fifteen or so when she would be there, told him for God's sake nothing to eat or drink, she would have had her fill of both. She had meant, let's go to bed, and he had known that: his eyes had acknowledged it, and the coverlet would be pulled down and he would be waiting for her, would greet her at the door, impatient and loverlike. She ran up the stone steps, going home, going to where she belonged, and pressed the buzzer.

He was on the landing, his arms reaching out for her.

"Did you have lunch?" she asked him. "The truth now."

"Yup. The machine is fed."

He untied the bow at the neck of her blouse, eased off her suit jacket. "I've had a good working day," he told her. "Fourteen pages, almost final draft caliber. I'm working smoothly of late, and I don't think I have to spell out why."

"Good, that's good."

"It's you, knowing you'll be here, or if not, at least on the other end of that phone line. I don't know what I did to deserve you."

"Oh, I love hearing you say that. Hang this up, will you? I can't very well leave here all crumpled and such. I must keep up my reputation as the well-dressed Mrs. Jennings who lives in 9E."

She stepped out of her skirt, spread it over a chair. "A nice lunch with friends, but it seemed endless," she told him. "I couldn't wait to get here. I love you. Oh, I'm so glad you're working well. Did you know I'm a very proficient typist? Can I do your manuscript?"

"You mean in about two years?"

"Oh? I guess I didn't realize—"

"It could be two years, Chris."

"Hell, that doesn't *throw* me. I just—well, I'd just like to help you in some way."

"You're doing that."

"Sometimes I think—"

"Don't think now, okay?"

"All right, I'll think tomorrow."

"What time do you have to leave?"

"Five. Or so."

"Would you stay on through dinner sometime?"

"Yes, I've already decided on that. Sometime soon. I promise, Jack."

"That's nice."

"We'll have a lovely time. Make room for me, you pig. Don't hog the whole bed."

"I thought you'd never get here."

"So did I."

It was not all screwing, though, not by a long shot. It was long, companionable walks, and going to the Abigail Adams house over near York Avenue, to refresh themselves with glowing woods and winking chandeliers and artifacts of the past, or stopping in for a movie at one of the art theaters, or window shopping, or the Cooper Hewitt — any one of a number of things, infinite variety.

Jack introduced her to Yorkville, the Yorkville he knew, and she helped him food shop at Schaller & Weber, where he ordered in German: *"Eine pfund süss Butter," "Halbe pfund Schinken, bitte."* It was certainly more than a stone's throw from where he lived, but he said it was worth it for the quality of the food, with which she heartily agreed, sampling the ham and the pure, sweet butter.

There was also, on Third Avenue, a bakery, Mrs. Herbst, where they went occasionally for its adamantly old-world atmosphere. It was many-mirrored, with a lincruster ceiling, its vast front counter offering all sorts of goodies, like Demel's in Vienna. Mrs. Herbst was really Vienna transplanted, a chip off the old block, and you never, ever heard English spoken there. Christine knew she would never dare to go in alone, she was sure she'd be shown the door if she had the temerity to ask for some of the bakery goods in English, as the women behind the counter were so intimidating.

But they did have mouth-watering wares: Rigo Yanchi, Dobos torte and Sacher torte, kipferln,

Milles feuilles, pig's ears and Florentines and whatall. In the rear were a few booths and tables, painted in a French blue, a dewy red rose in a bud vase on each. There you sat, after selecting your rich tidbit from the counter, chatting over Kaffee mit Schlagobers, whiling away a half hour.

New places for Christine, new scenes and ambiances. The Cafe Geiger, on Eighty-sixth Street, was another discovery for her. Jack said he really preferred Eine Kleine Konditorei, but he got a kick out of saying to her over the phone, "How about meeting me at the Geiger counter?"

The Geiger too had its big, overflowing display of sinful pastries for the Yorkville sweet tooth, its glass case presided over by starched and officious ladies with accents you could cut with a knife. Jack said they too were horrid if you didn't speak German, tried to pretend you weren't there, but then that was true of most of the tradespeople in this area, they looked down their noses at "foreigners," as if Yorkville was a separate and sanctified principality, like Vatican City.

Beyond the Geiger counter there were three or four tables for someone who wanted beer and a sandwich, or just a cup of coffee, then a short flight of steps led up to the main dining room, quite large and with every table swathed in a white linen cloth. The napkins were linen as well, very large and smelling slightly of the laundry room. The men and women dining at these tables were distinctly middle-European, as if they had just been imported from Berlin or Vienna or Munich, and they ate heavy lunches, taking their sweet time about it and conversing in German or Wienerische or Hungarian. Mostly these people looked coldly arrogant, with the women wearing hats that seemed peculiarly out of style. The men were brusque and peremptory when giving their order.

Jack said to listen for someone asking for Wiener Schnitzel. "Why?" Christine asked him. He said they all sounded like Peter Sellers doing his Viennese turn, but particularly with that dish. "They say 'buttocked,'" he told her. "Wiener Schnitzel viss buttocked noodles . . . ssss."

Her laugh sounded like a small explosion in the quiet restaurant. There were generally some thirty-odd diners at the white-clothed tables during a lunch hour, but their conversations were habitually in low tones, as if some secret agent might be listening, or perhaps a member of the Gestapo. Except for an occasional ebullient gentleman who had imbibed too freely on Löwenbrau, the Geiger dining room was stiffly genteel, many a pinkie extended with the coffee cup.

It was another world, really, though Jack said much of it was going by the board, with speculators and developers buying up whole blocks of the old tenements to replace them with high-rises. "I never gave much thought to it when I found myself down here," Christine confessed. "I just noticed that it was rather swarming, and quite ugly—you know, a Coney Island air. I guess I thought of it in terms of an eyesore. You've made me see it differently, and I enjoy it very much. It's like something out of Grosz, particularly in the stores and restaurants."

"It was a hotbed of Nazi Bunds at one time, of course. World War II. We weren't around then, but I guess the Teutonic mentality at its worst was very much in evidence. Well, never mind, you try to forget about that, and the thing is it's so damned easy. Anyway, I like it down here because it's not chic and glossy and artificial. They're mostly working class people, rough and ready, and you can believe New York's still a neighborhood kind of place, there's something so inhuman about the rest of it."

"There's Ninth Avenue and little Italy, the Village, still, or a lot of it, the West Village."

"Yeah, but where you live, where you walk around, you want a certain chummy coziness. Well, a home ground, like the *arrondissements* of Paris."

Jack said he liked to walk along Second Avenue from Eighty-sixth to Seventy-second Street on a Sunday morning. "When it's sunny, particularly. Then you get the feeling of old times, the turn of the century, Edward Hopper. Old red brick buildings, like some small town in middle America, and not very many people on the street. It must have been nice years ago, the clop-clop of horses drawing a milk wagon, the steam of fresh horse dung on cobbles—I like the smell of horse dung."

"I guess I do too, because I like the smell of stables. I used to go horseback in Central Park —oh, for about a year. With some friends. There was a riding academy on the West Side, I suppose it's still there. I wore jodhpurs, I looked pretty snazzy."

"I bet you did, you little witch."

"And I loved the smell in the place, I thought it was very refreshing. Very earthy."

"I like the smell of fresh gasoline too."

"As to that, I'm not sure."

"Oh, it's pure and pungent, it's only from the exhaust that it becomes putrid." He pointed out a cubbyhole of a store, its window dim and fly-specked. "That's my typewriter place, where I get it overhauled when necessary."

"Is that often, Jack?"

"Not now, the one I have is new. Or newish. The old one was a Smith Corona, I was very attached to it, but I worked it to death and the keys started popping off. First one, and I had that replaced, then a second one I had to see to. In the end, six of them gave up the ghost, just flew off. That was it. I think I got around fifty dollars off the new one, which was gratifying, and now I'm off the hook."

"Use it in good health."

"Both mine and the machine's, I hope. This guy's an old German, a character, he's straight out of Graham Greene. So's the shop. You get the feeling it's a 'safe' place, where spies and counterspies shamble in with hats pulled over their eyes and weather-stained trench coats. Some password or other. 'The cuckoo sings in the spring . . .' Eyes meeting eyes and a quick exchange of something—a microfilm concealed in a tube of toothpaste. Then the guy in the trench coat slips out a back door."

"Does the typewriter man look like Sidney Greenstreet?"

"No no, not at all. He's small and slight and short, with a goatee and heavy eyebrows. He looks quite a bit like Dr. Ohly."

"Dr. Who?"

"My father's eye doctor. Piercing gaze. I always found Dr. Ohly a bit sinister."

"Jack, you're a hell of a lot of fun."

"I try," he said modestly.

Carrying packages, leaving Yorkville and heading for Sixty-first Street. Up the stone steps and then the inside carpeted stairs. Setting the packages down and putting the groceries away in Jack's fridge, in the overhead cabinets, the toilet things in the bathroom. The newspaper, *TV Guide, New Yorker* in the magazine rack, then sitting down opposite each other at the kitchen table, tired from their ramblings and chatting idly.

Something said would lead to a silly joke or anecdote or reminiscence. Sometimes a *very* silly joke, springing into Jack's head in what seemed an arbitrary way, but which was generally connected to a previous observation. "This young girl came home at seven in the morning after staying out all night. She was confronted by her fuming father. 'Good morning, daughter of Satan,' he says. 'Good morning, father,' daughter replies."

"I heard that when I was I think about ten years old."

"Screw you."

"No, screw you."

"I said it first."

"All right, you win. What led up to that dumb story?"

266

"Let's see—oh yes, you said it was a wise child who knew its own father."

"Reasonable enough," she conceded.

Palindromes, he was fond of palindromes. The only one Christine knew before she met Jack was the classic "Able was I ere I saw Elba." He had an awesome collection, of which her favorite was "Naomi, sex at noon taxes, I moan." "Who makes these up, I wonder?" she pondered.

"People with nothing better to do."

"I guess. Did you ever try your hand at it?"

"Sure. I failed. It just kept me awake that night, trying to work something out. It's bad enough as it is. I write dialogue in my sleep. I'm not kidding. In my sleep I see typed sheets of paper. Occupational hazard."

He was a wonderful, endlessly absorbing companion. There was a bird in residence in some tree or other, he told her. "I can hear it in the mornings. First comes the sneeze from next door. Then the bird starts in. Same old refrain, tirelessly repeated. *Stop it, stop it, stop, stop, stop*, it says. It's like some prissy housewife being goosed by her spouse. "Stop it, stop it for goodness sake, Henry, not in front of the children."

He had an imaginative ear. Mendelssohn's Reformation Symphony, he informed her, had a passage in which the instruments clearly sounded the words "Good afternoon, good afternoon, good afternoon, good afternoon."

"I perforce have to wait for it," he said. " 'And good afternoon to you, Felix,' I respond. It would be impolite not to return the greeting."

Entertaining him in turn, she did her takeoffs of Brando and Barbara Walters, Jackie Onassis, John Belushi. "Cagney?" she said disdainfully when he suggested it. "Everyone does Cagney, I wouldn't lower myself."

Preludes and preambles to lovemaking, and after the lovemaking sitting up against the pillows, hair tumbled, played out and resting, a head on a shoulder, clasp of hands. It was good to be in bed with him, not doing anything even, just being close to him in his skin: she felt a new respect for bodies, the vulnerable bodies under the clothing, their demands and bothersome functions, and the restraints imposed on them, the pretenses respectability and taste dictated.

You said of someone that he/she had a good mind, but you didn't say they had a good bod, unless it was a film star or a stripper or Mr. America. Suits and ties met dresses and scarves: you recognized a friend on the street from something he/she was wearing. And all the while women walked about with Maxi pads, or a tampon whose string dangled: you never were aware of that. Men got in the wrong position and the apparatus became uncomfortably malplaced, but if they had good manners they didn't publicly squirm it back, so you never knew that either. You told people you had a headache, a tummyache, but you would never announce that you had a sore rectum or an irritated vulva: you might be in agony with a need to urinate, but you wouldn't consider it legitimate distress even if it hurt very much, and you'd go to any lengths to hide your plight, probably let your bladder burst, requiring a hospital stay. Only small children were not ashamed of the machinery of their bodies, a state quickly outgrown as they learned, from their elders, to hold it in low esteem.

Decorum was one thing, shame another. Or contempt, devaluation. It was because Christine, for really the first time, was able to shed herself in lovemaking unabashedly and with a hearty enthusiasm, that her preoccupation with the body which gave her such overwhelming pleasure — *carnal* pleasure — was so profound. Perhaps, she thought, she had grown up to it. There had never been anything wrong with her libido: she could be strongly attracted, but it was the wanting more than the getting that lured her. The getting generally had failed to measure up. She had a short attention span, it seemed, as in mathematics, when it came down to sexual performance.

Before she met Carl there had been a few experiments — some of them little more than sophomoric fumblings — with young and not very proficient men, but it hadn't been the men, it had been her own self-awareness that wrecked the sex, a kind of "let's get it over with" damper that got in the way of things. Or she would start thinking of something else. She had been accused of scratching her nose at the "crucial moment," which obviously had been crucial for him, but for her simply a welcome windup of this tiresome, disappointing business. Give me your undivided attention was the watchword, and rightly so, but since all the touted sensations seemed to be taking place in someone else and not in herself, it was difficult to comply. You can lead a horse to water but you can not make him drink.

As for Carl, she had enjoyed, still did, his nearness, and during the early years of joyous felicity had met him halfway. As far as she knew she had never scratched her nose, not even when she had a pile of undies soaking in the washbasin. He was the first man who gave her love and honor and respect without infatuation: other men went overboard for the perfection of her facial features and the color of her hair—that was, when they were not eyeing her legs and her bustline. He treated her as an adult personality and as a woman to be admired for her liveliness and sense of fun and, according to him, her goodness. Suddenly she had a partner, a very decent guy who saw things in her other men hadn't, and he didn't keep saying, God, you're so gorgeous, or surreptitiously put his hands here and put his hands there and pant in her ear.

They "went together" and met for dinner when Carl could manage it (he was doing his internship) and twice attended the opera: they saw *Boris Godounov* and *Forza del Destino*. She was living in the apartment at Ninety-second Street, but they didn't go whole hog in their lovemaking, even though they had complete privacy. The first time they did it was in his room, the size of a walk-in closet, at Montefiore, where there were items like a brain pickled in a big Mayonnaise jar, anatomy casts, great medical tomes that must have weighed ten pounds each, a skeleton with a silly smirk on its wobbly skull and a cot bed so slenderly proportioned that almost any normal person would have fallen to the floor just by turning over.

It was what they coupled on, however, and they managed exceedingly well. Her wholehearted attention was with him, no diversionary thoughts, and while she failed to achieve orgasm (hell, she didn't expect to, she half believed it was a myth) she was glad and happy and not one bit turned off, and he was so clean and fresh-smelling, nice and immaculate, and he didn't say the way dreary drips were wont to, "Did you come? Did you? *Did you come?*"

She knew she would marry him. If she hadn't been sure before she was that night. He couldn't even take her home, poor thing, being on call: she cabbed back to Ninety-second Street all the way from the Bronx. She felt secure and shielded forevermore from harm. She had Carl now, and the whole rest of her life was no longer a stretch of years with a question mark, but laid out and designed, rosy and glowing, everything was okeydokey.

Then when he didn't want to wait, but instead to be married as soon as he transferred to his third year residency at Cornell Medical, dissension raised its ugly head. That was when she got so cross and upset and everything began to get colored gray, and she didn't see him anymore because he told her he would bide his time, but she would have to be the one to make the overtures if she changed her mind. It was money, of course, he was paid a pittance in his internship and she would have to give up the apartment on Ninety-second Street because there was insufficient closet space, insufficient walking space for two, insufficient everything. She went down with a crash, started crying at the office file cabinets at work; it was horrible.

And of course she couldn't stand it. Neither could her mother, whose telephone calls became increasingly shrill. "Christine Elliott, you must be out of your head, a wonderful man like that, will you come to your *senses*!"

"It's me," she said over the phone. That was, after cooling her heels for about fifteen minutes, on hold and waiting for him to answer the beeper, also the paging system, she could hear it over the wires. "Dr. Jennings. Dr. Jennings . . ."

"I was wrong," she said when his voice finally came. "We'll do it your way, Carl."

So it was the two of them again; he seemed to be the other part of her and there was never again any thought of division. Bemused as she was now, in these latter and bewitching days of love, laughter and enchantment, there lay beyond it a reality she very carefully put aside, as in a vault, for safekeeping. She had locked it up, nobody could steal it, and it was intact.

What she felt for Carl was firm and solid and well established. It wasn't, never had been, anything like what she felt for Jack Allerton. This was the romance she had never had, it was exactly that, a romance, an enrapturing poem of love, with a fragility about it that haunted her. What is perfect is destructible — even diamonds, it had lately been revealed, were not forever. Was every beautiful thing doomed to fade and die? Well, of course a diamond was a coarse comparison, it had lustre and light but not the warmth and vibrancy of a human body, with its incredible intricacies, its network of veins and arteries, its ligaments, tissues, bones, glands and ganglia, all of these meshing pieces and parts sheathed, in the most masterly way, with muscle and fasciae and then layered with skin: no man-made material could approximate the skin of a man's body or a woman's body.

It had never been Carl's body Christine prized, it had never threaded through her dreams or seemed a miracle of creation. He was a big, sturdy, strong and comforting man, sitting across a table from her, going places with her, making babies with her, coming home from the office with a smiling hello, darling.

With Jack it was different. Walking home when she left him, she stifled laughter at something he had said, or they had both said, and a block later after successfully controlling this untimely mirth, would see before her—as if it were actually there, right out on the street, Lexington Avenue—his naked form limned on the horizon, the way he lay after coitus and sliding off her to relieve her of his pressure, arms outstretched on the pillow, legs spread, chest heaving, ribs and flat belly and navel, loins bathed in sweat and semen. The armpit hair, the luxuriant sprout at the crotch, the penis, having done its stint, shrunken and spent, faintly rosy.

The apparition vanished, or was banished, when she went through that outside door to the lobby of the Colonnade, and the transition to the other

Christine, the one who was married to Carl Jennings, took place. "Hi, Jimmy," in the elevator, then her key in the lock. Getting out of her street clothes and into pants and a shirt, opening the door of the fridge. It was like coming home from a job. Or it was like going to a job after hours of joyous freedom. Braising the eye of round, washing the lettuce. Coming down.

Carl arriving. "How was your day?"

"Fine. Yours?"

Bruce joining them, his day at the park concession over. "Something smells good."

"Sauerbraten."

"It smells like pot roast."

"Which it is, only with vinegar it's sauerbraten. Want to make something out of it?"

"You're cute, Mother. Can I help?"

"Not yet, dear. You can set the table later. Nothing to do now."

Even if you weren't going to see him tomorrow, or the day after that as well, perhaps, there would be his voice on the phone in the morning, it meant a lot. Even just his voice. He would say something amusing and she would laugh, then his own rumbling laugh would come over the wires. The sound of his voice would stay with her all day, in her ears and mind: she hoped it was the same for him, that what she had said and the way she said it would linger for him too, through all the day's hours.

14.

The first thing to do when she walked into Jack's apartment was to go to his desk, it was almost a compulsion. She had to see if the pile of typed sheets was increasing noticeably. A way to ease her conscience, she knew. If she saw a substantial rise in the stack she felt less guilty. He was spending time with her but he was also adding to his output.

"I think it's growing, Jack."

"It's grown by sixty-four pages since you were here."

"That's pretty good, isn't it?"

"That's damned good. What do you want, blood?"

"When are you going to let me read the books you've got out? You promised."

"Not at the moment."

"*Why* not? You said you weren't ashamed of them. Anyway, why should you be ashamed of them? Were they pornographic?"

He laughed. "No, they were far from that. I did have offers to do a line of raunchy stuff, it's wanted, sells well, plenty of demand. You write children's books, hard-core and science fiction, you're in business. I can't do any of the aforementioned. Sci fi—nothing is more alien to me. A pertinent adjective, isn't it, aliens from outer space? Aliens from outer space put me into a doze, they have no sense of humor in any of those yarns, Pompous and orotund or wearyingly diabolical."

"You never read comic books when you were a kid? That's un-American."

"The funny papers in the newspaper, that was it. I was a little snob, didn't you know that? I did read the Fu Manchu books, though. And my grandfather had a whole collection of books by a man named Karl May, a German author who wrote about the American West, cowboys and Indians. Old Sure Hand, old Fire Hand. I loved those. That was my mother's father."

"The one that was Czech."

"Yeah."

"You said the books you had published were suspense. Crime?"

"No. I mean, not police stuff, not procedurals. There are specialists in that genre, Wambaugh, Hunter, et al. And of course that wonder of wonders Simenon. I didn't do anything painstaking like that. A complex character with a psychological blemish, a frailty, a moral defect. Plot based on human weakness, mainly a character study of a soul gone wrong. No supermind solving the riddle, elementary, my dear Watson, nothing like that. Very primitive stuff, but it taught me some discipline."

"It also brings you some checks once in a while."

"Yup, it does that."

"You said children's books were a fertile field. Yes, I can believe that. I'd make a guess that those, plus cookbooks, top the field in overall sales."

"About right. Science fiction's right up there, as I said, and then I guess girlish gothics and those period epics with crinolines and bursting bosoms."

"And the raunchy stuff? Where does that stand?"

"Nickel and dime. It's women who buy books, and women want make-believe. They don't want it spelled out."

"But you said there was a demand for it."

"There is, but men won't shell out much for a book, they can get their kicks from the smut magazines, why pay $4.95 for a paperback? So the list price is low, peanuts really, and they can pick up four or five at a time. Which means that the author's advance is peanuts too. In order to make anything worthwhile out of it he has to turn them out a dozen or so a year. It's sweat work."

"Is that why you turned down writing for the market?"

"Hell no. Look, spelling it out is tough, it takes either a spectacularly dirty mind or a better writer than I am. Try and think up new and original ideas about the act of fornicating. Jeez, some of the stuff I read to brief myself on what they want — absolutely hilarious. I remember one that had me heehawing for days on end, I'd wake up in the middle of the night guffawing."

He chuckled. "Fantasies, you understand. Who has fantasies like that outside of a prepubescent kid with snot in his nose I couldn't venture to say. In this little opus a grocery boy has a high old time with some gal he delivers to. I think one day she meets him at the door in the altogether or something, and that paves the way for the didos that follow. None of your tired old banging away, no, that's too tame. A lot of eerie goings-on, but the really imaginative stuff is concerned with the victuals he delivers. This kid has really exotic ideas, such as stuffing food up her privates, hamburger meat, calves' liver. Like that. Yeah, and I do remember that a grapefruit was involved, I think that was an afterthought."

He shook his head. "I felt like asking some physician. Could you do that? A pound of calves' liver, mind you, plus another pound of ground beef. And the grapefruit besides? Also, this woman was partial to walking around with all those provisions nestled within; she got a big charge out of that.

Now you tell me, Christine, wouldn't they fall out? Or would the grapefruit act as a kind of plug?"

She was rocking with laughter. "Yeah," he said, shrugging. "Can you picture me wracking my brains to think up things like that?"

She finally wiped her eyes. "What I'd like to know is did she feed the stuff to her family afterwards? If so, the Board of Health should get after her. And did she eat it herself? Somehow there are cannibalistic overtones there."

"Also, was she able to get it all *out*? I just don't see how, without an X-ray picture, she could ever be sure. Besides, there were additional items on other days. I think a few Bermuda onions featured at one time. Don't you think she could get a bad infection that way? Possibly even gangrene."

"Well, Jack, don't ever get so desperate that you have to write raunchy novels. If that wouldn't put you in the loony bin I don't know what would. I'm not sure I'll ever have grapefruit again."

"It left me with a faint aversion to them myself."

Ah, yes, there was a lot of laughter along with the lovemaking, no lack of it. Walks and talks and fondness and laughter. Just the same Christine knew that Jack must have beleaguering thoughts about the position she had placed him in, that of a man compliant with a status quo which stripped him of superiority. And he with his psyche not in the best shape. *What time do you have to leave?* He always said that casually, without any noticeable trace of irony or anger, but she had begun to inwardly cringe, to feel that he was punishing her in the only way he knew how. That he was remind-

279

ing her of her deliberate and continued betrayal, and she herself had come to see that she had been incorrect in her assumption that Carl was the one who was getting the dirty end of the stick. Not true, she realized finally, or only technically true. It would have been so if her relationship with Jack Allerton was based solely on sex, a roll in the hay, a bang, laying and getting laid. When in fact it was being, in almost every sense, a wife to two men, rather than a wife to one and mistress to another.

It would be galling to any proud man, knowing that he was lavishing himself on a woman who was not separated, divorced or even disaffected with her own going concern, her marriage. She had never given Jack any reason to believe that the physical part of her life with Carl was over—or even distasteful—so it would follow as the night the day that she was in Carl's arms when his arms wanted her, which she was. Nor did it present any real problem for her (which probably meant she *was* of low moral fiber). It came as naturally for her to satisfy her husband's desires as it would have to give an ailing child the proper attention—a back rub, propped up pillows, soup and toast fingers.

All very well, but from Jack's point of view it would be of little comfort and, perversely enough, she wouldn't respect him if it did. She was sometimes, in a strange and eerily discomfiting way, like a spectator watching the progress of a play, or else as if she were cogitating a case presented to her for arbitration—an amicus curiae, a friend of the court: clearly the facts as furnished indicated

280

malicious mischief?

"I'll have dinner with you tonight," she told Jack on a day that was so particularly sparkling that she knew as soon as she greeted it in the morning she was not going to leave him at the usual time this afternoon. It was a day that made you think of your childhood, with everything seeming fresh and new and almost unbearably exciting, the way things used to seem then.

"Unless, of course, you're tied up this evening."

"You'll really stay?"

She said quickly, "Not overnight—"

"I didn't expect that. I might want it, but I don't expect it."

He was in the bed, waiting for her. "But you'll be here until much later on?"

"All day. We won't have to think of the time. Let's be together in bed for a while, then we can take a shower, we've never showered together, or are you anti such familiarity?"

"A man and a woman taking a shower together? I can't believe such a lewd invitation. Maybe, though if I steel myself—"

"You remember those buttons. 'Save water, shower with a friend.' "

"Yeah," he said, smiling anticipatively. "We ain't never done that, have we? Hey, that's nice."

"After that, how about going for a walk, let's go to Gracie Square, sit by the water."

"I could go for that."

"We'll come back with a fresh sunburn."

"Nice. Where shall we have lunch?"

"We can pick up some deli stuff and have it here."

"Whatever you say."

"Actually, it's whatever you say. I'm only making suggestions."

"I like you to make suggestions. Okay. Bed right now. Then a walk, sit in the sun, watch the Circle Line boats. A deli for lunch stuff. After lunch, what?"

"I sort of thought maybe bed again? Unless you'd rather sit on the sofa and discuss literature."

"I'd naturally prefer the latter, but we must please the lady. I know how avid you always are to get my hands on your body."

He laughed. "What I meant to say was get your hands on *my* body."

"Just for that we'll sit on the sofa and discuss literature."

"The hell we will."

"I wonder if we're overdoing it."

"That's something that never crossed *my* mind."

"Here we are, on this beautiful day, burying ourselves in bed."

"After we bury ourselves for a while we're going out for a walk into the beautiful day," he reminded her. "What more do you want?"

"That recurring phrase of Faulkner's. 'Fornication, sin and death.' I guess it made an impression on me all those years ago."

"Ever notice that Faulkner used the word 'ratiocination' a lot?"

"Yes, a lot. I wonder why."

"He liked it."

"He seemed to, yes."

"Wait," Jack said. She was undressed, ready to

join him in the bed. "Don't move."

She stood, arrested in motion. "What is it?"

"I just want to look at you. Just for a minute. Stand there. You're so lovely."

"You're making me self-conscious."

"Don't you know how yummy you are?"

"If you think so I'm glad."

"You know what I like to see you do? It's when you're wearing earrings, and you get undressed and then the last thing you do is take off the earrings. It's the most graceful, feminine gesture, the way your body moves, your hands move. Reaching up and taking off an earring. Then reaching up and taking off the other one."

"It sends you, does it?"

Grinning up at her. "Get down here, you witch."

"That was my original intention."

He didn't plunge into her prematurely anymore. He was disciplined now, artful, it was like being on a surfboard with him, breasting the waves. It was like learning to dance properly, she supposed, learning with the same partner, following the will and whim of another body, so that at last you became like one skilled entity. It was wonderful.

They didn't look for inventions, make a production of it: whatever they did was without thought or plan. They offered freely, took freely. Discussing erotic conversations, they ended up snickering. Jack said, "I guess I'm not geared to it and apparently neither are you. I guess we're not infantile enough. I know there are people who say things like, 'What am I doing to you? You're fucking me. What am I fucking you with? You're fucking me with your prick, your joystick, your big, swollen cock, fuck me, fuck me . . .' "

"I think it takes rather an unnecessary amount of time, if you want to know."

"Yeah, me too. Anyway, it's so damned manufactured."

He said there were also people who pretended they'd just met in a bar or a cafe, something like that, made believe it was a pickup. "Maybe they'd been to bed together for about a hundred thousand times and anything to make it something other than the same old thing. Desperation time. Also the rape fantasy. She sits there in their apartment over a drink and he lunges at her. 'How dare you,' she says. 'You asked me for a drink and now you—' "

"She's shocked to the core—"

"And scared, very scared. He pulls her dress down at the neck. Now she's terrified. 'Please, please—' "

"But he's merciless."

"Absolutely. He's going to take her by force. She can see it in his eyes, his teeth are drawn back . . ."

"She's going to be ravished!"

He laughed. "Maybe it works for some idiots. I was assured it did by a guy in my office, he went into great detail."

"Is that what men talk about in offices? I thought that kind of chitchat took place in locker rooms."

"You must be kidding. It's standard water cooler stuff."

But it was true that she and Jack didn't need to rely on artificial stimuli when the chemistry of their bodies and minds was so potent: it was clear that Jack enjoyed and feasted on her, that a sudden caress—idly, and in passing—sent the blood coursing through his veins and ventricles. He often erected with her hand slipped inside his shirt, she loved to do that, see him lose his preoccupation with something abruptly, feel his quick reaction.

As for herself, she was a hundred percent male-oriented, but had never felt she was phallus-worshipping, yet the fact was that the mass between his legs—or even just thinking about it—was very nearly an obsession, there was something almost embarrassing about it. She found herself, when alone, cupping her hands as if to imprison the weight of balls and penis between them. This fixation traveled into her dreams: she woke recalling night visions of male parts, like the exaggerated statuary in the Archaeological Museum at Naples, relics of libidinous Pompeii, those Priapus idolators who had tirelessly carved male genitalia in stone and marble and travertine, penis after penis in a state of upthrust tumescence, bigger and better their motto. The Neopolitans were still turning them out to this very day, on an assembly line basis, you could buy them at the souvenir stalls, take one home for a tittering conversation piece.

"I don't like the soap," she complained, when they got into the shower. "And the spray's too forceful. Hey! I don't want to get my hair wet! You should have a shower cap."

"How can you take a shower without getting

your hair wet?"

"I told you. Just hold my head away. Like this. The rest of me will get the water. Only turn down the spray a bit."

"How are we going to have exotic little adventures in here if there are all these prohibitions?"

"We'll just be like two dear little children."

His laugh echoed against the tiles. "You're the weirdest woman in the world, I could eat you up. Oh, and say, what's the matter with the soap?"

"It's drying," she said tersely. "Bad for the skin. You should use Keri or Lubriderm, I'll bring you some."

"Let me tell you, no gal I ever showered with objected to the quality of my soap."

"I'll wash your mouth out with this if you start talking about other women."

"Jealous, huh? Ah, the beautiful women I've showered with, m'dear. Fifty beautiful girls, fifty. A cast of thousands. The wolf of Sixty-first Street."

"Open your mouth!"

"You shove that cake of soap in my mouth, I'll stick your head under the water."

"Okay, uncle. Enough! My lovely curls—"

"This is fun," he said. "It's not ball-aching, but it's a hell of a lot of fun, being a dear little child with you."

"See? There are other ways to entertain oneself."

Drying off afterward, toweling. One of Jack's oversized bath towels, which today were a deep royal blue. "You need towels?" she asked him. "You need bed linen? I like to buy you things, you know. Please tell me what you need, Jack."

286

"A mink coat," he said. "Full-length."

"I'll have it sent over in the morning. *Seriously*. What are you in short supply on?"

"Why don't you shut your yap? Save your pennies for Christmas."

"Okay, what do you want for Christmas?"

He regarded her. "Oddly enough, I was thinking about that the other day," he said. "What I'm going to give you for Christmas. In a way I can hardly wait for it. It's been many a year since it meant something to me."

"Really, Jack?"

"Ah, yes. Well, there are a lot of shopping days until then, gives me time to think up something Christineish. By the way, let's not forget to get you a shower cap on our walk."

"And some decent soap."

"Nag, nag, nag. Get dressed, babe, it's Gracie Square time."

Walking over, the sun high in the sky, it was early, they had hours ahead of them. Passing Henderson Place, those magnificent old houses, ivy-trimmed, austere. Then the little park that led to the boardwalk, which was trimmed up with strollers and baby carriages and kids on roller skates, toddlers pedaling away on scooters. The sun on the water, small craft gliding along, the bridges that spanned the rippling blue expanse.

"I used to come here on Sunday mornings with my *Times*," Christine said when they sat down on one of the benches. "Deepen my summer tan at the same time. It's a nice place to have handy."

"I came here when the tall ships passed. Bi-

287

centennial year. Great show, that was something to take your mind off your troubles."

"Were you having troubles then, Jack?"

"Yes, quite a few."

Maybe, she thought, it pinpointed when the breakup came, Jack's breakup, his marriage pfft. It sounded rather like that. He didn't say. He never said anything, or at least hadn't to date. "There's that park on Sutton Place too," she said. "Very small, very pretty, do you know that one?"

"No, I guess not. There's John Jay, but farther down. I guess I haven't come across it."

"We'll go there sometime."

"Cigarette?"

"No, I'm too comfy to bother. Thanks."

"What a day."

"I love the sun. I love it. I know people who couldn't care less about the weather. So it's raining, they say. What's wrong with rain? So it's overcast. You wouldn't want it to be sunny all the time? But I would!"

"I'm not keen on cloudbursts myself," Jack said. "I even decided against basing myself in London because I wasn't sure I could stick the gray of it. The pea soupers and the drizzles."

"You did consider living in England, then?"

"I considered a lot of things. Get away seemed to be a solution. Most of us have periods when we want to run. So I guess at one time I wanted to run. I didn't get very far, I'm still in the place I started in."

"So am I."

"We could be in a worse place. New York seems

like home, I guess it always will."

"Oh, by the way, Jack. I've been to London three times, I never ran into a pea soup fog. Believe that if you will."

"Oh, I don't think they're all they're cracked up to be. I think they're mostly in Hitchcock thrillers. At least I've never been totally fogbound whenever I was there, not the kind where you can't see your hand in front of your face. Plenty of pouring rain, though. I find it rather daunting, and it would definitely add to your cleaning bills if you lived there."

"Suppose you made a big haul with some book of yours. Maybe the one you're writing now. More money than you ever dreamed of. I assume you'd have your *pièd a terre* here, in New York, and then what else besides? A lovely little chalet in Switzerland? A villa in Nice?"

He thought it over. "Both," he decided. "Let's see, now. Oh yeah, Fiesole. A villa in Fiesole, naturally. With that view. That view . . ."

"I remember that view well," she said. "Yes, I can picture you up there, in one of those crumbly-stuccoed houses with the red-tiled roofs, sitting in the garden typing, with a bottle of Punt é Mes on a table. You've grown a beard, and your face is now a famous face and you, too, have grown fond of the word 'ratiocination' and—"

"Can you tell me when all this is going to happen, I'd just as soon have a little advance notice. And how do I look with a beard display, adorable?"

"Most impressive. There goes one of your Circle

Line boats. People on the deck waving as if it were the *Q.E. II*. Bless them, they seem to be having a fine time."

"I don't suppose you're hungry?"

"Which means you are. Am I a selfish slob to take up a whole day of yours like this? How can you become famous sitting by the water in Gracie Square?"

"What makes you think that, Christine? That I want to become famous."

"You said it yourself. Nobody knows my name."

"Salinger's a household word, but he shuns the limelight. To the point of paranoia. Do you really think I'm the type to go on talk shows and bare my chest like Hemingway?"

"Why not, you've got a dandy chest."

He laughed, played with her hand. "Famous is fine, I'd settle for that, Chris. Nothing wrong with a few whiskers, either, maybe some day I'll cultivate a bunch. Right now I'm thinking about finding a deli and then going home and feeding our faces. We want to have plenty of time to discuss literature on the sofa before thinking of dinner."

"There seems to be a lot of eating on the agenda," she observed. "Where are we going for dinner, do you know?"

"Yeah. That is, if it's all right with you. Is it all right with you?"

"Just so long as it isn't a vegetarian place."

"It is. How'd you guess?"

"Okay. If you insist."

"It's a place called Eduardo's, to be serious. I

found it awhile ago, it doesn't look like much but it's great, I think very highly of it. Practically right around the corner from where I live. So okay?"

"Certainly, fine."

There was a delicatessen opposite Schaller & Weber, they went in and bought pastrami, potato salad, a jar of dill pickles. Jack said he had rye bread in the house, sweet butter. They sat in their ladderback chairs polishing it off, then had coffee. After that Jack led her to the bedroom. "Lie down, I want to talk to you," he said with a leer.

"It was nice down by the water," she said, when they were lying together. "I'll remember it, you know. There are some things you remember more than others."

"Yes, I'll think of that too."

"And taking that silly shower. Goddamn it, I forgot to get the soap!"

"The whole day blown to smithereens," he murmured. "You forgot the soap."

"Where is this Eduardo's?" she asked, when they at last got up and turned on lamps. "It's Italian, one gathers."

"First Avenue, Fifty-ninth. Yes, of course Italian."

She was in the bathroom, at the mirror. "My hair. I look like a Forty-second Street hooker."

"You look like Primavera."

"Some Primavera. At my age."

"Your age. You should know from age. I love your hair that way."

"Like this? A trollop out of Hogarth?"

"Do Marlon Brando."

"Shut your bloody trap. May I borrow your comb? Or maybe your egg beater?"

"I don't have a comb. I do have an egg beater, yes, I'll go get it."

"Naturally I was kidding. Naturally I have a comb, would you mind bringing me my handbag?"

"Born to fetch and carry, that's me."

"Never mind, I'll get it. I hate people who say would you mind bringing me this, would you mind bringing me that . . ."

"Shut up, here it is."

"Grudgingly, I notice."

"You're a crazy woman. When they made you, they—"

"Broke the mold. I know, I've heard that before about myself."

"You realize it's true."

"Listen, Jack. I'm somebody's mother, I really would like a little respect."

He sat on the edge of the tub laughing. She could see him in the mirror, grinning away. She glanced at her watch. It was after seven. They had had a whole day.

And now it was almost gone.

When they left she was all smooth and combed and fresh-faced. "What is it you use on your mouth?" Jack asked her. "It's not lipstick. Not the general kind, anyway."

"A Germaine Monteuil product. Designed to make the most of what nature gave you. You approve?"

"It's luscious. That wet look."

"It's not supposed to look wet! Just faintly moist!"

"That's what I said, faintly moist."

Going down the carpeted stairs. They looked different at this time of the evening, the color of the carpet subtly changed. There were round hanging bulbs at each landing, lit now, a soft light. "This is a steal what you've got here," Christine said. "When I think of some of the dumps Rodney and I went into. I wouldn't put my worst enemy into any of them."

"It's a good place, I'm pleased as punch. Look at this, we're going out to dinner for the first time. Will wonders never cease? Christ, I'm way up, like over and beyond the Van Allen belt. Dinner with Christine Jennings, who'd believe it?"

"Do they have soft-shelled crabs at Eduardo's?"

"They do indeed."

She called the house, pleasantly explaining that one of the girls had suggested staying "in town" for dinner. "You don't mind, Carl?"

"Have a good time, of course I don't mind."

Years ago, saying to Mother, "I won't be home to dinner, some friends—just dinner, that's all."

"Don't be too late, Christine."

The same sense of adventure, the same feeling that life held infinite promises, the bright night lights, dark pools of shadow where the light didn't penetrate, walking along arm in arm. "Balmy," Jack commented. "A balmy evening, listen to me with my eternal clichés."

"Well, it's balmy, who's criticizing? This is such fun."

There were cordial smiles at Eduardo's. Jack was

obviously a welcome guest, and there was a heady smell of garlic that greeted you when you opened the door and went inside. Very simpatico, and a jovial waiter who called her signora. *"Buona sera, signora."*

"No, not a martini," she said, when Jack gave the drink order. "I'll have a perfect Manhattan, because Italian restaurants know how to put together one of those."

"I'm learning something about you every day," he observed.

"But it's a fact. Dry vermouth and sweet vermouth, and they use the right brand for it, Stock's, I think. It's really my favorite drink, but you only get the real McCoy in an Eyetalian place."

When it arrived she took a sip and then circled two fingers in the air. "I told you so," she said triumphantly. To the waiter, "Couldn't be better, thanks, it's excellent."

"Bene, bene."

"So. What do you think of Eduardo's?" Jack demanded. "No plush and gilt-framed mirrors, but it's warm and welcoming, do you feel that?"

"Oh, yes, I like it very much. And thank God no piped music, though if they did have it it would probably be Italian, Neopolitan songs and so forth. I wouldn't mind that. Just the same I'd just as soon not have it, it's usually too loud anyway."

"I used to go to Monk's Court, music there, but on a stereo, and good stuff. Baroque, also Gregorian chants. Carl Orff too, *Carmina Burana.* You wouldn't mind that, would you?"

"No, I'd like that. Why that sort of thing? Oh,

Monks, I see. The motif, I take it."

"Naturally. The waiters wear rough-spun cassocks, rope-tied round the waist. They're all fat and jolly, like Friar Tuck."

"Good food?"

"*Very* old English, hearty fare, slabs of beef, Yorkshire pudding. Nice. You'd like it, want to go sometime?"

"If it's still in business, sure. So many places are going out of business. When were you there last?"

"About fifty years ago, come to think of it. I'll check it out."

"How about the food here, Jack? Veal piccata, I hope?"

"By all means. I thought you were set on the soft-shelled crabs."

"If the food's really good I'll have a hard time deciding. Italian's my favorite, but only when it's very special super duper."

"I would call the food here all of that."

"That good, huh? I guess I'm glad I came."

"I know someone else who is. Not mentioning any names."

"That's my Jack."

"*Your* Jack is right. I don't even ogle dames on the street anymore. That used to be one of my beloved pastimes."

"Their loss, my gain."

"You said once that you occasionally saw some man on the street, or on the bus . . . and were attracted to him. I remember that irked me very much."

"Did it really irk you? Forget it, Jack. I don't do

that anymore either."

"How can I believe you?"

"How can I believe *you?*"

"You have my word."

"You have mine. What's our waiter's name, do you know? He's eyeing us with a benevolent gaze, he seems to approve of our togetherness."

"He's probably spinning fantasies about what it would be like to take you to bed."

"Of course, why didn't I think of that? Why don't you go over and tell him what it's like?"

"Words would fail me."

"It would be the first time."

"I'm that verbose? Wrong again, you're the one who does the most talking."

"That's unfair. I'm a very good listener."

They smiled at each other. Unremarkable conversation, lovers' talk, silly, the two of them, fondly smirking—how wonderful it would be not to part at the end of the evening, just walk slowly back to Jack's place, have a nightcap and a few post mortems and then fall asleep together . . .

In the morning having him there, his warmth beside her.

They had another drink, this time scanning the menus as they downed it: Christine decided on the soft-shelled crabs after all. It was chicken cacciatore for Jack. She had a taste of it, it was delicious. A big, oregano-scented stuffed clam in its shell was added to each plate. Glancing up at the waiter, Christine felt sure it was an extra for them because he liked them.

"How's your crab?" Jack asked.

"Like poetry. Melt in your mouth. Here, try it."

He forked up a bit. "Yeah," he commented approvingly. "I told you, didn't I? Have some chicken."

"Great. Really great. Say, this is a find. And the clam. Fantastic. You're a good man to know, John Allerton."

"I have my talents."

Halfway through dinner the overhead lights dimmed. Jack's face, across from her, went darker and fainter. "Are you there?" she questioned.

"Yes, are you?"

"Could it be a power failure?"

"Some romantic you are. Atmosphere, my girl. Atmosphere."

"Oh, they always do that?"

"Yes, they always do. In a little while it will be dimmed some more. That's when everybody starts necking."

"Oh, it's *that* kind of place. I knew there must be some ulterior motives. Well, I like this light. Do I look mysterious and femme fatale this way?"

"You look like Ondine, under the sea."

"You look like the young Tolstoy, with your beard."

"Did the young Tolstoy sport a beard? I'm not sure. The beard again, huh? What is it, you want me to grow a beard?"

"Not until your *oeuvre* takes off. Stay the way you are."

"Thank you. It can't be the easiest thing eating Italian with a chin growth."

"I'm sure it wouldn't. This is lovely, Jack. I'm

having the most gorgeous time."

"Can we do it again?"

"Yes, darling. Sometime. Yes, we can and will."

"I hoped you'd say that."

"I suppose you knew I would."

"No. I didn't know that."

"We will come here again, Jack. Let's write off Monk's Court. I want to come here."

"So do I. They have a tasty rum cake, Chris. And the usual tortoni, spumone. That's about it."

"I guess it will be the spumone."

He put her in a cab afterwards. It was nearly eleven. "Talk to you in the morning."

"Yes. Jack, it was sublime."

"It was for me. Be careful, okay?"

"Yes, it is a splendid summer," she said to the cab driver. "Not too muggy so far, which is a blessing. Do you work nights as a rule?"

"As a rule," he agreed. "More money in it. Naturally more chance of being mugged and robbed. Killed, let's face it. You take your chances."

"Yes," she said soberly.

"City isn't getting any better."

"Unfortunately it isn't."

"I remember better. Other days, other times. What are you supposed to do, go to Arizona? Who's got the dough to do that? Anyway, this is my piece of the U.S.A. Which entrance, ma'am?"

"The one on the left, just head for the circular driveway, that's fine. How much do I owe you?"

"Two-ten."

"You made good time, thanks."

"Easy, not much traffic this time of night. Hey, thanks, you're a real doll."

That was because she gave him a dollar and a half tip.

And then inside. "Hello, Manuel," she said to the night elevator operator. "Ninth floor, remember?"

"Oh, yeah. I don't see you much, Mrs. Jennings."

"True. We don't go out that often at night."

Manhattan in this year of our Lord—no one went out that much at night. There was a whole bunch of spooks out on those streets. Carl was in the study, poring over some medical journals. "Well, hello," he greeted her. "I was beginning to get worried."

"Nothing to worry about, plenty of cabs around."

"Had a good time?"

"Yes, nice. You?"

"Just going over some material." He yawned. "I guess it's about time to turn in."

"Anything good on television this evening?"

"The usual, a not-bad TV film about school busing. Something you would have enjoyed, very creditable acting."

He had been waiting for her. He never went to bed until she was there, in the house, his security blanket. He didn't even ask where she had dinner. It didn't signify. She was home and now he could turn in, the Missus was where she belonged, it meant he could switch off the lights and get into his pajamas. "You going to read for a while?" he asked her, when they were settled in their beds.

"Not tonight."

"Sleep well, dearest."

"You too, darling."

You should think what you were doing, but you didn't think because it wouldn't have any bearing—thinking wouldn't change things, not one single thing. You lay a bed away from one man and your heart and mind was with another. You just learned to accept things the way they were, and you weren't hurting anyone if they didn't have an inkling of what was going on. She fell asleep with the sound of Carl's light snoring in her ears, not sawing away at a great rate, he never did that, but somehow comforting, quieting, like the sound of a faraway surf, like the murmur of the sea against some distant shore.

15.

Clover was a little late, though not by much and anyway it made no difference, you didn't mind waiting for a friend. Ten minutes or so after the hour she walked in breezily, looking charming as always, her smart skirt swaying as she swung toward Christine's table, her coppery tan an effective contrast to the sun-streaked hair. Clover was "petite" but beautifully proportioned: she had legs like a stripper. "Hiya," she said as she plumped herself down. "Jeez, this is the ticket. I love having lunch out on a Tuesday."

"Why on a Tuesday?"

"Also on a Monday, Wednesday, Thursday, Friday." A grin. "Let's face it, any day in the week. Thing is I'm not pally with anyone in the agency. So generally I wolf down some soggy sandwich either in a Soup Burg or at my desk."

"How come you're not pally with anyone there?"

"Tell you about that in a minute. You order your drink yet?"

"No, not until you came. I'm having a martini."

"That will be *deux*." She gave the order when the waiter came over. "Extra dry, please. Olives, yes, Chris?"

"Um hum."

"I'm very glad you called, Chris. You and I haven't had lunch together alone in a dog's age."

"Spur of the moment. I had nothing better to do so I phoned you. As a last resort, of course."

"I had nothing better to do so I said yes, let's. As a last resort, ditto."

"None of us ever grew up, did we? Same old wisecracks."

"With each other, anyway. It's a different idiom with other people, *we're* like a Quad group, sorority sisters or something. I still think of you as Elliott sometimes. When we worked together the five of us called each other by last names. I'm not sure when it was we left off doing that."

"And I quite often think of you as Martinson. 'Hey, Martinson, gettin' much?' The standard

302

Monday morning greeting."

"Dumb kids we were. Anyway, kidding aside, glad for your spur-of-the-moment impulse. This is great."

It had not been spur of the moment by any means. The truth was that Christine had been thinking of Clover Martinson a lot lately, for reasons that were only partly clear to her. It was probably mostly that Clover, who was unmarried and involved with a married man, was the very opposite of herself, who was married and involved with an *un*married man. Also Clover's lover was older, while Jack Allerton was younger.

At the same time there was a similarity she didn't need to spell out for herself: in neither case was there a *ménage a trois* but something vaguely approximating it. What she wanted was to sound Clover out, probe her true state of mind. Was she as carefree as she seemed with this long-term relationship, was it working? It had suddenly seemed imperative to talk to Clover, and so she had phoned her at the travel agency. "Well, all *right*," Clover said enthusiastically. "One o'clock? How about Chinese?"

They had agreed to meet at Sheila Chang's.

The drinks came and Clover said, *"L'chayim,"* and Christine said yes, to life, and they smiled at each other. "So what's the reason you don't have lunch with anyone in your agency, Clo?"

Prompt and concise. "They're the pits, the scabby end. They are *absolute* shitheads. I knew that when I went into travel. It didn't matter then and it doesn't matter now. Travel's my bag and the

303

hell with the people in it, I couldn't care less."

She picked up her glass and took a quick swallow. "For a Chink place you do get good drinks here, this one's no child's piss. Good, huh? But yes, I thought I'd dropped a hint or two about my confrères in the business, God knows I'm always griping about it. Not just my agency, it's all of them, the whole contingent, they're really a breed apart. Backbiting, small-minded, avaricious, all of them fighting to get the best perks possible. They stay in the fray till they're practically senile and they're the worst vultures in any business you can name. The rag trade? Pretty grim, but travel can go it one better. At least I think so."

"Doesn't it rub off on you? I don't mean make you the same way, but isn't it festering to work with people like that?"

"I close my eyes to it. You don't really work *with* them, you work around them. I have my own desk space, own phone, my own clients. I rub shoulders with them, that's about it. Oh, *and* they're all drunks, too. They must spend a fortune on booze alone. Anton and I met one of the women in my agency one evening when we were having dinner at Sea Fare of the Aegean."

She sipped again, laughed. "We passed by her table—she was with her husband, whom I happen to know is a first-class lecher—and she jumped up, almost spilling her drink, and fell all over me. Clover *Martinson*, hello *dear*, why'nt you join us, and somehow or other I was able to wrest her away from me, *and* him, he was feasting his eyes on my cleavage. Well. Next day at the agency I said politely, 'Good morning, Martha, nice to run into you last night at the restaurant.' She gave me this absolutely blank look, this long, vacant look, told me I must be mistaken, she was home last night with a migraine and skipped dinner completely."

Clover, chuckling, remarked that in Martha's mind it was undoubtedly the truth, as she obviously didn't remember one bit of the previous evening. She had probably blanked out after her one too many whatever-she-was-drinking. "Oh, they're a great bunch, and every one of them dyed in the wool racists."

Then she half emptied her glass with a big gulp. "As they say, I needed that." There was a hoot of laughter. "Here I am sounding off about lushes and I'm well on my way to a refill. With you just starting. But you know me, kiddo. I wouldn't give up my schnapps, I make no secret of it, but two's my limit on a working day. Take your time, Chris. How am I doing with my tan, do I look like a bushbaby?"

"No, like St. Tropez. Where do you go?"

"Well, I start, as soon as the weather indicates, on my terrace, you know there's no parapet over it, and I begin with half an hour, gradually lengthen the time after the first week. When I get a real good base Anton and I go to the beach. He's not a moneybags, you know, earns high but he's got family obligations need I tell you, and I'm no Rockefeller. So we catch the subway at Eighty-sixth the Street, express to Nevins, then change over to a local that takes us to the last stop, Flatbush Avenue. *Then* we go up the stairs, into the sunlight again, and take a bus to Riis Park. The whole trip is about an hour and a half each way, but Riis Park is beautifully unspoiled, or at least the part we head for, which is called the family section, and it's never crowded and noisy like Jones Beach."

"It's a long trip, Clover. But it sounds like fun."

"It's marvelous. I really can't tell you how much we enjoy it. Just a shirt and jeans over your bathing suit, your towels, a little cash for fares and lunch, a frank and a can of beer. A blanket to lie on. We both look forward to it all week."

"How is Anton these days?"

"A joy, an absolute joy. I don't know what I ever did without him. It's as if there never was anything else. Sounds like the title of an Albee play. *Nothing before Anton.*"

"Clover, I'm *very* glad that man made an appearance in your life. I know things were always very pleasant for you before, but there's nothing like that kind of, as you say, absolute joy."

"Yes. Yes, Chris. Funny how one day there's just ordinary, doing this and doing that, no great shakes and then a day later, tantara tantara, everything's like a rainbow, you want to strew flowers in his path. Well. A little lavender, that, but I tend to be Miss Ebullience these days."

"*Ms* Ebullience."

"Correction noted and point taken. I mean it, though, I'm sure it's an unmitigated bore, this kind of stars in the eyes palaver."

"On the contrary. It's lovely, so much more enjoyable than hearing about the deteriorating state of someone's liver, or how you can't get decent cleaning women anymore."

"They don't do windows. Yeah, you do hear a lot of that shit." She fiddled with her glass. "How's Carl, Chris?"

"Just fine. Busy. As usual."

"The kids? Nancy, Bruce?"

"Nancy's still in Mass. Bruce's summer job — I told you about that. As for me, it's summer and that's when I come completely alive."

"You should go to the beach with us. When's vacation this year, Chris?"

A pang. Vacation. Two and a half weeks parted from Jack. It was increasingly on her mind. It could very well be finis, Christine thought dejectedly. Almost three weeks for Jack to take stock of the situation, find it insupportable. It was beginning to disturb her sleep at night. "We're leaving on the 20th of September."

"Your birthday's on the 27th, isn't it?"

"Yes, must you remind me?"

If it makes you feel any better, *I* just turned forty. I never thought you were one to tear your hair out over things like that, Chris."

"I'd just as soon stop celebrating it. Carl will make a big production, some fancy restaurant, flowers, about twelve birthday cards."

"Good for Carl. Where are you going?"

"Italy again. A medical tour, as usual. That is for the flight, anyway. Carl likes to hobnob with other men of med'cin? I don't mind. The rest of the time we're on our own. I'd rather have you plan an itinerary for us."

"Don't give it a thought, we've been all through

this before. We women are friends, the guys and gals haven't ever socialized. I for one have always preferred it that way. What we have belongs to us, not to them. I like to keep my business separate. I really wouldn't like to dicker with friends, you must realize that. I've got my own regular group tours, faithful clients, a nice bit of change accruing therefrom. Oh, I'm off to Israel and Egypt in the autumn. Egypt, I've never been there. Giza, the Pyramids, the Sphinx, camel rides on licey blankets. Damn, I'm out of cigarettes. This pack's empty, I don't have a fresh one in my bag. Look, I'll be right back, I'll get some from the front desk."

"Don't be silly, Clover, help yourself to mine. I have another pack with me."

"I hate to sponge."

"What's mine is yours. What's got into you? Take these and I'll get the new pack out."

"Bring you some next time. Thanks, Chris. So, Egypt. Yes, the camel rides, I can just imagine the mangy state of those camel blankets. Wow. Plus sanitary conditions in general. My doctor's going to dose me up before I leave, with gamma globulin. And God knows there'll be any number of shots, anti everything you can think of. I suppose I'll be a mass of lumps. Then there's that horrid Nile worm."

"What's *that*?"

"Some ghastly crud. A worm, I guess, they call it the Nile worm. Dr. Enfield said, looking me straight in the eye to be sure I understood he meant business, that if I so as much dipped a toe into Nile waters I'd be sorry, that it would mean slow and irrevocable deterioration, a sure threat to my mental capacities as well, that I'd end up a mindless wreck."

"Well, happy vacation," Christine said, laughing. "Are you going alone or with Anton?"

"This year alone. Last year it was with Anton. Remember, we went to Spain and Portugal? We take turns, Madame and I—I should say the Frau and I. So you see it's all very fair and equitable."

"It doesn't seem to bother you."

"It doesn't bother me."

Was that said rather curtly, Christine wondered, tapping ashes into the tray. "That's fine," she murmured. "I didn't mean to sound inquisitive."

Clover raised astonished eyes. "Inquisitive? Hell, I don't think that! Why should I?"

"I guess I'm ready for that second drink now. Can you get his attention, honey?"

An arm up again, the waiter responding. "Two more of the same, please, and the menu, okay?"

When he padded away Christine said she didn't really think she'd ever get to Egypt, but that she'd very much like to go to Israel. "Yes, you should," Clover assured her. "All the Bible places, aside from anything else. And of course Israel's—to all intents and purposes—the end of the Diaspora. Anton nitpicks about it, he's not a Zionist, he says Herzl would turn over in his grave if he knew how the homeland turned out. Well, you don't want to hear about that, I know I talk about Anton too much. Me, I've been there before, I find much of it blatantly materialistic, but I'm kinda sentimental about it." She shrugged, "I guess I'm very sentimental about it."

"Because Anton's Jewish?"

"No, I was before. Rooting with my pompoms. Good for you, tiny country, you show them. Well, maybe more so because of Anton, yes, I suppose. I feel the weight of the infamy in a more personal way."

The waiter returned with their fresh drinks, the menus. "Let's order, shall we, Chris? It will take a while for the stuff to be ready."

They selected an assortment of dishes, Clover saying yes, chopsticks for her, Christine declining. She should learn, Clover told her, but Christine said she wasn't the most avid fan of Oriental cuisine, so why bother to take up an indoor sport that she would rarely use? "Oh, *I'm* sorry," Clover said apologetically. "I should have left it up to you."

"No, I have nothing against Chinese, don't be silly, it's fun once in a while and I particularly like this place."

"It's so pretty at Christmastime, lovely decorations, it's like fairyland."

"Years ago Luchow's was the place to go during the year-end holidays. I haven't been there for ages."

"It went down so. I understand new people have taken it over and it's good again."

"Let's all troop down there sometime for lunch."

"Yes, let's."

It was when their plates were set before them and they were dividing the steaming fare that

Christine decided to come to the point. She simply didn't want to settle for discussing the merits of various eating places, or make small talk about vacations and then go on to clothes or the latest art films. After two hearty drinks she now felt up to advancing the conversation. After all, it was what she had come here for.

Mentally clearing her throat, she said, "This isn't idle curiosity, Clover, but—well, Anton. It's going on five years since you met, and you established a—a relationship almost right away. I was wondering if—"

She was conscious of her friend's upturned look, then her steady regard, Clover's eyes on her, speculative and inquiring. She rushed on. "It's just that—"

And then came to a halt.

"It's just what?" Clover asked. "You don't have to pussyfoot with me. Don't you know that? What's this all about, huh?"

"Clover, I don't want you to think I'm *prying*—"

"You're not the prying kind," Clover said, picking up her chopsticks. "You never were."

"I guess I have a particular reason for asking about you and Anton. If you object, I'll retreat. Fools rush in . . ."

A warm smile from Clover when their eyes met. "I never thought of you as a fool either. Nor do I think you're concerned about my rashness, that you're going to advise me to think twice before I go on with this, this relationship, as you called it."

She popped a morsel of crisped pork in her mouth. "What's beginning to occur to me," she went on, "is that *you're* stewing about something. Something outside of me but in some way bearing on me and Anton. So it seems to be my turn now. Is Carl involved with someone else, Chris?"

She put up a quick hand. "You don't have to answer that. I only asked it because it seemed a possible reason for you to bring Anton into the conversation so persistently."

"No reason you shouldn't ask. And no, Carl's not up to any hankypanky. At least I see no indication of it."

"Oh, well, then. Let me take my foot out of my mouth."

That tactful look on Clover's face. She doesn't believe me, Christine thought. Or at best there's a doubt in her mind. "Don't you adore these roasted walnuts?" Clover murmured. "I could eat them till they came out of my ears."

"Yes, they're great," Christine agreed, and took the plunge. "It's I who's involved with someone," she said, out of a need to exempt Carl from censure. There, she had spilled the beans, and was neither glad nor sorry she had. Clover didn't turn a hair, she was pleased to see. Her friend just looked back at her, no change of expression: she might have been informing Clover that she had bought new dining room pieces.

"I didn't mean to tell anyone," she said quickly. "Or maybe I did. Maybe that's the reason I wanted to be with you today."

Clover's chopsticks were arrested in midair. "Oh?" she finally said. "But why me, Chris? You've always been closer to Ruth."

"That's a question of neighborhoods, Ruth and I live practically on each other's doorsteps. Anyway, I wouldn't tell Ruth. I've only told you because I feel I might learn something from you. About — well, to put it bluntly, an unorthodox —"

She forked up some sweet and sour pork, put it in her mouth, chewed and swallowed. "Oh, God, this isn't working."

"Now, come on," Clover said, in the tones of a patient piano teacher. "Take your time, feel your way. We're old friends, let's rap without confusion or embarrassment. Tell me anything or ask me anything. What are friends for? My life is the proverbial open book. I've never been one to conceal things. Go ahead and say whatever you've a mind to say."

She snickered. "We never used to be this reticent, did we? Staggering into work, discussing abortive love affairs. Gee, you're white as a sheet, what's wrong? I've got the curse, these cramps are killing me. Or jamming into the john to plot mayhem against the boss. Remember that bastard Tully? We all hated his guts, he was really a rotten man, and then he got Julie Johns knocked up and he was canned. Oh, joy in the morning! We all went out to lunch at Reidy's and came back bombed."

"Ah yes, I remember it well. He always had it in for us because we never gave him a tumble. He had this insane impression he was God's gift to girls."

"Then *continuez*, as my French teacher at P.S. whatever-it-was used to say. So you're getting it on

313

with someone else, Chris. I say that flippantly because, well—"

"The trouble is it's not that. Getting it on. That's the catch."

"What do you mean?"

"It's more than that. I could handle it if it were just *that*."

"Oh. I suppose I understand."

"It's more like something I didn't bargain for. Not that I bargained for any of it. I never went looking. I never wanted to go looking. I wasn't missing anything. Or at least so I thought. Anyway, it's not what I want to talk about. I don't want to be shriven. I'm in something deeper than I should be and I can't just say from one day to the next, cut it out, Christine, you're a naughty girl. I've presented myself with a problem and I've presented someone else with a problem. It's there and it's not going to go away."

She leaned forward. "I wanted, you know, to hear how it is with Anton and you. You've so often said, and without bile, that he'll never leave his wife."

"I don't want him to. If he did that might mean he'd leave me some day. Or no, that isn't really what I mean. It would make him not the man he is, the man I love and honor. I'd like it if she died, but it isn't all that important. I'm just as happy with the way things are. I love him, he loves me, who'd want better?"

"I used to think getting married was the answer to everything. Yes, I did. I didn't break my neck trying to land someone, but I did think it was what you were supposed to do. A husband and children. A *normal* life. Sometimes — well lately, I've thought it was exactly the trap the feminists say it is. It doesn't seem to be the answer."

"The answer? Answer to what?" Clover cried. "Like the old joke. *Religion's the answer, but what's the question?* There are answers to arithmetical questions, I grant you. Otherwise it's feeling around in the dark. What did I find this time? A treasure hunt. Maybe you come up with a guy who says let's get married and you get married. The altar, a husband, then cloning yourself. Okay, but what question is that an answer to? You're in this alone, why kid yourself. Who's going to stop the pain when you have pain? Maybe the doctor, or at least he has some means to make an attempt, but hell, you're the one with the pain, and if you're terminal you're terminal all by yourself, loved ones notwithstanding, they can't will good health to come to you. You've got children and I don't, but that's of relatively short duration because one of these days there ain't no children anymore, they're out and away and you're a little bit older, with no one to make chicken soup for anymore."

"Don't rub it in," Christine said wryly. "I've been through all that in my mind. You're doing it differently. I'm interested to hear how it works out *that* way."

"Okay," Clover said briskly. "Okay, maybe I'm a mutation from some women, though I do seem to be in fashion these days with my single-status shenanigans. I don't know how to say it in any other way, Chris, but I'm very, very fulfilled and very,

very content. That's putting it, deliberately, in an unromanticized way, even clinically, no hyperbole. I don't consider, however, that doing it *my* way means an answer to anything."

She pulled out another cigarette, lit it. "It just so happened, Chris, that a fortunate thing happened on the way to my fortieth birthday. I met Anton. Nothing wrong before, I had no bones to pick with my lot. But then I did meet Anton, a man I love so much that I'd do anything, short of inflicting pain or torture on another person, to keep what I have and keep it until I die. Unfortunately Anton is *quite* a bit older, so it seems a vain hope. But I don't want anything to change and I didn't really mean it when I said I'd like for her to die. Even that isn't so, because she's such a big part of him, he'd be losing a hell of lot if she died; it would mean suffering for him and I don't want him to suffer. He had his share of suffering, I've told you about that, the Third Reich and the way it touched him. Why should he lose her too?"

A speculative glance at Christine, a sip of her drink, some hesitation. Then she shrugged. "Chris, I don't know how deeply you feel about — well, this man you said you were involved with. That's as good a term for what we both mean as any, I suppose. Involved with. But you're not a shallow woman and I suspect there are flies in the ointment, even if you do look so radiant, as we all remarked just recently."

She threw down her chopsticks. "I'm finished and you've barely touched your lunch," she said. "Why don't you eat a little more? Come on, some more chicken."

316

"No, I don't think so. Not to worry, I've eaten plenty."

"Let's have cognac with our coffee, okay?"

"Yes, fine."

She held up a hand, the waiter trotted over to take away their plates and she said, "A fine lunch, thank you very much. We'd like coffee now, please, and two cognacs."

"Yes, madam."

"Am I talking too much?" Clover asked when they were waiting for the coffee and liqueurs. "Too much and to no avail? Like, is this all just sound and fury, signifying *nada*?"

"You're doing fine. Am I being a bore?"

"Never that. Well, here's our coffee, the cognacs. How about it, let's drink to you, Chris. And to your peace of mind."

"Many thanks."

They sipped. "Do you want to talk now?" Clover suggested.

"No. Except—well, the man I told you about is younger. A lot younger."

"You're *very* fond of him. . . ."

"Much too much, I'm afraid."

"I see. Younger then. Well, don't be afraid of younger, Chris. It's older that's a worry."

There was a little silence. Then, "Are you thinking of divorce?" Clover asked.

"Oh, my God, no!"

"But you don't want to give up this other man."

"No, I don't."

"So you're on the horns of a dilemma."

"And to add to the absurdity, his being so young—"

317

"Oh, Chris. I'd make a Faustian pact to have myself older than Anton. God, would I!" She gestured helplessly. "Or at least both of us the same age, instead of—"

Draining her glass, she set it back on the table with a small bang, shaking her head. "Because, you see, I'll lose him. Chris, he's almost sixty. He's fifty-six—my father died when he was fifty-eight. I always have that in my mind. And then where'll I be? Not young, not old. I'll never settle for a lesser man, Anton's a *mensch*. I'd die before I let another man touch me."

She pushed her glass back. "I'd like another, but I don't intend to join the Swill Club," she confided. "But you go ahead if you care to."

"No. This is fine."

"I had a dream the other night," Clover announced with a reflective smile. "Some dream, I woke up shaking. I was going to Anton's funeral. Which was ridiculous to begin with because naturally I wouldn't be invited to the proceedings, being 'the other woman.' Anyway, he died, and there was this funeral, a cemetery, you know, with those ornate white burial grounds benches, and the mounds and the headstones, and all the people stifling their weeping. Hushed voices, solemnity and the sun shining like crazy. I went up to the gravesite, this big, empty rectangle in the ground and the coffin there beside it covered with flowers. There I stood. They were going to put him in there, in that cavern in the earth, and leave him there after shoveling in the dirt and—"

She frowned. "It was so damned real. I guess I

think about it more than I want to, when it really could happen. I stood there, looking down at the place they'd made for Anton to lie eternally in, and I was saying—I kid you not—I was saying, 'Duncan is in his grave: After life's fitful fever he sleeps well.' "

She pulled a cigarette out of Christine's pack. "Christ, you'd think I'd remember to bring my own smokes," she said apologetically. "I don't usually do this. I've finished the whole pack, almost."

"Don't be a nut. Clover, you must stop worrying about his age! He's in the prime of life, for heaven's sake."

"A little too prime to suit me, kiddo." A sheepish grin. "It doesn't show, maybe, but I'm a worrier at heart. I guess that's why I seize on things like Old James and Lang's bracing postulations. It's mostly about small things. I'm always afraid when I have my period that I'll get up out of a chair with a spot of blood on my dress. Things like that. So it stands to reason when I have something important on my mind I'll worry about that too. Only more. I only cited that dumb dream because you said he—whoever he is—is younger than you. So long as he's of voting age I wouldn't consider it a drawback. Far from it."

She reached for Christine's hand. "By the way, your secret's safe with me. You must know that or you wouldn't have confided. I'll be thinking of you, Chris, wishing you well. I don't have to tell you how to conduct your life, nor would I presume to. You're an intelligent woman, you'll manage all right."

"Thanks, Clover. Really thanks. I appreciate your patience and forbearance and understanding. And I never doubted for a minute that my secret would be safe with you."

So Clover loved Anton that much, she was thinking, her mind reaching back to their earlier days, when they had been friends among other friends in a more irresponsible era, when they were young, really young, with nothing to dwell on except dates and fun and that occasional raise to boost their take-home pay. In the meantime life had touched them, left its marks, and today Clover Martinson, who had found happiness, dreamed of losing it. They sat now, certainly better dressed and probably better looking, in Sheila Chang's, making their own separate peace with what had happened to them and what was going to happen.

And of course they parted, after paying the check, just about the way they had met, casual and smiling, with promises to do this again sometime soon. It really had been so damned much fun. Clover walked off, in her stunning skirt with the matching silk pullover, in one direction and Christine in another.

She walked slowly, strolling really, looking into shop windows and thinking of Clover. What Clover had told her and what she had told Clover. I love her, she thought. More than I ever did, and I hope he fools her and lives to be ninety.

16.

Nancy returned to the city two weeks before
Labor Day, brown as a coffee bean and looking
taller. "I am," she stated. "Grew almost an inch.
Oh, I hope I'll be one of those statuesque amazons
who dazzle the bejeezus out of lesser mortals. What
do you think, Mother?"

"I'm tall, your father's tall, your brother's tall.
Why shouldn't you be too?" I'm sure you will,

Nancy and if that's what you want I hope it will be so."

"You're not tall!"

"I'm five six, what do you mean that's not tall?"

"Oh, *no*, I mean like five *eleven*."

"How many men are you going to find who are five eleven? Look around you, women are climbing up there, men are staying much the same."

"I don't care about *that*."

"Since when didn't you care about gents?"

"I didn't mean that, I just meant—anyway, yes, I grew, and I'll need some clothes for school. A lot of the stuff will be too skimpy from last year."

"Okay, what do we have to fill in on?"

"I've got a list. I'll have to try on things in my closet, see what's still suitable. So. Yes, now I made this list, but it's possible *nothing* I have will do, except for around the house. I can't tell until I find that out."

"Let me see that list."

Scanning it, Christine frowned. "It seems to me you've got everything possible itemized here. What more would you need besides this? As it is it will cost a fortune."

"Are we suddenly poor?"

"Nancy! I didn't say we couldn't afford this—or whatever else—but for heaven's sake you've put down everything but the kitchen sink. Sweaters, blouses, pullovers, slacks, shoes, boots. A jacket or two—I see you've got a question mark next to that."

"I may want to invest in more than one or two. It all depends on how I decide to coordinate things."

"Very well—besides these things, what possible other accoutrements could you have in mind?"

"You can't really know until you go through the stores!" She got that snide look on her face. "Are you going to tell me that when you were my age you—"

"No, I have no intention of doing that, if you don't mind, don't put words into my mouth." She handed back the list. "I'd like to say, though, that it offends me to hear you use phrases like 'are we suddenly poor.' It offends me for your sake. It makes you sound like some petulant brat who's a Dorian Gray at heart. Spoiled and vain and haughty. It's not one bit becoming, it sounds like 'let the servants do that, we don't have to dirty our hands.' That's not the way we are, Nancy, it's not the way I want you to be."

"Why should you make a federal case out of a perfectly simple *remark*? In the first place we don't have servants."

"I won't say anymore. Your behavior is your business, you're old enough to know what you want to be like. And what you want to sound like to other people. Very well, about these things. We can knock this off in no time. A day should do for the bulk of it, the rest can take care of itself a bit at a time. Like the tops, the pants too. You can fill in nicely as you go along, you'll certainly see things during the school term, right? Tomorrow we'll go to Bloomie's and you'll see, most of it will be accomplished."

"I fail to see *how*. What's the hurry? There's two whole weeks before school starts."

"Not quite that. But Nancy, surely I shouldn't have to point out that I have a million other things to attend to? Your father has needs too. *Our* vacation. I can't be expected to outfit the whole family at the very last minute."

"But you've had the whole summer!"

"So have you, may I remind you. You can't mean to say that Amy and her mother didn't go shopping for Amy's school things? Why couldn't you have done the same?"

"I don't have a charge card. Do I have a charge card?"

"You could have phoned me and we would have arranged something. Two short letters from you all summer, and not a word to Bruce, not so much as a post card."

"I'm sure a postcard would have sent him into the stratosphere. A post card from Sis—now I can die happy."

"Let's skip the irony. Make me a copy of that list."

"How about xeroxing it in triplicate? Then we can frame one of them."

"Just what we need to hang over the fireplace."

"What fireplace?"

"The one we don't have. You be ready at nine-thirty sharp tomorrow morning, we'll be there when the store opens."

"Am I permitted to have breakfast first?"

"If you can fit it in. Come on, honey, we'll have a good time buying lovely things and the sooner we leave the house the better. No reason in the world why we can't do just about all of it tomorrow."

"In one *day?*"

"Why not, I know every nook and cranny of that store." She smiled hearteningly. "And so do you. I still don't see why you couldn't have had fun with Amy buying things in Northampton, they have such lovely shops there."

"I didn't go to Massachusetts to spend my time in stores." She cast a cold eye on her mother. "You sound as if you were peeved with me for being away and having a good time. Which is grossly unjust. You were tickled pink to get me out of the city during the long hot summer. Now you're throwing a fit."

"Oh, jump in the lake, darling," Christine said pleasantly, which was something of an effort. "Don't worry, everything you need will simply appear on the racks before our very eyes, and we'll come home staggering under the weight of your loot."

"I'm terribly sorry to be such a bother," Nancy said with exaggerated politeness. "Forgive me for—"

"Honey, will you please go and *unpack?*"

"Just one thing more. Not that I begrudge you and Daddy your European trip, did I ever? But I assure you it's no big uplift being left with Mrs. Chamberlain to preside over this happy little household. She has her TV blaring every night in that den and I'm sure flakes off when you're away, like the hell with the baseboards. I just thought you ought to know that."

"Maybe it's a kind of vacation for Mrs. Chamberlain too."

"You can say that again, and in spades."

Nancy, flouncing out: please God give me strength, Christine thought, on edge. Why couldn't they be easy with each other, easy *on* each other. Nancy was back and it was like having another woman in the house, a steely, determined woman whose aim was to take over the whole kit and kaboodle, like a rival, or a Mormon second wife, an *ambitious* second wife.

You're being unfair, a voice inside her warned, You're in favor of abdicating a mother's responsibility because you're up to your neck in forbidden pleasures. And you're frantic because September the twentieth is just around the corner, and you haven't said a word to Jack about your vacation. Now it is time to prepare him and you are in a flap about it.

I won't take it out on Nancy, she thought contritely. Nancy needed love more than she cared to admit. She had always been a defiant little thing, difficult to cuddle: she had, in a way, been born old. Everyone needed love, though, people like Nancy—who held affection at arm's length —needed it perhaps far more than those who accepted it easily, without question. I'll make her a whopping dinner, Christine decided. Let's see, Nancy was a sucker for slaughter-in-the-pan, so how about that?

Not that the name of the dish could be found in any cookbook: Carl had coined it, with one of his dry smiles. It was apt enough, because it was a succulent, runny affair, one of her specialties and a fair amount of work. It was pork chops, center cut, apples, small new potatoes, onion slices, done in a roasting pan and swimming in a rich dark gravy.

She looked in on Nancy, to tell her what they were having for dinner, soon gave that idea up. Nancy, whose bag was opened but still crammed with the clothes of her summer holiday, lay sprawled on the bed, on the phone and laughing into it, clad only in a bra and panties that were little more than a wisp of nothing, long, nut-brown legs scissored, magnificent young torso without a blemish.

Did I really make this beautiful creature? Christine thought, dazzled. Did I actually really create this perfect specimen? How could you not be aburst with pride about such an achievement? She left the doorway with a glow inside her, smiling with pleasure. Okay, she'd just surprise Nance with the special dinner when it came time. Nancy would be on the phone for a while, there would be a half dozen other calls after this one as Nancy caught up with the summer activities of her friends and brought them up to date on her own.

She went out and bought pork chops.

It was a good dinner. Nancy, without access to junk food, (Mrs. Longworth was a stickler for health items, had things like dulse and bean sprouts for nibbles and noshes) seemed starved, and asked for a third helping. A big success, Christine thought contentedly as she watched her daughter stuff herself, looking so well and happy, summer-tanned and my goodness, so much taller!

"Nice to have you back, chicken," Carl said, reaching over for Nancy's hand.

"Yes, and to *be* back, Daddy. Mid pleasures and palaces, there's no place like the old homestead."

"That's my girl."

"Ugh. I'm sodden with food. I ate too much. Or as some would say I et too much. Pork's got to be the best. Now I must go on an anorexia kick. If I want to be like the wand I want to be like."

"Thank God there's a doctor in the house," Carl murmured.

"I'm at a dangerous age, just the time when you have to begin counting calories. After all that I'm scared to get on the scales."

Bruce, as always, helped with the clearing up, then stacked things in the washer as Christine rinsed them. "Are you sorry your summer job's over?" she asked him.

"Yes. I really am. I did dig it. Getting wages, too. I should have done it before, other summers."

"You were too young."

"I'll miss the guys."

"Bruce, what do *you* need for school?"

"Don't worry about that. Sometime this next week I'll go foraging, now I'm not tied down anymore. There's not too much, I know just about what's lacking in my dandy's wardrobe."

"Shall I go with you?"

"Why should you worry your pretty little head? It would only be a drag for you, I have everything pretty well settled in my mind, what I need."

The washer was filled, the door closed and Christine turned the ON dial. "That's it, Brucey, thanks."

He put his arms around her. "When I get married, will you teach my wife to make slaughter-in-the-pan?"

"Oh, Bruce, I can't imagine you married! Gone away . . ."

"I'll be gone away next year," he reminded her.

"Yes, but not forever. Married's a different can of worms. Me a mother-in-law. I suppose she'll hate me."

"She'll probably side with you against *me*. Since it happens to be about ten years away let's not malign the poor thing, whoever she may turn out to be. A lot of water has to go under the bridge before then. A lot of grind too, you betcha. You finished in here?"

"Just about."

"The roasting pan?"

"Let it soak. I'm not going to tackle *that* tonight. I'll just tidy up a little more in here. Go along, get started on whatever you're doing tonight. And thanks, love."

She was just about to snap out the light, after putting away unused napkins and inserting a fresh roll of paper towels in the rack when the swinging doors opened. It was Carl.

"What?" she asked. "A glass of water?"

"No, I—" He regarded her, a kind of quizzical regard. She was rubbing Keri lotion into her hands, thinking of nothing in particular. She wriggled her fingers idly: she had used too much of the lotion, it was slow to absorb into the skin.

"Anything on TV?" she asked abstractedly, and he moved a little nearer. "I just thought," he said, "that after all it's Nancy's first day back home, did you have to light into her?"

Her eyes widened. "What are you talking about?"

"She said you're upset about some things she needs for school. She said—"

"*When* did she say?" Christine demanded, her jaw set. "And why? Does she report every conversation she and I have? Who am I, Jean Valjean? And you Inspector Javert?"

His jaw fell open. You read in books that someone's jaw falls open. It was true, sometimes people's jaws did fall open. He looked at her as if she were a species he had heretofore not encountered. And a mean, sadistic little thrill ran through her.

"Oh," she said. "Of course. Talking above your head again. I can't seem to remember, for the life of me, that you couldn't possibly know what I'm talking about nine-tenths of the time. You've never read *Les Miserables*, have you? How could you be expected to? What room could you make for literature, or music, or any of the fine arts in a mind filled with locomotor ataxia and lupus erythematosis and glomerula nephritis?"

Her hands, on which the lotion was fully dry now, waved in the air, as if she were conducting an orchestra. She was doing that because they were shaking so: she was absolutely furious with him. *Nancy said, Nancy said.* And she had made Nancy's very favorite meal, painstakingly cutting up apples, slicing onions, peeling potatoes, slaving over the gravy, with the heat from the oven beading her forehead. And he came in here and—

"All she said was—Chris, what's the beef? God,

honey, she had a good time and then you light into her . . ."

Little red dots danced in front of her eyes. "Work it off," she said between her teeth. "Don't talk to me about lighting into anyone. She's my daughter too, so butt out. Keep your sophomoric little grievances to yourself. You want to do something constructive? Just work it off, whatever's eating you, scrub that roasting pan, that ought to keep you busy and out of mischief for a while."

"Now wait," he said, his own jaw extending. "I want to know what all this is about."

"What's it about? What it's about is if you don't appreciate me maybe some men would," she flung at him. "Why don't you put *that* in your pipe and smoke it? And when you're finished washing that roasting pan it belongs in the lower cupboard. See? Right down there. Have fun."

Judas, she thought in the bathroom. My own daughter a Judas. Treated as if she were a bath-mat. The worm turneth, it was said. Seething, she filled the basin and stuck her face in it. And Clover Martinson was setting out on an evening walk, with her Anton. Or maybe this was a night they wouldn't be together. Anyway, Clover was her own woman, no buttinskys, she would stay young far longer than the rest of them, never any wearying nights of holding steam kettles over a child's croupy cough, no sitting for endless hours in a hospital waiting for an appendectomy to be over. No thousands of little agonies . . .

When she finally went out to the living room Carl had clammed up. He had that look on his

331

face, as if he had been beaten senseless by some insane assailant. He didn't turn her way. The evening closed in, two people in a room, with the faint sound of Nancy's chatter drifting in from her bedroom, phone calls. Bruce, the quiet one, had Mahler on his stereo.

Italy, where they would be going in so short a time. She'd make a Faustian pact, the way Clover said she would for what she wanted, if she were going to Italy with Jack Allerton. Rome, with Jack. Florence and Verona, with Jack. Bologna, Naples . . .

She felt as if little drops of blood were trying to ooze through her skin. If she could only not love Carl, if she could only not feel that he was meshed into her, so much a part of herself that they were like a four-armed, four-legged creature. After all, seventeen years. Seventeen years were almost half her life. He held out a hand after a while, from one Buddha chair to the other, and they laced fingers together. Nothing more was said, but when they went to their beds it was with the customary affability. After all, what else?

"Good night, honey."

"Good night, Carl, sleep well."

The house was quiet and so, in this part of town, was the city. Only an occasional footfall, from some rash idiot walking the streets at this time of night, sounded from time to time. Christine wondered if Jack was lying wakeful too, and then dozed off not much later, with the moon, in its first quarter, raying in from out of doors.

17.

"So you'll be away for almost a month," Jack said slowly.

"No, no! Two and a half weeks, that's all."

"Between your getting ready and then getting squared away again when you come back it will be a good month, let's face it."

"Believe me Jack, I'd give anything if I didn't have to go."

"Then don't go."

"Jack—"

They were at his kitchen table, after shopping in Yorkville, a coffee cup in front of each and nibbling on ham sandwiches, Schaller & Weber ham and Peppridge Farm bread. It was the first week in September, Christine had put it off as long as possible. Now something would have to be said, she had been thinking worriedly. She had started to frame the words days ago, was unable to, but getting up this morning decided it was simply not fair to wait any longer.

It hadn't been easy to come out with it. Jack hadn't given her any openings. After all, he must know that they took a yearly vacation, how could he imagine otherwise? "It will give you some time to forge way ahead on your book," she pointed out. "Uninterrupted by—"

"Thank you very much for handing out small favors."

"Jack—"

He drummed on the table. She waited nervously. He looked *very* grim. Silent and grim. And that rat tat tat—she wanted to tear his fingers away from the table top. "Jack, please," she implored. "Say something."

He looked steadily at her, long and steadily, but he stopped drumming. "All right," he said at last. "All right, Chris. I made promises, which I've kept, and to the letter. No mishmash about your life, your life when you're not with me. Not once have I showed you, by word or deed, how damned tough it's been to keep my mouth shut, accept things on your terms, be a pleasant fellow. Do you agree?"

"Yes, I do agree. You've—"

"Now it's got to be different. Probation time's over. I won't settle for second best, Chris. Sorry, but I have to put it that way. Love in the afternoon—"

"Oh no," she cried vehemently. "It's never been that, you know it! Never! Let me tell you there have been a few temptations over the years, for that kind of thing—"

She leaned toward him. "Jack, it's been tough for me too. Falling in love . . . being in love . . . and the dishonesty—my God, I've tried to show you, in every conceivable way, what you mean to me, that it's not balling, a bed thing, not just a bed thing."

"You're in love with me? You love me? Is that what you're saying? It certainly sounds like it."

"Yes. Yes! And yes again, for God's sake."

He tilted back his chair. "Then there's no problem," he said calmly. "I love you. You love me. I want us to be married."

She stared at him. She almost said, after absorbing what she had just heard, *how can I marry you when I'm already married*? She felt, for a befuddled moment, like a slow child, trying to understand what the grownups were talking about.

She must really be slightly retarded not to have guessed he wanted that. If he were her own age, instead of a decade younger, she would have thought of it. Another time-honored inculcation: the man must always be older, or at least the same age. *Younger is better*, Clover had said.

"Well," she was finally able to answer, "this seems to be a clear case of jacta alea est. The die is cast. Just let me ask you. If I weren't going away for those two and a half weeks, would you have presented me with this new development?"

He seemed to ponder it. Then he nodded, in a judicious way, said yes of course, sooner or later. "What did you think?" he demanded. "It's been over three months. It's not balling for me either, a bed thing, just a bed thing. And *you* know *that*. As you yourself once pointed out, I'm a free agent, there are plenty of obliging women in town, if that was what I wanted it would be easy as falling off a log. However, it was not what I wanted or would want. I'd jerk off before I'd go the singles bars route. Chris, don't tell me you don't know what I'm after. You know damned well I want to build, I want my woman, mine, part of me, continuity . . .

"I'd better go home," she said shakily. "Apparently I'm being asked to do some heavy thinking. So I'd better go home and think."

"Home," he echoed, his face going dark. "That's what I meant. There's here and there's there. *There* is home. This is a hideaway, a place for lovers."

"That's unfair. That's unfair and cruel. You know what I meant."

"All too well," he said, getting up.

She still sat there. He was clearing the table, stacking the dishes in the sink. She watched him moving about purposefully, stiff as a ramrod, his face set. Why had she told him about the vacation?

336

She could have told him one of her parents was sick: she could have said, I'm needed there, my parents aren't young anymore.

She felt like a lump of soggy dough. Her throat was tight. She couldn't even seem to stir herself. All the dishes were in the sink now and he was leaning against the refrigerator.

She looked up at him. "Jack, I'm so much older," she heard herself saying. "It wouldn't be fair to you."

"Uh uh," he said, tightening his mouth. "Don't put it on me, Chris. It's fair to keep me dangling, you seem to think, to come and go at your own convenience. It's fair to give so much and at the same time so little. Withhold yourself in the most important ways. Christ, I've never seen you brushing your teeth, or in a nightgown. I've never turned over in bed at night or in the early morning and found you beside me, felt your warmth. Don't give me that age shit, it's just a copout. I want my wife and I want you for my wife, I've finished with being your stud."

"You shouldn't have said that," she whispered, going white. "No matter what your gripes are you shouldn't have said that."

He came over to her right away. Put his arms around her. "No I shouldn't have said that," he told her, his face against her hair. "I'm sorry. I'm sorry, darling."

His fingers on her face. "You're crying."

"Of course I'm crying," she said choked. "What did you think I'd do, burst out laughing?"

He pulled the other chair over, sat down

alongside her. "Chris. Darling. Okay, I lashed out when you used those words. 'Fair to me, it wouldn't be fair to me.' When we both know it's you it wouldn't be fair to. You think I'm deaf, dumb and blind? Anyone can see you've got it all right now, not a worry in the world. Why should you give that up? And for what? This apartment, after what you have now, both of us scurrying around looking for a wardrobe for your clothes—two of them, most likely—and, hell, fitting yourself *in*, not enough room to breathe in."

He gestured. "And then do what all day? A little tidying up, making the bed, and then watching me work? Hell, that's some offer. You think I don't know what it must sound like to you, me saying let's get married and then—"

He stopped her when she started to reply. "No, wait, just let me finish," he said. "Well, of course I know it's no offer at all. But I know now, Chris, that it can't be any two years to get this book done. The best and most valuable thing a writer can have going for him is incentive, we're all of us motivated at bottom by the carrot on the stick. I know where I'm going with it now, I have most of the key scenes written, they're good, it's pulling together. Once it's finished I think it will be a winner. I can't promise it will be on the best seller list for fifty-two weeks, but I'm willing to bet it will do a lot for me, I'm sure it will make it in a more than modest way. If I weren't, I wouldn't be saying any of these things. And it will be off the agenda, I can work things out by that time."

"Jack, none of this has any bearing on—"

"Oh, yes," he said instantly. "*All* of this has a bearing on *all* of it. Remember too, I can draw on my trust fund if it should ever become necessary. All *that* takes is a conference with the lawyer. Chris, I was wondering too if you'd like to be a reader for one of the pub firms or a film company. It doesn't pay much but it's interesting work and you're well qualified. I have a feeling it would set well with you. We could put a desk in the other corner, and—"

He searched her face eagerly. She felt exhausted with the outpouring of words, the whole thing was just so unexpected, so swift and sudden. He was so touching, so intense, so young. Tears started up again, she couldn't seem to stop *crying*. "Come," he said gently. "Lie with me. Let's hold each other. Quiet and together, just holding each other. Chris, I love you so much. Or cry then if you want to. Let's just lie together for the rest of the afternoon. Okay? You must know what you mean to me. How could I let you go? How could I ever let you go? Didn't you know I couldn't let you go?"

"You should let me go," she said bleakly. "There oughtn't to be anyone like me in your life. You should be spending your time with either a tart or a malleable young girl who'd be waiting in bed for you at night. And who'd fix you a decent supper after a day's work. And take your wash to a laundromat. What the hell do you want with someone like me?"

"It isn't someone like you, it happens to be you. Why do you question that? That girl I was married to—I hurt her bad. It wasn't her fault she'll want her Mommy until the day she dies. Ten years old emotionally, a Radcliffe education and the mind, notwithstanding, of a summer squash. She stopped maturing when she started menstruating, she never got over that, it meant she had to grow up. She didn't want a man, she wanted her mother, I could have been kinder, though. Which I was not."

He held both her hands. "Then there was you, Christine. From that first day I knew. And here you are asking me why. And of course I know why. It's because you're programmed. You're programmed to the life you know. God—"

He rubbed his forehead. "I can *understand* that. You looked at me in that puzzled way when I said I was trying to drag you down. You must remember that, it was the day we became lovers. I'm very conscious of it, that I'd be taking you away from safety, security, the things you've earned. I'm conscious of the fact that there are two kids in your scheme of things. *I* can't provide for them. I'm offering you nothing but my life, and what's that? Here I am, nobody at all, throwing down my cloak for you to walk on, big deal, big fat deal. There's no way I can prove I'll reach the apex, make it into a document, signed and sealed. I know I will because nothing else is acceptable to me. I'll do it, and be able to give you everything you have now. But I can't do it by the end of next week. So essentially I'm asking you to relinquish everything you have and start in all over again."

He put his hands on her shoulders. "Yeah, and knowing all that, I'll go on asking you. Hoping for it. I just couldn't go on any longer without making some kind of statement. A statement, and that's it for now. I won't torture you. You know how I feel, so now it has to be up to you. All right, I've said it, you know how it is with me, but you won't come back from your two and a half weeks to find me out of the picture. Not a chance. Somehow or other I'm just not going to let you go."

He didn't try to make love to her. They must have slept, because the next thing she knew the day was darkening outside. She got up and dressed. Just before she left he said, "We've had it out, Chris, and I'll be true to my word. I've said all there is to say. From now on it's your decision, I've made mine. I'd like to see you tomorrow, as a matter of fact may I insist on it, please? I want to be with you tomorrow, laughing again and loving. I wouldn't want it any other way. Don't shut me out because I've asked something that's difficult. And no more discussions. You'll tell me when your mind's made up. I never set any time limits, you'll notice."

She nodded. "I'll be here tomorrow, then."

"And it will be just as usual."

"I promise."

How could it be just as usual? she wondered, walking home. And yet she must have known there would be a cutoff point. As a matter of fact for her as well. It was like being sawed in half, as in some magic show, and she marveled now that she had ever thought this kind of attachment was easy, a joyous adventure, the only culpabilities mechanical ones, lies and excuses and a few half-truths thrown in.

And yet it was accomplished. They had almost two weeks before Christine's departure date, spent almost every one of those days together. Jack was no different from his habitual self, it was almost as if not a word had been spoken. She was tremulous with gratitude. He seemed to be the older and more responsible of them, and here she was shortly going off to Italy with Carl, underlining her status as another man's wife in still another way.

Not that he knew she would be going to Italy, his beloved Italy. He had refrained from asking, as he scrupulously refrained from any mention of her life outside his orbit. He was possibly more possessive, though, as if by making his "statement" he had asserted certain rights and was therefore to be considered more than a part-time adjunct in her life. He had adopted a way of discussing what he was buying in stores, things for his own use, own fridge or pantry, asking if she was sure it would do, as though he wanted to make clear to the person behind the counter that it was for both of them, that they were a legitimatized "couple."

Otherwise it was the same carefree kind of thing, meeting somewhere or her going to his apartment first, then leaving for a walk or whatever, later returning to his apartment to go to bed.

It was a swiftly-passing two weeks, during which Christine had the disorienting feeling more than once that Jack was going off to fight a war, that he might never come back, that he would fall on the battlefield, never to rise again, and so this last time together must be doubly precious because it might be all they would ever have. She seemed to remember every single thing he said, as if she must have mental tape recordings of it all. You could love two men and possibly three or four at the same time, but you only loved one of them in this particular kind of aching way, that was for sure.

The only thing she could hang onto was that when she arrived back at Kennedy Airport she would call him from there. It was rehearsed in her mind. She would say to Carl, "Why don't you see to the luggage, I'll just phone the kids, see how everything is."

But she would phone Jack first. At least there was that to look forward to.

18.

It was good to have Christine back, Rodney thought. He had missed her in the worst way, not that he saw her all that much, but at least she was there, within reach of a phone, and during the time she was in Italy he had felt frightfully deprived, knowing that calling her number would only yield Bruce or Nancy, or else that housekeeper, who never could understand a word he said. Because of his accent, she told him, which had ultimately brought forth a sharp and shirty retort from him. "I believe it's you have the accent, not I, madam." It had left her, to his gratification, speechless.

Christine had been home for a week: he had immediately invited her to lunch, but she had asked for a "rain check," which he now learned meant people had something better to do, ask them another time when they didn't have something better to do. Chris had claimed to have a million and one things to attend to, sort out vacation clothes and get some cleaned, film to be developed — "You name it," she added. She said she needed a vacation after her vacation and was going to take it easy for a bit. Appending all this with, "Sometime next week I want you over to dinner, see what you've been up to while we were away."

He had given her enough time now, he would call her this morning. Take her somewhere and tell her he hadn't been up to anything, more was the pity, that boredom had begun to set in and he thought it might be time to acquaint himself with another part of the country, maybe California. And if California, then San Francisco seemed the logical place. He had seen television shows based in San Francisco and it looked very smashing, with that Golden Gate bridge and all those precipitous hills climbing up steeply. Cable cars. Interesting restaurants. More than likely outdoor cafes.

It occurred to him that perhaps he could cajole Christine into accompanying him out there. She might worry about him otherwise, off on his own and who knew what trouble he might get into. On the one hand he didn't care for her thinking in such condescending terms, such *maternal* terms, but on the other hand if it would be a selling point—

He had just finished his breakfast, now began to have glowing visions of the two of them flying out to San Francisco, where they would stay at that hotel—what was the name? Ah yes, the Mark Hopkins, with the famous restaurant on the roof.

Warming to the glorious picture of himself and the divine Mrs. Jennings occupying adjoining rooms, Rodney sat on the arm of his Brown Jordan settee, smoking a cigarette with quick, enthusiastic drags and dreaming a little. She must have smashing evening frocks: he would invest in a dinner jacket and they'd dine at posh places at night, drink champagne and inevitably Christine would loosen up. Maybe it would take him a while, but sooner or later she would turn to him with glistening eyes and say in a passionate whisper, "Why don't we just give into this thing, haven't we waited long enough, Rodney?"

Thinking about it, he erected. He toyed with the idea of playing out his fantasy, give into the mood he had put himself into, spin out a long sequence of events between himself and Christine. It wouldn't be the first time and it wouldn't be the last. But he was now too fixated on the notion of a real-life adventure—what do you think, he asked himself with quickening breath, was it an actual possibility?

Or was he a wish-thinking ass?

It was difficult to be even remotely certain of such things. At least so far as he was concerned. There were no comparisons for him to make, no backlog of experience to bring into play. His education was purely academic: as a man of the world he hadn't got started yet.

The fact was that he was a quasi-virgin, of which he was angrily ashamed, not only because of his virginity but also because of the circumstances under which he had not actually, one hundred percent, lost it. The girl in question had been a little beauty, one of those bewitching Dorsetshire lasses he met on a country holiday while bicycling with a friend, Mark Macmillan.

They had put up at rural homes during the trip: Molly was the daughter of the farmer who provided accommodations for two nights of the fortnight's journey. She was a tease, like so many of those girls in out-of-the-way, secluded villages, girls who had faces like Raphael Madonnas and the sexual appetites of a sow, which was probably only to be expected considering their opportunity to observe the activities of the animals with which they were surrounded. They married early, frequently when they were impregnated by some over-acquiescent yokel, losing their deceptive physical frailty to a robust overripeness. Then they became like the sows themselves, bursting with fat, like Rowlandson sluts.

But when they were young they were charming. "Hands off," Mark Macmillan warned, needlessly expounding what Rodney already knew, that you didn't lay a hand on a country girl if you wanted to keep your hide intact, or else be saddled with a wife you'd have to hide in the attic. Or if you were lucky, just having them bleed you for a bundle to pay for your transgression.

It was good advice, reinforcing Rodney's own caution, but Molly, who made no secret of its being, not Mark but his friend who titillated her, was persistent. So persistent, in fact, that she had her way with him, as Rodney's blood was hot and young too: she cornered him in a woody glade one early morning when he was alone and communing with nature. She must have followed him, all intent and guile, and before Rodney knew it, he was disrobing as rapidly as the girl, conscious of only one thing—her slenderwaisted, full-bosomed form on the loamy ground, her legs spread wantonly, revealing what he had never before set eyes on, the moist and blossomy lobes that led to the dark gates of an Elysian entrance and which, as he stared, exuded further moisture. On Molly's saintly little face a Circe smile spread slowly: eyes filmed, she drew her legs farther apart and deliberately, with the fingers of both hands, parted the fleshy lips that were crowned with curly chestnut hair and invited him in.

He needed no further coaxing. There was birdsong in the trees, the sun rayed through leaf and branch, warmth came from the summer day. It should have been Arcadian, but the boy was inexpert: his body was not accustomed to the real thing. Alone, unobserved, you could draw it out, slow up to prolong the delicious proceedings, then heat up once more and decide now was the time, now we'll work it up to the finish. But he was operating on a two-way basis now, and there was a decided difference.

It was predetermined in his mind, before he actually went down on her, to withdraw when he felt the approach of climax. The decision was made in a desire-haze, but was firm: the consequences of an "accident" were dire.

His body raced ahead of his mind, however, and he missed his target. The sight, the smell, the proximity of this rich and eloquent body sent him into a tailspin, he had no command over his performance. With his bursting member imperatively demanding quick release he went disconcertingly bleary-eyed, as if he had on a blindfold and was playing pin the tail on the donkey. He got himself part way into Molly and then shot out again, a victim of the very liquids that were designed to aid him in his entry, and found himself exploding, in great jets, over the Dorsetshire girl's belly.

He wanted very much, after he was able to breathe again in a more normal way, to kill her quickly and dispose of her body somewhere. An irrational but not entirely unreasonable longing. His first fuck and look what happened. Furthermore, she was shaking with laughter. Her legs were now clamping about his own, in a punishing grip, like that of a victorious wrestler underlining the punier strength of a defeated opponent. She was laughing audibly not long after that, throaty and rhythmical, plus tossing about his hair, tangling it up in a friendly frenzy, saying maddening, condescending things like better luck next time, li'ul man.

He would infinitely have preferred her shoveling into her clothes and stalking off in contempt.

It was a horrid memory, a quite wretched one, and for long afterwards it had plucked him out of sleep at night, firing his face with shame and humiliation. Molly had laughed, but Christine was a kinder person, and no crude country girl. It would be in the dark, in her room or his at the Mark Hopkins, and he was no longer a callow eighteen-year-old. A more sophisticated woman, such as Christine, would not expect clockwork efficiency, but instead would entice him slowly and leisurely, one seductive step at a time until, with masterful expertise, he gave it to her, and gave it to her . . . and gave it . . .

Whoops. Just in time he thrust his breakfast napkin against himself, puffing like a locomotive. Bloody close that, almost inundated the settee. He came back to the present, not without some chagrin. Ah, the divine Mrs. J. Ah so near and yet so far. How the bloody hell was he ever going to accomplish that which he so yearned for?

He got rid of the sopping napkin, cleaned up his breakfast dishes, told himself it was time to become really serious about starting up something it was clear the lady was obviously not going to instigate on her own, and dialed her number.

After six rings he sagged. Out. She was out. *As* usual. Damn bloody damn. Teeth set, he kept at it. Maybe she was in the bath. Give her a little more time. Wrath replaced disappointment. She wasn't out, it was too early, it was only just past ten. She was always home at this hour, she was a late riser. He'd just keep on until he drove her crazy, and if she was in the bath she would have, in desperation, to get out of the tub and answer the phone that was screeching away.

"Hello, hello," a voice suddenly said in his ear, so unexpectedly, by this time, that he jumped.

"Oh," he said jerkily. "Is that you, Christine?"

"Is that you, Rodney?"

"Yes, did I get you out of the bath?"

"Out of the bath? No, I went downstairs to get our mail."

"How about lunch," he asked. "I've given you a good bit of time to rest up after your hols."

"Wish I could, Rodney, but I'm meeting my friends at oneish. You know, my women's group. Oh. Can you come to dinner this week? You say what night, any's okay for me."

"I'm disappointed," he said slowly. "I had particularly wanted to see you today."

"Why today?"

"I'm at loose ends today. Not feeling up to par a-*tall*." He made his voice just the right shade of forlorn. "I wanted, very much wanted to be with you today, Christine. Can't you rearrange your plans?"

After a minimal silence she said, with gentle concern, "Are you sick or something?"

"Just lonely." The dolor deepened in his voice. "Just a little lonely."

Heartlessly, she laughed. "Oh, *Rodney*. Why should you be lonely? What's the matter with Jeannie, has she given you the gate?"

"It isn't Jeannie I wanted to see. If it was I'd see her."

"Then find some other girl. Nothing like a little variety. Silly boy—why, you're the most eligible bachelor in town." Then she became maternal and brisk. "Darling, I'll call you tomorrow. No, tonight, I'll call you tonight. Meanwhile, when can you come for dinner?"

"We'll see," he said coolly.

"What's the matter with you, dear?"

"And don't call me dear in that patronizing way," he said, dropping the cool and making it icy. "I expected better from you, Christine."

With that he hung up.

She'll call right back, he thought, waiting expectantly. She would of course instantly call right back. Certainly. She wouldn't ignore his plaint, her heart was too soft for that. So now she'd call him back and say, Rodney, we can't have you so upset, of course I'll change my plans and meet you.

She didn't call right back, however. She didn't call back at all.

He considered rushing over to her apartment and raping her on the spot.

Getting dressed, he began to really weigh this thought in his mind. She was clearly alone, otherwise the phone would have been picked up before it had been. That meant it wasn't the housekeeper's day to be there. Bruce and Nancy would be at school. Even if he didn't rape her he could make some kind of headway with her, soften her up in some clever way. She would be dressing too, half naked, she would throw a robe over herself and hurry to the door. "Hello," he would say nonchalantly. He debonair, dangerous, his eyes

352

intent. "Why, Rodney, you look so strange, so — I've never seen you like this."

No, we are not going to build up a head of steam again, he told himself disgustedly, tightening his legs. What the hell was he going to do with himself today anyway? Suddenly New York City seemed an alien place. Now that he had canvassed its purlieus it remained that he was, in all the real ways, just another tourist. He had had fun, but he hadn't made a striking dent in the businesslike tenor of this gleaming metropolis; he was just another face in the crowd.

Dressed, brushed and walking tall, he locked up and went out to the street. Once there a surge of confidence gushed up in him. He had no way of knowing that this was a common Manhattan reaction, that once out of the confines of the studio or one-bedroom — little boxes made of ticky-tacky — a New Yorker gained a sense of heady power, mingling with the throng and under the impression that he was now in his rightful place, in the mainstream of the city he not only inhabited but also possessed — *his* property, *his* sward and, for that matter, his very living room. What's to worry, look at all this, and now we'll dance. The arrogant smile wreathed his handsome features once again and he strode untroubled downtown. Downtown because even if Christine refused to succumb to his entreaties today, maybe Jack Allerton would not.

He hadn't seen Jack since that afternoon in early June when he and Christine had been invited there. Chris, of course, had helped him find a few things for his flat, which she said looked very nice when finished. Aside from that she hadn't seen him either, for he had asked her, but she said Jack was busy carving out a writing career and the best thing was to leave him alone to do it.

All very well, Rodney thought, but it remained that Jack Allerton had done him a quite stupendous favor: if it weren't for Jack he might still be looking for a flat. He wondered if Jack had been to Windows on the World yet, at the Trade Center; it would be a good way to show his appreciation by taking him there to lunch. The poor chap must need a break anyway, crouched over his typewriter. It must be a most restricted life: Rodney was far from sure that it would suit himself, though the rewards could be great, and he would dearly love to see himself on the back cover of a book. The blurbs—"a fresh, new, blazing talent . . ."

He had a feeling Jack had *not* been to Windows on the World, many people had not, the view was fabulous, and so were the prices. A writer carving out a career almost certainly would not favor the latter.

Well, then, should he phone first?

He had a feeling—call it a hunch—that if he did, Jack would look at all the work he had to do and say, Rodney, I'm afraid I simply can't take the time, I'm bogged down in a chapter.

Or something like that.

Very well, no phone call. Just drop in. Ring the bell, rouse him from his labors and insist he get some fresh air and a good, hearty lunch. Just dropping in would be a *fait accompli*. Jack wouldn't have time to mull it over. He stepped up his pace, striding on. It would be pleasant to see Jack again. He was looking forward to it.

He got sidetracked at Alexander's, where they were having a fall sale. All the stores were having fall sales, but leave it to Alexander's to make theirs sound more alluring. EXCITING FALL SALE! DESIGNER COATS, DRESSES, SUITS! ITALIAN KNITS!

He went in and an hour later came out with a big, filled shopping bag. He preferred Bloomingdale's shopping bags, with those femme fatale faces, beautiful ladies with luscious lips, but anyway he had some good bargains in his hot little hands, and it dawned on him that it could be a selling point too, he'd explain to Jack Allerton that he ought to hurry right over to Alexander's, look what he himself had garnered. And then take him to lunch.

It was just short of noon when he turned into Jack's street. There was a man with a dog just ahead of him, a cute little bugger, one of those endearing Schnauzers New York was awash with, everyone seemed to have a Schnauzer on a leash. He caught up with the man and the dog and, just before going on past them, stooped to put a hand on the dog's head. "Hey there, little thing."

He was still half crouched when he spotted her. Christine. Christine Jennings, walking lightly up the stone steps of Jack's building. He lost balance slightly, astonished as he was and then, righting himself quickly, saw her gain the entrance. He watched, convinced he must be going off his rocker, as she pushed open the front door and disappeared inside.

What was this?

What *was* this? Why, she was having lunch with her friends. "You know, my women's group." Uncomprehension seized him and then, not much more than a second or two later, a peculiar feeling. A very peculiar feeling. His mouth felt dry. There could be an explanation? Jack too had called Christine. Jack was under some sort of stress, worse than his, Rodney's distress. Something so serious that Christine, ever the good samaritan, had hurried over to see what she could do. Maybe Jack had pneumonia or something. Though that seemed unlikely at this time of year. Well, then, maybe he had a *crise*, some ghastly bit of news.

Like what? Rodney thought, chilled. And in any case why should Jack Allerton turn to a casual acquaintance for whatever ghastly news had fallen on him? Why? Would he turn to Rodney, who was also a casual acquaintance? How could either of them solve his problem, or whatever it was.

Very odd, thought Rodney, standing indecisive on the street. The man and the Schnauzer had long since passed, in fact had turned the corner at Second Avenue. What the bloody devil was all this about, Rodney pondered, but at the bottom of his mind was a cold and stony supposition that didn't stay at the bottom of his mind for very much longer, but instead began to surface in quickening stages, like water flooding a basement floor, at first sluggishly and then with increasing rapidity.

Jack got there first.

This was put aside at once. No, he would not settle for that. And no, it was not possible. If it

356

was, he would have guessed it, seen some signs. She would have tipped her hand in some way. Mentioned Jack inadvertently. Then flushed, been disconcerted. And he would have been alerted.

It just was not possible.

It took him a long time to acknowledge that yes, it was not only possible but even probable. The way she had slid out of his invitations, always returning to the tried and true, and safe for her. "Not today, I'm so sorry, Rodney, but I'm longing to see you, so please, please come to dinner, you name the evening."

He felt a trifle faint. Dizzy and faint. There was a ringing in his ears, his head felt as if someone had tied a band round it and was pulling it tighter and tighter. It couldn't be that way, he silently insisted. It simply could not be anything like that, he must be crackers to even give it a moment's consideration.

In the next second his thoughts swung full circle to this conviction: his imagination had been running away with him. Your imagination is running away with you, he told himself. The situation he was picturing was—*must* be—out of the question, a by-product of his overactive preoccupation with Christine's desirability. He had been fantasizing about her too much and now he could find no other reason for her to be visiting Jack Allerton than a sexual one. It was all in his mind.

Maybe it wasn't Christine?

A hope that was dismissed almost at once. Reluctantly, but with resignation. He knew that of course it had been Christine going up those steps and vanishing into the doorway beyond. He might mistake someone else for her a block or so away, but—

It was Christine, all right.

He realized after a while that he had been standing, in the precise same spot, for something like fifteen minutes. Which meant that Christine had been, for those fifteen or so minutes, upstairs in Jack's flat. *What were they doing up there?*

A wave of blind anger swept over him. There was hurt mixed in with that violent fury, but he subdued the hurt. The anger was what was sustaining him and he held on to it, which was not at all difficult, as the more he let the hostility build the more vehement it became. It was a way of protecting himself from the terrible letdown, the enormity of his loss. He was unconsciously casting himself in the role of betrayed lover: the fact that this was somewhat uncalled for escaped his attention. He simply would not sit still for this, he decided in a white heat of rage. He would just go up those steps himself and ring that doorbell. Which he would have done in any case a quarter of an hour ago had he not seen Christine precede him in her ascent.

Okay, here we go. You just bet I shall find out what's going on. You just bet on it, my fine friends; we shall just haul out your dirty laundry; how will you like that?

Okay. He still stood there, however, his hands in his pockets and sketching out an opening gambit. Jack would answer the bell and he would open the door quickly, dash up the stairs to Jack's landing before the chap knew what hit him. It would be too late for Jack to dissemble, because there would be Christine, large as life, and nothing either of them could do.

Apparently your friends were all at death's door, Christine, and couldn't make it for lunch today?

Why, Rodney. Her white face, her shaking hands.

He gained the flight of steps in front of Jack's building and stopped. Suppose Jack answered the door in a bathrobe? Suppose Christine wasn't in the living room. Suppose she was concealing herself in the bedroom, cowering there when she heard the familiar voice of her onetime lodger?

Rodney paled. If he were thus confronted so baldly and blatantly with such a contretemps, would he be able to handle it? Would he be able to deliver a speech heavy with irony, dripping with sarcasm?

Would he be able to say anything at all?

His heart began to pump away unpleasantly; abruptly he felt nauseated. For a ghastly moment he thought he might be about to barf. This compulsion was conquered by sheer force of his will, then another thought, heretofore not occurring to him, rushed into his mind. My God, if someone were at the window in Jack's apartment they would be able to see him standing down here! He was in plain sight of anyone standing at the window!

This latest possibility sent him up the steps two at a time. At the top he hesitated, mentally feeling his way. On the one hand, if he had been seen from above he would have to go ahead and ring the bell. On the other hand, he was increasingly loath to face the truth. It seemed to Rodney that if Jack opened the door in a state of dishabille he would turn tail and make for the stairs again, speechless and ashen. Like a whipped cur.

He opened the outer door and stepped quickly into the vestibule. Chances were no one had been standing at the window. Also—a faint touch of cheer—if he, or she were at the window in the living room it would mean they were not in the bedroom.

Yes, what about *that*? A casual visit only, maybe on her way to meet her friends she was having lunch with them after all. And on an impulse had stopped in to see how Jack Allerton was doing, it could be that, couldn't it?

Let's think it over, he told himself, buying time. Perhaps after all it was nothing, an eerie coincidence only, and he was torturing himself for no reason.

Well, then? Shall we go ahead and ring the bell?

A finger hovering over the bell, Rodney saw in his peripheral vision a shadow to his left which, when he turned to look, proved to be someone coming up the steps from the street. Ah, Christ!

He had to make a hasty decision. Either press the bell or, if he after all was not going to, open the door and go out, make as if he had just left someone's flat, was now departing. Which was it going to be, and it had to be fast because the person outside—it was a middle-aged woman—was at the top step now.

His uncertainty was the reason he finally pressed

it. She came in too quickly for him to mull it over any longer. The fact that she gave him a thorough, comprehensive glance didn't help matters any: she looked as if she were a suspicious sort, not happy about seeing a stranger standing in her vestibule.

"Good morning," he said, and plunged his finger down on the bell.

She said, "Good afternoon," and made an elaborate fuss about finding her keys, groping in her handbag and keeping her eye on him. The keys appeared to be elusive, she was fishing about in the depths of her bag, shuffling through its contents. Rodney had heard a few New York stories: people—particularly women—didn't like to open the door with an unknown person—particularly an unknown man—standing outside on the threshold.

"Why don't you ring it again," she suggested, edging a little closer to the outer door. He gave her a look of utter hatred. This lady seemed intent on making things even more difficult for him.

He rang again, and his mind shifted suddenly from the woman as he realized that when someone rings your doorbell you generally didn't take all day to answer it, unless you were in the bath, and if Jack had a visitor he wouldn't be in the bath, would he? The only reason Jack wouldn't answer the doorbell if he had a visitor—which in this case happened to be Christine—would be that he simply did not want to be disturbed.

There was still no response to either of Rodney's rings.

"Patently," woman said, "patently your friend is not at home."

"Yes, patently," he echoed, abusing her mentally for only a second or two and then too infuriated with the status quo to give her another thought. "Thank you," he said, and let himself out. This time he took the steps slowly, funereally, walking down with stately steps with his legs feeling heavy and thick. Into his turbulent muddle of thoughts popped the story of "The Little Mermaid." by Hans Christian Andersen, where the lovely little sea nymph, falling in love with a mortal, prayed for limbs instead of her fish tail, so that she might be mortal too. She got her legs, but pain along with them, as every step she took proved to be excruiating agony.

Well, he had fallen in love with a mortal too, though he had thought of her as goddess (with a few earthly appetites). Just a mortal after all, weak and designing and corrupt. They were up there and they hadn't answered the bell. Was any further corroboration needed?

He was all purpose now. He was Nemesis, shadowing a sinner. She would not go unscathed. He took up a position at the foot of the street, on the corner of Second Avenue, which was nearer Jack's building than Third. He would bide his time, and bide his time he did, even though his legs began to feel more and more like the little mermaid's after an hour or so of shifting from one foot to the other. Also his eyes, from constant concentration on that building up the block, were strained and bleary.

There was a pizza store across the avenue. He would like a slice, not that he had the slightest desire to *eat*, it would probably stick in his throat, but simply to help pass the time and take his mind off his misery.

There was no question of his leaving his post, however. That would be foolhardy. Nevertheless, when his watch told him it was now past two, he surrendered to hunger pangs, telling himself that the body had to be refueled; it was a matter of obeying the laws of nature.

The phrase, laws of nature, suddenly made him want to pee. If he were a street urchin in Naples he would go ahead and pee against the wall of the corner building. Hell. Well, he wasn't going to pee, he wasn't going to leave this spot, and that was final. He tightened his sphincter and determination, and the compulsion passed.

A kid, about nine or ten, crossed the street and reached the place where Rodney was standing. He stopped the kid. "I say," he hazarded. "I was wondering—you see I have to stay here, I can't move, I'm on the watch for someone. It's very important, don'tcha know."

He reached in a pants pocket and pulled out a handful of change. "I was wondering if you would be so kind as to go in that pizza place and bring me back a slice?"

"You want a slice? One enough?"

"One will be fine. Thank you very much. Here's the money, then." He counted out two dollars in quarters and dimes. handed it over. "You won't mind?"

"Nope. You gave me too much."

"Oh. That's perfectly all right. You keep whatever is left for yourself. I do thank you."

"Be right back."

It wasn't long before he returned, skipping across

the avenue. "Here ya go," he said, tough and street-wise. "This is left over, you want me to keep it?"

"Yes, of course, of course. And many thanks."

"You a cop? Plainclothes?"

"A cop?"

The kid smirked knowingly. "Okay, let it go," he said. "Your business. Good luck, I hope you catch him."

Then he bounced off and Rodney, hooking the Alexander's bag over an arm, folded the slice the way he had learned to do and ate it, saving the end crust for the last; all the while keeping his eyes on Jack's building. It couldn't be long now, he thought wearily, she's been there for over two hours.

The kid had thought he was a cop. Plainclothes. Maybe that would make his day. He probably watched crime shows on the telly one after the other and today was sure he had met a real live Avenger. He should have asked that boy to get him a coke too, now he was thirsty.

Half an hour later, at a little after three, Rodney gave up the ghost. The spirit was willing but the flesh was weak. It was asking too much of his muscles and his feet and his fortitude. He felt utterly defeated, weary and impotent. He had tried, but he wasn't up to another minute of this death watch. It was all for nothing, he had stood here, like one of the guards at Buckingham Palace, to no end. All he knew was that Christine Jennings was still in Jack's flat and they weren't answering the doorbell.

With a long last, bitter look up the street he left the corner and crossed to the other side of the street, no destination in mind but heading uptown because he lived uptown and he supposed he might as well go home now. He could scarcely believe his eyes when, at that precise moment, two people came out of the house he had been watching, two people who were, mirabile dictu, Christine and Jack. They came out, stood for a brief moment at the top and then, hand in hand, walked down the steps, with Christine's handbag dangling from one arm and Jack saying something to her. Her face was upturned and even from this distance he could see the warm coral lips curved in a smile.

Rodney, tense and hugging the corner building for concealment, stared bugeyed, wanting to take in everything he could and yet fearful of being spotted. They stood, Christine and Jack Allerton, at the bottom of the steps for à moment, as if conferring about something, then he saw Christine nod. Right after that they turned left and strolled up to Third, close together and hands brushing.

Stunned and sick, Rodney—his eyes strained and a crick in the neck from the prolonged vigil—walked up Second, in his mind a monotonous, thudding refrain. *Guilty as charged. Guilty. Guilty as charged*. So. Well, there you were. They had been tried and found guilty. As charged.

He was very well aware that none of this was his business, that what he had discovered was none of his concern. He was ashamed and disgusted at his half-baked adoration of Christine Jennings, like a kid crush, a dumb pash. He was ashamed and disgusted with his self-image and felt he would not be able to face himself in a mirror. He was a wog and a jackass and he wanted to go home. Back home, where home really was.

But he had his pride. He had said a year and, by Christ, it would be a year. He would find a good whorehouse and learn the ropes and then he would go to every singles bar in Manhattan and lay a different girl every night.

He would show her.

First he would go to San Francisco, find his way around another town. He would do something spectacular right away, right away fast.

Where had his bravado gone? His urbanity? His nonchalance? He felt sick at his stomach again, and then his eyes smarted, which galled him almost to the breaking point. Tears too?

When he let himself in his flat the place mocked him. Everything in it was practically labelled with the person who had helped him find these pieces. The *Vogue* poster, the Steinberg *New Yorker* cover taking up a whole side wall. The Brown Jordan settee and the Beylerian stackers and the brass étagère. The Saarinen chair.

It had started out so splendidly. *Hello, Rodney, my dear, kiss kiss. And where shall we have lunch today, love?* He had even, at odd and sundry times, felt sorry for Carl Jennings who, when Christine fell prey to the inevitable, would be a thorn in his conscience. After all Carl was Mum's friend as well as Christine.

Woolgathering, all of it woolgathering. Dreams of glory. He felt himself a pitiable object, a clod, with neither machismo nor clout of any kind. He was a British Holden Caulfield, he belonged in a nursery, riding a rocking horse.

Be that as it may, he would get his digs in. She had said she would call him tonight. If she didn't he would call her.

He would most assuredly get his digs in.

And then cut her out of his heart.

19.

The telephone rang at a quarter to eleven. "Who's calling at this hour?" Carl asked.

"For Nancy, one supposes."

"Or another wrong number. You notice how often that's happening lately?"

"Um hum."

Right after that Nancy came to the doorway of the living room. "For you, Mother, it's Rodney."

"Rodney? Oh, gosh, I promised to call him this evening. He'll be reproachful. I'll take it in my bedroom, Nancy."

She lit a cigarette on the way. He'd be reproachful, of course. Lonely, he'd said this morning. Well, we must do something about that. When did I ask him to dinner, or didn't I say?

"Rodney, I'm very sorry," she said, picking up the receiver. She settled herself on the side of the bed and heard the other extension click off. "I said I'd call, didn't I? I'm afraid the time got away from me. Now what is this about your not being up to par, hum? First, though, you are coming to dinner this week? How about Friday, is that all right for you?"

"Under the circumstances it would seem contraindicated," he said, sounding like one of Carl's medical colleagues. She laughed, amused. "Contraindicated, Rodney? Why so?"

"You can't guess?"

"Guess what?"

"What it means, what I said."

"You're not making much sense," she pointed out, then added, the thought suddenly occurring to her, "Rodney, are you drinking?"

"No, I'm not drinking."

"You seem to be somewhat incoherent, however. Do you mean you have a date on Friday and that's why it's contraindicated? But bring your date, I'd be delighted. So what's the problem?"

"I do hope you don't mind my calling this late, Christine."

"I don't mind. You should know, having lived with us, that we don't go to bed with the chickens."

She smiled. "You're mad at me for not calling

you tonight when I said I would. Please forgive me, dear. The time somehow got away from me. You know how it is sometimes. So you'll come on Friday with a girl, all right? Is it Jeannie or a new girl?"

"I don't have a new girl, I don't want a new girl, I don't want any girl at all and I'm going to San Francisco."

"Does your mother know that?" she asked sharply.

"Not yet."

"Why are you going to San Francisco?"

"Because this town's Sodom and Gomorrah, that's why."

"When did you discover that?" she asked dryly.

"Today."

"Rodney, I'm sure you're drinking and you'll end up sick as a dog. We're coming right over. Carl and I will be right over. In the meantime don't take another swallow, you hear?"

His voice suddenly had something ugly in it. Some weird undertone that came over the wires when he answered. "Don't come over," he said, in that strange, hard, ugly voice. "I won't open the door to you."

"Rodney, my God, what is this all about?" she demanded, really alarmed. "What could possess you to say a thing like that? What could possibly—"

"Christine? I just thought I'd ask you if you enjoyed your lunch today. Your lunch with your friends. The women's group, I believe you said."

The tone of his voice and the sudden switch to her day's activities, which should be of no import or interest to him, gave her pause. Did it mean that he was, for some petulant reason, really angry at her for not cancelling the plans she said she had, was he actually going to hold that against her? He had said, to be fair, that he was not up to par—did it mean that he was in some kind of emotional dither, the way kids got into so suddenly, with their lightning changes of mood?

"Yes, I did," she said slowly. "Why do you ask? That is to say, Rodney, why do you ask something like that at this late hour?"

"Oh," he replied. "I thought you said you weren't jarred by a call at this hour."

"Something's wrong," she said flatly. "Something's wrong and I want to know what it is, Rodney. I'm waiting, love. If you don't tell me what it is, I promise Carl and I will hop into a cab and if you don't let us in I'll call the super."

"One moment," he said. Clear and distinct. "Just one moment, if you please, Christine."

"Yes. Go ahead. Speak up, Rodney. I want to know what's wrong with you, what you're talking about."

"I'm talking about your group lunch," he said. "Your group lunch on Sixty-first Street. With a mutual friend, name of Jack Allerton."

"I beg your pardon?" she said, a flutter setting up in her chest. "Would you mind repeating that?"

"Why would you want me to repeat it, Christine?"

"You're right, I don't want you to. What I do want is that you retract it. Unsay it, Rodney. I have no idea what you think you know but I assure you you're barking up the wrong tree. And now, if you don't mind, apologize, please. Apologize and say you're sorry."

"A pleonasm," he informed her. "Apologizing and saying you're sorry is the same thing."

"Don't trifle with someone who's your good and true friend, and don't be rude and uncouth, you were brought up better than that. Rodney, how dare you be unkind to me, who loves you! Flooding me with accusations, how *could* you?"

"How could *you?*" he countered, and the recollection, nothing at all but now meaning so much, flashed in on her. The bell rang: "Aren't you going to answer it, Jack?"

"Not expecting any deliveries these days," he said. "It's just someone who forgot their keys, they want to be buzzed in. I won't do that, uh uh. It's just the way goons get in, you can't be too careful in these brownstones. Well, you must know that, you lived in one once."

"How could you is more to the point," Rodney went on. "I saw you, Christine. I saw you going in there. I was on my way to his flat myself, wanting some company, which you had denied me, and there you were, just ahead of me on the street. I saw you going in. And now I know you're having an affair with him."

"Whatever you saw, or whatever you think you saw, is meaningless," she said, her voice hard and determined. "Also—*also*, if I *were* having an affair with someone it would have nothing whatever to do with you. Don't interfere in my life, Rodney, don't ever do that. I'm sorry you felt called upon to spy on me, and I'm sorry your imaginings led you to believe that I was at Jack Allerton's today. When I tell you I'm going to do something, that's what I'm going to do, and if you should happen to think otherwise, why it's unfortunate as well as insulting. I'm a big girl, Rodney, and I conduct my life as I see fit. It's time, high time, that the same should apply to you. That is, if you want to attain the status of a responsible adult."

"Are you telling me you weren't *there*?" he asked belligerently.

"I'm telling you that I was having lunch with my friends at a midtown restaurant and that's what you're going to accept."

"Can you explain why I should accept it?"

"Because I insist you do. A final period after that, Rodney. I'll try not to hold this against you, because your mother is a cherished friend of mine. But you've succeeded in hurting me deeply, as well as blemishing yourself in my eyes because of your flagrant intrusion into my private life."

At the other end of the line silence now. He was there, though, the wires still hummed. After a second or two she said, "Rodney?"

"Yes, what?"

"Did you understand what I said?"

"Very well indeed. You want me to keep my mouth shut."

She closed her eyes. God. Who would have thought? Rodney. Upsetting the apple cart. She knew now that Jack had been right. "He's in love with you too."

Of course she had sensed it, his youthful admiration, the goo-goo eyes. It was such an *everyday* occurrence. Such a dreary cliché, a young boy responding to an older woman who somehow put ideas, all unwittingly, into his head. Rodney had gotten it into his mind that he might charm her into some sort of flirtation, innocent or otherwise, but at least something he could dream about, a love object, maybe not available but *there*, where he could give into his fantasies.

And then, somehow, he had come to know about her and Jack. Had seen her today. Had actually *seen* her.

And now he was vengeful.

She cleared her throat. "I want you to act like a decent human being," she said quietly. "And that, my friend, is that. Either you give me some assurance that you *can* behave in such a manner or else you bow out of our lives. I can't have it any other way. If you want to think about it, do so, then call me when you've made your decision. And now, Rodney, I'm going to say good night."

She didn't hang up right away. She waited, to give him time to recollect himself. It didn't appear to be going to happen, so she started to put down the receiver.

"Don't hang up," he said quickly.

"I'm still here."

"You want me to apologize for what's only the truth?"

She said, "Good night, Rodney."

"No. Wait. I apologize. I apologize because—"

"It doesn't matter because why. You've apologized and I take it you mean it."

"At the same time it's bitter fruit," he said in a defeated voice. "I just would like you to understand that."

"I just would like *you* to understand that it's of no importance to me what your opinion is. And if that's bitter fruit too, there's plenty of that in a lifetime, as we all come to discover. One thing more, Rodney. In spite of this breach of friendship and good faith you're still part of our lives. If you wish to be. You're Peggy's son, and at heart a fine boy, only you've gone into spheres that don't have anything to do with you. We'll skip dinner on Friday, because it's better for both of us to wait for a while. Just the same, try to remember that you are very much loved by me and my family, always will be. And now go to bed."

She waited, but nothing more seemed to be forthcoming.

"Good night, Rodney," she said, and put down the receiver.

She hadn't bothered to switch on a lamp when she came in. The room had sufficient illumination from the light that shone in from out of doors. She was glad to be sheltered in shadows, the way she felt and the way she knew she was going to feel when she had been able to sort this all out. Her heart was pounding away, she could see its acceleration stirring her shirt.

How could such a rotten coincidence come about, that Rodney had been on his way to Jack's today too. How sick and sad and besmirched she felt, how robbed.

There was a slight sound from the other bed, a faint creak of springs. She turned slightly. "Who's there?"

Carl's voice. "Me."

"How long have you been in here?"

"Long enough," he said. "I didn't mean to eavesdrop, I though you knew I was here."

"I didn't know, but it's all right. This is your room too."

"Also my life. What's up Christine?"

"You must have heard. And now you know."

"Do I? All I heard was denials."

"There was nothing to do but deny. It's nothing to do with him. Just me. Us."

"You are seeing someone else, then?"

"Yes, I have been."

"Somehow," he said quietly, "somehow, in my fatuous way, I never anticipated anything like this."

"I never anticipated anything like this either."

"What happens now?"

"Nothing. Unless you want a divorce."

"Why would I want that?"

"You've just learned that your wife is having an affair with another man. That's considered A-one grounds for divorce."

He didn't say anything. She didn't know whether he was sitting stiffly, as she was, or lying down, what his face looked like, what expression he wore, if it was angry or wounded or uncomprehending. "It wouldn't change things to say how sorry I am that you had to know about this," she told him. "But I am sorry, terribly, agonizingly sorry, Carl.

That you had to be hit over the head so swiftly and brutally. I never wanted to hurt you, just as I never wanted you to hurt me. And now I have."

"You sure have," he said then. "You sure as hell have. I must have been cockeyed not to have sensed something was going on. Seventeen years—you think you know someone. Especially if you're a fatuous ass like me. You don't expect anything to go wrong."

"I never have stopped loving you," she said. "Maybe you won't be able to believe that. But it's true."

"You must admit it isn't the easiest thing to believe."

"Carl, this has happened to other couples and it will happen until the end of time. I can't demand that you live with it, though, I realize that."

"Do *you* want a divorce?"

"I don't know what I want. Maybe to be dead."

A creak of the springs again as he rose and came over to her, sat down beside her. "Would you like a cigarette?" he asked.

"Yes."

He got up again. "Be right back, I'll get some from inside."

"Don't turn on the light."

"I won't."

When he returned he lit one for her and positioned the ashtray on the bedside table. Then sat down. "Please don't say that again," he said urgently. "That maybe you want to be dead. And please don't think of me as the enemy."

"The enemy? You? I should think I would seem the enemy," she cried.

377

"Neither of us should think that. No matter what's happened, or what will happen. For God's sake, darling, we've been in each others' lives for a long, long span of years. Two intelligent, caring people. I know you're not, and couldn't be, a promiscuous woman, so what I meant was if you consider that I'd be standing in your way, if you're into something that's more than just, just an affair—"

He looked down and then up again and went on. "If that should be the case, then—"

"Are you telling me that you'd step aside? Or are you saying that you want to? You can't hack the status quo and you want out. For which I assure you I wouldn't blame you, Carl. There are lots of things we don't know about each other, just as there are lots of things we don't know about ourselves. Surprises are constantly in store. God, I didn't really believe I'd get to be this age, but here I am, things being taken away from me bit by bit, things you always took for granted. I'm a figurehead, I'm an empty paper bag, I have no place in the scheme of things."

"Why?" he asked quietly. "Why do you feel that way, Chris?"

"Why not," she said bitterly. "I'm your average, everyday, garden variety of anxiety-ridden middle-aged womanhood. I've done my job, it's over and I can only look forward to long and empty years, that's why."

"Somehow," he said, "somehow your saying that is worse than the, the other thing. That you're unhappy. That everything we've built up hasn't been enough."

His arms dangled between his knees. "And that I haven't known it. I just thought — well, you had a rich life, a fulfilling life. Like me. *With* me. For me it's been, and *is*, the whole ball game. I never, for a minute, got restless and dissatisfied. Maybe I should have told you that more often. What you meant to me. Mean to me."

"It isn't that," she said tightly. "It isn't you, Carl. You haven't failed me, don't think that, for Christ's sake. You haven't done anything but be good to me. It's true, though, that you have something I don't, you're part of the outside world. I'm not."

"So you went into that outside world and found something else."

"No. It happened. It was an accident. It could have happened to you."

"Nothing just happens. It happens because you decide it will happen."

"Maybe."

She saw his quick pain. So she wanted to hurt him after all. But it wasn't cruelty; she absolved herself of that. He would have to know, really know, that she was wretched, that she was up shit creek, not just a petulant protestor, the mad housewife. "I have to know, Carl. Do you want a divorce?"

A prolonged silence. Long enough for her to prepare herself for his answer. She knew, with certainty, that everything would be different if she and Jack were the same age. She had married young — according today's standards — lived her young life with Carl. It would be painful, perhaps crucifying and a mistake after all, to leave him, but she would be halfway sure, right this minute, that she would do it if she and Jack were in the same time of life.

They weren't. Those years between them meant far more than just the number of them. Jack himself had commented that she had "gotten there," meaning financial security, upward mobility, the end of the economic struggle. In ten more years or so it would be the same story for Jack, in all likelihood, the race run, the uncertainty over. Nobody knows my name, he had said. Most people's names weren't known, in the way he meant, but Jack Allerton wouldn't be satisfied with that. He was aiming for literary éclat, either critical or popular, or both. It would be a long time before he achieved that goal, and he needed a young courageous girl who would nourish his drives single-mindedly, share his vie do Bohème with zest and strength.

It was that old bugaboo, the time machine. It was either too early or too late. You could fight a lot of things, but you couldn't fight time. Forward you went, like it or not, but you could never go back.

"I don't want a divorce, no," Carl finally said. "Don't make the mistake of thinking I took so long to answer because I was thinking it over. I took so long because I'm afraid of what you might say when I throw it back to you. I don't know whether I'm up to it. I don't want a divorce, I can't even imagine it, but it's for you to say too. Christine, do you want it?"

She shook her head. "No." It was almost inaudible. "No, I don't," she said more clearly.

"You're sure?"

"If I weren't I'd say so. I'm sure, yes. I hope you are."

"How can I say it more emphatically?" There was a quick movement of his hands. "My God, it's not even in the realm of my imagining, Chris. I'm not a complex man, Chris, I'm pretty much a plodding sort, an everyday kind of guy, but I've always felt I got the brass ring on the merry-go-round when I got you. Oh, Christ, yes, I want you to stay with me. If you do, I'll try, try very hard to put everything out of my mind except my love for you. My love and deep, deep concern for your welfare. We've got two kids who are almost ready to be out on their own. You don't think that's a change in my life too? I'm not getting any younger either, you know. Men have their own hangups, they cut deep. The big prizes are never going to come your way, you know that after a while."

He put his arms around her, tentative, unsure. "I've always depended on you," he said. "We all have, you're the star that guides the ship. Asking too much, accepting too much. And now I've gotten my lumps. A brick falling on my head when I least expected it. A lot of bewildering things to accept. It hurts. Sure it hurts. You've made no explanations and I take it you're not going to offer any, about what's been going on, and I suppose that's the way it's going to be."

He withdrew his arm and sat now with his hands on his knees. "I said it hurts," he repeated. "Not as

381

much as it will later, on, though. I'm still in the trauma stage. Shock and all that. The real hurt will come creeping up on me little by little, but that's for me to handle. But divorce? Oh, no. No. I love you. God, you're as much a part of me as my arms, as my legs, my bicuspids. I'll lose the bicuspids one of these days, I guess, though I hope not for a long time. But I don't want to lose you. Not ever, if I'm that lucky."

"I don't want to lose you either," she said. "You're too much a part of me too." She nodded. "That's the God's honest truth. If it helps any."

"Yeah, it helps," he told her, and got up. "Let's not talk anymore tonight."

She put a hand on his arm. "Wait."

He sat down again. She swallowed. "Are you going to trust me?"

A hesitant silence, a quick glance at her. She persisted. "You said let's not talk anymore tonight. I assume you mean about this, about Rodney's phone call. Carl, I will never talk about it. It was—it happened. That's all I'll ever say. I'm sorry, but you'll have to accept that. If you can't, I want to know now."

After a while he said, "If that's the way you want it."

"It's the only way I can handle it." She put a hand over his. "Thank you for being a very fine man. I've always thought I got the brass ring on the merry-go-round too, Carl."

He didn't answer because he was evidently unable to speak. He just returned the pressure of her hand and got up again. She heard him going out of the room. She sat there for a while longer, knowing he had left her to compose herself, knowing too that he had to compose himself as well.

She got up finally, went to the bathroom, ran the tap and splashed water on her face. Cold and stinging. Then she toweled it, stood thinking. That boy, who would have dreamed that Rodney would stumble on her today, see her go into *that* building, who would have *dreamed*? God in heaven, it was just too horrible and bizarre. I must see Clover, she thought dully, I have to talk to someone. How could she tell Jack, what would she say to him? She must get a job, change her hours, get out of this house, this house, this house.

Of course it was over. How could it be otherwise? What could she say to Jack—don't you understand, I don't have the impetus any more, I don't have the stamina, something's gone out of me?

Mentally, she stood at the front window in Jack's apartment, looking out at the handsome maple tree, the green of its leaves lightly burnished with the colors of autumn, the row houses across the way, old and gracious, as New York used to be, small-scaled and individualistic. The slender saplings that had been planted earlier in the year flushed with gold that mingled with their tender green. The pistachio-tinted town house farther down, with its six-on-six windows. A street that had come to be part of her life and to which she was going to say goodbye.

How? How could she bring herself to do that?

She undressed, got into her nightgown, crept into bed. She was calmer now, or she was rallying, regaining a sense of proportion. The only decision made was to see Clover, talk to her, ask some advice about looking for work. The rest would be by ear. Tonight's emotional scene would eventually be simply a part of the past: its impact would lessen, its nightmare quality dim. For all she knew there would be no substantial changes, and she might go right on seeing Jack.

But it could never be the same. The bloom was off the rose. It was messy, it had become public knowledge, and it had lost its loveliness. Just like everything else. Everything always turned sour in the end.

20.

"So you've ended it," Clover said slowly. "Shut the door on it. It's over, then."

"It was over the minute Carl found out about it. After that it would have been cheating." Christine smiled. "That must sound weird. That it wasn't cheating until Carl learned about it."

"No, not weird at all. I understand what you mean. Chris, I'm so sorry."

"Well. Nothing else to do. When I got up this morning, after a very rotten night tossing and turning, I knew it was what had to be done."

"Easy as that."

"Easy? Clover—"

A shrug. "It's just that from the way you spoke the other day I thought it was something—well, not just your here today and gone tomorrow kind of ado."

"It isn't, wasn't."

"Okay, then, it wasn't easy."

"*Won't* be easy. I haven't—"

Clover waited. Christine felt her heart thumping painfully. "I haven't had it out with—we weren't meeting today, you see." She cleared her throat. "We will be tomorrow. I'll have to tell him tomorrow."

Her smile this time was forced. "Sounds as if I had an appointment for a D and C, with the threat of cancer in the back of my mind. Somehow even that might be easier."

She took a swallow of her drink. She felt sick, or dying, or she felt as if someone else had died, someone whose death she wouldn't be able to survive. She lit a cigarette, exhaled. "And then that will be that."

"For him too? He'll just say what a shame and then go his way with admirable equanimity?"

First she was hurt, then she was angry. Why was Clover saying things like this? "No," she replied shortly. "I told you it wouldn't be easy."

When she looked up, Clover's face was soft and kind. "Okay, I wouldn't for the world try to influence you, Christine. You must act as you must, same as I have to live according to my lights. Why don't you finish that drink and we'll order another? Talk away and I'll listen. I won't say another word."

She held up a hand. A few minutes later they had their refills. "What did you mean by influence me?" Christine demanded. "In what way?"

"No," Clover said firmly. "Just tell me what your plans are now. You said something over the phone about looking for a job."

"Yes, I'm going to. I've been trying to pretend that nothing was very different, even if my children are shooting up and soon to go their own separate ways. So what, I've been trying to rationalize, nothing will be very different, they'll still be under my aegis, in a way, and—"

She made an impatient gesture. "Pretending and knowing it isn't so at the same time. Knowing I'd have to face it and do something about it. What else is there but getting out and finding a new place for myself? I've been scared about it, but I'm not scared anymore. What I'm scared of is becoming one of those women who dribble their time away buying clothes and wracking their brains trying to find a way to fill their days. I won't do that. I simply will not. Ergo, a job."

Then she leaned forward. "First, though, tell me, please, what you meant about influencing me. Are you in some way indicating that you think I'm wrong to end this affair?"

"You said it wasn't an affair. Just an affair."

"Of course it's an affair! For lack of a better word! What else can I call it?"

A grin. "I guess I don't know."

"If you think I shouldn't end it, what would you do?"

"I'm me and you're you, it's as simple as that."

"If you were *me*, what would you do?"

"I'm not you, Chris, so there's no way for me to answer that question. All I can tell you is that I think if you find something that makes your life a joy, a splendid joy, then you should hold on to it. I think it's monstrous to kill a living thing, I couldn't do it, I just couldn't. To me it would be wrong, far more wrong than cheating, put quotes around that word. I'd pay the price. There's a price when you deal two ways, but then nothing comes free if you'll stop to think about it. We're not junior misses any longer, Chris, it's *bonjour tristesse* time, we both know that. Carl Jung claimed that it was impossible to live through the second half of life by the same standards that served so well during the first half. Maybe he was right. I'm inclined to think so."

She lit a cigarette, exhaled the smoke. It drifted upward in small circles, then thinned out. There was the pungent smell of the burning tobacco. "Whatever I do, however, has no bearing on whatever you do. The last thing in the world I'd want is to sway another person, it's not my mission in life. You have your own strong mind, you'll act, now and always, as it befits you. I *am* sorry about your dilemma, I can't do anything about that, but if you're really serious about work I'll be delighted to put out feelers. Between Anton and me, we'll find you something, and it won't be as a lowly file clerk. I've worked with you, I know your caliber. I would say Anton would be the one to come up with something good, really good. You must set your sights high. If by any chance you get placed in An-

388

ton's office, he'll probably end up working for *you*. I remember how you used to dig in there and put the pieces together — you're a natural-born organizer. You'll do fine, kiddo, you'll do just fine."

She beamed. "Soon as I get back to the office I'll call Anton, tell him to get on his stick."

"I just don't know how to say thanks, Clo. Please don't pressure him!"

"I won't need to. He'll come through without fail, one of my friends is the same as asking for myself. Take heart. Now finish that drink and let's get our order in. Old Clover will put that smile back on your face, if she has to die trying."

They said goodbye outside the restaurant an hour later: Christine spent the rest of the afternoon walking. It was mainly to tire herself out; she wanted very much to have a little sleep tonight. Last night had been a horror, falling off and then waking almost immediately, the whole sordid business rushing back into her mind. So the best thing to do was walk until your legs gave out, just put one foot in front of the other and trudge ahead. Like some old army mule.

One morning you got up and all was fine and dandy, next morning it was a sinkhole. You couldn't believe how fast it happened, the transition from perfect to execrable. It was unreal, but then it seemed to Christine that just about everything outside of making a meatloaf or taking a bath or dusting off a surface or planning a week's menu was unreal, that only the homespun little tasks of a day had any reality. The rest was *True Confessions,* cheap and trivial and luridly illustrated.

389

She walked down to Thirty-third Street, passing the Greek Orthodox Church, with its gilded dome, and the sprout of new highrises, then turned and walked back uptown. She wanted very much not to go home for the dinner hour, so as not to sit opposite Carl at the table and try to make conversation-as-usual with all of them. But she couldn't do that: if she did, Carl would think she was with "the other man." When she came to Jack's street she slowed up. She realized that she had turned off First Avenue in order to walk back up to Third, that it had been a compulsion to look up at that street, to see his house, and maybe Jack would be outside, waiting for her.

He was, of course, not standing there, and she went on. It was almost six when she passed through the lobby of the Colonnade, with a nod to the concierge, then rode up in the elevator. "Hi, Jimmy." The apartment was quietly humming. Both the kids were at home, sounds issuing from behind their doors. She didn't bother changing her street clothes but set about attending to the evening meal. A short time later Carl came home, his key in the lock, and shortly after that he pushed through the swinging doors to the kitchen.

She stiffened, feeling a quick hostility, even hatred. "Hello, darling," he said. "How was your day?"

"Uneventful. I didn't sleep very well last night. Neither did you. How was your day?"

"About as usual."

He opened the fridge, but then closed it right away. She was at the counter, chopping up shallots. She felt a hand on her shoulder, then his lips on her cheek. "Hey," he said. "Can I make you a drink?"

"Oh. Well, no. Thanks, dear, but not tonight. Go ahead if you want one, but we're having a pretty robust red wine tonight with the beef."

He still stood there, making her edgy, uneasy. He touched her shoulders lightly, just the faintest of pressures. "I love you so much, Chris," he said. Then his hands dropped.

She wanted to say she loved him too. It was certainly called for. Only she couldn't. Not at the moment, because the only thing she felt right now was a wild desolation, a sense of total defeat. She nodded, sweeping the chopped shallots into a bowl, and Carl went out, the door swinging behind him.

So much for that. It was a truce for now, but she knew enough about people—and particularly her husband—to be grimly sure that no matter how understanding, or tolerant, or generous Carl was, it remained that nothing could ever again be as it had been, that there might not be censure but there would always be doubt, and that from now on there would be an invisible barrier between them, a Berlin wall between two parts of the same country. A similar division probably occurred in nine out of ten marriages and was, she supposed, only to be expected.

It was an evening on which she and Anton were not meeting, since it was one of his "at home" nights. He would call her later on, just for a hello and only for a minute or two, that was, if the opportunity presented itself. It didn't matter, really. Just knowing he was in her life was enough. In her life, alive and hearty and supportive. Dear, darling Anton. Clover walked home as usual, a grocery list in the pocket of her jacket. Not much, just milk and Boston lettuce and salted nuts and some Peppridge Farm goldfish. She would have to pay by check, as she had neglected to go to the bank for a cash withdrawal. Let's see now, she would wash her hair tonight, get that done for the weekend.

In the grocery store, getting herself a cart, she revised her thinking. As long as she had to write a check she might as well do the bulk of next week's shopping, rather than simply fill in on immediate necessities. She walked up and down the aisles, pushing the shopping cart, inwardly humming. It was autumn, which was her favorite time of the year, and the limpid light of outdoors filtered in, competing with the fluorescent overhead bulbs of the supermarket. Winter would make its appearance one of these days but not for a long while yet. Meanwhile, after an unusually even-tempered summer, Manhattan was enjoying an unusually rich and golden fall. Who could ask for anything more?

At the checkout counter Geraldo, the friendly Chicano boy, asked after Anton, who was thought to be her husband. "And how is Mr. Martinson?"

"Fine, thanks. Goodness, did I buy *that* much? I wonder when double-digit inflation will become triple digit?"

"Maybe soon," he said fatalistically. "Terrible."

"I'd hate to be on a fixed income."

"You gotta be a millionaire."

She staggered home with two heavy bags. Fortunately her building was only a step away, just off Madison and about a third of the way down the street. She had to put both bags down in order to open the entrance door then, angered, found it was off the latch anyway. Some people were born stupid, didn't take even the most rudimentary precautions, just let the door swing to instead of slamming it shut. She really must tell the super to instruct the tenants about things like this.

She hefted the grocery bags and went inside. Paused for a moment: the woman on the street floor was playing the piano. Her hours were much like Clover's; they left very often at the same time in the morning and frequently arrived home simultaneously. She was a pleasant woman, not in the first blush of youth but attractive, well dressed and casually friendly. She also played piano very well: tonight it was a Brahms Ballade, one Clover particularly liked.

Sounds nice, Clover thought, and started up the the stairs. Her apartment was on the second floor, which Anton called the *premier étage*, which it was in a European flat, the ground floor being the *rez-de-chaussée*. Anton was not only fluent in French as well as German, he was inclined to fall back on Gallic terms far more frequently than his native tongue. "Let's make a *saut*," he said, when he meant let's make a quick stop at this place or that place. She liked such cosmopolitan sprinklings, had added quite a number of them to her own vocabulary.

She also liked to return home after her day's work, as she was inordinately fond of her apartment. It was in the rear, with a southern exposure and an open-to-the-sun terrace, on which there was an umbrella table, four Deauville chairs and a glider. For as long as the weather permitted she and Anton dined out there. It was a lovely addition to have and a great place for sunbathing. There was also a little grill, where they broiled steaks or chicken parts.

She was humming aloud now, very mellow and chipper. It had been a long day but a profitable one, with a new client who was obviously well-heeled and who promised to be good for some lengthy European trips. I *am* doing well, she reflected, glad she had started in travel early rather than late; it would be difficult to establish oneself in these more precarious times.

She could probably find a niche in the business for Christine, for example, but it would be hard going for a newcomer at this point. Better by far for Anton to get Chris settled, which he had faithfully promised to do when she called him this afternoon. It would be dandy if he could find her something in his own firm: if Chris located in the Genesco Building she and Chris would be near each other; they could meet for lunch now and then. It would be a bonanza for both of them.

Poor Chris—she had looked so sad today at the restaurant. Sad and pale and oh, so tense. Imagine that boy, that Rodney, finding out about it, Chris getting a kick in the pants from someone she had been so kind to. What she must be going through.

She set down the shopping bags in front of her door and put the key in the lock. She was wondering belatedly if she had enough shampoo in the house for her hair later on and then, with a horrid shock, felt the knob turn of its own accord. Not with the key but all by itself: the door simply swung open, slowly and eerily, and she stood transfixed, not immediately comprehending.

After that everything happened with lightning rapidity. She was never to recapitulate exactly *how* it happened because she had reached the end of her life on this pleasant autumn afternoon, the last afternoon she was to know. Her brain, in those final few moments, transmitted the truth, that someone was inside her apartment, but before she could move, or even tell herself that she must run, turn and run, a figure loomed suddenly, darkening the doorway, a shocking apparition that short-circuited her mind as it sent her reeling back in the hurry of its flight.

There was a bend in the stairs toward the top: she landed there and, as her hands groped for something to grab onto, the intruder stumbled over her sprawled form. An excruciating pain as one of her hands was ground under a heavy foot, then she hurtled down the stairs like a sack of flour. Her mind whirled with the plummeting and the pounding footsteps and finally, as the interloper tangled with her helpless body near the bottom, she was swiftly knocked out by a foot flying against her jaw.

The piano-playing neighbor, alerted by the horrendous commotion, found her there, looking quite peaceful though in a gruesome position, with her head knocked through the wall and one of her hands mangled and pulpy. A grocery bag on the story above had tumbled over in the melee, spilling some of its contents through the wicks of the railing: a bottle of Ocean Spray cranberry juice, in splinters and slowly flooding the vinyl floor, dripped down in crimson splashes.

The neighbor, shaking, ashen, brought cold towels, chafed the girl's wrists, but after a while she realized that Miss Martinson was dead, so she ran back inside her apartment and called the police. They were there in five minutes, a siren announcing their arrival. "This lousy city," the neighbor said, her teeth chattering. She would not be playing any more Brahms Ballades tonight. The police questioned her.

"No, she was single."

"Family?"

"I don't know much about her. She was a lovely girl."

"Do you know of anyone we can contact?"

"She has a friend. Yes, I know his name. Ehrenberg. Anton Ehrenberg."

"A boyfriend, is he?"

"Something like that. They were together a lot."

"He live here too?"

"No, she lives alone. Lived alone."

"Do you mind coming up to her apartment with us?"

"Yes, all right."

Between them they found Clover's address book.

Under E, Anton Ehrenberg's number. Clover's keys were still in the lock. The police locked the door and gave the keys to the neighbor. Also Clover's pocketbook. "I'm Lieutenant Malone," one of the officers said. "We'll be in touch with you. Just a formality, you understand. Thank you very much, ma'am. You have any tranquillizers, you better take one. You look beat."

"I'm all right."

They had called Lenox Hill Hospital from Clover's apartment. The neighbor got a little hysterical about it: she said, "The hospital, get her to the hospital. If you take her to the morgue I'll raise a stink about it. That man has to go and see her this way, and it's not going to be on some marble slab. Call the hospital—"

"Don't worry," they soothed her. "Of course it will be the hospital, ma'am."

Soon a second siren shrilled up the street. Two attendants took Clover away on a gurney and put her inside the ambulance. Then everyone went away and the neighbor closeted herself inside her street-floor flat and locked the door, leaned against it.

This lousy city . . .

After a while her mind began to accept the facts. That lovely-looking Miss Martinson. Such a nice girl. How could you live in this lousy city? Sooner or later it could happen to you too.

She checked the locks again and got out the bottle of scotch.

21

The Martinson family cremated its dead, and so there was a quiet noonday service at Fresh Pond on Long Island. No eulogies, just a few words from the Bible, the ones applicable to death. *I am the Resurrection and the Life* . . . Mrs. Martinson and her other daughter, the married one, April. April's husband. Mrs. Martinson's sister and her sister's husband. Anton

Ehrenberg. There was no "viewing," the casket was closed, with sprays of red roses blanketing it. There was a profusion of flowers overall, scenting the air and bright as the day itself, which was ablaze with sun. April told them that her mother had been against it, but people wanted to "do something," and flowers, being the traditional offering, seemed the logical thing.

Ruth and Helene and Christine and Meryl had driven out in a rented limo, which would take them back again: after that they were going to be together for a while, probably at the Carlyle, for a quiet talk. Nobody wanted to think of food, it would be just coffee and brandy. There were quite a few people from Clover's agency and numerous others whom April said were clients of her sister's. An organist played "Jesu, Joy of Man's Desiring."

Anton sat with Clover's family, accepted, one of them. He was a handsome, distinguished-looking man, they all agreed, a fine-looking man. He wore a white carnation in his buttonhole and there was an earnest, attentive expression on his face as though, if he attended carefully to everything that was said it might be explained to him why his Clover was dead.

After a while the music came to a stop and then a young man in a cassock recited his little litany in a soft and cultured voice. Without the sound of the organ it was very, very quiet in the small chapel. "Whosoever believeth in me shall never die," the minister asserted. He had a hairline with a widow's peak and the hint of a cowlick at the crown of his head: he seemed shockingly young.

He held a handsome, gilt-edged, leather-bound copy of The Book in his hands, not reading from it but just clasping it loosely. He had memorized the passages, as if out of respect to the mourners, or maybe to show that he was no novice at these obsequies. Then he finished speaking. The organist improvised softly. Soon two tall gentlemen (attendants of the mortuary, one supposed) took charge of the casket and bore it to a door that had been unobtrusively opened at the left of the chapel, into which it disappeared, to be consigned to the flames and eternity.

Once again the organ. *Sheep Shall Safely Graze.* People seemed uncertain for a few minutes, and then one by one slowly got up, looking as if they were suffering from low back pain, as if it were difficult and distressful to move. A low murmur of voices as sympathy was offered to Clover's family. April came over and asked if they would come back to her aunt's house, her mother would like them to, Ruth and Helene and Christine and Meryl. "Just a few friends," she said.

Yes, of course they would, though they would have preferred different, each of them knew, longing for escape from the palpable presence of affliction that hung about, like a fog, like a miasma. Hollow-eyed, drawn and numbed, they climbed back into the limo again and rode back to Manhattan.

Mrs. Martinson's sister lived in Manhattan House, which was a replica of the Colonnade, or rather the reverse, as the former had been the first to go up. The rooms were large and gracious and well appointed, with any number of plants that clearly thrived in the abundance of light and air. April showed those who had not visited before where the bathrooms were, coats were deposited on a bed in the master bedroom and the fog had lifted a bit because when someone died you made every effort to cling to the comfort and solace of others for as long as you could, before the visits and the cards and the letters tapered off, so you made the most of it, the faces and bodies and proximity of friends and strangers. That was why these gatherings so often appeared to be festivities rather than keenings — to quell for as long as possible the full force of grief and anguish.

There was a tasteful buffet laid out on the dining room table and, perversely, appetite returned as you did the civilized thing, observed the amenities and helped yourself to a slice of succulent ham, filled your plate with olives and stuffed celery and a wedge of quiche. "You girls were such good friends to Clover," Mrs. Martinson said, her eyes dry but bloodshot, the little veins etched in pink. Ruth's eyes filled. Ruth, the disciplined one, the toughie, looking at life through a vision unclouded by sentiment. "We've been friends," Meryl said, "for a very long time. Mrs. Martinson, will you be in New York for a while?"

"Yes, I do think I will. I'm a widow, you know, no reason to hurry home. I'll be staying here with my sister for a while."

"I hope we'll see you again. If there's any possibility, would you let one of us know? Just a quiet lunch some day."

"That's very thoughtful, and thank you. I shall have to see how things go." She was sitting on a high-backed chair, a slender woman in a tailored suit. Beside her was her sister, Mrs. Bradley, and on her other side her brother-in-law. "You must eat something," both were urging her, though they were plateless themselves.

"Yes, of course, later. Not just yet."

"Not later, this won't do," her brother-in-law insisted, jumping up. "Just a few nibbles, or else you'll be sick."

"Perhaps some coffee. Please, don't fuss, Howard, all right, coffee then. And girls, please have some more quiche, more ham, there's enough for an army."

"I think I'd like coffee," Meryl said. "Mrs.

Bradley, may I get you a cup?"

"I'm going to skip coffee but thanks, dear."

"I think I'll skip the coffee too," Christine said. The aroma of it, which she generally found enticing, was making her a little ill. Her friends were queuing up at the urn, at which April was in attendance.

"Does it keep you awake?" Mrs. Martinson asked earnestly, as if her very life depended on the answer. You could see she was speaking mechanically, that her responses were purely automatic, polite and pertinent. She was talking to one of Clover's friends, but afterwards would never remember which one of them it had been.

"I'm afraid it might, yes."

"Wouldn't you like a drink?" her sister suggested.

"Oh yes, do have a drink," Mrs. Martinson said. "I'd very much like one myself, but the doctor's shot me up with sedatives, so I don't dare. My son-in-law is being bartender, April's husband." She patted Christine's hand. "You go have a nice, hearty scotch, it will do you good."

"You're sure there's nothing I can get for you?"

"Nothing at all, my dear. You're very sweet."

On the way to the drink table Anton Ehrenberg was suddenly at her side. She had observed him, as had her friends, standing talking to one or another of the guests and acting, in a quiet way, as a kind of host. He seemed to be very much a part of the Bradley household, and Christine realized that he and Clover must have been frequent visitors to this apartment.

"We met briefly at the ceremony," he said.

"Yes, of course. You're Anton. I'm Christine."

"May I get you something to drink?"

"Yes, thank you. I was just on my way to the table for one."

He introduced her to April's husband. "I've heard your name often," the younger man said with a smile. "What can I give you? Scotch, bourbon? Vodka—"

"Scotch, please. Just ice and water, no soda. Thanks very much."

"Anton?"

"Nothing for me, thanks." Anton, his hand on Christine's arm, looked about. "We can sit over there," he suggested. "A little out of the way from the others. You don't mind?"

"No, of course not." She saw that his bouton- niere was drooping. He guided her toward a secluded corner of the room. "Now we can talk," he said, giving her a quick look. "I hope you don't mind?"

"Of course I don't mind, Anton." Why should she mind, she thought, bleeding for him. Poor soul, he looked ravaged, and desolation washed over her, the way things turned out, your props taken away from you at the very drop of a hat and always when you least expected it. Clover dreaming that she was standing at his gravesite and now it was Clover who was dead.

"Mrs. Martinson is lovely," she said. "I've never met her before. I hope she will stay for a while, it would be so much better for her to be with her sister for a bit."

"Oh, yes."

"Particularly alone as she is."

"Yes, indeed."

"She has April, fortunately. And her grandchildren."

"Yes, that is a—a blessing."

"I suppose April didn't bring the children?"

"No, I understand they're in the care of some friends."

That took care of Mrs. Martinson, Christine thought. But what about Anton? We can talk, he had said, but this bereaved gentleman had nothing to talk about, it seemed. What the hell was there to talk about for either of them? A vision of Jack's apartment flashed in on her, so vivid that everything else seemed to fall away, the crowded room and the people and the buffet table and Mrs. Martinson sitting there in her high-backed chair with her pink-veined eyes.

"What are you going to do?" she asked Anton, the words saying themselves aloud, the words she was really asking herself. She wanted to bite them back, because of course he could never understand what lay at the bottom of them. "I'm sorry," she rushed on. "I shouldn't have—"

His face changed, dark Austrian eyes flickering, first with shock and then with such a look of pain that she had to turn away. After a while there was an audible swallow, as if he were drinking his tears.

"I don't know," he said. "I can't imagine what I will do."

When she looked back at him he leaned toward her. "What will you do?" he asked. "Clover told me about your problem, that you were disturbed and unhappy."

"Do you mean she told you about—she told you that—"

"That there was a love affair? Yes. I heard a lot about her friends, they meant a great deal to her. I hope you don't mind."

"Oh. No, I don't mind, of course not."

"She said you had decided to end it."

"Yes."

"Did you want to?"

"No, but I can't see any other honorable way. As a matter of fact I'm still wavering, not really out of indecision but because—well, this—"

She gestured toward the room. "Clover. How can I think of anything else right now? If ever—"

She turned away again, tears scalding her eyes. Please, not in front of suffering Anton, she prayed, and mastered herself. When she faced him again she was composed and, God knew, he certainly was. He nodded, as if acknowledging her regained self-possession.

"Well—" He felt his carnation tentatively, then glanced down at it. "This seems to have had it," he remarked, and pulled it out of his lapel. He regarded it briefly and then put it in his jacket pocket.

"You and Clover had lunch together the day —the day it happened," he said. "I wonder, did she say anything special that day?" He smiled apologetically. "You always hope for some revelation, you understand, something you can remember, cling to. It's, of course, simply a shot in the dark."

He had singled her out, and now Christine knew why. It was she who had been the last to see Clover, she with whom Clover had spent a few of her last hours. He was waiting now, with a pathetic eagerness, a desperate hope.

"Yes," she said, remembering back. "She said that if you found something that made your life a joy, a splendid joy, you must hold on to it. She said it was monstrous to kill a living thing, that the price, whatever it might be, was worth it."

A flicker in Anton's eyes again, then a searching look, speculative and grave. After a while he said, "Do you think she paid a price? I mean, that we couldn't be married?"

"I think both of you did, Anton. But I feel that, without a doubt, it was worth it. Anton, she was the happiest of women. You must know that."

It was late afternoon when they left the gathering: most of the others had taken their leave earlier, but Mrs. Martinson seemed loath to relinquish the company of her daughter's close friends. They talked quietly until well after four-thirty. "Yes, please do call me," Clover's mother said. "I really think that yes, I shall be here for a good while longer."

At the door Anton grasped Christine's hand. "I understand you're looking for a job," he said. "Clover told me that too. She asked me to help you."

"It was one of the things we talked about that—that day."

"I told her that certainly, I would be delighted to help you find something. You'll allow me, I hope?"

"I will certainly be very grateful, it's kind of you, Anton."

"Not at all, simply a pleasure, and it might take my mind off things a bit. You can understand that. I don't like to lose track of Clover's friends. Fortunately I'm in touch with quite a few people in the business world, even if I am a foreigner."

He reached in an inner vest pocket and pulled out a leather case from which he extracted a card. "If you'll call me on Monday morning, Christine, I'll have something lined up—a few things."

"I'm so grateful."

"No, I am. In a way I'm looking for a lifeline. I guess you can understand that too."

"Yes, very well."

"You've helped me a bit, you know."

"I hope so. But as a matter of fact, it was you who helped me, Anton." She leaned forward and kissed his cheek, which was that of an older man whose skin was starting, very slowly, to groove, and he suddenly seemed to be worn, and tired, and in a sad and irrevocable way somewhat wilted, like the white carnation which rested now in his pocket.

She left Ruth at Ruth's street corner, both of them white and drained, and continued on home. But she didn't go all the way up, instead turned her steps downtown again. It was early enough to table dinner preparations for a while and she was in no hurry to return to that apartment. She had had no walk that day, no reason why she shouldn't have one now.

Along Lex as far as Sixty-first Street, then veering over to Third. Jack's street just ahead. Not to see him. Just to stand, for a moment or two, looking down toward Second. Just—well, because it gave her some small comfort to do it.

The street where John Allerton lived, a street almost identical to that of Clover's. Quiet, tree-trimmed, deceitfully peaceful, almost—in the welter of Manhattan's glass and steel towers—rural, somnolent in the sunny afternoon. Yet danger stalked streets like this, loomed menacingly, ready to strike. In a city, and a world, that was so filled with boobytraps you might as well rig your own. You made your way between the twin perils of Scylla and Charybdis just about every day of your life, and the moral imperative took on new contours. You learned to compromise because in any event whatever you might do was invariably met with the primal scream: if you accommodated one person you discommoded another, robbed Peter to pay Paul; you were damned if you did and damned if you didn't.

Even if she decided not to give up Jack (*if* she decided that) she would still have to spell out the latest, shall we say, developments. Rodney had found out, her husband had found out and no, she could not see her way clear to throw in her lot with someone so much younger. He would accept the new rules, she was almost sure, but it would diminish him in his own eyes, it would be a hollow victory. So in a way it *was* over: there was a loss of innocence, it would never be the same again. She and Jack would pretend it was, but it would have lost its ripe robustness, its earthy richness. Blight had darkened its glow, staled it, like the fading carnation in Anton Ehrenberg's buttonhole.

She walked back up to the Colonnade and on the way saw Clover Martinson twice, once going into a cheese store and again at the Third Avenue

410

corner of her own street, standing in front of the Sixty-eighth Street Playhouse, in a line waiting for the doors to open for the next showing. She would see her friend for a long time to come, she knew, just as she would see Jack Allerton, if their separation became inevitable, for a long time to come, maybe for the rest of her life.

FICTION FOR TODAY'S WOMAN!

GOODBYE IS JUST THE BEGINNING   (442, $2.50)
by Gail Kimberly
After twenty-two years of marriage Abby's life suddenly falls apart when she finds her husband with another woman. From seduction scenes and singles' bars to the problems, successes, and independence of being an "unmarried woman," Abby rediscovers life and her own identity.

WHAT PRICE LOVE by Alice Lent Covert   (491, $2.25)
Unhappy and unfulfilled, Shane plunges into a passionate, all-consuming affair. And for the first time in her life she realizes that there's a dividing line between what a woman owes her husband and what she owes herself, and is willing to take the consequences no matter what the cost.

LOVE'S TENDER TEARS by Kate Ostrander   (504, $1.95)
A beautiful woman caught between the bonds of innocence and womanhood, loyalty and love, passion and fame, is too proud to fight for the man she loves and risks her lifelong dream of happiness to save her pride.

WITHOUT SIN AMONG YOU   (506, $2.50)
by Katherine Stapleton
Vivian Wright, the overnight success, the superstar writer who was turning the country upside down by exposing her most intimate adventures was on top of the world—until she was forced to make a devastating choice: her career or her fiance?

ALWAYS, MY LOVE by Dorothy Fletcher   (517, $2.25)
Iris thought there was to be only one love in her lifetime—until she went to Paris with her widowed aunt and met Paul Chandon who quickly became their constant companion. But was Paul really attracted to her, or was he a fortune hunter after her aunt's money?

Available wherever paperbacks are sold, or direct from the Publisher. Send cover price plus 40¢ per copy for mailing and handling to Zebra Books, 21 East 40th Street, New York, N.Y. 10016 DO NOT SEND CASH!